THE WARNING OF LORD FOUL

Fear and bewilderment sucked at Thomas Covenant. He was sinking in nightmare.

The unbodied voice of Lord Foul went on remorselessly: "You will bear a message to the Council of Lords. Do not fail, groveler, or every human in the Land will be dead before ten seasons have passed. Drool Rockworm has the Staff of Life, and that is cause for terror. But that is not the worst peril. There are banes buried in the deeps of Earth too potent for any mortal to control; they would make the universe a hell forever. Such a bane Drool seeks. He searches for the Illearth Stone!"

The voice paused. Covenant shuddered with the force of his desire for escape.

"One more word," Foul said. "I shall not rest until I have eradicated hope from the Land. Think of that—and be dismayed!"

"An intricately crafted fantasy that presents a most unusual and memorable anti-hero in Thomas Covenant. But it is the spellbinding tapestry of the Land through which he journeys that will linger on in the reader's imagination long after the last page is turned. It will be turned all too quickly."

—Terry Brooks, author of
The Sword of Shannara

The Chronicles of Thomas

Covenant the Unbeliever

"The *War and Peace* of fantasy literature."
—Kansas City Star

"The books are filled with wondrous beings. There is a special warmth in Donaldson's feeling for the Land, and for the power and life inherent to it. Because his eye for detail is good and his feeling for the Land authentic, the Land is as real and substantial as the more prosaic ground we walk upon."
—Chicago Tribune Book World

"Here is classical fantasy with just enough of the modern to give it an added dimension. The background is carefully built, the writing has a sweep of grandeur, the imaginative factors display a depth that is seldom seen."
—Clifford D. Simak

"Stephen R. Donaldson meets the novelist's major challenge—fashioning a whole new fantasy world of his own to share with readers who esteem creative imagination."
—Robert Bloch

*The Chronicles of Thomas Covenant
the Unbeliever*
Published by Ballantine Books:

LORD FOUL'S BANE

THE ILLEARTH WAR

THE POWER THAT PRESERVES

*The Second Chronicles of
Thomas Covenant*

THE WOUNDED LAND

The Chronicles of Thomas Covenant the Unbeliever

Lord Foul's Bane

STEPHEN R. DONALDSON

A Del Rey Book

BALLANTINE BOOKS • NEW YORK

A Del Rey Book
Published by Ballantine Books

Copyright © 1977 by Stephen R. Donaldson
Map Copyright © 1977 by Lynn K. Plagge

All rights reserved under International and Pan-American
Copyright Conventions. Published in the United States by
Ballantine Books, a division of Random House, Inc., New
York, and simultaneously in Canada by Random House of
Canada, Limited, Toronto, Canada.

Library of Congress Catalog Card Number: 77-3533

ISBN 0-345-31011-X

Published in hardcover by Holt, Rinehart and Winston.

Manufactured in the United States of America

First Ballantine Books Edition: August 1978
Sixteenth Printing: September 1982

Cover art by Darrell K. Sweet

For Dr. James R. Donaldson, M.D.,
whose life expressed compassion and commitment
more eloquently than any words

Something there is in beauty

Contents

THE LAND

Outer Earth

North Plains

Westron
Mountains

Grimmerdhore
Forest

Revelstone

Guards
Gap

Trothgard

Maerl R.

White R.

Gray R.

Soulsease R.

Llurallin R.

Rill R.

Revelwood

Andelainian
Hills

Last Hills

Center Plains

Garroting Deep

Black River

Melenkurion
Skyweir

South Plains

Mithil R.

Kevin's
Watch

Rivenrock

N

Doom's
Retreat

Mithil
Stonedown

Cravenhaw

Doriendor
Corishev

Southron Wastes

Map by Lynn K. Plagge

ONE: Golden Boy

SHE came out of the store just in time to see her young son playing on the sidewalk directly in the path of the gray, gaunt man who strode down the center of the walk like a mechanical derelict. For an instant, her heart quailed. Then she jumped forward, gripped her son by the arm, snatched him out of harm's way.

The man went by without turning his head. As his back moved away from her, she hissed at it, "Go away! Get out of here! You ought to be ashamed!"

Thomas Covenant's stride went on, as unfaltering as clockwork that had been wound to the hilt for just this purpose. But to himself he responded, *Ashamed? Ashamed?* His face contorted in a wild grimace. *Beware! Outcast unclean!*

But he saw that the people he passed, the people who knew him, whose names and houses and hand-clasps were known to him—he saw that they stepped aside, gave him plenty of room. Some of them looked as if they were holding their breath. His inner shouting collapsed. These people did not need the ancient ritual of warning. He concentrated on restraining the spasmodic snarl which lurched across his face, and let the tight machinery of his will carry him forward step by step.

As he walked, he flicked his eyes up and down himself, verifying that there were no unexpected tears or snags in his clothing, checking his hands for scratches, making sure that nothing had happened to the scar which stretched from the heel of his right palm across

1

where his last two fingers had been. He could hear the doctors saying, "VSE, Mr. Covenant. Visual Surveillance of Extremities. Your health depends upon it. Those dead nerves will never grow back—you'll never know when you've hurt yourself unless you get in the habit of checking. Do it all the time—think about it all the time. The next time you might not be so lucky."

VSE. Those initials comprised his entire life.

Doctors! he thought mordantly. But without them, he might not have survived even this long. He had been so ignorant of his danger. Self-neglect might have killed him.

Watching the startled, frightened or oblivious faces—there were many oblivious faces, though the town was small—that passed around him, he wished he could be sure that his face bore a proper expression of disdain. But the nerves in his cheeks seemed only vaguely alive, though the doctors had assured him that this was an illusion at the present stage of his illness, and he could never trust the front which he placed between himself and the world. Now, as women who had at one time chosen to discuss his novel in their literary clubs recoiled from him as if he were some kind of minor horror or ghoul, he felt a sudden treacherous pang of loss. He strangled it harshly, before it could shake his balance.

He was nearing his destination, the goal of the affirmation or proclamation that he had so grimly undertaken. He could see the sign two blocks ahead of him: Bell Telephone Company. He was walking the two miles into town from Haven Farm in order to pay his phone bill. Of course, he could have mailed in the money, but he had learned to see that act as a surrender, an abdication to the mounting bereavement which was being practiced against him.

While he had been in treatment, his wife, Joan, had divorced him—taken their infant son and moved out of the state. The only thing in which he, Thomas Covenant, had a stake that she had dared handle had been the car; she had taken it as well. Most of her clothing she had left behind. Then his nearest neighbors, half a mile away on either side, had complained shrilly about his presence among them; and when he had refused to sell his property, one of them moved from the county. Next, within three weeks of his return home, the grocery store—he was walking past it now, its windows full of frenetic advertisements—had begun delivering his supplies, whether or not he ordered them—and, he suspected, whether or not he was willing to pay.

Now he strode past the courthouse, its old gray columns looking proud of their burden of justice and law—the building in which, by proxy, of course, he had been reft of his family. Even its front steps were polished to guard against the stain of human need which prowled up and down them, seeking restitution. The divorce had been granted because no compassionate law could force a woman to raise her child in the company of a man like him. *Were there tears?* he asked Joan's memory. *Were you brave? Relieved?* Covenant resisted an urge to run out of danger. The gaping giant heads which topped the courthouse columns looked oddly nauseated, as if they were about to vomit on him.

In a town of no more than five thousand, the business section was not large. Covenant crossed in front of the department store, and through the glass front he could see several high-school girls pricing cheap jewelry. They leaned on the counters in provocative poses, and Covenant's throat tightened involuntarily. He found himself resenting the hips and breasts of the girls—curves for other men's caresses, not his. He was impotent. In the decay of his nerves, his sexual capacity was just another amputated member. Even the release of lust was denied to him; he could conjure up desires until insanity threatened, but he could do nothing about them. Without warning, a memory of his wife flared in his mind, almost blanking out the sunshine and the sidewalk and the people in front of him. He saw her in one of the opaque nightgowns he had bought for her, her breasts tracing circles of invitation under the thin fabric. His heart cried, *Joan!*

How could you do it? Is one sick body more important than everything?

Bracing his shoulders like a strangler, he suppressed the memory. Such thoughts were a weakness he could not afford; he had to stamp them out. Better to be bitter, he thought. Bitterness survives. It seemed to be the only savor he was still able to taste.

To his dismay, he discovered that he had stopped moving. He was standing in the middle of the sidewalk with his fists clenched and his shoulders trembling. Roughly, he forced himself into motion again. As he did so, he collided with someone.

Outcast unclean!

He caught a glimpse of ocher; the person he had bumped seemed to be wearing a dirty, reddish-brown robe. But he did not stop to apologize. He stalked on down the walk so that he would not have to face that particular individual's fear and loathing. After a moment, his stride recovered its empty, mechanical tick.

Now he was passing the offices of the Electric Company—his last reason for coming to pay his phone bill in person. Two months ago, he had mailed in a check to the Electric Company—the amount was small; he had little use for power—and it had been returned to him. In fact, his envelope had not even been opened. An attached note had explained that his bill had been anonymously paid for at least a year.

After a private struggle, he had realized that if he did not resist this trend, he would soon have no reason at all to go among his fellow human beings. So today he was walking the two miles into town to pay his phone bill in person—to show his peers that he did not intend to be shriven of his humanity. In rage at his outcasting, he sought to defy it, to assert the rights of his common mortal blood.

In person, he thought. What if he were too late? If the bill had already been paid? What did he come in person for then?

The thought caught his heart in a clench of trepidation. He clicked rapidly through his VSE, then returned his gaze to the hanging sign of the Bell

Telephone Company, half a block away. As he moved forward, conscious of a pressure to surge against his anxiety, he noticed a tune running in his mind along the beat of his stride. Then he recollected the words:

> Golden boy with feet of clay,
> Let me help you on your way.
> A proper push will take you far—
> But what a clumsy lad you are!

The doggerel chuckled satirically through his thoughts, and its crude rhythm thumped against him like an insult, accompanied by slow stripper's music. He wondered if there were an overweight goddess somewhere in the mystical heavens of the universe, grinding out his burlesque fate: A proper push *leer* will take you far—but what a clumsy lad you are! *mock pained dismay*. Oh, right, golden boy.

But he could not sneer his way out of that thought, because at one time he had been a kind of golden boy. He had been happily married. He had had a son. He had written a novel in ecstasy and ignorance, and had watched it spend a year on the best-seller lists. And because of it, he now had all the money he needed.

I would be better off, he thought, if I'd known I was writing that kind of book.

But he had not known. He had not even believed that he would find a publisher, back in the days when he had been writing that book—the days right after he had married Joan. Together, they did not think about money or success. It was the pure act of creation which ignited his imagination; and the warm spell of her pride and eagerness kept him burning like a bolt of lightning, not for seconds or fractions of seconds, but for five months in one long wild discharge of energy that seemed to create the landscapes of the earth out of nothingness by the sheer force of its brilliance—hills and crags, trees bent by the passionate wind, night-ridden people, all rendered into being by that white bolt striking into the heavens from the lightning rod of his writing. When he was done, he felt as drained and satisfied as all of life's love uttered in one act.

That had not been an easy time. There was an anguish in the perception of heights and abysses that gave each word he wrote the shape of dried, black blood. And he was not a man who liked heights; unconstricted emotion did not come easily to him. But it had been glorious. The focusing to that pitch of intensity had struck him as the cleanest thing that had ever happened to him. The stately frigate of his soul had sailed well over a deep and dangerous ocean. When he mailed his manuscript away, he did so with a kind of calm confidence.

During those months of writing and then of waiting, they lived on her income. She, Joan Macht Covenant, was a quiet woman who expressed more of herself with her eyes and the tone of her skin than she did with words. Her flesh had a hue of gold which made her look as warm and precious as a sylph or succuba of joy. But she was not large or strong, and Thomas Covenant felt constantly amazed at the fact that she earned a living for them by breaking horses.

The term *breaking,* however, did not do justice to her skill with animals. There were no tests of strength in her work, no bucking stallions with mad eyes and foaming nostrils. It seemed to Covenant that she did not break horses; she seduced them. Her touch spread calm over their twitching muscles. Her murmuring voice relaxed the tension in the angle of their ears. When she mounted them bareback, the grip of her legs made the violence of their brute fear fade. And whenever a horse burst from her control, she simply slid from its back and left it alone until the spasm of its wildness had worn away. Then she began with the animal again. In the end, she took it on a furious gallop around Haven Farm, to show the horse that it could exert itself to the limit without surpassing her mastery.

Watching her, Covenant had felt daunted by her ability. Even after she taught him to ride, he could not overcome his fear of horses.

Her work was not lucrative, but it kept her and her

husband from going hungry until the day a letter of acceptance arrived from the publisher. On that day, Joan decided that the time had come to have a child.

Because of the usual delays of publication, they had to live for nearly a year on an advance on Covenant's royalties. Joan kept her job in one way or another for as long as she could without threatening the safety of the child conceived in her. Then, when her body told her that the time had come, she quit working. At that point, her life turned inward, concentrated on the task of growing her baby with a single-mindedness that often left her outward eyes blank and tinged with expectation.

After he was born, Joan announced that the boy was to be named Roger, after her father and her father's father.

Roger! Covenant groaned as he neared the door of the phone company's offices. He had never even liked that name. But his son's infant face, so meticulously and beautifully formed, human and complete, had made his heart ache with love and pride—yes, pride, a father's participation in mystery. And now his son was gone—gone with Joan he did not know where. Why was he so unable to weep?

The next instant, a hand plucked at his sleeve. "Hey, mister," a thin voice said fearfully, urgently. "Hey, mister." He turned with a yell in his throat— Don't touch me! Outcast unclean!—but the face of the boy who clutched his arm stopped him, kept him from pulling free. The boy was young, not more than eight or nine years old—surely he was too young to be so afraid? His face was mottled pale-and-livid with dread and coercion, as if he were somehow being forced to do something which terrified him.

"Hey, mister," he said, thinly supplicating. "Here. Take it." He thrust an old sheet of paper into Covenant's numb fingers. "He told me to give it to you. You're supposed to read it. Please, mister?"

Covenant's fingers closed involuntarily around the paper. He? he thought dumbly, staring at the boy. He?

"Him." The boy pointed a shaking finger back up the sidewalk.

Covenant looked, and saw an old man in a dirty ocher robe standing half a block away. He was mumbling, almost singing a dim nonsense tune; and his mouth hung open, though his lips and jaw did not move to shape his mutterings. His long, tattered hair and beard fluttered around his head in the light breeze. His face was lifted to the sky; he seemed to be staring directly at the sun. In his left hand he held a wooden beggar-bowl. His right hand clutched a long wooden staff, to the top of which was affixed a sign bearing one word: "Beware."

Beware?

For an odd moment, the sign itself seemed to exert a peril over Covenant. Dangers crowded through it to get at him, terrible dangers swam in the air toward him, screaming like vultures. And among them, looking toward him through the screams, there were eyes—two eyes like fangs, carious and deadly. They regarded him with a fixed, cold and hungry malice, focused on him as if he and he alone were the carrion they craved. Malevolence dripped from them like venom. For that moment, he quavered in the grasp of an inexplicable fear.

Beware!

But it was only a sign, only a blind placard attached to a wooden staff. Covenant shuddered, and the air in front of him cleared.

"You're supposed to read it," the boy said again.

"Don't touch me," Covenant murmured to the grip on his arm. "I'm a leper."

But when he looked around, the boy was gone.

TWO: "You Cannot Hope"

IN his confusion, he scanned the street rapidly, but the boy had escaped completely. Then, as he turned back toward the old beggar, his eyes caught the door, gilt-lettered: Bell Telephone Company. The sight gave him a sudden twist of fear that made him forget all distractions. Suppose— This was his destination; he had come here in person to claim his human right to pay his own bills. But suppose—

He shook himself. He was a leper; he could not afford suppositions. Unconsciously, he shoved the sheet of paper into his pocket. With grim deliberateness, he gave himself a VSE. Then he gripped himself, and started toward the door.

A man hurrying out through the doorway almost bumped into him, then recognized him and backed away, his face suddenly gray with apprehension. The jolt broke Covenant's momentum, and he almost shouted aloud, Leper outcast unclean! He stopped again, allowed himself a moment's pause. The man had been Joan's lawyer at the divorce—a short, fleshy individual full of the kind of bonhomie in which lawyers and ministers specialize. Covenant needed that pause to recover from the dismay of the lawyer's glance. He felt involuntarily ashamed to be the cause of such dismay. For a moment, he could not recollect the conviction which had brought him into town.

But almost at once he began to fume silently. Shame and rage were inextricably bound together in him. I'm not going to let them do this to me, he rasped. By hell! They have no right. Yet he could not so

9

easily eradicate the lawyer's expression from his
thoughts. That revulsion was an accomplished fact,
like leprosy—immune to any question of right or justice. And above all else a leper must not forget the
lethal reality of facts.

As Covenant paused, he thought, I should write a
poem.

> These are the pale deaths
> which men miscall their lives:
> for all the scents of green things growing,
> each breath is but an exhalation of the grave.
> Bodies jerk like puppet corpses,
> and hell walks laughing—

Laughing—now there's a real insight. Hellfire.

Did I do a whole life's laughing in that little time?

He felt that he was asking an important question.
He had laughed when his novel had been accepted
—laughed at the shadows of deep and silent thoughts
that had shifted like sea currents in Roger's face—
laughed over the finished product of his book—
laughed at its presence on the best-seller lists. Thousands of things large and small had filled him with
glee. When Joan had asked him what he found so
funny, he was only able to reply that every breath
charged him with ideas for his next book. His lungs
bristled with imagination and energy. He chuckled
whenever he had more joy than he could contain.

But Roger had been six months old when the novel
had become famous, and six months later Covenant
still had somehow not begun writing again. He had
too many ideas. He could not seem to choose among
them.

Joan had not approved of this unproductive lux-
uriance. She had packed up Roger, and had left her
husband in their newly purchased house, with his office newly settled in a tiny, two-room hut overlooking
a stream in the woods that filled the back of Haven
Farm—left him with strict orders to start writing
while she took Roger to meet his relatives.

That had been the pivot, the moment in which the

rock had begun rolling toward his feet of clay—begun with rumbled warnings the stroke which had cut him off as severely as a surgeon attacking gangrene. He had heard the warnings, and had ignored them. He had not known what they meant.

No, rather than looking for the cause of that low thunder, he had waved good-bye to Joan with regret and quiet respect. He had seen that she was right, that he would not start to work again unless he were alone for a time; and he had admired her ability to act even while his heart ached under the awkward burden of their separation. So when he had waved her plane away over his horizons, he returned to Haven Farm, locked himself in his office, turned on the power to his electric typewriter, and wrote the dedication of his next novel:

"For Joan, who has been my keeper of the possible."

His fingers slipped uncertainly on the keys, and he needed three tries to produce a perfect copy. But he was not sea-wise enough to see the coming storm.

The slow ache in his wrists and ankles he also ignored; he only stamped his feet against the ice that seemed to be growing in them. And when he found the numb purple spot on his right hand near the base of his little finger, he put it out of his mind. Within twenty-four hours of Joan's departure, he was deep into the plotting of his book. Images cascaded through his imagination. His fingers fumbled, tangled themselves around the simplest words, but his imagination was sure. He had no thought to spare for the suppuration of the small wound which grew in the center of that purple stain.

Joan brought Roger home after three weeks of family visits. She did not notice anything wrong until that evening, when Roger was asleep, and she sat in her husband's arms. The storm windows were up, and the house was closed against the chill winter wind which prowled the Farm. In the still air of their living room, she caught the faint, sweet, sick smell of Covenant's infection.

Months later, when he stared at the antiseptic

walls of his room in the leprosarium, he cursed himself for not putting iodine on his hand. It was not the loss of two fingers that galled him. The surgery which amputated part of his hand was only a small symbol of the stroke which cut him out of his life, excised him from his own world as if he were some kind of malignant infestation. And when his right hand ached with the memory of its lost members, that pain was no more than it should be. No, he berated his carelessness because it had cheated him of one last embrace with Joan.

But with her in his arms on that last winter night, he had been ignorant of such possibilities. Talking softly about his new book, he held her close, satisfied for that moment with the press of her firm flesh against his, with the clean smell of her hair and the glow of her warmth. Her sudden reaction had startled him. Before he was sure what disturbed her, she was standing, pulling him up off the sofa after her. She held his right hand up between them, exposed his infection, and her voice crackled with anger and concern.

"Oh, Tom! Why don't you take care of yourself?"

After that, she did not hesitate. She asked one of the neighbors to sit with Roger, then drove her husband through the light February snow to the emergency room of the hospital. She did not leave him until he had been admitted to a room and scheduled for surgery.

The preliminary diagnosis was gangrene.

Joan spent most of the next day with him at the hospital, during the time when he was not being given tests. And the next morning, at six o'clock, Thomas Covenant was taken from his room for surgery on his right hand. He regained consciousness three hours later back in his hospital bed, with two fingers gone. The grogginess of the drugs clouded him for a time, and he did not miss Joan until noon.

But she did not come to see him at all that day. And when she arrived in his room the following morning, she was changed. Her skin was pale, as if her heart were hoarding blood, and the bones of her forehead seemed to press against the flesh. She had the look of a trapped animal. She ignored his outstretched hand. Her voice was low, constrained; she had to exert force to make even that much of herself reach toward him. Standing as far away as she could in the room, staring emptily out the window at the slushy streets, she told him the news.

The doctors had discovered that he had leprosy.

His mind blank with surprise, he said, "You're kidding."

Then she spun and faced him, crying, "Don't play stupid with me now! The doctor said he would tell you, but I told him no, I would do it. I was thinking of you. But I can't—I can't stand it. You've got leprosy! Don't you know what that means? Your hands and feet are going to rot away, and your legs and arms will twist, and your face will turn ugly like a fungus. Your eyes will get ulcers and go bad after a while, and I can't stand it—it won't make any difference to you because you won't be able to feel anything, damn you! And—oh, Tom, Tom! It's catching."

"Catching?" He could not seem to grasp what she meant.

"Yes!" she hissed. "Most people get it because"— for a moment she choked on the fear which impelled her outburst—"because they were exposed when they were kids. Children are more susceptible than adults. Roger— I can't risk— I've got to protect Roger from that!"

As she ran, escaped from the room, he answered, "Yes, of course." Because he had nothing else to say. He still did not understand. His mind was empty. He did not begin to perceive until weeks later how much of him had been blown out by the wind of Joan's passion. Then he was simply appalled.

Forty-eight hours after his surgery, Covenant's surgeon pronounced him ready to travel, and sent him to the leprosarium in Louisiana. On their drive to the leprosarium, the doctor who met his plane talked flatly about various superficial aspects of leprosy. *Mycobacterium leprae* was first identified by Armauer Hansen in 1874, but study of the bacillus has been consistently foiled by the failure of the researchers to meet two of Koch's four steps of analysis: no one had been able to grow the microorganism artificially, and no one had discovered how it is transmitted. However, certain modern research by Dr. O. A. Skinsnes of Hawaii seemed promising. Covenant listened only vaguely. He could hear abstract vibrations of horror in the word *leprosy,* but they did not carry conviction. They affected him like a threat in a foreign language. Behind the intonation of menace, the words themselves communicated nothing. He watched the doctor's earnest face as if he were staring at Joan's incomprehensible passion, and made no response.

But when Covenant was settled in his room at the leprosarium—a square cell with a white blank bed and antiseptic walls—the doctor took another tack. Abruptly, he said, "Mr. Covenant, you don't seem to understand what's at stake here. Come with me. I want to show you something."

Covenant followed him out into the corridor. As they walked, the doctor said, "You have what we call a primary case of Hansen's disease—a native case, one that doesn't seem to have a—a genealogy. Eighty percent of the cases we get in this country involve people—immigrants and so on—who were exposed to the disease as children in foreign countries—tropical climates. At least we know where they contracted it, if not why or how.

"Of course, primary or secondary, they can take the same general path. But as a rule people with secondary cases grew up in places where Hansen's disease is less arcane than here. They recognize what they've got when they get it. That means they have a better chance of seeking help in time.

"I want you to meet another of our patients. He's the only other primary case we have here at present. He used to be a sort of hermit—lived alone away from everyone in the West Virginia mountains. He didn't know what was happening to him until the army tried to get in touch with him—tell him his son was killed in the war. When the officer saw this man, he called in the Public Health Service. They sent the man to us."

The doctor stopped in front of a door like the one to Covenant's cell. He knocked, but did not wait for an answer. He pushed open the door, caught Covenant by the elbow, and steered him into the room.

As he stepped across the threshold, Covenant's nostrils were assaulted by a pungent reek, a smell like that of rotten flesh lying in a latrine. It defied mere carbolic acid and ointments to mask it. It came from a shrunken figure sitting grotesquely on the white bed.

"Good afternoon," the doctor said. "This is Thomas Covenant. He has a primary case of Hansen's disease, and doesn't seem to understand the danger he's in."

Slowly, the patient raised his arms as if to embrace Covenant.

His hands were swollen stumps, fingerless lumps of pink, sick meat marked by cracks and ulcerations from which a yellow exudation oozed through the medication. They hung on thin, hooped arms like awkward sticks. And even though his legs were covered by his hospital pajamas, they looked like gnarled wood. Half of one foot was gone, gnawed away, and in the place of the other was nothing but an unhealable wound.

Then the patient moved his lips to speak, and Covenant looked up at his face. His dull, cataractal eyes sat in his face as if they were the center of an eruption. The skin of his cheeks was as white-pink as an albino's; it bulged and poured away from his eyes in waves, runnulets, as if it had been heated to the melting point; and these waves were edged with thick tubercular nodules.

"Kill yourself," he rasped terribly. "Better than this."

Covenant broke away from the doctor. He rushed out into the hall and the contents of his stomach spattered over the clean walls and floor like a stain of outrage.

In that way, he decided to survive.

Thomas Covenant lived in the leprosarium for more than six months. He spent his time roaming the corridors like an amazed phantasm, practicing his VSE and other survival drills, glaring his way through hours of conferences with the doctors, listening to lectures on leprosy and therapy and rehabilitation. He soon learned that the doctors believed patient psychology to be the key to treating leprosy. They wanted to counsel him. But he refused to talk about himself. Deep within him, a hard core of intransigent fury was growing. He had learned that by some bitter trick of his nerves the two fingers he had lost felt more alive to the rest of his body than did his remaining digits. His right thumb was always reaching for those excised fingers, and finding their scar with an awkward, surprised motion. The help of the doctors seemed to resemble this same trick. Their few sterile images of hope struck him as the gropings of an unfingered imagination. And so the conferences, like the lectures, ended as long speeches by experts on the problems that he, Thomas Covenant, faced.

For weeks the speeches were pounded into him until he began to dream them at night. Admonitions took over the ravaged playground of his mind. Instead of stories and passions, he dreamed perorations.

"Leprosy," he heard night after night, "is perhaps the most inexplicable of all human afflictions. It is a mystery, just as the strange, thin difference between living and inert matter is a mystery. Oh, we know some things about it: it is not fatal; it is not contagious in any conventional way; it operates by destroying the nerves, typically in the extremities and in the cornea of the eye; it produces deformity, largely because it negates the body's ability to protect itself by feeling and reacting against pain; it may result in complete disability, extreme deformation of the face and limbs, and blindness; and it is irreversible, since the nerves that die cannot be restored. We also know that, in almost all cases, proper treatment using DDS —diamino-diphenyl-sulfone—and some of the new synthetic antibiotics can arrest the spread of the disease, and that, once the neural deterioration has been halted, the proper medication and therapy can keep the affliction under control for the rest of the patient's life. What we do not know is why or how any specific person contracts the illness. As far as we can prove, it comes out of nowhere for no reason. And once you get it, you cannot hope for a cure."

The words he dreamed were not exaggerated—they could have come verbatim from any one of a score of lectures or conferences—but their tolling sounded like the tread of something so unbearable that it should never have been uttered. The impersonal voice of the doctor went on: "What we have learned from our years of study is that Hansen's disease creates two unique problems for the patient—interrelated difficulties that do not occur with any other illness, and that make the mental aspect of being a leprosy victim more crucial than the physical.

"The first involves your relationships with your fellow human beings. Unlike leukemia today, or tuberculosis in the last century, leprosy is not, and has never been, a 'poetic' disease, a disease which can be romanticized. Just the reverse. Even in societies that hate their sick less than we Americans do, the leper has always been despised and feared—outcast even by his most-loved ones because of a rare bacillus no one can predict or control. Leprosy is not fatal, and the average patient can look forward to as much as thirty or fifty years of life as a leper. That fact, combined with the progressive disability which the disease inflicts, makes leprosy patients, of all sick people, the ones most desperately in need of human support. But virtually all societies condemn their lepers to isolation and despair—denounced as criminals and degenerates, as traitors and villains—cast out of the human race because science has failed to unlock the mystery of this affliction. In country after country, culture after culture around the world, the leper has been considered the personification of everything people, privately and communally, fear and abhor.

"People react this way for several reasons. First, the disease produces an ugliness and a bad smell that are undeniably unpleasant. And second, generations of medical research notwithstanding, people fail to believe that something so obvious and ugly and so mysterious is not contagious. The fact that we cannot answer questions about the bacillus reinforces their fear—we cannot be sure that touch or air or food or water or even compassion do not spread the disease. In the absence of any natural, provable explanation of the illness, people account for it in other ways, all bad—as proof of crime or filth or perversion, evidence of God's judgment, as the horrible sign of some psychological or spiritual or moral corruption or guilt. And they insist it's catching, despite evidence that it is minimally contagious, even to children. So many of you are going to have to live without one single human support to bear the burden with you.

"That is one reason why we place such an emphasis on counseling here; we want to help you learn to cope with loneliness. Many of the patients who leave this institution do not live out their full years. Under the shock of their severance, they lose their motivation; they let their self-treatments slide, and become either actively or passively suicidal; few of them come back here in time. The patients who survive find someone somewhere who is willing to help them want to live. Or they find somewhere inside themselves the strength to endure.

"Whichever way you go, however, one fact will remain constant: from now until you die, leprosy is the biggest single fact of your existence. It will control how you live in every particular. From the moment you awaken until the moment you sleep, you will have to give your undivided attention to all the hard corners and sharp edges of life. You can't take vacations from it. You can't try to rest yourself by daydreaming, lapsing. Anything that bruises, bumps, burns, breaks, scrapes, snags, pokes, or weakens you can maim, cripple, or even kill you. And thinking about all the kinds of life you can't have can drive you to despair and suicide. I've seen it happen."

Covenant's pulse was racing, and his sweat made the sheets cling to his limbs. The voice of his nightmare had not changed—it made no effort to terrify him, took no pleasure in his fear—but now the words were as black as hate, and behind them stretched a great raw wound of emptiness.

"That brings us to the other problem. It sounds

simple, but you will find it can be devastating. Most people depend heavily on their sense of touch. In fact, their whole structure of responses to reality is organized around their touch. They may doubt their eyes and ears, but when they touch something they know it's real. And it is not an accident that we describe the deepest parts of ourselves—our emotions—in terms of the sense of touch. Sad tales *touch* our *feelings*. Bad situations *irritate* us or *hurt* us. This is an inevitable result of the fact that we are biological organisms.

"You must fight and change this orientation. You're intelligent creatures—each of you has a brain. Use it. Use it to recognize your danger. Use it to train yourself to stay alive."

Then he woke up alone in his bed drenched with sweat, eyes staring, lips taut with whimpers that tried to plead their way between his clenched teeth. Dream after dream, week after week, the pattern played itself out. Day after day, he had to lash himself with anger to make himself leave the ineffectual sanctuary of his cell.

But his fundamental decision held. He met patients who had been to the leprosarium several times before—haunted recidivists who could not satisfy the essential demand of their torment, the requirement that they cling to life without desiring any of the recompense which gave life value. Their cyclic degeneration taught him to see that his nightmare contained the raw materials for survival. Night after night, it battered him against the brutal and irremediable law of leprosy; blow by blow, it showed him that an entire devotion to that law was his only defense against suppuration and gnawing rot and blindness. In his fifth and sixth months at the leprosarium, he practiced his VSE and other drills with manic diligence. He stared at the blank antiseptic walls of his cell as if to hypnotize himself with them. In the back of his mind, he counted the hours between doses of his medication. And whenever he slipped, missed a beat of his defensive rhythm, he excoriated himself with curses.

In seven months, the doctors were convinced that his diligence was not a passing phase. They were reasonably sure that the progress of his illness had been arrested. They sent him home.

As he returned to his house on Haven Farm in late summer, he thought that he was prepared for everything. He had braced himself for the absence of any communication from Joan, the dismayed revulsions of his former friends and associates—though these assaults still afflicted him with a vertiginous nausea of rage and self-disgust. The sight of Joan's and Roger's belongings in the house, and the desertion of the stables where Joan had formerly kept her horses, stung his sore heart like a corrosive—but he had already set his heels against the pull of such pains.

Yet he was not prepared, not for everything. The next shock surpassed his readiness. After he had double- and triple-checked to be sure he had received no mail from Joan, after he had spoken on the phone with the lawyer who handled his business—he had heard the woman's discomfort throbbing across the metallic connection—he went to his hut in the woods and sat down to read what he had written on his new book.

Its blind poverty left him aghast. To call it ridiculously naive would have been a compliment. He could hardly believe that he was responsible for such supercilious trash.

That night, he reread his first novel, the best-seller. Then, moving with extreme caution, he built a fire in his hearth and burned both the novel and the new manuscript. Fire! he thought. Purgation. If I do not write another word, I will at least rid my life of these lies. Imagination! How could I have been so complacent? And as he watched the pages crumble into gray ash, he threw in with them all thought of further writing. For the first time, he understood part of what the doctors had been saying; he needed to crush out his imagination. He could not afford to have an imagination, a faculty which could envision Joan, joy, health. If he tormented himself with unattainable desires, he would cripple his grasp on the law which enabled him to survive. His imagination could kill him, lead or seduce or trick him into suicide: seeing all the things he could not have would make him despair.

When the fire went out, he ground the ashes underfoot as if to make their consummation irrevocable.

The next morning, he set about organizing his life.

First, he found his old straight razor. Its long, stainless-steel blade gleamed like a leer in the fluorescent light of his bathroom; but he stropped it deliberately, lathered his face, braced his timorous bones against the sink, and set the edge to his throat. It felt like a cold line of fire across his jugular, a keen threat of blood and gangrene and reactivated leprosy. If his half-unfingered hand slipped or twitched, the consequences might be extreme. But he took the risk consciously to discipline himself, enforce his recognition of the raw terms of his survival, mortify his recalcitrance. He instituted shaving with that blade as a personal ritual, a daily confrontation with his condition.

For the same reason, he began carrying around a sharp penknife. Whenever he felt his discipline faltering, felt threatened by memories or hopes or love, he took out the knife and tested its edge on his wrist.

Then, after he had shaved, he worked on his house. He neatened it, rearranged the furniture to minimize the danger of protruding corners, hard edges, hidden obstacles; he eliminated everything which could trip, bruise, or deflect him, so that even in the dark his rooms would be navigable, safe; he made his house as much like his cell in the leprosarium as possible. Anything that was hazardous, he threw into the guest room; and when he was done he locked the guest room and threw away the key.

After that he went to his hut and locked it also. Then he pulled its fuses, so that there would be no risk of fire in the old wiring.

Finally he washed the sweat off his hands. He washed them grimly, obsessively; he could not help himself—the physical impression of uncleanness was too strong.

Leper outcast unclean.

He spent the autumn stumbling around the rims of madness. Dark violence throbbed in him like a *picar* thrust between his ribs, goading him aimlessly. He felt an insatiable need for sleep, but could not heed it because his dreams had changed to nightmares of gnawing; despite his numbness, he seemed to feel himself being eaten away. And wakefulness confronted him with a vicious and irreparable paradox. Without the support or encouragement of other people, he did not believe he could endure the burden of his struggle against horror and death; yet that horror and death explained, made comprehensible, almost vindicated the rejection which denied him support or encouragement. His struggle arose from the same passions which produced his outcasting. He hated what would happen to him if he failed to fight. He hated himself for having to fight such a winless and interminable war. But he could not hate the people who made his moral solitude so absolute. They only shared his own fear.

In the dizzy round of his dilemma, the only response which steadied him was vitriol. He clung to his bitter anger as to an anchor of sanity; he needed fury in order to survive, to keep his grip like a stranglehold on life. Some days he went from sun to sun without any rest from rage.

But in time even that passion began to falter. His outcasting was part of his law; it was an irreducible fact, as totally real and compulsory as gravity and pestilence and numbness. If he failed to crush himself to fit the mold of his facts, he would fail to survive.

When he looked out over the Farm, the trees which edged his property along the highway seemed so far away that nothing could bridge the gap.

The contradiction had no answer. It made his fingers twitch helplessly, so that he almost cut himself shaving. Without passion he could not fight—yet all his passions rebounded against him. As the autumn passed, he cast fewer and fewer curses at the impossibilities imprisoning him. He prowled through the woods behind Haven Farm—a tall, lean man with haggard eyes, a mechanical stride, and two fingers gone from his right hand. Every cluttered trail, sharp rock, steep slope reminded him that he was keeping himself alive with caution, that he had only to let his surveillance slip to go quietly unmourned and painless out of his troubles.

It gave him nothing but an addition of sorrow to touch the bark of a tree and feel nothing. He saw clearly the end that waited for him; his heart would become as affectless as his body, and then he would be lost for good and all.

Nevertheless, he was filled with a sudden sense of focus, of crystallization, as if he had identified an enemy, when he learned that someone had paid his electric bill for him. The unexpected gift made him abruptly aware of what was happening. The townspeople were not only shunning him, they were actively cutting off every excuse he might have to go among them.

When he first understood his danger, his immediate reaction was to throw open a window and shout into the winter, "Go ahead! By hell, I don't need you!" But the issue was not simple enough to be blown away by bravado. As winter scattered into an early March spring, he became convinced that he needed to take some kind of action. He was a person, human like any other; he was kept alive by a personal heart. He did not mean to stand by and approve this amputation.

So when his next phone bill came, he gathered his courage, shaved painstakingly, dressed himself in clothes with tough fabrics, laced his feet snugly into sturdy boots, and began the two-mile walk into town to pay his bill in person.

That walk brought him to the door of the Bell Telephone Company with trepidation hanging around his head like a dank cloud. He stood in front of the gilt-lettered door for a time, thinking,

These are the pale deaths . . .

and wondering about laughter. Then he collected himself, pulled open the door like the gust of a gale, and stalked up to the girl at the counter as if she had challenged him to single combat.

He put his hands palms down on the counter to steady them. Ferocity sprang across his teeth for an instant. He said, "My name is Thomas Covenant."

The girl was trimly dressed, and she held her arms crossed under her breasts, supporting them so that they showed to their best advantage. He forced himself to look up at her face. She was staring blankly past him. While he searched her for some tremor of revulsion, she glanced at him and asked, "Yes?"

"I want to pay my bill," he said, thinking, She doesn't know, she hasn't heard.

"Certainly, sir," she answered. "What is your number?"

He told her, and she moved languidly into another room to check her files.

The suspense of her absence made his fear pound in his throat. He needed some way to distract himself, occupy his attention. Abruptly, he reached into his pocket and brought out the sheet of paper the boy had given him. *You're supposed to read it.* He smoothed it out on the counter and looked at it.

The old printing said:

A real man—real in all the ways that we recognize as real—finds himself suddenly abstracted from the world and deposited in a physical situation which could not possibly exist: sounds have aroma, smells have color and depth, sights have texture, touches have pitch and timbre. There he is informed by a disembodied voice that he has been brought to that place as a champion for his world. He must fight to the death in single combat against a champion from another world. If he is defeated, he will die, and his world—the real world—will be destroyed because it lacks the inner strength to survive.

The man refuses to believe that what he is told

is true. He asserts that he is either dreaming or hallucinating, and declines to be put in the false position of fighting to the death where no "real" danger exists. He is implacable in his determination to disbelieve his apparent situation, and does not defend himself when he is attacked by the champion of the other world.

Question: is the man's behavior courageous or cowardly? This is the fundamental question of ethics.

Ethics! Covenant snorted to himself. Who the hell makes these things up?

The next moment, the girl returned with a question in her face. "Thomas Covenant? Of Haven Farm? Sir, a deposit has been made on your account which covers everything for several months. Did you send us a large check recently?"

Covenant staggered inwardly as if he had been struck, then caught himself on the counter, listing to the side like a reefed galleon. Unconsciously he crushed the paper in his fist. He felt light-headed, heard words echoing in his ears: Virtually all societies condemn, denounce, cast out—you cannot hope.

He focused his attention on his cold feet and aching ankles while he fought to keep the violence at bay. With elaborate caution, he placed the crumpled sheet on the counter in front of the girl. Striving to sound conversational, he said, "It isn't catching, you know. You won't get it from me—there's nothing to worry about. It isn't catching. Except for children."

The girl blinked at him as if she were amazed by the vagueness of her thoughts.

His shoulders hunched, strangling fury in his throat. He turned away with as much dignity as he could manage, and strode out into the sunlight, letting the door slam behind him. Hellfire! he swore to himself. Hellfire and bloody damnation.

Giddy with rage, he looked up and down the street. He could see the whole ominous length of the town from where he stood. In the direction of Haven

Farm, the small businesses stood close together like
teeth poised on either side of the road. The sharp
sunlight made him feel vulnerable and alone. He
checked his hands quickly for scratches or abrasions,
then hurried down the gauntlet, as he moved, his
numb feet felt unsure on the sidewalk, as if the cement were slick with despair. He believed that he
displayed courage by not breaking into a run.

In a few moments the courthouse loomed ahead
of him. On the sidewalk before it stood the old beggar. He had not moved. He was still staring at the
sun, still muttering meaninglessly. His sign said, Beware, uselessly, like a warning that came too late.

As Covenant approached, he was struck by how
dispossessed the old man looked. Beggars and fanat-
ics, holy men, prophets of the apocalypse did not
belong on that street in that sunlight; the frowning,
belittling eyes of the stone columns held no toler-
ance for such preterite exaltation. And the scant coins
he had collected were not enough for even one
meal. The sight gave Covenant an odd pang of
compassion. Almost in spite of himself, he stopped
in front of the old man.

The beggar made no gesture, did not shift his
contemplation of the sun; but his voice altered, and
one clear word broke out of the formless hum:

"Give."

The order seemed to be directed at Covenant
personally. As if on command, his gaze dropped to
the bowl again. But the demand, the effort of coercion, brought back his anger. *I don't owe you anything,* he snapped silently.

Before he could pull away, the old man spoke
again.

"I have warned you."

Unexpectedly, the statement struck Covenant like
an insight, an intuitive summary of all his experi-
ences in the past year. Through his anger, his decision came immediately. With a twisted expression
on his face, he fumbled for his wedding ring.

He had never before removed his white gold wedding band; despite his divorce, and Joan's unanswer-

ing silence, he had kept the ring on his finger. It was an icon of himself. It reminded him of where he had been and where he was—of promises made and broken, companionship lost, helplessness—and of his vestigial humanity. Now he tore it off his left hand and dropped it in the bowl. "That's worth more than a few coins," he said, and stamped away.

"Wait."

The word carried such authority that Covenant stopped again. He stood still, husbanding his rage, until he felt the man's hand on his arm. Then he turned and looked into pale blue eyes as blank as if they were still studying the secret fire of the sun. The old man was tall with power.

A sudden insecurity, a sense of proximity to matters he did not understand, disturbed Covenant. But he pushed it away. "Don't touch me. I'm a leper."

The vacant stare seemed to miss him completely, as if he did not exist or the eyes were blind; but the old man's voice was clear and sure.

"You are in perdition, my son."

Moistening his lips with his tongue, Covenant responded, "No, old man. This is normal—human beings are like this. Futile." As if he were quoting a law of leprosy, he said to himself, Futility is the defining characteristic of life. "That's what life is like. I just have less bric-a-brac cluttering up the facts than most people."

"So young—and already so bitter."

Covenant had not heard sympathy for a long time, and the sound of it affected him acutely. His anger retreated, leaving his throat tight and awkward. "Come on, old man," he said. "We didn't make the world. All we have to do is live in it. We're all in the same boat—one way or another."

"Did we not?"

But without waiting for an answer the beggar went back to humming his weird tune. He held Covenant there until he had reached a break in his song. Then a new quality came into his voice, an aggressive tone that took advantage of Covenant's unexpected vulnerability.

"Why not destroy yourself?"

A sense of pressure expanded in Covenant's chest, cramping his heart. The pale blue eyes were exerting some kind of peril over him. Anxiety tugged at him. He wanted to jerk away from the old face, go through his VSE, make sure that he was safe. But he could not; the blank gaze held him. Finally, he said, "That's too easy."

His reply met no opposition, but still his trepidation grew. Under the duress of the old man's will, he stood on the precipice of his future and looked down at jagged, eager dangers—rough damnations multiplied below him. He recognized the various possible deaths of lepers. But the panorama steadied him. It was like a touchstone of familiarity in a fantastic situation; it put him back on known ground. He found that he could turn away from his fear to say, "Look, is there anything I can do for you? Food? A place to stay? You can have what I've got."

As if Covenant had said some crucial password, the old man's eyes lost their perilous cast.

"You have done too much. Gifts like this I return to the giver."

He extended his bowl toward Covenant.

"Take back the ring. Be true. You need not fail."

Now the tone of command was gone. In its place, Covenant heard gentle supplication. He hesitated, wondering what this old man had to do with him. But he had to make some kind of response. He took the ring and replaced it on his left hand. Then he said, "Everybody fails. But I am going to survive—as long as I can."

The old man sagged, as if he had just shifted a load of prophecy or commandment onto Covenant's shoulders. His voice sounded frail now.

"That is as it may be."

Without another word, he turned and moved away. He leaned on his staff like an exhausted prophet, worn out with uttering visions. His staff rang curiously on the sidewalk, as if the wood were harder than cement.

Covenant gazed after the wind-swayed ocher robe

and the fluttering hair until the old man turned a corner and vanished. Then he shook himself, started into his VSE. But his eyes stopped on his wedding ring. The band seemed to hang loosely on his finger, as if it were too big for him. *Perdition,* he thought. *A deposit has been made.* I've got to do something before they barricade the streets against me.

For a while, he stood where he was and tried to think of a course of action. Absently, he looked up the courthouse columns to the stone heads. They had careless eyes and on their lips a spasm of disgust carved into perpetual imminence, compelling and forever incomplete. They gave him an idea. Casting a silent curse at them, he started down the walk again. He had decided to see his lawyer, to demand that the woman who handled his contracts and financial business find some legal recourse against the kind of black charity which was cutting him off from the town. Get those payments revoked, he thought. It's not possible that they can pay my debts—without my consent.

The lawyer's office was in a building at the corner of a cross street on the opposite side of the road. A minute's brisk walking brought Covenant to the corner and the town's only traffic light. He felt a need to hurry, to act on his decision before his distrust of lawyers and all public machinery convinced him that his determination was folly. He had to resist a temptation to cross against the light.

The signal changed slowly, but at last it was green his way. He stepped out onto the crosswalk.

Before he had taken three steps, he heard a siren. Red lights flaring, a police car sprang out of an alley into the main street. It skidded and swerved with the speed of its turn, then aimed itself straight at Covenant's heart.

He stopped as if caught in the grip of an unseen fist. He wanted to move, but he could only stand suspended, trapped, looking down the muzzle of the hurtling car. For an instant, he heard the frantic scream of brakes. Then he crumbled.

As he dropped, he had a vague sense that he was

falling too soon, that he had not been hit yet. But he could not help himself; he was too afraid, afraid of being crushed. After all his self-protections, to die like this! Then he became aware of a huge blackness which stood behind the sunlight and the gleaming store-windows and the shriek of tires. The light and the asphalt against his head seemed to be nothing more than paintings on a black background; and now the background asserted itself, reached in and bore him down. Blackness radiated through the sunlight like a cold beam of night.

He thought that he was having a nightmare. Absurdly, he heard the old beggar saying, *Be true. You need not fail.*

The darkness poured through, swamping the day, and the only thing that Covenant was sure he could see was a single red gleam from the police car—a red bolt hot and clear and deadly, transfixing his forehead like a spear.

THREE: Invitation to a Betrayal

FOR a time that he could only measure in heartbeats, Covenant hung in the darkness. The red, impaling light was the only fixed point in a universe that seemed to seethe around him. He felt that he might behold a massive moving of heaven and earth, if only he knew where to look; but the blackness and the hot red beam on his forehead prevented him from turning away, and he had to let the currents that swirled around him pass unseen.

Under the pressure of the ferocious light, he could feel every throb of his pulse distinctly in his temples, as if it were his mind which hammered out his life, not his heart. The beats were slow—too slow for the amount of apprehension he felt. He could not conceive what was happening to him. But each blow shook him as if the very structure of his brain were under assault.

Abruptly, the bloody spear of light wavered, then split in two. He was moving toward the light—or the light was approaching him. The two flaming spots were eyes.

The next instant, he heard laughter—high, shrill glee full of triumph and old spite. The voice crowed like some malevolent rooster heralding the dawn of hell, and Covenant's pulse trembled at the sound.

"Done it!" the voice cackled. "I! Mine!" It shrilled away into laughter again.

Covenant was close enough to see the eyes clearly now. They had no whites or pupils; red balls filled the sockets, and light moiled in them like lava. Their heat was so close that Covenant's forehead burned.

Then the eyes flared, seemed to ignite the air around them. Flames spread out, sending a lurid glow around Covenant.

He found himself in a cavern deep in stone. Its walls caught and held the light, so that the cave stayed bright after the single flare of the eyes. The rock was smooth, but broken into hundreds of irregular facets, as if the cavern had been carved with an erratic knife. Entrances gaped in the walls around the circumference of the cave. High above his head, the roof gathered into a thick cluster of stalactites, but the floor was flat and worn as if by the passing of many feet. Reflections sprang through the stalactites above, so that the cluster swarmed with red gleamings.

The chamber was full of a rank stench, an acrid odor with a sickly sweet under-smell—burning sulfur over the reek of rotting flesh. Covenant gagged on it, and on the sight of the being whose eyes had held him.

Crouched on a low dais near the center of the cave was a creature with long, scrawny limbs, hands as huge and heavy as shovels, a thin, hunched torso, and a head like a battering ram. As he crouched, his knees came up almost to the level of his ears. One hand was braced on the rock in front of him, the other gripped a long wooden staff shod with metal and intricately carved from end to end. His grizzled mouth was rigid with laughter, and his red eyes seemed to bubble like magma.

"Ha! Done it!" he shrieked again. "Called him. My power. Kill them all!" As his high voice ranted, he slavered hungrily. "Lord Drool! Master! Me!"

The creature leaped to his feet, capering with mad pride. He strode closer to his victim, and Covenant recoiled with a loathing he could not control.

Holding his staff near the center with both hands, the creature shouted, "Kill you! Take your power! Crush them all! Be Lord Drool!" He raised his staff as if to strike Covenant with it.

Then another voice entered the cavern. It was deep and resonant, powerful enough to fill the air without effort, and somehow deadly, as if an abyss were speaking. "Back, Rockworm!" it commanded. "This prey is too great for you. I claim him."

The creature jabbed his face toward the ceiling and cried, "Mine! My Staff! You saw. I called him. You saw!"

Covenant followed the red eyes upward, but he could see nothing there except the dizzy chiaroscuro of the clustered stone spikes.

"You had aid," the deep voice said. "The Staff was too hard a matter for you. You would have destroyed it in simple irritation, had I not taught you some of its uses. And my aid has its price. Do whatever else you wish. I claim this prize. It belongs to me."

The creature's rage subsided, as if he had suddenly remembered some secret advantage. "My Staff," he muttered darkly. "I have it. You are not safe."

"You threaten me?" The deep voice bristled, and its dangers edged closer to the surface. "Watch and ward, Drool Rockworm! Your doom grows upon you. Behold! I have begun!"

There was a low, grinding noise, as of great teeth breaking against each other, and a chilling mist intervened between Covenant and Drool, gathered and swirled and thickened until Drool was blocked from Covenant's sight. At first, the mist glowed with the light of the burning stones, but as it swirled the red faded into the dank, universal gray of fogs. The vile reek melted into a sweeter smell—attar, the odor of funerals. Despite the blindness of the mist, Covenant felt that he was no longer in Drool's cavern.

The change gave him no relief. Fear and bewilderment sucked at him as if he were sinking in nightmare. That unbodied voice dismayed him. As the fog blew around him his legs shuddered and bent, and he fell to his knees.

"You do well to pray to me," the voice intoned. Its deadliness shocked Covenant like a confrontation with grisly murder. "There are no other hopes or helps for a man amid the wrack of your fate. My Enemy will not aid you. It was he who chose you for this doom. And when he has chosen, he does not give; he takes." A raw timbre of contempt ran through the voice, scraping Covenant's nerves as it passed. "Yes, you would do well to pray to me. I might ease you of your burden. Whatever health or strength you ask is mine to give. For I have begun my attack upon this age, and the future is mine. I will not fail again."

Covenant's mind lay under the shock of the voice. But the offer of health penetrated him, and his heart jumped. He felt the beat clearly in his chest, felt his heart laboring against the burden of his fear. But he was still too stricken to speak.

Over his silence, the voice continued, "Kevin was a fool—fey, anile and gutless. They are all fools. Look you, groveler. The mighty High Lord Kevin, son of Loric and great-grandson of Berek Lord-Fatherer whom I hate, stood where you now kneel, and he thought to destroy me. He discovered my designs, recognized some measure of my true stature—though the dotard had set me on his right side in the Council for long years without sensing his peril—saw at the last who I was. Then there was war between us, war that

blasted the west and threatened his precious Keep itself. The feller fist was mine and he knew it. When his
armies faltered and his power waned, he lost himself
in despair—he became mine in despair. He thought
that he still might utterly undo me. Therefore he met
me in that cavern from which I have rescued you—
Kiril Threndor, Heart of Thunder.

"Drool Rockworm does not know what a black rock
it is on which he stands. And that is not his only ignorance—but of my deeper plans I say nothing. He
serves me well in his way, though he does not intend
service. Likewise will you and those timid Lords serve
me, whether you choose or no. Let them grope through
their shallow mysteries for a time, barely fearing that
I am alive. They have not mastered the seventh part
of dead Kevin's Lore, and yet in their pride they dare
to name themselves Earthfriends, servants of Peace.
They are too blind to perceive their own arrogance.
But I will teach them to see.

"In truth it is already too late for them. They will
come to Kiril Threndor, and I will teach them things
to darken their souls. It is fitting. There Kevin met and
dared me in his despair. And I accepted. The fool!
I could hardly speak the words for laughing. He
thought that such spells might unbind me.

"But the Power which upholds me has stood since
the creation of Time. Therefore when Kevin dared me
to unleash the forces that would strike the Land and
all its accursed creations into dust, I took the dare.
Yes, and laughed until there was doubt in his face
before the end. That folly brought the age of the Old
Lords to its ruin—but I remain. I! Together we stood
in Kiril Threndor, blind Kevin and I. Together we
uttered the Ritual of Desecration. Ah, the fool! He
was already enslaved to me and knew it not. Proud
of his Lore, he did not know that the very Law which
he served preserved me through that cataclysm,
though all but a few of his own people and works were
stricken into death.

"True, I was reduced for a time. I have spent a
thousand years gnawing my desires like a beaten cur.
The price of that has yet to be paid—for it and other

things I shall exact my due. But I was not destroyed. And when Drool found the Staff and recognized it, and could not use it, I took my chance again. I will have the future of this life, to waste or hold as I desire. So pray to me, groveler. Reject the doom that my Enemy has created for you. You will not have many chances to repent."

The fog and the attar-laden air seemed to weaken Covenant, as if the strength were being absorbed from his blood. But his heart beat on, and he clung to it for a defense against the fear. He wrapped his arms about his chest and bent low, trying to shelter himself from the cold. "What doom?" he forced himself to say. His voice sounded pitiful and lost in the mist.

"He intends you to be my final foe. He chose you—you, groveler, with a might in your hands such as no mortal has ever held before—chose you to destroy me. But he will find that I am not so easily mastered. You have might—wild magic which preserves your life at this moment—but you will never know what it is. You will not be able to fight me at the last. No, you are the victim of his expectations, and I cannot free you by death—not yet. But we can turn that strength against him, and rid him of the Earth entirely."

"Health?" Covenant looked painfully up from the ground. "You said health."

"Whatever health you lack, groveler. Only pray to me, while I am still patient."

But the voice's contempt cut too deep. Covenant's violence welled up in the wound. He began to fight. Heaving himself up off his knees, he thought, No. I'm not a groveler. With his teeth gritted to stop his trembling, he asked, "Who are you?"

As if sensing its mistake, the voice became smoother. "I have had many names," it said. "To the Lords of Revelstone, I am Lord Foul the Despiser; to the Giants of Seareach, Satansheart and Soulcrusher. The Ramen name me Fangthane. In the dreams of the Bloodguard, I am Corruption. But the people of the Land call me the Gray Slayer."

Distinctly, Covenant said, "Forget it."

"Fool!" ground the voice, and its force flattened

Covenant on the rock. Forehead pressed against the
stone, he lay and waited in terror for the anger of the
voice to annihilate him. "I do not take or eschew
action at your bidding. And I will not forget this. I
see that your pride is offended by my contempt.
Groveler! I will teach you the true meaning of contempt before I am done. But not now. That does not
meet my purpose. Soon I will be strong enough to
wrest the wild magic from you, and then you will learn
to your cost that my contempt is without limit, my
desires bottomless.

"But I have wasted time enough. Now to my pur-
pose. Heed me well, groveler. I have a task for you.
You will bear a message for me to Revelstone—to the
Council of Lords.

"Say to the Council of Lords, and to High Lord
Prothall son of Dwillian, that the uttermost limit of
their span of days upon the Land is seven times seven
years from this present time. Before the end of those
days are numbered, I will have the command of life
and death in my hand. And as a token that what I say
is the one word of truth, tell them this: Drool
Rockworm, Cavewight of Mount Thunder, has found
the Staff of Law, which was lost ten times a hundred
years ago by Kevin at the Ritual of Desecration. Say
to them that the task appointed to their generation is
to regain the Staff. Without it, they will not be able to
resist me for seven years, and my complete victory
will be achieved six times seven years earlier than it
would be else.

"As for you, groveler: do not fail with this message. If you do not bring it before the Council, then
every human in the Land will be dead before ten seasons have passed. You do not understand—but I tell
you Drool Rockworm has the Staff, and that it is a
cause for terror. He will be enthroned at Lord's Keep
in two years if the message fails. Already, the Cavewights are marching to his call; and wolves, and ur-
viles of the Demondim, answer the power of the Staff.
But war is not the worst peril. Drool delves ever deeper
into the dark roots of Mount Thunder—Gravin
Threndor, Peak of the Fire-Lions. And there are banes

buried in the deeps of the Earth too potent and terrible for any mortal to control. They would make of the universe a hell forever. But such a bane Drool seeks. He searches for the Illearth Stone. If he becomes its master, there will be woe for low and high alike until Time itself falls.

"Do not fail with my message, groveler. You have met Drool. Do you relish dying in his hands?"

The voice paused, and Covenant held his head in his arms, trying to silence the echo of Foul's threats. This is a dream, he thought. A dream! But the blindness of the mist made him feel trapped, encapsulated in insanity. He shuddered with the force of his desire for escape and warmth. "Go away! Leave me alone!"

"One word more," Foul said, "a final caution. Do not forget whom to fear at the last. I have had to be content with killing and torment. But now my plans are laid, and I have begun. I shall not rest until I have eradicated hope from the Earth. Think on that, and be dismayed!"

Dismayed hung prolonged in the air, while around it grew the noise of grinding, great boulders crushing lesser rocks between them. The sound rushed down onto Covenant, then passed over him and away, leaving him on his knees with his head braced between his arms and his mind blank with panic. He remained rigid there until the grinding was gone, and a low hum of wind rose through the new silence. Then he opened his eyes fearfully, and saw sunlight on the rock before his face.

FOUR: Kevin's Watch

HE stretched himself flat and lay still for a long time, welcoming the sun's warmth into his fog-chilled bones. The wind whistled a quiet monody around him, but did not touch him; and soon after the trouble of Foul's passing had ended, he heard the call of faraway birds. He lay still and breathed deeply, drawing new strength into his limbs—grateful for sunshine and the end of nightmare.

Eventually, however, he remembered that there had been several people nearby during his accident in the street. They were strangely silent; the town itself seemed hushed. The police car must have injured him worse than he realized. Leper's anxiety jerked him up onto his hands and knees.

He found himself on a smooth stone slab. It was roughly circular, ten feet broad, and surrounded by a wall three feet high. Above him arched an unbroken expanse of blue sky. It domed him from rim to rim of the wall as if the slab were somehow impossibly afloat in the heavens.

No. His breath turned to sand in his throat. Where—?

Then a panting voice called, "Hail!" He could not locate it; it sounded vague with distance, like a hallucination. "Hail!"

His heart began to tremble. What is this?

"Kevin's Watch! Are you in need?"

What the hell is this?

Abruptly, he heard a scrambling noise behind him. His muscles jumped; he dove to the wall and flipped around, put his back to it.

Opposite him, across a gap of open air beyond the wall, stood a mountain. It rose hugely from cliffs level with his perch to a sun-bright peak still tipped with snow high above him, and its craggy sides filled nearly half the slab's horizons. His first impression was one of proximity, but an instant later he realized that the cliff was at least a stone's throw away from him.

Facing squarely toward the mountain, there was a gap in the wall. The low, scrambling sound seemed to come from this gap.

He wanted to go across the slab, look for the source of the noise. But his heart was laboring too hard; he could not move. He was afraid of what he might see.

The sound came closer. Before he could react, a girl thrust her head and shoulders up into the gap, braced her arms on the stone. When she caught sight of him, she stopped to return his stare.

Her long full hair—brown with flashes of pale honey scattered through it—blew about her on the breeze; her skin was deeply shaded with tan, and the dark blue fabric of her dress had a pattern of white leaves woven into the shoulders. She was panting and flushed as if she had just finished a long climb, but she met Covenant's gaze with frank wonder and interest.

She did not look any older than sixteen.

The openness of her scrutiny only tightened his distress. He glared at her as if she were an apparition.

After a moment's hesitation, she panted, "Are you well?" Then her words began to hurry with excitement. "I did not know whether to come myself or to seek help. From the hills, I saw a gray cloud over Kevin's Watch, and within it there seemed to be a battle. I saw you stand and fall. I did not know what to do. Then I thought, better a small help soon than a large help late. So I came." She stopped herself, then asked again, "Are you well?"

Well?

He had been hit—!

His hands were only scraped, bruised, as if he had used them to absorb his fall. There was a low

ache of impact in his head. But his clothing showed
no damage, no sign that he had been struck and sent
skidding over the pavement.

He jabbed his chest with numb fingers, jabbed his
abdomen and legs, but no sharp pain answered his
probing. He seemed essentially uninjured.

But that car must have hit him somewhere.

Well?

He stared at the girl as if the word had no meaning.

Faced with his silence, she gathered her courage
and climbed up through the gap to stand before him
against the background of the mountain. He saw that
she wore a dark blue shift like a long tunic, with a
white cord knotted at the waist. On her feet she had
sandals which tied around her ankles. She was slim,
delicately figured; and her fine eyes were wide with
apprehension, uncertainty, eagerness. She took two
steps toward him as if he were a figure of peril,
then knelt to look more closely at his aghast incomprehension.

What the bloody hell is this?

Carefully, respectfully, she asked, "How may I
aid you? You are a stranger to the Land—that I
see. You have fought an ill cloud. Command me."
His silence seemed to daunt her. She dropped her
eyes. "Will you not speak?"

What's happening to me?

The next instant, she gasped with excitement,
pointed in awe at his right hand. "Halfhand! Do
legends live again?" Wonder lit her face. "Berek
Halfhand!" she breathed. "Is it true?"

Berek? At first, he could not remember where he
had heard that name before. Then it came back to
him. Berek! In cold panic he realized that the nightmare was not over, that this girl and Lord Foul the
Despiser were both part of the same experience.

Again he saw darkness crouching behind the brilliant blue sky. It loomed over him, beat toward his
head like vulture wings.

Where—?

Awkwardly, as if his joints were half frozen with dread, he lurched to his feet.

At once, an immense panorama sprang into view below him, attacked his sight like a bludgeon of exhilaration and horror. He was on a stone platform four thousand feet or more above the earth. Birds glided and wheeled under his perch. The air was as clean and clear as crystal, and through it the great sweep of the landscape seemed immeasurably huge, so that his eyes ached with trying to see it all. Hills stretched away directly under him; plains unrolled toward the horizons on both sides; a river angled silver in the sunlight out of the hills on his left. All was luminous with spring, as if it had just been born in that morning's dew.

Bloody hell!

The giddy height staggered him. Vulture wings of darkness beat at his head. Vertigo whirled up at him, made the earth veer.

He did not know where he was. He had never seen this before. How had he come here? He had been hit by a police car, and Foul had brought him here. Foul had brought him here?

Brought me here?

Uninjured?

He reeled in terror toward the girl and the mountain. Three dizzy steps took him to the gap in the parapet. There he saw that he was on the tip of a slim splinter of stone—at least five hundred feet long—that pointed obliquely up from the base of the cliff like a rigid finger accusing the sky. Stairs had been cut into the upper surface of the shaft, but it was as steep as a ladder.

For one spinning instant, he thought dumbly, *I've got to get out of here. None of this is happening to me.*

Then the whole insanity of the situation recoiled on him, struck at him out of the vertiginous air like the claws of a condor. He stumbled; the maw of the fall gaped below him. He started to scream silently:

No!!

As he pitched forward, the girl caught his arm, heaved at him. He swung and toppled to the stone within the parapet, pulled his knees up against his chest, covered his head.

Insane! he cried as if he were gibbering.

Darkness writhed like nausea inside his skull. Visions of madness burned across his mindscape.

How?

Impossible!

He had been crossing the street. He insisted upon that desperately. The light had been green.

Where?

He had been hit by a police car.

Impossible!

It had aimed itself straight for his heart, and it had hit him.

And not injured him?!

Mad. I'm going mad mad mad.

And not injured him?

Nightmare. None of this is happening, is happening, is happening.

Through the wild whirl of his misery, another hand suddenly clasped his. The grip was hard, urgent; it caught him like an anchor.

Nightmare! I'm dreaming. Dreaming!

The thought flared through his panic like a revelation. Dreaming! Of course he was dreaming. Juggling furiously, he put the pieces together. He had been hit by a police car—knocked unconscious. Concussion. He might be out for hours—days. And while he was out, he was having this dream.

That was the answer. He clutched it as if it were the girl's grip on his straining hand. It steadied him against his vertigo, simplified his fear. But it was not enough. The darkness still swarmed at him as if he were carrion Foul had left behind.

How?

Where do you get dreams like this?

He could not bear to think about it; he would go mad. He fled from it as if it had already started to gnaw on his bones.

Don't think about it. Don't try to understand. Madness—madness is the only danger. Survive! Get going. Do something. Don't look back.

He forced his eyes open; and as he focused on the sunlight, the darkness receded, dropped away into the background and came hovering slowly behind him as if it were waiting for him to turn and face it, fall prey to it.

The girl was kneeling beside him. She had his maimed right hand clamped in both of hers, and concern stood like tears in her eyes. "Berek," she murmured painfully as he met her gaze, "oh, Berek. What ill assails you? I know not what to do."

She had already done enough—helped him to master himself, resist the pull of the dangerous questions he could not answer. But his fingers were numb; parts of her clasp on his hand he could not feel at all. He dredged himself into a sitting position, though the exertion made him feel faint. "I'm a leper," he said weakly. "Don't touch me."

Hesitantly, she loosened her grip, as if she were not sure he meant what he said, not sure he knew what he was saying.

With an effort that seemed harsh because of his weakness, he withdrew his hand.

She caught her lower lip between her teeth in chagrin. As if she feared she had offended him, she moved back and sat down against the opposite wall.

But he could see that she was consumed with interest in him. She could not remain silent long. After a moment, she asked softly, "Is it wrong to touch you? I meant no harm. You are Berek Halfhand, the Lord-Fatherer. An ill I could not see assailed you. How could I bear to see you tormented so?"

"I'm a leper," he repeated, trying to conserve his strength. But her expression told him that the word conveyed nothing to her. "I'm sick—I have a disease. You don't know the danger."

"If I touch you, will I become—'sick'?"

"Who knows?" Then, because he could hardly believe the evidence of his eyes and ears, he asked, "Don't you know what leprosy is?"

"No," she answered with a return of her earlier

wonder. "No." She shook her head, and her hair swung lightly about her face. "But I am not afraid."

"Be afraid!" he rasped. The girl's ignorance or innocence made him vehement. Behind her words, he heard wings beating like violence. "It's a disease that gnaws at you. It gnaws at you until your fingers and toes and hands and feet and arms and legs turn rotten and fall off. It makes you blind and ugly."

"May it be healed? Perhaps the Lords—"

"There's no cure."

He wanted to go on, to spit out some of the bitterness Foul had left in him. But he was too drained to sustain anger. He needed to rest and think, explore the implications of his dilemma.

"Then how may I aid you? I know not what to do. You are Berek Ha—"

"I'm not," he sighed. The girl started, and into her surprise he repeated, "I'm not."

"Then who? You have the omen of the hand, for the legends say that Berek Earthfriend may come again. Are you a Lord?"

With a tired gesture he held her question at bay. He needed to think. But when he closed his eyes, leaned his head back against the parapet, he felt fear crowding up in him. He had to move, go forward—flee along the path of the dream.

He pulled his gaze back into focus on the girl's face. For the first time, he noticed that she was pretty. Even her awe, the way she hung on his words, was pretty. And she had no fear of lepers.

After a last instant of hesitation, he said, "I'm Thomas Covenant."

"Thomas Covenant?" His name sounded ungainly in her mouth. "It is a strange name—a strange name to match your strange apparel. Thomas Covenant." She inclined her head in a slow bow to him.

Strange, he thought softly. The strangeness was mutual. He still had no conception of what he would have to deal with in this dream. He would have to find out where he stood. Following the girl's lead, he asked, "Who are you?"

"I am Lena," she replied formally, "daughter of

Atiaran. My father is Trell, Gravelingas of the *rhadhamaerl*. Our home is in Mithil Stonedown. Have you been to our Stonedown?"

"No." He was tempted to ask her what a *Stonedown* was, but he had a more important question in mind. "Where—" The word caught in his throat as if it were a dangerous concession to darkness. "Where are we?"

"We are upon Kevin's Watch." Springing lightly to her feet, she stretched her arms to the earth and the sky. "Behold."

Gritting his resolve, Covenant turned and knelt against the parapet. With his chest braced on the rim, he forced himself to look.

"This is the Land," Lena said joyfully, as if the outspread earth had a power to thrill her. "It reaches far beyond seeing to the north, west, and east, though the old songs say that High Lord Kevin stood here and saw the whole of the Land and all its people. So this place is named Kevin's Watch. Is it possible that you do not know this?"

Despite the coolness of the breeze, Covenant was sweating. Vertigo knuckled his temples, and only the hard edge of the stone against his heart kept it under control. "I don't know anything," he groaned into the open fall.

Lena glanced at him anxiously, then after a moment turned back to the Land. Pointing with one slim arm to the northwest, she said, "There is the Mithil River. Our Stonedown stands beside it, but hidden behind this mountain. It flows from the Southron Range behind us to join the Black River. That is the northern bound of the South Plains, where the soil is not generous and few people live. There are only five Stonedowns in the South Plains. But in this north-going line of hills live some Woodhelvennin.

"East of the hills are the Plains of Ra." Her voice sparkled as she went on: "That is the home of the wild free horses, the Ranyhyn, and their tenders the Ramen. For fifty leagues across the Plains they gallop, and serve none that they do not themselves choose.

"Ah, Thomas Covenant," she sighed, "it is my dream to see those horses. Most of my people are too content—they do not travel, and have not seen so much as a Woodhelven. But I wish to walk the Plains of Ra, and see the horses galloping."

After a long pause, she resumed: "These mountains are the Southron Range. Behind them are the Wastes, and the Gray Desert. No life or passage is there; all the Land is north and west and east from us. And we stand on Kevin's Watch, where the highest of the Old Lords stood at the last battle, before the coming of the Desolation. Our people remember that, and avoid the Watch as a place of ill omen. But Atiaran my mother brought me here to teach me of the Land. And in two years I will be old enough to attend the Loresraat and learn for myself, as my mother did. Do you know," she said proudly, "my mother has studied with the Lorewardens?" She looked at Covenant as if she expected him to be impressed. But then her eyes fell, and she murmured, "But you are a Lord, and know all these things. You listen to my talk so that you may laugh at my ignorance."

Under the spell of her voice, and the pressure of his vertigo, he had a momentary vision of what the Land must have looked like after Kevin had unleashed the Ritual of Desecration. Behind the luminous morning, he saw hills ripped barren, soil blasted, rank water trickling through vile fens in the riverbed, and over it all a thick gloom of silence—no birds, no insects, no animals, no people, nothing living to raise one leaf or hum or growl or finger against the damage. Then sweat ran into his eyes, blurred them like tears. He pulled away from the view and seated himself again with his back to the wall. "No," he murmured to Lena, thinking, You don't understand. "I did all my laughing—long ago."

Now he seemed to see the way to go forward, to flee the dark madness which hovered over him. In that brief vision of Desolation, he found the path of the dream. Skipping transitions so that he would not have to ask or answer certain questions, he said, "I've got to go to the Council of Lords."

He saw in her face that she wanted to ask him why. But she seemed to feel that it was not her place to question his purpose. His mention of the Council only verified his stature in her eyes. She moved toward the stair. "Come," she said. "We must go to the Stonedown. There a way will be found to take you to Revelstone." She looked as if she wanted to go with him.

But the thought of the stair hurt him. How could he negotiate that descent? He could not so much as look over the parapet without dizziness. When Lena repeated, "Come," he shook his head. He lacked the courage. Yet he had to keep himself active somehow. To Lena's puzzlement, he said, "How long ago was this Desolation?"

"I do not know," she replied soberly. "But the people of the South Plains came back across the mountains from the bare Wastes twelve generations past. And it is said that they were forewarned by High Lord Kevin—they escaped, and lived in exile in the wilderness by nail and tooth and *rhadhamaerl* lore for five hundred years. It is a legacy we do not forget. At fifteen, each of us takes the Oath of Peace, and we live for the life and beauty of the Land."

He hardly heard her; he was not specifically interested in what she said. But he needed the sound of her voice to steady him while he searched himself for strength. With an effort, he found another question he could ask. Breathing deeply, he said, "What were you doing in the mountains—why were you up where you could see me here?"

"I was stone-questing," she answered. "I am learning *suru-pa-maerl*. Do you know this craft?"

"No," he said between breaths. "Tell me."

"It is a craft I am learning from Acence my mother's sister, and she learned it from Tomal, the best Craftmaster in the memory of our Stonedown. He also studied for a time in the Loresraat. But *suru-pa-maerl* is a craft of making images from stones without binding or shaping. I walk the hills and search out the shapes of rocks and pebbles. And when I discover a form that I understand, I take it home and find a place for it, balancing or interlocking with other forms until a new form is made.

"Sometimes, when I am very brave, I smooth a roughness to make the joining of the stones steadier. In this way, I remake the broken secrets of the Earth, and give beauty to the people."

Vaguely, Covenant murmured, "It must be hard—think of a shape and then find the rocks to fit it."

"That is not the way. I look at the stones, and seek for the shapes that are already in them. I do not ask the Earth to give me a horse. The craft is in learning to see what it is the Earth chooses to offer. Perhaps it will be a horse."

"I would like to see your work." Covenant paid no attention to what he was saying. The stairs beckoned him like the seductive face of forgetfulness, in which lepers lost their self-protective disciplines, their hands and feet, their lives.

But he was dreaming. The way to endure a dream was to flow with it until it ended. He had to make that descent in order to survive. That need outweighed all other considerations.

Abruptly, convulsively, he hauled himself to his feet. Planting himself squarely in the center of the circle, he ignored the mountain and the sky, ignored the long fall below him, and gave himself a thorough examination. Trembling, he probed his still-living nerves for aches or twinges, scanned his clothing for snags, rents, inspected his numb hands.

He had to put that stair behind him.

He could survive it because it was a dream—it could not kill him—and because he could not stand all this darkness beating about his ears.

"Now, listen," he snapped at Lena. "I've got to go first. And don't give me that confused look. I told you I'm a leper. My hands and feet are numb—no feeling. I can't grip. And I'm—not very good at heights. I might fall. I don't want you below me. You—" He balked, then went on roughly, "You've been decent to me, and I haven't had to put up with that for a long time."

She winced at his tone. "Why are you angry? How have I offended you?"

By being nice to me! he rasped silently. His face was gray with fear as he turned, dropped to his hands and knees, and backed out through the gap.

In the first rush of trepidation, he lowered his feet to the stairs with his eyes closed. But he could not face the descent without his eyes; the leper's habit of watching himself, and the need to have all his senses alert, were too strong. Yet with his eyes open the height made his head reel. So he strove to keep his gaze on the rock in front of him. From the first step, he knew that his greatest danger lay in the numbness of his feet. Numb hands made him feel unsure of every grip, and before he had gone fifty feet he was clenching the edges so hard that his shoulders began to cramp. But he could see his hands, see that they were on the rock, that the aching in his wrists and elbows was not a lie. His feet he could not see—not unless he looked down. He could only tell that his foot was on a stair when his ankle felt the pressure of his weight. In each downward step he lowered himself onto a guess. If he felt an unexpected flex in his arch, he had to catch himself with his arms and get more of his foot onto the unseen stair. He tried kicking his feet forward so that the jar of contact would tell him when his toes were against the edge of the next stair; but when he misjudged, his shins or knees struck the stone corners, and that sharp pain nearly made his legs fold.

Climbing down stair by stair, staring at his hands with sweat streaming into his eyes, he cursed the fate which had cut away two of his fingers—two fingers less to save himself with if his feet failed. In addition, the absence of half his hand made him feel that his right hold was weaker than his left, that his weight was pulling leftward off the stair. He kept reaching his feet to the right to compensate, and kept missing the stairs on that side.

He could not get the sweat out of his eyes. It stung

him like blindness, but he feared to release one hand to wipe his forehead, feared even to shake his head because he might lose his balance. Cramps tormented his back and shoulders. He had to grit his teeth to keep from crying for help.

As if she sensed his distress, Lena shouted, "Half-way!"

He crept on downward, step by step.

Helplessly, he felt himself moving faster. His muscles were failing—the strain on his knees and elbows was too great—and with each step he had less control over his descent. He forced himself to stop and rest, though his terror screamed for him to go on, get the climb over with. For a wild instant, he thought that he would simply turn and leap, hoping he was close enough to land on the mountain slope and live. Then he heard the sound of Lena's feet approaching his head. He wanted to reach up and grab her ankles, force her to save him. But even that hope seemed futile, and he hung where he was, quivering.

His breath rattled harshly through his clenched teeth, and he almost did not understand Lena's shout:

"Thomas Covenant! Be strong! Only fifty steps remain!"

With a shudder that almost tore him loose from the rock, he started down again.

The last steps passed in a loud chaos of cramps and sweat blindness—and then he was down, lying flat on the level base of the Watch and gasping at the cries of his limbs. For a long time, he covered his face and listened to the air lurching in and out of his lungs like sobs—listened until the sound relaxed and he could breathe more quietly.

When he finally looked up, he saw the blue sky, the long black finger of Kevin's Watch pointing at the noon sun, the towering slope of the mountain, and Lena bending over him so low that her hair almost brushed his face.

FIVE: Mithil Stonedown

COVENANT felt strangely purged, as if he had passed through an ordeal, survived a ritual trial by vertigo. He had put the stair behind him. In his relief, he was sure that he had found the right answer to the particular threat of madness, the need for a real and comprehensible explanation to his situation, which had surrounded him on Kevin's Watch. He looked up at the radiant sky, and it appeared pure, untainted by carrion eaters.

Go forward, he said to himself. Don't think about it. Survive.

As he thought this, he looked up into Lena's soft brown eyes and found that she was smiling.

"Are you well?" she asked.

"Well?" he echoed. "That's not an easy question." It drew him up into a sitting position. Scanning his hands, he discovered blood on the heels and finger-tips. His palms were scraped raw, and when he probed his knees and shins and elbows they burned painfully.

Ignoring the ache of his muscles, he pushed to his feet. "Lena, this is important," he said. "I've got to clean my hands."

She stood also, but he could see that she did not understand. "Look!" He brandished his hands in front of her. "I'm a leper. I can't feel this. No pain." When she still seemed confused, he went on, "That's how I lost my fingers. I got hurt and infected, and they had to cut my hand apart. I've got to get some soap and water."

Touching the scar on his right hand, she said, "The sickness does this?"

"Yes!"

"There is a stream on the way toward the Stonedown," said Lena, "and hurtloam near it."

"Let's go." Brusquely, Covenant motioned for her to lead the way. She accepted his urgency with a nod, and started at once down the path.

It went west from the base of Kevin's Watch along a ledge in the steep mountain slope until it reached a cluttered ravine. Moving awkwardly because of the clenched stiffness of his muscles, Covenant followed Lena up the ravine, then stepped gingerly behind her down a rough-hewn stair in the side of a sharp cut which branched away into the mountain. When they reached the bottom of the cut, they continued along it, negotiating its scree-littered floor while the slash of sky overhead narrowed and the sides of the cut leaned together. A rich, damp smell surrounded them, and the cool shadows deepened until Lena's dark tunic became dim in the gloom ahead of Covenant. Then the cut turned sharply to the left and opened without warning into a small, sun-bright valley with a stream sparkling through the center and tall pines standing over the grass around the edges.

"Here," said Lena with a happy smile. "What could heal you more than this?"

Covenant stopped to gaze, entranced, down the length of the valley. It was no more than fifty yards long, and at its far end the stream turned left again and filed away between two sheer walls. In this tiny pocket in the vastness of the mountain, removed from the overwhelming landscapes below Kevin's Watch, the earth was comfortably green and sunny, and the air was both fresh and warm—pine-aromatic, redolent with springtime. As he breathed the atmosphere of the place, Covenant felt his chest ache with a familiar grief at his own sickness.

To ease the pressure in his chest, he moved forward. The grass under his feet was so thick and springy that he could feel it through the strained ligaments of his knees and calves. It seemed to encourage him toward the stream, toward the cleansing of his hurts.

The water was sure to be cold, but that did not

concern him. His hands were too numb to notice cold very quickly. Squatting on a flat stone beside the stream, he plunged them into the current and began rubbing them together. His wrists felt the chill at once, but his fingers were vague about the water; and it gave him no pain to scrub roughly at his cuts and scrapes.

He was marginally aware that Lena had moved away from him up the stream, apparently looking for something, but he was too preoccupied to wonder what she was doing. After an intense scrubbing he let his hands rest, and rolled up his sleeves to inspect his elbows. They were red and sore, but the skin was not broken.

When he pulled up his pant legs, he found that his shins and knees were more battered. The discoloration of his bruises was already darkening, and would be practically black before long; but the tough fabric of his trousers had held, and again the skin was unbroken. In their way, bruises were as dangerous to him as cuts, but he could not treat them without medication. He made an effort to stifle his anxiety, and turned his attention back to his hands.

Blood still oozed from the heels and fingertips, and when he washed it off he could see bits of black grit lodged deep in some of the cuts. But before he started washing again, Lena returned. Her cupped hands were full of thick brown mud. "This is hurtloam," she said reverently, as if she were speaking of something rare and powerful. "You must put it on all your wounds."

"Mud?" His leper's caution quivered. "I need soap, not more dirt."

"This is hurtloam," repeated Lena. "It is for healing." She stepped closer and thrust the mud toward him. He thought he could see tiny gleams of gold in it.

He stared at it blankly, shocked by the idea of putting mud in his cuts.

"You must use it," she insisted. "I know what it is. Do you not understand? This is hurtloam. Listen. My father is Trell, Gravelingas of the *rhadhamaerl*.

His work is with the fire-stones, and he leaves healing to the Healers. But he is a *rhadhamaerl*. He comprehends the rocks and soils. And he taught me to care for myself when there is need. He taught me the signs and places of hurtloam. This is healing earth. You must use it."

Mud? He glared. In my cuts? Do you want to cripple me?

Before he could stop her, Lena knelt in front of him and dropped a handful of the mud onto his bare knee. With that hand free, she spread the brown loam down his shin. Then she scooped up the remainder and put it on his other knee and shin. As it lay on his legs, its golden gleaming seemed to grow stronger, brighter.

The wet earth was cool and soothing, and it seemed to stroke his legs tenderly, absorbing the pain from his bruises. He watched it closely. The relief that it sent flowing through his bones gave him a pleasure that he had never felt before. Bemused, he opened his hands to Lena, let her spread hurtloam over all his cuts and scrapes.

At once, the relief began to run up into him through his elbows and wrists. And an odd tingling started in his palms, as if the hurtloam were venturing past his cuts into his nerves, trying to reawaken them. A similar tingling danced across the arches of his feet. He stared at the glittering mud with a kind of awe in his eyes.

It dried quickly; its light vanished into the brown. In a few moments Lena rubbed it off his legs. Then he saw that his bruises were almost gone—they were in the last, faded yellow stages of healing. He slapped his hands into the stream, washed away the mud, looked at his fingers. They had become whole again. The heels of his hands were healed as well, and the abrasions on his forearms had disappeared completely. He was so stunned that for a moment he could only gape at his hands and think, Hellfire. Hellfire and bloody damnation. What's happening to me?

After a long silence, he whispered, "That's not possible."

In response, Lena grinned broadly.

"What's so funny?"

Trying to imitate his tone, she said, " 'I need soap, not more dirt.' " Then she laughed, a teasing sparkle in her eyes.

But Covenant was too full of surprise to be distracted. "I'm serious. How can this happen?"

Lena dropped her eyes and answered quietly, "There is power in the Earth—power and life. You must know this. Atiaran my mother says that such things as hurtloam, such powers and mysteries, are in all the Earth—but we are blind to them because we do not share enough, with the Land and with each other."

"There are—other things like this?"

"Many. But I know only a few. If you travel to the Council, it may be that the Lords will teach you everything. But come"—she swung lightly to her feet—"here is another. Are you hungry?"

As if cued by her question, an impression of emptiness opened in his stomach. How long had it been since he had eaten? He adjusted his pant legs, rolled down his sleeves, and shrugged himself to his feet. His wonder was reinforced to find that almost every ache was gone from his muscles. Shaking his head in disbelief, he followed Lena toward one side of the valley.

Under the shade of the trees, she stopped beside a gnarled, waist-high shrub. Its leaves were spread and pointed like a holly's, but it was scattered with small viridian blooms, and nestled under some of the leaves were tight clusters of a blue-green fruit the size of blueberries.

"This is *aliantha*," said Lena. "We call them treasure-berries." Breaking off a cluster, she ate four or five berries, then dropped the seeds into her hand and threw them behind her. "It is said that a person can walk the whole length and breadth of the Land eating only treasure-berries, and return home stronger and better fed than before. They are a great gift of the Earth. They bloom and bear fruit in all seasons. There is no part of the Land in which they do not grow—except, perhaps, in the east, on the Spoiled Plains. And they are the hardiest of growing things— the last to die and the first to grow again. All this my mother told me, as part of the lore of our people. Eat," she said, handing Covenant a cluster of the berries, "eat, and spread the seeds over the Earth, so that the *aliantha* may flourish."

But Covenant made no move to take the fruit. He was lost in wonder, in unanswerable questions about the strange potency of this Land. For the moment, he neglected his danger.

Lena regarded his unfocused gaze, then took one of the berries and put it in his mouth. By reflex, he broke the skin with his teeth; at once, his mouth was filled with a light, sweet taste like that of a ripe peach faintly blended with salt and lime. In another moment he was eating greedily, only occasionally remembering to spit out the seeds.

He ate until he could find no more fruit on that bush, then looked about him for another. But Lena put her hand on his arm to stop him. "Treasure-berries are strong food," she said. "You do not need many. And the taste is better if you eat slowly."

But Covenant was still hungry. He could not remember ever wanting food as much as he now wanted that fruit—the sensations of eating had never been so vivid, so compulsory. He snatched his arm away as if he meant to strike her, then abruptly caught himself.

What is this? What's happening?

Before he could pursue the question, he became aware of another feeling—overpowering drowsiness. In the space of one instant, he passed almost without transition from hunger to a huge yawn that made him seem top-heavy with weariness. He tried to turn, and stumbled.

Lena was saying, "The hurtloam does this, but I did not expect it. When the wounds are very deadly, hurtloam brings sleep to speed the healing. But cuts on the hands are not deadly. Do you have hurts that you did not show me?"

Yes, he thought through another yawn. *I'm sick to death.*

He was asleep before he hit the grass.

When he began to drift slowly awake, the first thing that he became conscious of was Lena's firm thighs pillowing his head. Gradually, he grew aware of other things—the tree shade bedizened with glints of declining sunlight, the aroma of pine, the wind murmuring, the grass thickly cradling his body, the sound of a tune, the irregular tingling that came and went from his palms like an atavism—but the warmth of his cheek on Lena's lap seemed more important. For the time, his sole desire was to clasp Lena in his arms and bury his face in her thighs. He resisted it by listening to her song.

In a soft and somehow naive tone, she sang:

> Something there is in beauty
> which grows in the soul of the beholder
> like a flower:
> fragile—
> for many are the blights
> which may waste
> the beauty
> or the beholder—
> and imperishable—
> for the beauty may die,
> or the beholder may die,
> or the world may die,
> but the soul in which the flower grows
> survives.

Her voice folded him in a comfortable spell which he did not want to end. After a pause full of the scent of pine and the whispering breeze, he said softly, "I like that."

"Do you? I am glad. It was made by Tomal the Craftmaster, for the dance when he wed Imoiran Moiran-daughter. But ofttimes the beauty of a song is in the singing, and I am no singer. It may be that tonight Atiaran my mother will sing for the Stonedown. Then you will hear a real song."

Covenant gave no answer. He lay still, only wishing to nestle in his pillow for as long as he could. The tingling in his palms seemed to urge him to embrace

Lena, and he lay still, enjoying the desire and wondering where he would find the courage.

Then she began to sing again. The tune sounded familiar, and behind it he heard the rumor of dark wings. Suddenly he realized that it was very much like the tune that went with "Golden Boy."

He had been walking down the sidewalk toward the offices of the phone company—the Bell Telephone Company; that name was written in gilt letters on the door—to pay his bill in person.

He jerked off Lena's lap, jumped to his feet. A mist of violence dimmed his vision. "What song is that?" he demanded thickly.

Startled, Lena answered, "No song. I was only trying to make a melody. Is it wrong?"

The tone of her voice steadied him—she sounded so abandoned, so made forlorn by his quick anger. Words failed him, and the mist passed. No business, he thought. I've got no business taking it out on her. Extending his hands, he helped her to her feet. He tried to smile, but his stiff face could only grimace. "Where do we go now?"

Slowly the hurt faded from her eyes. "You are strange, Thomas Covenant," she said.

Wryly, he replied, "I didn't know it was this bad."

For a moment, they stood gazing into each other's eyes. Then she surprised him by blushing and dropping his hands. There was a new excitement in her voice as she said, "We will go to the Stonedown. You will amaze my mother and father." Gaily, she turned and ran away down the valley.

She was lithe and light and graceful as she ran, and Covenant watched her, musing on the strange new feelings that moved in him. He had an unexpected sense that this Land might offer him some spell with which he could conjure away his impotence, some rebirth to which he could cling even after he regained consciousness, after the Land and all its insane implications faded into the miasma of half-remembered dreams. Such hope did not require that the Land be real, physically actual and independent of his own unconscious, uncontrolled dream-weaving. No, leprosy was an incurable disease, and if he did not die from his accident, he would have to live with that fact. But a dream might heal other afflictions. It might. He set off after Lena with a swing in his stride and eagerness in his veins.

The sun was down far enough in the sky to leave the lower half of the valley in shadow. Ahead of him, he could see Lena beckoning, and he followed the stream toward her, enjoying the spring of the turf under his feet as he walked. He felt somehow taller than before, as if the hurtloam had done more to him than simply heal his cuts and scrapes. Nearing Lena, he seemed to see parts of her for the first time—the delicacy of her ears when her hair swung behind them—the way the soft fabric of her shift hung on her breasts and hips—her slim waist. The sight of her made the tingling in his palms grow stronger.

She smiled at him, then led the way along the stream and out of the valley. They moved down a crooked file between sheer walls of rock which climbed above them until the narrow slit of the sky was hundreds of feet away. The trail was rocky, and Covenant had to watch his feet constantly to keep his balance. The effort made the file seem long, but within a couple hundred yards he and Lena came to a crevice that ascended to the right away from the stream. They climbed into and along the crevice. Soon it leveled, then sloped gradually downward for a long way, but it bent enough so that Covenant could not see where he was headed.

At last, the crevice took one more turn and ended, leaving Lena and Covenant on the mountainside high above the river valley. They were facing due west into the declining sun. The river came out of the mountains to their left, and flowed away into the plains on their right. There was a branch of the mountain range across the valley, but it soon shrank into the plains to the north.

"Here is the Mithil," said Lena. "And there is Mithil Stonedown." Covenant saw a tiny knot of huts north of him on the east side of the river. "It is not a great distance," Lena went on, "but the path travels up the valley and then back along the river. The sun will be gone when we reach our Stonedown. Come."

Covenant had an uneasy moment looking down the slope of the mountain—still more than two thousand feet above the valley—but he mastered it, and followed Lena to the south. The mountainside relaxed steadily, and soon the path lay along grassy slopes and behind stern rock buttresses, through dells and ravines, among mazes of fallen boulders. And as the trail descended, the air became deeper, softer, and less crystalline. The smells slowly changed, grew greener; pine and aspen gave way to the loam of the grasslands. Covenant felt that he was alive to every gradation of the change, every nuance of the lowering altitude. Through the excitement of his new alertness, the descent passed quickly. Before he was ready to leave the mountains, the trail rolled down a long hill, found the river, and then swung north along it.

The Mithil was narrow and brisk where the path first joined it, and it spoke with wet rapidity to itself in a voice full of resonances and rumors. But as the river drew toward the plains, it broadened and slowed, became more philosophical in its low, self-communing mutter. Soon its voice no longer filled the air. Quietly it told itself its long tale as it rolled away on its quest for the sea.

Under the spell of the river, Covenant became slowly more conscious of the reassuring solidity of the Land. It was not an intangible dreamscape; it was concrete, susceptible to ascertainment. This was an illusion, of course—a trick of his wracked and smitten mind. But it was curiously comforting. It seemed to promise that he was not walking into horror, chaos—that this Land was coherent, manageable, that when he had mastered its laws, its peculiar facts, he would be able to travel unscathed the path of his dream, retain his grip on his sanity. Such thoughts made him feel almost bold as he followed Lena's lithe back, the swaying appeal of her hips.

While Covenant wandered in unfamiliar emotions, the Mithil valley dropped into shadow. The sun crossed behind the western mountains, and though light still glowed on the distant plains, a thin veil of darkness thickened in the valley. As he watched, the rim of the shadow stretched itself high up the mountain on his right, climbing like a hungry tide the shores of day. In the twilight, he sensed his peril sneaking furtively closer to him, though he did not know what it was.

Then the last ridge of the mountains fell into dusk, and the glow on the plains began to fade.

Lena stopped, touched Covenant's arm, pointed. "See," she said, "here is Mithil Stonedown."

They stood atop a long, slow hill, and at its bottom were gathered the buildings of the village. Covenant could see the houses quite clearly, although lights already shone faintly behind some of the windows. Except for a large, open circle in the center of the village, the Stonedown looked as erratically laid out as if it had fallen off the mountain not long ago. But this impression was belied by the smooth sheen of the stone walls and the flat roofs. And when he looked more closely, Covenant saw that the Stonedown was not in fact unorganized. All the buildings faced in toward the center.

None of them had more than one story, and all were stone, with flat slabs of rock for roofs; but they varied considerably in size and shape—some were round, others square or rectangular, and still others so irregular from top to bottom that they seemed more like squat hollow boulders than buildings.

As she and Covenant started down toward the Stonedown, Lena said, "Five times a hundred people of the South Plains live here—*rhadhamaerl,* Shepherds, Cattleherds, Farmers, and those who Craft. But Atiaran my mother alone has been to the Loresraat." Pointing, she added, "The home of my family is there—nearest the river."

Walking together, she and Covenant skirted the Stonedown toward her home.

SIX: Legend of Berek Halfhand

Dusk was deepening over the valley. Birds gathered to rest for the night in the trees of the foothills. They sang and called energetically to each other for a while, but their high din soon relaxed into a quiet, satisfied murmur. As Lena and Covenant passed behind the outer houses of the Stonedown, they could again hear the river contemplating itself in the distance. Lena was silent, as if she were containing some excitement or agitation, and Covenant was too immersed in the twilit sounds around him to say anything. The swelling night seemed full of soft communions—anodynes for the loneliness of the dark. So they came quietly toward Lena's home.

It was a rectangular building, larger than most in the Stonedown, but with the same polished sheen on the walls. A warm yellow light radiated from the windows. As Lena and Covenant approached, a large figure crossed one of the windows and moved toward a farther room.

At the corner of the house, Lena paused to take Covenant's hand and squeezed it before she led him up to the doorway.

The entry was covered with a heavy curtain. She held it aside and drew him into the house. There she halted. Looking around swiftly, he observed that the room they had entered went the depth of the house, but it had two curtained doors in either wall. In it, a stone table and benches with enough space to seat six or eight people occupied the middle of the floor. But the room was large enough so that the table did not dominate it.

Cut into the rock walls all around the room were shelves, and these were full of stoneware jars and utensils, some obviously for use in cooking and eating, others with functions which Covenant could not guess. Several rock stools stood against the walls. And the warm yellow light filled the chamber, glowing on the smooth surfaces and reflecting off rare colors and textures in the stone.

The light came from fires in several stone pots, one in each corner of the room and one in the center of the table; but there was no flicker of flames—the light was as steady as its stone containers. And with the light came a soft smell as of newly broken earth.

After only a cursory glance around the chamber, Covenant's attention was drawn to the far end of the room. There on a slab of stone against the wall sat a huge granite pot, half as tall as a man. And over the pot, peering intently at its contents, stood a large man, a great pillar of a figure, as solid as a boulder. He had his back to Lena and Covenant, and did not seem to be aware of them. He wore a short brown tunic with brown trousers under it, but the leaf pattern woven into the fabric at his shoulders was identical to Lena's. Under the tunic, his massive muscles bunched and stretched as he rotated the pot. It looked prodigiously heavy, but Covenant half expected the man to lift it over his head to pour out its contents.

There was a shadow over the pot which the brightness of the room did not penetrate, and for some time the man stared into the darkness, studying it while he rotated the pot. Then he began to sing. His voice was too low for Covenant to make out the words, but as he listened he felt a kind of invocation in the sound, as if the contents of the pot were powerful. For a moment, nothing happened. Then the shadow began to pale. At first, Covenant thought that the light in the room had changed, but soon he saw a new illumination starting from the pot. The glow swelled and deepened, and at last shone out strongly, making the other lights seem thin.

With a final mutter over his work, the man stood upright and turned around. In the new brightness, he

seemed even taller and broader than before, as if
his limbs and shoulders and deep chest drew strength,
stature, from the light; and his forehead was ruddy
from the heat of the pot. Seeing Covenant, he started
in surprise. An uneasy look came into his eyes, and
his right hand touched his thick reddish beard. Then
he extended the hand, palm forward, toward Covenant, and said to Lena, "Well, daughter, you bring a
guest. But I remember that our hospitality is in your
charge today." The strange potency of a moment before was gone from his voice. He sounded like a
man who did not speak much with people. But though
he was treating his daughter sternly, he seemed essentially calm. "You know I promised more graveling
today, and Atiaran your mother is helping deliver the
new child of Odona Murrin-mate. The guest will be
offended by our hospitality—with no meal ready to
welcome the end of his day." Yet while he repri-
manded Lena, his eyes studied Covenant cautiously.

Lena bowed her head, trying, Covenant felt sure,
to look ashamed for her father's benefit. But a moment later she hurried across the room and hugged
the big man. He smiled softly at her upturned face.
Then, turning toward Covenant, she announced, "Trell
my father, I bring a stranger to the Stonedown. I
found him on Kevin's Watch." A lively gleam shone
in her eyes, although she tried to keep her voice
formal.

"So," Trell responded. "A stranger—that I see.
And wonder what business took him to that ill-blown
place."

"He fought with a gray cloud," answered Lena.

Looking at this bluff, hale man, whose muscle-
knotted arm rested with such firm gentleness on
Lena's shoulder, Covenant expected him to laugh at
the absurd suggestion—a man fighting a cloud. Trell's
presence felt imperturbable and earthy, like an assertion of common sense that reduced the nightmare
of Foul to its proper unreality. So Covenant was put
off his balance by hearing Trell ask with perfect
seriousness, "Which was the victor?"

The question forced Covenant to find a new footing for himself. He was not prepared to deal with the memory of Lord Foul—but at the same time he felt obscurely sure that he could not lie to Trell. He found that his throat had gone dry, and he answered awkwardly, "I lived through it."

Trell said nothing for a moment, but in the silence Covenant felt that his answer had increased the big man's uneasiness. Trell's eyes shifted away, then came back as he said, "I see. And what is your name, stranger?"

Promptly, Lena smiled at Covenant and answered for him, "Thomas Covenant. Covenant of Kevin's Watch."

"What, girl?" asked Trell. "Are you a prophet, that you speak for someone higher than you?" Then to Covenant he said, "Well, Thomas Covenant of Kevin's Watch—do you have other names?"

Covenant was about to respond negatively when he caught an eager interest in the question from Lena's eyes. He paused. In a leap of insight, he realized that he was as exciting to her as if he had in fact been Berek Halfhand—that to her yearning toward mysteries and powers, all-knowing Lords and battles in the clouds, his strangeness and his unexplained appearance on the Watch made him seem like a personification of great events out of a heroic past. The message of her gaze was suddenly plain; in the suspense of her curiosity she was hanging from the hope that he would reveal himself to her, give her some glimpse of his high calling to appease her for her youth and ignorance.

The idea filled him with strange reverberations. He was not used to such flattery; it gave him an unfamiliar sense of possibility. Quickly, he searched for some high-sounding title to give himself, some name by which he could please Lena without falsifying himself to Trell. Then he had an inspiration. "Thomas Covenant," he said as if he were rising to a challenge, "the Unbeliever."

Immediately, he felt that with that name he had committed himself to more than he could measure at present. The act made him feel pretentious, but Lena

rewarded him with a beaming glance, and Trell ac-
cepted the statement gravely. "Well, Thomas Cove-
nant," he replied, "you are welcome to Mithil
Stonedown. Please accept the hospitality of this home.
I must go now to take my graveling as I promised.
It may be that Atiaran my wife will return soon.
And if you prod her, Lena may remember to offer
you refreshment while I am gone."

While he spoke, Trell turned back to his stone pot.
He wrapped his arms about it, lifted it from its base.
With red-gold flames reflecting a dance in his hair
and beard, he carried the pot toward the doorway.
Lena hurried ahead of him to hold open the curtain,
and in a moment Trell was gone, leaving Covenant
with one glimpse of the contents of the pot. It was
full of small, round stones like fine gravel, and they
seemed to be on fire.

"Damnation," Covenant whispered. "How heavy is
that thing?"

"Three men cannot lift the pot alone," replied Lena
proudly. "But when the graveling burns, my father
may lift it easily. He is a Gravelingas of the
rhadhamaerl, deep with the lore of stone."

Covenant stared after him for a moment, appalled
by Trell's strength.

Then Lena said, "Now, I must not fail to offer
you refreshment. Will you wash or bathe? Are you
thirsty? We have good springwine."

Her voice brought back the scintillation of Covenant's nerves. His instinctive distrust of Trell's might
dissipated under the realization that he had a power
of his own. This world accepted him; it accorded
him importance. People like Trell and Lena were prepared to take him as seriously as he wanted. All he
had to do was keep moving, follow the path of his
dream to Revelstone—whatever that was. He felt
giddy at the prospect. On the impetus of the moment,
he determined to participate in his own importance,
enjoy it while it lasted.

To cover his rush of new emotions, he told Lena
that he would like to wash. She took him past a curtain into another room, where water poured con-

tinuously from a spout in the wall. A sliding stone valve sent the water into either a washbasin or a large tub, both formed of stone. Lena showed him some fine sand to use as soap, then left him. The water was cold, but he plunged his hands and head into it with something approaching enthusiasm.

When he was done, he looked around for a towel, but did not see one. Experimentally, he eased a hand over the glowing pot that lit the room. The warm yellow light dried his fingers rapidly, so he leaned over the pot, rubbing the water from his face and neck, and soon even his hair was dry. By force of habit, he went through his VSE, examining the nearly invisible marks where his hands had been cut. Then he pushed the curtain out of his way and reentered the central chamber.

He found that another woman had joined Lena. As he returned, he heard Lena say, "He says he knows nothing of us." Then the other woman looked at him, and he guessed immediately that she was Atiaran. The leaf pattern at the shoulders of her long brown robe seemed to be a kind of family emblem; he did not need such hints to see the long familiarity in the way the older woman touched Lena's shoulder, or the similarities in their posture. But where Lena was fresh and slim of line, full of unbroken newness, Atiaran appeared complex, almost self-contradictory. Her soft surface, her full figure, she carried as if it were a hindrance to the hard strength of experience within her, as if she lived with her body on the basis of an old and difficult truce. And her face bore the signs of that truce; her forehead seemed prematurely lined, and her deep spacious eyes appeared to open inward on a weary battleground of doubts and uneasy reconciliations. Looking at her over the stone table, Covenant received a double impression of a frowning concern—the result of knowing and fearing more than other people realized—and an absent beauty that would rekindle her face if only she would smile.

After a brief hesitation, the older woman touched her heart and raised her hand toward Covenant as Trell had done. "Hail, guest, and welcome. I am

Atiaran Trell-mate. I have spoken with Trell, and with Lena my daughter—you need no introduction to me, Thomas Covenant. Be comfortable in our home."

Remembering his manners—and his new determination—Covenant responded, "I'm honored."

Atiaran bowed slightly. "Accepting that which is offered honors the giver. And courtesy is always welcome." Then she seemed to hesitate again, uncertain of how to proceed. Covenant watched the return of old conflicts to her eyes, thinking that gaze would have an extraordinary power if it were not so inward. But she reached her decision soon, and said, "It is not the custom of our people to worry a guest with hard questions before eating. But the food is not ready"— she glanced at Lena—"and you are strange to me, Thomas Covenant, strange and disquieting. I would talk with you if I may, while Lena prepares what food we have. You seem to bear a need that should not wait."

Covenant shrugged noncommittally. He felt a twinge of anxiety at the thought of her questions, and braced himself to try to answer them without losing his new balance.

In the pause, Lena began moving around the room. She went to the shelves to get plates and bowls for the table, and prepared some dishes on a slab of stone heated from underneath by a tray of graveling. She turned her eyes toward Covenant often as she moved, but he did not always notice. Atiaran compelled his attention.

At first, she murmured uncertainly, "I hardly know where to begin. It has been so long, and I learned so little of what the Lords know. But what I have must be enough. No one here can take my place." She straightened her shoulders. "May I see your hands?"

Remembering Lena's initial reaction to him, Covenant held up his right hand.

Atiaran moved around the table until she was close enough to touch him, but did not. Instead, she searched his face. "Halfhand. It is as Trell said. And some say that Berek Earthfriend, Hearthew and Lord-

Fatherer, will return to the Land when there is need. Do you know these things?"

Covenant answered gruffly, "No."

Still looking into his face, Atiaran said, "Your other hand?"

Puzzled, he raised his left. She dropped her eyes to it.

When she saw it, she gasped, and bit her lip and stepped back. For an instant, she seemed inexplicably terrified. But she mastered herself, and asked with only a low tremble in her voice, "What metal is that ring?"

"What? This?" Her reaction startled Covenant, and in his surprise he gaped at a complicated memory of Joan saying, *With this ring I thee wed,* and the old ocher-robed beggar replying, *Be true, be true.* Darkness threatened him. He heard himself answer as if he were someone else, someone who had nothing to do with leprosy and divorce, "It's white gold."

Atiaran groaned, clamped her hands over her temples as if she were in pain. But again she brought herself under control, and a bleak courage came into her eyes. "I alone," she said, "I alone in Mithil Stonedown know the meaning of this. Even Trell has not this knowledge. And I know too little. Answer, Thomas Covenant—is it true?"

I should've thrown it away, he muttered bitterly. A leper's got no right to be sentimental.

But Atiaran's intensity drew his attention toward her again. She gave him the impression that she knew more about what was happening to him than he did—that he was moving into a world which, in some dim, ominous way, had been made ready for him. His old anger mounted. "Of course it's true," he snapped. "What's the matter with you? It's only a ring."

"It is white gold." Atiaran's reply sounded as forlorn as if she had just suffered a bereavement.

"So what?" He could not understand what distressed the woman. "It doesn't mean a thing. Joan—" Joan had preferred it to yellow gold. But that had not prevented her from divorcing him.

"It is white gold," Atiaran repeated. "The Lords

sing an ancient lore-song concerning the bearer of white gold. I remember only a part of it, thus:

> And he who wields white wild magic gold
> is a paradox—
> for he is everything and nothing,
> hero and fool,
> potent, helpless—
> and with the one word of truth or treachery,
> he will save or damn the Earth
> because he is mad and sane,
> cold and passionate,
> lost and found.

Do you know the song, Covenant? There is no white gold in the Land. Gold has never been found in the Earth, though it is said that Berek knew of it, and made the songs. You come from another place. What terrible purpose brings you here?"

Covenant felt her searching him with her eyes for some flaw, some falsehood which would give the lie to her fear. He stiffened. *You have might,* the Despiser had said, *wild magic— You will never know what it is.* The idea that his wedding band was some kind of talisman nauseated him like the smell of attar. He had a savage desire to shout. None of this is happening! But he only knew of one workable response: don't think about it, follow the path, survive. He met Atiaran on her own ground. "All purposes are terrible. I have a message for the Council of Lords."

"What message?" she demanded.

After only an instant's hesitation, he grated, "The Gray Slayer has come back."

When she heard Covenant pronounce that name, Lena dropped the stoneware bowl she was carrying, and fled into her mother's arms.

Covenant stood glowering at the shattered bowl. The liquid it had contained gleamed on the smooth stone floor. Then he heard Atiaran pant in horror, "How do you know this?" He looked back at her, and saw the two women clinging together like children threatened by the demon of their worst dreams. Leper outcast unclean! he thought sourly. But as he watched, Atiaran seemed to grow solider. Her jaw squared, her broad glance hardened. For all her fear, she was a strong woman comforting her child—and bracing herself to meet her danger. Again she asked, "How do you know?"

She made him feel defensive, and he replied, "I met him on Kevin's Watch."

"Ah, alas!" she cried, hugging Lena. "Alas for the young in this world! The doom of the Land is upon them. Generations will die in agony, and there will be war and terror and pain for those who live! Alas, Lena my daughter. You were born into an evil time, and there will be no peace or comfort for you when the battle comes. Ah, Lena, Lena."

Her grief touched an undefended spot in Covenant, and his throat thickened. Her voice filled his own image of the Land's Desolation with a threnody he had not heard before. For the first time, he sensed that the Land held something precious which was in danger of being lost.

This combination of sympathy and anger tightened his nerves still further. He vibrated to a sharper pitch, trembled. When he looked at Lena, he saw that a new awe of him had already risen above her panic. The unconscious offer in her eyes burned more disturbingly than ever.

He held himself still until Atiaran and Lena slowly released each other. Then he asked, "What do you know about all this? About what's happening to me?"

Before Atiaran could reply, a voice called from outside the house, "Hail! Atiaran Tiaran-daughter. Trell Gravelingas tells us that your work is done for this day. Come and sing to the Stonedown!"

For a moment, Atiaran stood still, shrinking back into herself. Then she sighed, "Ah, the work of my life has just begun," and turned to the door. Holding aside the curtain, she said into the night, "We have not yet eaten. I will come later. But after the gathering I must speak with the Circle of elders."

"They will be told," the voice answered.

"Good," said Atiaran. But instead of returning to Covenant, she remained in the doorway, staring into the darkness for a while. When she closed the curtain at last and faced Covenant, her eyes were moist, and they held a look that he at first thought was defeat. But then he realized that she was only remembering defeat. "No, Thomas Covenant," she said sadly, "I know nothing of your fate. Perhaps if I had remained at the Loresraat longer—if I had had the strength. But I passed my limit there, and came home. I know a part of the old Lore that Mithil Stonedown does not guess, but it is too little. All that I can remember for you are hints of a wild magic which destroys peace—

wild magic graven in every rock,
contained for white gold to unleash or control—

but the meaning of such lines, or the courses of these times, I do not know. That is a double reason to take you to the Council." Then she looked squarely into his face, and added, "I tell you openly, Thomas Covenant—if you have come to betray the Land, only the Lords may hope to stop you."

Betray? This was another new thought. An instant passed before he realized what Atiaran was suggesting. But before he could protest, Lena put in for him, "Mother! He fought a gray cloud on Kevin's Watch. I saw it. How can you doubt him?" Her defense controlled his belligerent reaction. Without intending to, she had put him on false ground. He had not gone so far as to fight Lord Foul.

Trell's return stopped any reply Atiaran might have made. The big man stood in the doorway for a moment, looking between Atiaran and Lena and Covenant. Abruptly, he said, "So. We are come on hard times."

"Yes, Trell my husband," murmured Atiaran. "Hard times."

Then his eyes caught the shards of stoneware on the floor. "Hard times, indeed," he chided gently, "when stoneware is broken, and the pieces left to powder underfoot."

This time, Lena was genuinely ashamed. "I am sorry, Father," she said. "I was afraid."

"No matter." Trell went to her and placed his big hands, light with affection, on her shoulders. "Some wounds may be healed. I feel strong today."

At this, Atiaran gazed gratefully at Trell as if he had just undertaken some heroic task.

To Covenant's incomprehension, she said, "Be seated, guest. Food will be ready soon. Come, Lena." The two of them began to bustle around the cooking stone.

Covenant watched as Trell started to pick up the pieces of the broken pot. The Gravelingas' voice rumbled softly, singing an ancient subterranean song. Tenderly, he carried the shards to the table and set them down near the lamp. Then he seated himself. Covenant sat beside him, wondering what was about to happen.

Singing his cavernous song between clenched teeth, Trell began to fit the shards together as if the pot were a puzzle. Piece after piece he set in place, and each piece held where he left it without any adhesive Covenant could see. Trell moved painstakingly, his touch delicate on every fragment, but the pot seemed to grow quickly in his hands, and the pieces fit together perfectly, leaving only a network of fine black lines to mark the breaks. Soon all the shards were in place.

Then his deep tone took on a new cadence. He began to stroke the stoneware with his fingers, and everywhere his touch passed, the black fracture-marks vanished as if they had been erased. Slowly, he covered every inch of the pot with his caress. When he had completed the outside, he stroked the inner surface. And finally he lifted the pot, spread his touch over its base. Holding the pot between the fingers of both hands, he rotated it carefully, making sure he had missed nothing. Then he stopped singing, set the pot down gently, took his hands away. It was as complete and solid as if it had never been dropped.

Covenant pulled his awed stare away from the pot to Trell's face. The Gravelingas looked haggard with strain, and his taut cheeks were streaked with tears. "Mending is harder than breaking," he mumbled. "I could not do this every day." Wearily, he folded his arms on the table and cradled his head in them.

Atiaran stood behind her husband, massaging the heavy muscles of his shoulders and neck, and her eyes were full of pride and love. Something in her expression made Covenant feel that he came from a very poor world, where no one knew or cared about healing stoneware pots. He tried to tell himself that he was dreaming, but he did not want to listen.

After a silent pause full of respect for Trell's deed, Lena started to set the table. Soon Atiaran brought bowls of food from the cooking stone. When everything was ready, Trell lifted his head, climbed tiredly to his feet. With Atiaran and Lena, he stood beside the table. Atiaran said to Covenant, "It is the custom of our people to stand before eating, as a sign of our respect for the Earth, from which life and food and power come." Covenant stood as well, feeling awkward and out of place. Trell and Atiaran and Lena closed their eyes, bowed their heads for a moment. Then they sat down. When Covenant had followed them to the bench, they began to pass around the food.

It was a bountiful meal: there was cold salt beef covered with a steaming gravy, wild rice, dried apples, brown bread, and cheese; and Covenant was given a tall mug of a drink which Lena called springwine. This beverage was as clear and light as water, slightly effervescent, and it smelled dimly of *aliantha*; but it tasted like a fine beer which had been cured of all bitterness. Covenant had downed a fair amount of it before he realized that it added a still keener vibration to his already thrumming nerves. He could feel himself tightening. He was too full of unusual pressures. Soon he was impatient for the end of the meal, impatient to leave the house and expand in the night air.

But Lena's family ate slowly, and a pall hung over them. They dined as deliberately as if this meal marked the end of all their happiness together. In the silence, Covenant realized that this was a result of his presence. It made him uneasy.

To ease himself, he tried to increase what he knew about his situation. "I have a question," he said stiffly. With a gesture, he took in the whole Stonedown. "No wood. There's plenty of trees all over this valley, but I don't see you using any wood. Are the trees sacred or something?"

After a moment, Atiaran replied, "Sacred? I know that word, but its meaning is obscure to me. There is Power in the Earth, in trees and rivers and soil and stone, and we respect it for the life it gives. So we have sworn the Oath of Peace. Is that what you ask? We do not use wood because the wood-lore, the *lillianrill,* is lost to us, and we have not sought to regain it. In the exile of our people, when Desolation was upon the Land, many precious things were lost. Our people clung to the *rhadhamaerl* lore in the Southron Range and the Wastes, and it enabled us to endure. The wood-lore seemed not to help us, and it was forgotten. Now that we have returned to the Land, the stone-lore suffices for us. But others have kept the *lillianrill.* I have seen Soaring Woodhelven, in the hills far north and east of us, and it is a fair place—their people understand wood, and flourish. There is some trade between Stonedown and Woodhelven, but wood and stone are not traded."

When she stopped, Covenant sensed a difference in the new silence. A moment passed before he was sure that he could hear a distant rumor of voices. Shortly, Atiaran confirmed this by saying to Trell, "Ah, the gathering. I promised to sing tonight."

She and Trell stood together, and he said, "So. And then you will speak with the Circle of elders. Some preparations for tomorrow I will make. See"

—he pointed at the table—"it will be a fine day —there is no shadow on the heart of the stone."

Almost in spite of himself, Covenant looked where Trell pointed. But he could see nothing.

Noticing his blank look, Atiaran said kindly, "Do not be surprised, Thomas Covenant. No one but a *rhadhamaerl* can foretell weather in such stones as this. Now come with me, if you will, and I will sing the legend of Berek Halfhand." As she spoke, she took the pot of graveling from the table to carry with her. "Lena, will you clean the stoneware?"

Covenant got to his feet. Glancing at Lena, he saw her face twisted with unhappy obedience; she clearly wanted to go with them. But Trell also saw her expression and said, "Accompany our guest, Lena my daughter. I will not be too busy to care for the stoneware."

Pleasure transformed her instantly, and she leaped up to throw her arms around her father's neck. He returned her embrace for a moment, then lowered her to the floor. She straightened her shift, trying to look suddenly demure, and moved to her mother's side.

Atiaran said, "Trell, you will teach this girl to think she is a queen." But she took Lena's hand to show that she was not angry, and together they went past the curtain. Covenant followed promptly, went out of the house into the starry night with a sense of release. There was more room for him to explore himself under the open sky.

He needed exploration. He could not understand, rationalize, his mounting excitement. The spring-wine he had consumed seemed to provide a focus for his energies; it capered in his veins like a raving satyr. He felt inexplicably brutalized by inspiration, as if he were the victim rather than the source of his dream. White gold! he sputtered at the darkness between the houses. Wild magic! Do they think I'm crazy?

Perhaps he was crazy. Perhaps he was at this moment wandering in dementia, tormenting himself with false griefs and demands, the impositions of an illusion. Such things had happened to lepers.

I'm not! he shouted, almost cried out aloud. I know the difference—I know I'm dreaming.

His fingers twitched with violence, but he drew cool air deep into his lungs, put everything behind him. He knew how to survive a dream. Madness was the only danger.

As they walked together between the houses, Lena's smooth arm brushed his. His skin felt lambent at the touch.

The murmur of people grew quickly louder. Soon Lena, Atiaran, and Covenant reached the circle, moved into the gathering of the Stonedown.

It was lit by dozens of hand-held graveling pots, and in the illumination Covenant could see clearly. Men, women, and children clustered the rim of the circle. Covenant guessed that virtually the entire Stonedown had come to hear Atiaran sing. Most of the people were shorter than he was—and considerably shorter than Trell—and they had dark hair, brown or black, again unlike Trell. But they were a stocky, broad-shouldered breed, and even the women and children gave an impression of physical strength; centuries of stone-work had shaped them to suit their labor. Covenant felt the same dim fear of them that he had of Trell. They seemed too strong, and he had nothing but his strangeness to protect him if they turned against him.

They were busy talking to each other, apparently waiting for Atiaran, and they gave no sign of noticing Covenant. Reluctant to call attention to himself, he hung back at the outer edges of the gathering. Lena stopped with him. Atiaran gave her the graveling pot, then moved away through the crowd toward the center of the circle.

After he had scanned the assembly, Covenant turned his attention to Lena. She stood by his right side, the top of her head just an inch or two higher than his shoulder, and she held the graveling pot at her waist with both hands, so that the light empha- sized her breasts. She was clearly unconscious of the effect, but he felt it intensely, and his palms itched again with an eager and fearful desire to touch her.

As if she felt his thoughts, she looked up at him with a solemn softness in her face that made his heart lurch as if it were too big for his constraining ribs. Awkwardly, he took his eyes away, stared around the circle without seeing anything. When he glanced back at her, she seemed to be doing just what he had done—pretending to look elsewhere. He tightened his jaw and forced himself to wait for something to happen.

Soon the gathering became still. In the center of the open circle, Atiaran stood up on a low stone platform. She bowed her head to the gathering, and the people responded by silently raising their graveling pots. The lights seemed to focus around her like a penumbra.

When the pots were lowered, and a last ripple of shuffling had passed through the gathering, Atiaran began: "I feel I am an old woman this night—my memory seems clouded, and I do not remember all the song I would like to sing. But what I remember I will sing, and I will tell you the story, as I have told it before, so that you may share what lore I have." At this, low laughter ran through the gathering—a humorous tribute to Atiaran's superior knowledge. She remained silent, her head bowed to hide the fear that knowledge had brought her, until the people were quiet again. Then she raised her eyes and said, "I will sing the legend of Berek Halfhand."

After a last momentary pause, she placed her song into the welcoming silence like a rough and rare jewel.

In war men pass like shadows that stain the
    grass,
    Leaving their lives upon the green:
    While Earth bewails the crimson sheen,
Men's dreams and stars and whispers all helpless
    pass.

In one red shadow by woe and wicked cast,
    In one red pool about his feet,

Berek mows the vile like ripe wheat,
Though of all of Beauty's guarders he is last:

Last to pass into the shadow of defeat,
    And last to feel the full despair,
    And leave his weapons lying there—
Take his half unhanded hand from battle seat.

Across the plains of the Land they all swept—
    Treachers lust at faltering stride
    As Berek fled before the tide,
Till on Mount Thunder's rock-mantled side he
    wept.

Berek! Earthfriend!—Help and weal,
Battle-aid against the foe!
    Earth gives and answers Power's peal,
    Ringing, Earthfriend! Help and heal!
Clean the Land from bloody death and woe!

The song made Covenant quiver, as if it concealed
a specter which he should have been able to recognize. But Atiaran's voice enthralled him. No instru-
ments aided her singing, but before she had finished
her first line, he knew that she did not need them.
The clean thread of her melody was tapestried with
unexpected resonances, implied harmonies, echoes of
silent voices, so that on every rising motif she seemed
about to expand into three or four singers, throats
separate and unanimous in the song.

It began in a minor mode that made the gold-hued,
star-gemmed night throb like a dirge; and through it
blew a black wind of loss, in which things cherished
and consecrated throughout the Stonedown seemed to
flicker and go out. As he listened, Covenant felt that
the entire gathering wept with the song, cried out as
one in silent woe under the wide power of the singer.

But grief did not remain long in that voice. After a
pause that opened in the night like a revelation,
Atiaran broke into her brave refrain—"Berek!
Earthfriend!"—and the change carried her high in a
major modulation that would have been too wrench-

ing for any voice less rampant with suggestions, less
thickly woven, than hers. The emotion of the gathering continued, but it was reborn in an instant from
grief to joy and gratitude. And as Atiaran's long,
last high note sprang from her throat like a salute to
the mountains and the stars, the people held up their
graveling pots and gave a resounding shout:

"Berek! Earthfriend! Hail!"

Then, slowly, they lowered their lights and began
to press forward, moving closer to Atiaran to hear
her story. The common impulse was so simple and
strong that Covenant took a few steps as well before
he could recollect himself. Abruptly, he looked about
him—focused his eyes on the faint glimmering stars,
smelled the pervasive aroma of the graveling. The
unanimous reaction of the Stonedown frightened him;
he could not afford to lose himself in it. He wanted to
turn away, but he needed to hear Berek's story, so he
stayed where he was.

As soon as the people had settled themselves,
Atiaran began.

"It came to pass that there was a great war in the
eldest days, in the age that marks the beginning of the
memory of mankind—before the Old Lords were
born, before the Giants came across the Sunbirth Sea
to make the alliance of Rockbrothers—a time before
the Oath of Peace, before the Desolation and High
Lord Kevin's last battle. It was a time when the Viles
who sired the Demondim were a high and lofty race,
and the Cavewights smithed and smelted beautiful
metals to trade in open friendship with all the people
of the Land. In that time, the Land was one great
nation, and over it ruled a King and Queen. They
were a hale pair, rich with love and honor, and for
many years they held their sway in unison and
peace.

"But after a time a shadow came over the heart of
the King. He tasted the power of life and death over
those who served him, and learned to desire it. Soon
mastery became a lust with him, as necessary as food.
His nights were spent in dark quests for more power,

and by day he exercised that power, becoming hungrier and more cruel as the lust overcame him.

"But the Queen looked on her husband and was dismayed. She desired only that the health and fealty of the past years should return. But no appeal, no suasion or power of hers, could break the grip of cruelty that degraded the King. And at last, when she saw that the good of the Land would surely die if her husband were not halted, she broke with him, opposed his might with hers.

"Then there was war in the Land. Many who had felt the cut of the King's lash stood with the Queen. And many who hated murder and loved life joined her also. The chiefest of these was Berek—strongest and wisest of the Queen's champions. But the fear of the King was upon the Land, and whole cities rose up to fight for him, killing to protect their own slavery.

"Battle was joined across the Land, and for a time it seemed that the Queen would prevail. Her heroes were mighty of hand, and none were mightier than Berek, who was said to be a match for any King. But as the battle raged, a shadow, a gray cloud from the east, fell over the hosts. The Queen's defenders were stricken at heart, and their strength left them. But her enemies found a power of madness in the shadow. They forgot their humanity—they chopped and trampled and clawed and bit and maimed and defiled until their gray onslaught whelmed the heroes, and Berek's comrades broke one by one into despair and death. So the battle went until Berek was the last hater of the shadow left alive.

"But he fought on, heedless of his fate and the number of his foes, and souls fell dead under his sword like autumn leaves in a gale. At last, the King himself, filled with the fear and madness of the shadow, challenged Berek, and they fought. Berek stroked mightily, but the shadow turned his blade. So the contest was balanced until one blow of the King's ax cleft Berek's hand. Then Berek's sword fell to the ground, and he looked about him—looked and saw the shadow, and all his brave comrades dead. He cried a great cry of despair, and, turning, fled the battleground.

"Thus he ran, hunted by death, and the memory of the shadow was upon him. For three days he ran—never stopping, never resting—and for three days the King's host came behind him like a murderous beast, panting for blood. At the last of his strength and the extremity of his despair, he came to Mount Thunder. Climbing the rock-strewn slope, he threw himself down atop a great boulder and wept, saying, 'Alas for the Earth. We are overthrown, and have no friend to redeem us. Beauty shall pass utterly from the Land.'

"But the rock on which he lay replied, 'There is a Friend for a heart with the wisdom to see it.'

" 'The stones are not my friends,' cried Berek. 'See, my enemies ride the Land, and no convulsion tears the earth from under their befouling feet.'

" 'That may be,' said the rock. 'They are alive as much as you, and need the ground to stand upon. Yet there is a Friend for you in the Earth, if you will pledge your soul to its healing.'

"Then Berek stood upon the rock, and beheld his enemies close upon him. He took the pledge, sealing it with the blood of his riven hand. The Earth replied with thunder; from the heights of the mountain came great stone Fire-Lions, devouring everything in their path. The King and all his host were laid waste, and Berek alone stood above the rampage on his boulder like a tall ship in the sea.

"When the rampage had passed, Berek did homage to the Lions of Mount Thunder, promising respect and communion and service for the Earth from himself and all the generations which followed him upon the Land. Wielding the first Earthpower, he made the Staff of Law from the wood of the One Tree, and with it began the healing of the Land. In the fullness of time, Berek Halfhand was given the name Heartthew, and he became the Lord-Fatherer, the first of the Old Lords. Those who followed his path flourished in the Land for two thousand years."

For a long moment, there was silence over the gathering when Atiaran finished. Then together, as if their pulses moved to a single beat, the Stonedownors began to surge forward, stretching out their hands to touch her in appreciation. She spread her arms to hug as many of her friends as she could, and those who could not reach her embraced each other, sharing the oneness of their communal response.

SEVEN: Lena

ALONE in the night—alone because he could not share the spontaneous embracing impulse of the Stonedown — Covenant felt suddenly trapped, threatened. A pressure of darkness cramped his lungs; he could not seem to get enough air. A leper's claustrophobia was on him, a leper's fear of crowds, of unpredictable behavior. Berek! he panted with mordant intensity. These people wanted him to be a hero. With a stiff jerk of repudiation, he swung away from the gathering, went stalking in high dudgeon between the houses as if the Stonedownors had dealt him a mortal insult.

Berek! His chest heaved at the thought. Wild magic! It was ridiculous. Did not these people know he was a leper? Nothing could be less possible for him than the kind of heroism they saw in Berek Halfhand.

But Lord Foul had said, *He intends you to be my final foe. He chose you to destroy me.*

In stark dismay, he glimpsed the end toward which the path of the dream might be leading him; he saw himself drawn ineluctably into a confrontation with the Despiser.

He was trapped. Of course he could not play the hero in some dream war. He could not forget himself that much; forgetfulness was suicide. Yet he could not escape this dream without passing through it, could not return to reality without awakening. He knew what would happen to him if he stood still and tried to stay sane. Already, only this far from the lights of the gathering, he felt dark night beating toward him, circling on broad wings out of the sky at his head.

He lurched to a halt, stumbled to lean against a wall, caught his forehead in his hands.

I can't—he panted. All his hopes that this Land might conjure away his impotence, heal his sore heart somehow, fell into ashes.

Can't go on.

Can't stop.

What's happening to me?

Abruptly, he heard steps running toward him. He jumped erect, and saw Lena hurrying to join him. The swing of her graveling pot cast mad shadows across her figure as she moved. In a few more strides, she slowed, then stopped, holding her pot so that she could see him clearly. "Thomas Covenant?" she asked tentatively. "Are you not well?"

"No," he lashed at her, "I'm not *well*. Nothing's *well,* and it hasn't been since"—the words caught in his throat for an instant—"since I was divorced." He glared at her, defying her to ask what a *divorce* was.

The way she held her light left most of her face in darkness; he could not see how she took his outburst. But some inner sensitivity seemed to guide her. When she spoke, she did not aggravate his pain with crude questions or condolences. Softly, she said, "I know a place where you may be alone."

He nodded sharply. Yes! He felt that his distraught nerves were about to snap. His throat was thick with violence. He did not want anyone to see what happened to him.

Gently, Lena touched his arm, led him away from the Stonedown toward the river. Under the dim starlight they reached the banks of the Mithil, then turned downriver. In half a mile, they came to an old stone bridge that gleamed with a damp, black reflection, as if it had just arisen from the water for Covenant's use. The suggestiveness of that thought made him stop. He saw the span as a kind of threshold; crises lurked in the dark hills beyond the far riverbank. Abruptly, he asked, "Where are we going?" He was afraid that if he crossed that bridge he would not be able to recognize himself when he returned.

"To the far side," Lena said. "There you may be alone. Our people do not often cross the Mithil—it is said that the western mountains are not friendly, that the ill of Doom's Retreat which lies behind them has bent their spirit. But I have walked over all the western valley, stone-questing for *suru-pa-maerl* images, and have met no harm. There is a place nearby where you will not be disturbed."

For all its appearance of age, the bridge had an untrustworthy look to Covenant's eye. The un-mortared joints seemed tenuous, held together only by dim, treacherous, star-cast shadows. When he stepped onto the bridge, he expected his foot to slip, the stones to tremble. But the arch was steady. At the top of the span, he paused to lean on the low side wall of the bridge and gaze down at the river.

The water flowed blackly under him, grumbling over its long prayer for absolution in the sea. And he looked into it as if he were asking it for courage. Could he not simply ignore the things that threatened him, ignore the opposing impossibilities, madnesses, of his situation—return to the Stonedown and pretend with blithe guile that he was Berek Halfhand reborn?

He could not. He was a leper; there were some lies he could not tell.

With a sharp twist of nausea, he found that he was pounding his fists on the wall. He snatched his hands up, tried to see if he had injured himself, but the dim stars showed him nothing.

Grimacing, he turned and followed Lena down to the western bank of the Mithil.

Soon they reached their destination. Lena led Covenant directly west for a distance, then up a steep hill to the right, and down a splintered ravine toward the river again. Carefully, they picked their way along the ragged bottom of the ravine as if they were balancing on the broken keel of a ship; its shattered hull rose up on either side of them, narrowing their horizons. A few trees stuck out of the sides like spars, and near the river the hulk lay aground on a swath of smooth sand which faded toward a flat rock promontory jutting into the river. The Mithil complained around this rock, as if annoyed by the brief constriction of its banks, and the sound blew up the ravine like a sea breeze moaning through a reefed wreck.

Lena halted on the sandy bottom. Kneeling, she scooped a shallow basin in the sand and emptied her pot of graveling into it. The fire-stones gave more light from the open basin, so that the ravine bottom was lit with yellow, and shortly Covenant felt a quiet warmth from the graveling. The touch of the stones' glow made him aware that the night was cool, a pleasant night for sitting around a fire. He squatted beside the graveling with a shiver like the last keen quivering of imminent hysteria.

After she had settled the graveling in the sand, Lena moved away toward the river. Where she stood on the promontory, the light barely reached her, and her form was dark; but Covenant could see that her face was raised to the heavens.

He followed her gaze up the black face of the mountains, and saw that the moon was rising. A silver sheen paled the stars along the rim of rock, darkening the valley with its shadow; but the shadow soon passed down the ravine, and moonlight fell on the river, giving it the appearance of old argent. And as the full moon arose from the mountains, it caught Lena, cast a white haze like a caress across her head and shoulders. Standing still by the river, she held her head up to the moon, and Covenant watched her with an odd grim jealousy, as if she were poised on a precipice that belonged to him.

Finally, when the moonlight had crossed the river into the eastern valley, Lena lowered her head and returned to the circle of the graveling. Without meeting Covenant's gaze, she asked softly, "Shall I go?"

Covenant's palms itched as if he wanted to strike her for even suggesting that she might stay. But at the same time he was afraid of the night; he did not want to face it alone. Awkwardly he got to his feet, paced a short distance away from her. Scowling up the hulk of the ravine, he fought to sound neutral as he said, "What do you want?"

Her reply, when it came, was quiet and sure. "I want to know more of you."

He winced, ducked his head as if claws had struck at him out of the air. Then he snatched himself erect again.

"Ask."

"Are you married?"

At that, he whirled to face her as if she had stabbed him in the back. Under the hot distress of his eyes and his bared teeth, she faltered, lowered her eyes and turned her head away. Seeing her uncertainty, he felt that his face had betrayed him again. He had not willed the snarling contortion of his features. He wanted to contain himself, not give way like this—not in front of her. Yet she aggravated his distress more than anything else he had encountered. Striving for self-control, he snapped, "Yes. No. It doesn't matter. Why ask?"

Under his glare, Lena dropped to the sand, sat on her feet by the graveling, and watched him obliquely from beneath her eyebrows. When she said nothing immediately, he began to pace up and down the swath of sand. As he moved, he turned and pulled fiercely at his wedding ring.

After a moment, Lena answered with an air of irrelevance, "There is a man who desires to marry me. He is Triock son of Thuler. Though I am not of age he woos me, so that when the time comes I will make no other choice. But if I were of age now I would not marry him. Oh, he is a good man in his way—a good Cattleherd, courageous in defense of his kine. And he is taller than most. But there are too many wonders in the world, too much power to know and beauty to share and to create—and I have not seen the Ranyhyn. I could not marry a Cattleherd who de-

sires no more than a *suru-pa-maerl* for wife. Rather,
I would go to the Loresraat as Atiaran my mother did,
and I would stay and not falter no matter what trials
the Lore put upon me, until I became a Lord. It is
said that such things may happen. Do you think so?"

Covenant scarcely heard her. He was pacing out his
agitation on the sand, enraged and undercut by an
unwanted memory of Joan. Beside his lost love, Lena
and the silver night of the Land failed of significance.
The hollowness of his dream became suddenly obvious to his inner view, like an unveiled wilderland,
a new permutation of the desolation of leprosy. This
was not real—it was a torment that he inflicted upon
himself in subconscious, involuntary revolt against his
disease and loss. To himself, he groaned, Is it being
outcast that does this? Is being cut off such a shock?
By hell! I don't need any more. He felt that he was
on the edge of screaming. In an effort to control himself, he dropped to the sand with his back to Lena
and hugged his knees as hard as he could. Careless of
the unsteadiness of his voice, he asked, "How do your
people marry?"

In an uncomplicated tone, she said, "It is a simple thing, when a man and a woman choose each
other. After the two have become friends, if they wish
to marry they tell the Circle of elders. And the elders
take a season to assure themselves that the friendship
of the two is secure, with no hidden jealousy or failed
promise behind them to disturb their course in later
years. Then the Stonedown gathers in the center, and
the elders take the two in their arms and ask, 'Do
you wish to share life, in joy and sorrow, work and
rest, peace and struggle, to make the Land new?'

"The two answer, 'Life with life, we choose to share
the blessings and the service of the Earth.' "

For a moment, her star-lit voice paused reverently.
Then she went on, "The Stonedown shouts together,
'It is good! Let there be life and joy and power while
the years last!' Then the day is spent in joy, and the
new mates teach new games and dances and songs
to the people, so that the happiness of the Stonedown

is renewed, and communion and pleasure do not fail in the Land."

She paused again shortly before continuing: "The marriage of Atiaran my mother with Trell my father was a bold day. The elders who teach us have spoken of it many times. Every day in the season of assurance, Trell climbed the mountains, searching forgotten paths and lost caves, hidden falls and new-broken crevices, for a stone of *orcrest*—a precious and many-powered rock. For there was a drought upon the South Plains at that time, and the life of the Stonedown faltered in famine.

"Then, on the eve of the marriage, he found his treasure—a piece of *orcrest* smaller than a fist. And in the time of joy, after the speaking of the rituals, he and Atiaran my mother saved the Stonedown. While she sang a deep prayer to the Earth—a song known in the Loresraat but long forgotten among our people—he held the *orcrest* in his hand and broke it with the strength of his fingers. As the stone fell into dust, thunder rolled between the mountains, though there were no clouds, and one bolt of lightning sprang from the dust in his hand. Instantly, the blue sky turned black with thunderheads, and the rain began to fall. So the famine was broken, and the Stonedownors smiled on the coming days like a people reborn."

Though he clenched his legs with all his strength, Covenant could not master his dizzy rage. Joan! Lena's tale struck him like a mockery of his pains and failures.

I can't—

For a moment, his lower jaw shuddered under the effort he made to speak. Then he leaped up and dashed toward the river. As he covered the short distance, he bent and snatched a stone out of the sand. Springing onto the promontory, he hurled the stone with all the might of his body at the water.

Can't—!

A faint splash answered him, but at once the sound died under the heedless plaint of the river, and the ripples were swept away.

Softly at first, Covenant said to the river, "I gave

Joan a pair of riding boots for a wedding present."
Then, shaking his fists wildly, he shouted, "Riding
boots! Does my impotence surprise you?!"

Unseen and incomprehending, Lena arose and
moved toward Covenant, one hand stretched out as if
to soothe the violence knotted in his back. But she
paused a few steps away from him, searching for the
right thing to say. After a moment, she whispered,
"What happened to your wife?"

Covenant's shoulders jerked. Thickly, he said,
"She's gone."

"How did she die?"

"Not her—me. She left me. Divorced. Terminated.
When I needed her."

Indignantly, Lena wondered, "Why would such a
thing happen while there is life?"

"I'm not alive." She heard fury climbing to the top
of his voice. "I'm a leper. Outcast unclean. Lepers
are ugly and filthy. And abominable."

His words filled her with horror and protest. "How
can it be?" she moaned. "You are not—abominable.
What world is it that dares treat you so?"

His muscles jumped still higher in his shoulders, as
if his hands were locked on the throat of some tormenting demon. "It's real. That is reality. Fact. The
kind of thing that kills you if you don't believe it."
With a gesture of rejection toward the river, he gasped,
"This is a nightmare."

Lena flared with sudden courage. "I do not believe
it. It may be that your world—but the Land—ah, the
Land is real."

Covenant's back clenched abruptly still, and he said
with preternatural quietness, "Are you trying to drive
me crazy?"

His ominous tone startled her, chilled her. For an
instant, her courage stumbled; she felt the river and
the ravine closing around her like the jaws of a trap.
Then Covenant whirled and struck her a stinging slap
across the face.

The force of the blow sent her staggering back into
the light of the graveling. He followed quickly, his
face contorted in a wild grin. As she caught her bal-

ance, got one last, clear, terrified look at him, she felt sure that he meant to kill her. The thought paralyzed her. She stood dumb and helpless while he approached.

Reaching her, he knotted his hands in the front of her shift and rent the fabric like a veil. She could not move. For an instant, he stared at her, at her high, perfect breasts and her short slip, with grim triumph in his eyes, as though he had just exposed some foul plot. Then he gripped her shoulder with his left hand and tore away her slip with his right, forcing her down to the sand as he uncovered her.

Now she wanted to resist, but her limbs would not move; she was helpless with anguish.

A moment later, he dropped the burden of his weight on her chest, and her loins were stabbed with a wild, white fire that broke her silence, made her scream. But even as she cried out she knew that it was too late for her. Something that her people thought of as a gift had been torn from her.

But Covenant did not feel like a taker. His climax flooded him as if he had fallen into a Mithil of molten fury. Suffocating in passion, he almost swooned. Then time seemed to pass him by, and he lay still for moments that might have been hours for all he knew —hours during which his world could have crumbled, unheeded.

At last he remembered the softness of Lena's body under him, felt the low shake of her sobbing. With an effort, he heaved himself up and to his feet. When he looked down at her in the graveling light, he saw the blood on her loins. Abruptly, his head became giddy, unbalanced, as though he were peering over a precipice. He turned and hurried with a shambling, unsteady gait toward the river, pitched himself flat on the rock, and vomited the weight of his guts into the water. And the Mithil erased his vomit as cleanly as if nothing had happened.

He lay still on the rock while the exhaustion of his exacerbated nerves overcame him. He did not hear Lena arise, gather the shreds of her clothing, speak, or climb away out of the shattered ravine. He heard nothing but the long lament of the river—saw nothing but the ashes of his burnt-out passion—felt nothing but the dampness of the rock on his cheeks like tears.

EIGHT: The Dawn of the Message

THE hard bones of the rock slowly brought Thomas Covenant out of dreams of close embraces. For a time, he drifted on the rising current of the dawn—surrounded on his ascetic, sufficient bed by the searching self-communion of the river, the fresh odors of day, the wheeling cries of birds as they sprang into the sky. While his self-awareness returned, he felt at peace, harmonious with his context; and even the uncompromising hardness of the stone seemed apposite to him, a proper part of a whole morning.

His first recollections of the previous night were of orgasm, heartrending, easing release and satisfaction so precious that he would have been willing to coin his soul to make such things part of his real life. For a long moment of joy, he reexperienced that sensation. Then he remembered that to get it he had hurt Lena.

Lena!

He rolled over, sat up in the dawn. The sun had not yet risen above the mountains, but enough light reflected into the valley from the plains for him to see that she was gone.

She had left her fire burning in the sand up the ravine from him. He lurched to his feet, scanned the ravine and both banks of the Mithil for some sign of her—or, his imagination leaped, of Stonedownors seeking vengeance. His heart thudded; all those rock-strong people would not be interested in his explanations or apologies. He searched for evidence of pursuit like a fugitive.

But the dawn was as undisturbed as if it contained no people, no crimes or desires for punishment. Gradually, Covenant's panic receded. After a last look around, he began to prepare for whatever lay ahead of him.

He knew that he should get going at once, hurry along the river toward the relative safety of the plains. But he was a leper, and could not undertake solitary journeys lightly. He needed to organize himself.

He did not thing about Lena; he knew instinctively that he could not afford to think about her. He had violated her trust, violated the trust of the Stonedown; that was as close to his last night's rage as he could go. It was past, irrevocable—and illusory, like the dream itself. With an effort that made him tremble, he put it behind him. Almost by accident on Kevin's Watch, he had discovered the answer to all such insanity: keep moving, don't think about it, survive. That answer was even more necessary now. His "Berek" fear of the previous evening seemed relatively unimportant. His resemblance to a legendary hero was only a part of a dream, not a compulsory fact or demand. He put it behind him also. Deliberately, he gave himself a thorough scrutiny and VSE.

When he was sure that he had no hidden injuries, no dangerous purple spots, he moved out to the end of the promontory. He was still trembling. He needed more discipline, mortification; his hands shook as if they could not steady themselves without his usual shaving ritual. But the penknife in his pocket was inadequate for shaving. After a moment, he took a deep breath, gripped the edge of the rock, and dropped himself, clothes and all, into the river for a bath.

The current tugged at him seductively, urging him to float off under blue skies into a spring day. But the water was too cold; he could only stand the chill long enough to duck and thrash in the stream for a mo-

ment. Then he hauled himself onto the rock and
stood up, blowing spray off his face. Water from his
hair kept running into his eyes, blinding him momentarily to the fact that Atiaran stood on the sand
by the graveling. She contemplated him with a grave,
firm glance.

Covenant froze, dripping as if he had been caught
in the middle of a flagrant act. For a moment, he and
Atiaran measured each other across the sand and
rock. When she started to speak, he cringed inwardly,
expecting her to revile, denounce, hurl imprecations.
But she only said, "Come to the graveling. You must
dry yourself."

In surprise, he scrutinized her tone with all the
high alertness of his senses, but he could hear nothing
in it except determination and quiet sadness. Suddenly
he guessed that she did not know what had happened to her daughter.

Breathing deeply to control the labor of his heart,
he moved forward and huddled down next to the
graveling. His mind raced with improbable specula-
tions to account for Atiaran's attitude, but he kept
his face to the warmth and remained silent, hoping
that she would say something to let him know where
he stood with her.

Almost at once, she murmured, "I knew where to
find you. Before I returned from speaking with the
Circle of elders, Lena told Trell that you were here."

She stopped, and Covenant forced himself to ask,
"Did he see her?"

He knew that it was a suspicious question. But
Atiaran answered simply, "No. She went to spent
the night with a friend. She only called out her message as she passed our home."

Then for several long moments Covenant sat still
and voiceless, amazed by the implications of what
Lena had done. Only called out! At first, his brain
reeled with thoughts of relief. He was safe—temporarily, at least. With her reticence, Lena had purchased
precious time for him. Clearly, the people of this
Land were prepared to make sacrifices—

After another moment, he understood that she had

not made her sacrifice for him. He could not imagine
that she cared for his personal safety. No, she chose
to protect him because he was a Berek-figure, a
bearer of messages to the Lords. She did not want his
purpose to be waylaid by the retribution of the
Stonedown. This was her contribution to the defense
of the Land from Lord Foul the Gray Slayer.

It was a heroic contribution. In spite of his discipline, his fear, he sensed the violence Lena had done
herself for the sake of his message. He seemed to see
her huddling naked behind a rock in the foothills
throughout that bleak night, shunning for the first time
in her young life the open arms of her community—
bearing the pain and shame of her riven body alone
so that he would not be required to answer for it. An
unwanted memory of the blood on her loins writhed
in him.

His shoulders bunched to strangle the thought.
Through locked teeth, he breathed to himself, I've
got to go to the Council.

When he had steadied himself, he asked grimly,
"What did the elders say?"

"There was little for them to say," she replied in a
flat voice. "I told them what I know of you—and of
the Land's peril. They agreed that I must guide you to
Lord's Keep. For that purpose I have come to you
now. See"—she indicated two packs lying near her
feet—"I am ready. Trell my husband has given me
his blessing. It grieves me to go without giving my love
to Lena my daughter, but time is urgent. You have
not told me all your message, but I sense that from
this day forward each delay is hazardous. The elders
will give thought to the defense of the plains. We must
go."

Covenant met her eyes, and this time he understood
the sad determination in them. She was afraid, and
did not believe that she would live to return to her
family. He felt a sudden pity for her. Without fully
comprehending what he said, he tried to reassure her.
"Things aren't as bad as they might be. A Cavewight
has found the Staff of Law, and I gather he doesn't

really know how to use it. Somehow, the Lords have got to get it away from him."

But his attempt miscarried. Atiaran stiffened and said, "Then the life of the Land is in our speed. Alas that we cannot go to the Ranyhyn for help. But the Ramen have little countenance for the affairs of the Land, and no Ranyhyn has been ridden, save by Lord or Bloodguard, since the age began. We must walk, Thomas Covenant, and Revelstone is three hundred long leagues distant. Is your clothing dry? We must be on our way."

Covenant was ready; he had to get away from this place. He gathered himself to his feet and said, "Fine. Let's go."

However, the look that Atiaran gave him as he stood held something unresolved. In a low voice as if she were mortifying herself, she said, "Do you trust me to guide you, Thomas Covenant? You do not know me. I failed in the Loresraat."

Her tone seemed to imply not that she was undependable, but that he had the right to judge her. But he was in no position to judge anyone. "I trust you," he rasped. "Why not? You said yourself—" He faltered, then forged ahead. "You said yourself that I come to save or damn the Land."

"True," she returned simply. "But you do not have the stink of a servant of the Gray Slayer. My heart tells me that it is the fate of the Land to put faith in you, for good or ill."

"Then let's go." He took the pack that Atiaran lifted toward him and shrugged his shoulders into the straps. But before she put on her own pack, she knelt to the graveling in the sand. Passing her hands over the fire-stones, she began a low humming—a soft tune that sounded ungainly in her mouth, as if she were unaccustomed to it—and under her waving gestures the yellow light faded. In a moment, the stones had lapsed into a pale, pebbly gray, as if she had lulled them to sleep, and their heat dissipated. When they were cold, she scooped them into their pot, covered it, and stored it in her pack.

The sight reminded Covenant of all the things he

did not know about this dream. As Atiaran got to
her feet, he said, "There's only one thing I need. I
want you to talk to me—tell me all about the
Loresraat and the Lords and everything I might be
interested in." Then because he could not give her
the reason for his request, he concluded lamely, "It'll
pass the time."

With a quizzical glance at him, she settled her pack
on her shoulders. "You are strange, Thomas Covenant.
I think you are too eager to know my ignorance. But
what I know I will tell you—though without your
raiment and speech it would pass my belief to think
you an utter stranger to the Land. Now come. There
are treasure-berries aplenty along our way this morning. They will serve as breakfast. The food we carry
must be kept for the chances of the road."

Covenant nodded, and followed her as she began
climbing out of the ravine. He was relieved to be
moving again, and the distance passed quickly. Soon
they were down by the river, approaching the bridge.

Atiaran strode straight onto the bridge, but when
she reached the top of the span she stopped. A moment after Covenant joined her, she gestured north
along the Mithil toward the distant plains. "I tell you
openly, Thomas Covenant," she said, "I do not mean
to take a direct path to Lord's Keep. The Keep is west
of north from us, three hundred leagues as the eye
sees across the Center Plains of the Land. There many
people live, in Stonedown and Woodhelven, and it
might chance that both road and help could be found
to take us where we must go. But we could not hope
for horses. They are rare in the Land, and few folk
but those of Revelstone know them.

"It is in my heart that we may save time by journeying north, across the Mithil when it swings east,
and so into the land of Andelain, where the fair
Hills are the flower of all the beauties of the Earth.
There we will reach the Soulsease River, and it may
be that we will find a boat to carry us up that sweet
stream, past the westland of Trothgard, where the
promises of the Lords are kept, to great Revelstone
itself, the Lord's Keep. All travelers are blessed by

the currents of the Soulsease, and our journey will
end sooner if we find a carrier there. But we must pass
within fifty leagues of Mount Thunder—Gravin
Threndor." As she said the ancient name, a shiver
seemed to run through her voice. "It is there or
nowhere that the Staff of Law has been found, and
I do not wish to go even as close as Andelain to the
wrong wielder of such might."

She paused for a moment, hesitating, then went
on: "There would be rue unending if a corrupt Cavewight gained possession of the ring you bear—the evil
ones are quick to unleash such forces as wild magic.
And even were the Cavewight unable to use the ring,
I fear that ur-viles still live under Mount Thunder.
They are lore-wise creatures, and white gold would
not surpass them.

"But time rides urgently on us, and we must save it
where we may. And there is another reason for seeking the passage of Andelain at this time of year—if
we hasten. But I should not speak of it. You will see it
and rejoice, if no ill befall us on our way."

She fixed her eyes on Covenant, turning all their
inward strength on him, so that he felt, as he had the
previous evening, that she was searching for his weak-
nesses. He feared that she would discover his night's
work in his face, and he had to force himself to
meet her gaze until she said, "Now tell me, Thomas
Covenant. Will you go where I lead?"

Feeling both shamed and relieved, he answered,
"Let's get on with it. I'm ready."

"That is well." She nodded, started again toward
the east bank. But Covenant spent a moment looking
down at the river. Its soft plaint sounded full of
echoes, and they seemed to moan at him with serene
irony, *Does my impotence surprise you?* A cloud of
trouble darkened his face, but he clenched himself,
rubbed his ring, and stalked away after Atiaran, leaving the Mithil to flow on its way like a stream of forgetfulness or a border of death.

As the sun climbed over the eastern mountains,
Atiaran and Covenant were moving north, downstream along the river toward the open plains. At

first, they traveled in silence. Covenant was occupied with short forays into the hills to his right, gathering *aliantha*. He found their tangy peach flavor as keenly delicious as before; a fine essence in their juice made hunger and taste into poignant sensations. He refrained from taking all the berries off any one bush—he had to range away from Atiaran's sternly forward track often to get enough food to satisfy him—and he scattered the seeds faithfully, as Lena had taught him. Then he had to trot to catch up with Atiaran. In this way, he passed nearly a league, and when he finished eating, the valley was perceptibly broader. He made one last side trip—this time to the river for a drink—then hurried to take a position beside Atiaran.

Something in the set of her features seemed to ask him not to talk, so he disciplined himself to stillness with survival drills. Then he strove to regain the mechanical ticking stride which had carried him so far from Haven Farm. Atiaran appeared resigned to a trek of three hundred leagues, but he was not. He sensed that he would need all his leper's skills to hike for even a day without injuring himself. In the rhythm of his steps, he struggled to master the unruliness of his situation.

He knew that eventually he would have to explain his peculiar danger to Atiaran. He might need her help, at least her comprehension. But not yet—not yet. He did not have enough control.

But after a while, she changed direction, began angling away from the river up into the northeastern foothills. This close to the mountains, the hills were steep and involuted, and she seemed to be following no path. Behind her, Covenant scrambled up and staggered down the rocky, twisting slopes, though the natural lay of the land tried constantly to turn them westward. The sides of his neck started to ache from the weight of his pack, and twitches jumped like incipient cramps under his shoulder blades. Soon he was panting heavily, and muttering against the folly of Atiaran's choice of directions.

Toward midmorning, she stopped to rest on the downward curve of a high hill. She remained standing, but Covenant's muscles were trembling from the exertion, and he dropped to the ground beside her, breathing hard. When he had regained himself a little, he panted, "Why didn't we go around, north past these hills, then east? Save all this up and down."

"Two reasons" she said shortly. "Ahead there is a long file north through the hills—easy walking so that we will save time. And again"—she paused while she looked around—"we may lose something. Since we left the bridge, there has been a fear in me that we are followed."

"Followed?" Covenant jerked out. "Who?"

"I do not know. It may be that the spies of the Gray Slayer are already abroad. It is said that his highest servants, his Ravers, cannot die while he yet lives. They have no bodies of their own, and their spirits wander until they find living beings which they can master. Thus they appear as animals or humans, as chance allows, corrupting the life of the Land. But it is my hope that we will not be followed through these hills. Are you rested? We must go."

After adjusting her robe under the straps of her pack, she set off again down the slope. A moment later, Covenant went groaning after her.

For the rest of the morning, he had to drive himself to persevere in the face of exhaustion. His legs grew numb with fatigue, and the weight on his back seemed to constrict his breathing so that he panted as if he were suffocating. He was not conditioned for such work; lurching unsteadily, he stumbled up and down the hills. Time and again, only his boots and tough trousers saved him from damage. But Atiaran moved ahead of him smoothly, with hardly a wasted motion or false step, and the sight of her drew him onward.

But finally she turned down into a long ravine that ran north as far as he could see, like a cut in the hills. A small stream flowed down the center of the file, and they stopped beside it to drink, bathe their faces, and rest. This time, they both took off their packs and dropped to the ground. Groaning deeply, Covenant lay flat on his back with his eyes closed.

For a while he simply relaxed, listened to his own hoarse respiration until it softened and he could hear behind it the wind whistling softly. Then he opened his eyes to take in his surroundings.

He found himself looking up four thousand feet at Kevin's Watch.

The view was unexpected; he sat up as if to look at it more closely. The Watch was just east and south from him, and it leaned out into the sky from its cliff face like an accusing finger. At that distance, the stone looked black and fatal, and it seemed to hang over the file down which he and Atiaran would walk. It reminded him of the Despiser and darkness.

"Yes," Atiaran said, "that is Kevin's Watch. There stood Kevin Landwaster, High Lord and wielder of the Staff, direct descendant of Berek Halfhand, in the last battle against the Gray Slayer. It is said that there he knew defeat, and mad grief. In the blackness which whelmed his heart he—the most powerful champion in all the ages of the Land—even he, High Lord Kevin, sworn Earthfriend, brought down the Desecration, the end of all things in the Land for many generations. It is not a good omen that you have been there."

As she spoke, Covenant turned toward her, and saw that she was gazing, not up at the rock, but inward, as if she were considering how badly she would have failed in Kevin's place. Then, abruptly, she gathered herself and stood up. "But there is no help for it," she said. "Our path lies under the shadow of the Watch for many leagues. Now we must go on." When Covenant moaned, she commanded, "Come. We dare not go slowly, for fear that we will be too late at the end. Our way is easier now. And if it will help your steps, I will talk to you of the Land."

Reaching for his pack, Covenant asked, "Are we still being followed?"

"I do not know. I have neither heard nor seen any

sign. But my heart misgives me. I feel some wrong upon our path this day."

Covenant pulled on his pack and staggered wincing to his feet. His heart misgave him also, for reasons of its own. Here under Kevin's Watch, the humming wind sounded like the thrum of distant vulture wings. Settling the pack straps on his raw shoulders, he bent under the weight, and went with Atiaran down the bottom of the file.

For the most part, the cut was straight and smooth-floored, though never more than fifteen feet across. However, there was room beside the narrow stream for Atiaran and Covenant to walk together. As they traveled, pausing at every rare *aliantha* to pick and eat a few berries, Atiaran sketched in a few of the wide blanks in Covenant's knowledge of the Land.

"It is difficult to know how to speak of it," she began. "Everything is part of everything, and each question which I can answer raises three more which I cannot. My lore is limited to what all learn quickly in their first years in the Loresraat. But I will tell you what I can.

"Berek Heartthew's son was Damelon Giantfriend, and his son was Loric Vilesilencer, who stemmed the corruption of the Demondim, rendering them impotent." As she spoke, her voice took on a cadence that reminded Covenant of her singing. She did not recite dry facts; she narrated a tale that was of sovereign importance to her, to the Land. "And Kevin, whom we name Landwaster more in pity than in condemnation of his despair, was the son of Loric, and High Lord in his place when the Staff was passed on. For a thousand years, Kevin stood at the head of the Council, and he extended the Earthfriendship of the Lords beyond anything known before in the Land, and he was greatly honored.

"In his early years, he was wise as well as mighty and knowledgeable. When he saw the first hints that the ancient shadow was alive, he looked far into the chances of the future, and what he saw gave him cause to fear. Therefore he gathered all his Lore into Seven Wards—

Seven Wards of ancient Lore
For Land's protection, wall and door—

and hid them, so that his knowledge would not pass from the Land even if he and the Old Lords fell.

"For many many long years the Land lived on in peace. But during that time, the Gray Slayer rose up in the guise of a friend. In some way, the eyes of Kevin were blinded, and he accepted his enemy as a friend and Lord. And for that reason, the Lords and all their works passed from the Earth.

"But when Kevin's betrayal had brought defeat and Desolation, and the Land had lain under the bane for many generations, and had begun to heal, it called out to the people who lived in hiding in the Wastes and the Northron Climbs. Slowly, they returned. As the years passed, and the homes and villages became secure, some folk traveled, exploring the Land in search of half-remembered legends. And when they finally braved Giant Woods, they came to the old land of Seareach, and found that the Giants, Rockbrothers of the people of the Land, had survived the Ritual of Desecration.

"There are many songs, old and new, praising the fealty of the Giants—with good reason. When the Giants learned that people had returned to the Land, they began a great journey, sojourning over all the Land to every new Stonedown and Woodhelven, teaching the tale of Kevin's defeat and renewing the old Rockbrotherhood. Then, taking with them those people who chose to come, the giants ended their journey at Revelstone, the ageless castle-city which they had riven out of the rock of the mountain for High Lord Damelon, as surety of the bond between them.

"At Revelstone, the Giants gave a gift to the gathered people. They revealed the First Ward, the fundamental store of the beginnings of Kevin's Lore. For he had trusted it to the Giants before the last battle. And the people accepted that Ward and consecrated themselves, swearing Earthfriendship and loyalty to the Power and beauty of the Land.

"One thing more they swore—Peace, a calmness of self to protect the Land from destructive emotions like those that maddened Kevin. For it was clear to all there gathered that power is a dreadful thing, and that the knowledge of power dims the seeing of the wise. When they beheld the First Ward, they feared a new Desecration. Therefore they swore to master the Lore, so that they might heal the Land—and to master themselves, so that they would not fall into the anger and despair which made Kevin his own worst foe.

"These oaths were carried back to all the people of the Land, and all the people swore. Then the few who were chosen at Revelstone for the great work took the First Ward to Kurash Plenethor, Stricken Stone, where the gravest damage of the last battle was done. They named the land Trothgard, as a token of their promise of healing, and there they founded the Loresraat—a place of learning where they sought to regain the knowledge and power of the Old Lords, and to train themselves in the Oath of Peace."

Then Atiaran fell silent, and she and Covenant walked down the file in stillness textured by the whispering of the stream and by the occasional calls of the birds. He found that her tale did help him to keep up their pace. It caused him to forget himself somewhat, forget the raw ache of his shoulders and feet. And her voice seemed to give him strength; her tale was like a promise that any exhaustion borne in the Land's service would not be wasted.

After a time, he urged her to continue. "Can you tell me about the Loresraat?"

The bitter vehemence of her reply surprised him. "Do you remind me that I am of all people the least worthy to talk of these matters? You, Thomas Covenant, Unbeliever and white gold wielder—do you reproach me?"

He could only stare dumbly at her, unable to fathom the years of struggling that filled her spacious eyes.

"I do not need your reminders."

But a moment later she faced forward again, her expression set to meet the north. "Now you reproach me indeed," she said. "I am too easily hurt that the whole world knows what I know so well myself. Like a guilty woman, I fail to believe the innocence of others. Please pardon me—you should receive better treatment than this."

Before he could respond, she forged ahead. "In this way I describe the Loresraat. It stands in Trothgard in the Valley of Two Rivers, and it is a community of study and learning. To that place go all who will, and there they consecrate themselves to Earthfriendship and the Lore of the Old Lords.

"This Lore is a deep matter, not mastered yet despite all the years and effort that have been given to it. The chiefest problem is translation, for the language of the Old Lords was not like ours, and the words which are simple at one place are difficult at another. And after translation, the Lore must be interpreted, and then the skills to use it must be learned. When I"—she faltered briefly—"when I studied there, the Lorewardens who taught me said that all the Loresraat had not yet passed the surface of Kevin's mighty knowledge. And that knowledge is only a seventh part of the whole, the First Ward of Seven."

Covenant heard an unwitting echo of Foul's contempt in her words, and it made him listen to her still more closely.

"Easiest of translation," she went on, "has been the Warlore, the arts of battle and defense. But there much skill is required. Therefore one part of the Loresraat deals solely with those who would follow the Sword, and join the Warward of Lord's Keep. But there have been no wars in our time, and in my years at the Loresraat the Warward numbered scarcely two thousand men and women.

"Thus the chief work of the Loresraat is in teaching and studying the language and knowledge of the Earthpower. First, the new learners are taught the history of the Land, the prayers and songs and legends—in time, all that is known of the Old Lords and their struggles against the Gray Slayer. Those who master this become Lorewardens. They teach others, or search out new knowledge and power from the First

Ward. The price of such mastery is high—such purity and determination and insight and courage are required by Kevin's Lore—and there are some," she said as if she were resolved not to spare her own feelings, "who cannot match the need. I failed when that which I learned made my heart quail—when the Lorewardens led me to see, just a little way, into the Despite of the Gray Slayer. That I could not bear, and so I broke my devotion, and returned to Mithil Stonedown to use the little that I knew for my people. And now, when I have forgotten so much, my trial is upon me."

She sighed deeply, as if it grieved her to consent to her fate. "But that is no matter. In the Loresraat, those who follow and master both Sword and Staff, who earn a place in the Warward and among the Lorewardens, and who do not turn away to pursue private dreams in isolation, as do the Unfettered—those brave hearts are named Lords, and they join the Council which guides the healing and protection of the Land. From their number, they choose the High Lord, to act for all as the Lore requires:

> And one High Lord to wield the Law
> To keep all uncorrupt Earth's Power's core.

"In my years at the Loresraat, the High Lord was Variol Tamarantha-mate son of Pentil. But he was old, even for a Lord, and the Lords live longer than other folk—and our Stonedown has had no news of Revelstone or Loresraat for many years. I do not know who leads the Council now."

Without thinking, Covenant said, "Prothall son of Dwillian."

"Ah!" Atiaran gasped. "He knows me. As a Lorewarden he taught me the first prayers. He will remember that I failed, and will not trust my mission." She shook her head in pain. Then, after a moment's reflection, she added, "And you have known this. You know all. Why do you seek to shame the rudeness of my knowledge? That is not kind."

"Hellfire!" Covenant snapped. Her reproach made

him suddenly angry. "Everybody in this whole business, you and"—but he could not bring himself to say Lena's name—"and everyone keep accusing me of being some sort of closet expert. I tell you, I don't know one damn thing about this unless someone explains it to me. I'm not your bloody Berek."

Atiaran gave him a look full of skepticism—the fruit of long, harsh self-doubt—and he felt an answering urge to prove himself in some way. He stopped, pulled himself erect against the weight of his pack. "This is the message of Lord Foul the Despiser: 'Say to the Council of Lords, and to High Lord Prothall son of Dwillian, that the uttermost limit of their span of days upon the Land is seven times seven years from this present time. Before the end of those days are numbered, I will have the command of life and death in my hand.' "

Abruptly, he caught himself. His words seemed to beat down the file like ravens, and he felt a hot leper's shame in his cheeks, as though he had defiled the day. For an instant, complete stillness surrounded him—the birds were as silent as if they had been stricken out of the sky, and the stream appeared motionless. In the noon heat, his flesh was slick with sweat.

For that instant, Atiaran gaped aghast at him. Then she cried, *"Melenkurion abatha!* Do not speak it until you must! I cannot preserve us from such ills."

The silence shuddered, passed; the stream began chattering again, and a bird swooped by overhead. Covenant wiped his forehead with an unsteady hand. "Then stop treating me as if I'm something I'm not."

"How can I?" she responded heavily. "You are closed to me, Thomas Covenant. I do not see you."

She used the word *see* as if it meant something he did not understand. "What do you mean, you don't see me?" he demanded sourly. "I'm standing right in front of you."

"You are closed to me," she repeated. "I do not know whether you are well or ill."

He blinked at her uncertainly, then realized that she had unwittingly given him a chance to tell her about his leprosy. He took the opportunity; he was angry enough for the job now. Putting aside his incomprehension, he grated, "Ill, of course. I'm a leper."

At this, Atiaran groaned as if he had just confessed to a crime. "Then woe to the Land, for you have the wild magic and can undo us all."

"Will you cut that out?" Brandishing his left fist, he gritted, "It's just a ring. To remind me of everything I have to live without. It's got no more—wild magic—than a rock."

"The Earth is the source of all power," whispered Atiaran.

With an effort, Covenant refrained from shouting his frustration at her. She was talking past him, reacting to him as if his words meant something he had not intended. "Back up a minute," he said. "Let's get this straight. I said I was ill. What does that mean to you? Don't you even have diseases in this world?"

For an instant, her lips formed the word *diseases*. Then a sudden fear tightened her face, and her gaze sprang up past Covenant's left shoulder.

He turned to see what frightened her. He found nothing behind him; but as he scanned the west rim of the file, he heard a scrabbling noise. Pebbles and shale fell into the cut.

"The follower!" Atiaran cried. "Run! Run!"

Her urgency caught him; he spun and followed her as fast as he could go down the file.

Momentarily, he forgot his weakness, the weight of his pack, the heat. He pounded after Atiaran's racing heels as if he could hear his pursuer poised above him on the rim of the file. But soon his lungs seemed to be tearing under the exertion, and he began to lose his balance. When he stumbled, his fragile body almost struck the ground.

Atiaran shouted, "Run!" but he hauled up short, swung trembling around to face the pursuit.

A leaping figure flashed over the edge of the cut and dropped toward him. He dodged away from the plummet, flung up his arms to ward off the figure's swinging arm.

As the attacker passed, he scored the backs of Covenant's fingers with a knife. Then he hit the ground and rolled, came to his feet with his back to the east wall of the cut, his knife weaving threats in front of him.

The sunlight seemed to etch everything starkly in Covenant's vision. He saw the unevennesses of the wall, the shadows stretched under them like rictus.

The attacker was a young man with a powerful frame and dark hair—unmistakably a Stonedownor, though taller than most. His knife was made of stone, and woven into the shoulders of his tunic was his family insignia, a pattern like crossed lightning. Rage and hate strained his features as if his skull were splitting. "Raver!" he yelled. "Ravisher!"

He approached swinging his blade. Covenant was forced to retreat until he stood in the stream, ankle-deep in cool water.

Atiaran was running toward them, though she was too far away to intervene between Covenant and the knife.

Blood welled from the backs of his fingers. His pulse throbbed in the cuts, throbbed in his fingertips.

He heard Atiaran's commanding shout: "Triock!"

The knife slashed closer. He saw it as clearly as if it were engraved on his eyeballs.

His pulse pounded in his fingertips.

The young man gathered himself for a killing thrust.

Atiaran shouted again, "Triock! Are you mad? You swore the Oath of Peace!"

In his fingertips?

He snatched up his hand, stared at it. But his sight was suddenly dim with awe. He could not grasp what was happening.

That's impossible, he breathed in the utterest astonishment. Impossible.

His numb, leprosy-ridden fingers were aflame with pain.

Atiaran neared the two men and stopped, dropped

her pack to the ground. She seemed to place a terrible restraint on Triock; he thrashed viciously where he stood. As if he were choking on passion, he spat out, "Kill him! Raver!"

"I forbid!" cried Atiaran. The intensity of her command struck Triock like a physical blow. He staggered back a step, then threw up his head and let out a hoarse snarl of frustration and rage.

Her voice cut sharply through the sound. "Loyalty is due. You took the Oath. Do you wish to damn the Land?"

Triock shuddered. In one convulsive movement, he flung down his knife so that it drove itself to the hilt in the ground by his feet. Straightening fiercely, he hissed at Atiaran, "He has ravished Lena. Last night."

Covenant could not grasp the situation. Pain was a sensation, a splendor, his fingers had forgotten; he had no answer to it except, Impossible. Impossible. Unnoticed, his blood ran red and human down his wrist.

A spasm twitched across his face. Darkness gathered in the air about him; the atmosphere of the file seethed as if it were full of beating wings, claws which flashed toward his face. He groaned, "Impossible."

But Atiaran and Triock were consumed with each other; their eyes avoided him as if he were a plague spot. As Triock's words penetrated her, she crumbled to her knees, covered her face with her hands, and dropped her forehead to the ground. Her shoulders shook as if she were sobbing, though she made no sound; and over her anguish he said bitterly, "I found her in the hills when this day's sun first touched the plains. You know my love for her. I observed her at the gathering, and was not made happy by the manner in which this fell stranger dazzled her. It wrung my heart that she should be so touched by a man whose comings and goings no one could ever know. So, late at night, I inquired of Trell your husband, and learned that she said she meant to sleep with a friend—Terass daughter of

Annoria. Then I inquired of Terass—and she knew nothing of Lena's purpose. Then a shadow of fear came upon me—for when have any of the people been liars? I spent the whole of the night searching for her. And at first light I found her, her shift rent and blood about her. She strove to flee from me, but she was weak from cold and pain and sorrow, and in a moment she clung in my arms and told me what —what this Raver had done.

"Then I took her to Trell her father. While he cared for her I went away, purposing to kill the stranger. When I saw you, I followed, believing that my purpose was yours also—that you led him into the hills to destroy him. But you meant to save him —him, the ravisher of Lena your daughter! How has he corrupted your heart? You forbid? Atiaran Trell-mate! She was a child fair enough to make a man weep for joy at seeing her—broken without consent or care. Answer me. What have Oaths to do with us?"

The wild, rabid swirl of dark wings forced Covenant down until he was huddled in the stream. Images reeled across his brain—memories of the leprosarium, of doctors saying, *You cannot hope.* He had been hit by a police car. He had walked into town to pay his phone bill—to pay his phone bill in person. In a voice abstract with horror, he murmured, "Can't happen."

Slowly, Atiaran raised her head and spread her arms, as if opening her breast to an impaling thrust from the sky. Her face was carved with pain, and her eyes were dark craters of grief, looking inward on her compromised humanity. "Trell, help me," she breathed weakly. Then her voice gathered strength, and her anguish seemed to make the air about her ache. "Alas! Alas for the young of the world! Why is the burden of hating ill so hard to bear? Ah, Lena my daughter! I see what you have done. I understand. It is a brave deed, worthy of praise and pride! Forgive me that I cannot be with you in this trial."

But after a while, her gaze swung outward again. She climbed unsteadily to her feet, and stood swaying for a moment before she rasped hoarsely, "Loyalty is due. I forbid your vengeance."

"Does he go unpunished?" protested Triock.

"There is peril in the Land," she answered. "Let the Lords punish him." A taste of blood sharpened her voice. "They will know what to think of a stranger who attacks the innocent." Then her weakness returned. "The matter is beyond me. Triock, remember your Oath." She gripped her shoulders, knotted her fingers in the leaf pattern of her robe as if to hold her sorrow down.

Triock turned toward Covenant. There was something broken in the young man's face—a shattered or wasted capacity for contentment, joy. He snarled with the force of an anathema, "I know you, Unbeliever. We will meet again." Then abruptly he began moving away. He accelerated until he was sprinting, beating out his reproaches on the hard floor of the file. In a moment, he reached a place where the west wall sloped away, and then he was out of sight, gone from the cut into the hills.

"Impossible," Covenant murmured. "Can't happen. Nerves don't regenerate." But his fingers hurt as if they were being crushed with pain. Apparently nerves did regenerate in the Land. He wanted to scream against the darkness and the terror, but he seemed to have lost all control of his throat, voice, self.

As if from a distance made great by abhorrence or pity, Atiaran said, "You have made of my heart a wilderland."

"Nerves don't regenerate." Covenant's throat clenched as if he were gagging, but he could not scream. "They don't."

"Does that make you free?" she demanded softly, bitterly. "Does it justify your crime?"

"Crime?" He heard the word like a knife thrust through the beating wings. "Crime?" His blood ran from the cuts as if he were a normal man, but the flow was decreasing steadily. With a sudden convulsion, he caught hold of himself, cried miserably, "I'm in pain!"

The sound of his wail jolted him, knocked the swirling darkness back a step. *Pain!* The impossibility bridged a gap for him. Pain was for healthy people, people whose nerves were alive.

Can't happen. Of course it can't. That proves it —proves this is all a dream.

All at once, he felt an acute desire to weep. But he was a leper, and had spent too much time learning to dam such emotional channels. Lepers could not afford grief. Trembling feverishly, he plunged his cut hand into the stream.

"Pain is pain," Atiaran grated. "What is your pain to me? You have done a black deed, Unbeliever— violent and cruel, without commitment or sharing. You have given me a pain that no blood or time will wash clean. And Lena my daughter—! Ah, I pray that the Lords will punish—punish!"

The running water was chill and clear. After a moment, his fingers began to sting in the cold, and an ache spread up through his knuckles to his wrist. Red plumed away from his cuts down the stream, but the cold water soon stopped his bleeding. As he watched the current rinse clean his injury, his grief and fear turned to anger. Because Atiaran was his only companion, he growled at her, "Why should I go? None of this matters—I don't give a damn about your precious Land."

"By the Seven!" Atiaran's hard tone seemed to chisel words out of the air. "You will go to Revel-stone if I must drag you each step of the way."

He lifted his hand to examine it. Triock's knife had sliced him as neatly as a razor; there were no jagged edges to conceal dirt or roughen the healing. But the cut had reached bone in his middle two fingers, and blood still seeped from them. He stood up. For the first time since he had been attacked, he looked at Atiaran.

She stood a few paces from him, with her hands clenched together at her heart as if its pulsing hurt her. She glared at him abominably, and her face was taut with intimations of fierce, rough strength. He could see that she was prepared to fight him to

Revelstone if necessary. She shamed him, aggravated his ire. Belligerently, he waved his injury at her. "I need a bandage."

For an instant, her gaze intensified as if she were about to hurl herself at him. But then she mastered herself, swallowed her pride. She went over to her pack, opened it, and took out a strip of white cloth, which she tore at an appropriate length as she returned to Covenant. Holding his hand carefully, she inspected the cut, nodded her approval of its condition, then bound the soft fabric firmly around his fingers. "I have no hurtloam," she said, "and cannot take the time to search for it. But the cut looks well, and will heal cleanly."

When she was done, she went back to her pack. Swinging it onto her shoulders, she said, "Come. We have lost time." Without a glance at Covenant, she set off down the file.

He remained where he was for a moment, tasting the ache of his fingers. There was a hot edge to his hurt, as if the knife were still in the wound. But he had the answer to it now. The darkness had receded somewhat, and he could look about him without panic. Yet he was still afraid. He was dreaming healthy nerves; he had not realized that he was so close to collapse. Helpless, lying unconscious somewhere, he was in the grip of a crisis—a crisis of his ability to survive. To weather it he would need every bit of discipline or intransigence he could find.

On an impulse, he bent and tried to pull Triock's knife from the ground with his right hand. His half-grip slipped when he tugged straight up on the handle, but by working it back and forth he was able to loosen it, draw it free. The whole knife was shaped and polished out of one flat sliver of stone, with a haft leather-bound for a secure hold, and an edge that seemed sharp enough for shaving. He tested it on his left forearm, and found that it lifted off his hair as smoothly as if the blade were lubricated.

He slipped it under his belt. Then he hitched his pack higher on his shoulders and started after Atiaran.

NINE: Jehannum

BEFORE the afternoon was over, he had lapsed into a dull, hypnotized throb of pain. His pack straps constricted the circulation in his arms, multiplied the aching of his hand; his damp socks gave him blisters to which his toes were acutely and impossibly sensitive; weariness made his muscles as awkward as lead. But Atiaran moved constantly, severely, ahead of him down the file, and he followed her as if he were being dragged by the coercion of her will. His eyes became sightless with fatigue; he lost all sense of time, of movement, of everything except pain. He hardly knew that he had fallen asleep, and he felt a detached, impersonal sense of surprise when he was finally shaken awake.

He found himself lying in twilight on the floor of the file. After rousing him, Atiaran handed him a bowl of hot broth. Dazedly, he gulped at it. When the bowl was empty, she took it and handed him a large flask of springwine. He gulped it also.

From his stomach, the springwine seemed to send long, soothing fingers out to caress and relax each of his raw muscles, loosening them until he felt that he could no longer sit up. He adjusted his pack as a pillow, then lay down to sleep again. His last sight before his eyes fell shut was of Atiaran, sitting enshadowed on the far side of the graveling pot, her face set relentlessly toward the north.

The next day dawned clear, cool, and fresh. Atiaran finally succeeded in awakening Covenant as darkness was fading from the sky. He sat up painfully,

rubbed his face as if it had gone numb during the
night. A moment passed before he recollected the new
sensitivity of his nerves; then he flexed his hands,
stared at them as if he had never seen them before.
They were alive, alive.

He pushed the blanket aside to uncover his feet.
When he squeezed his toes through his boots, the pain
of his blisters answered sharply. His toes were as alive
as his fingers.

His guts twisted sickly. With a groan, he asked himself, How long—how long is this going to go on? He
did not feel that he could endure much more.

Then he remembered that he had not had on a
blanket when he went to sleep the night before.
Atiaran must have spread it over him.

He winced, avoided her eyes by shambling
woodenly to the stream to wash his face. Where did
she find the courage to do such things for him? As he
splashed cold water on his neck and cheeks, he found
that he was afraid of her again.

But she did not act like a threat. She fed him,
checked the bandage on his injured hand, packed up
the camp as if he were a burden to which she had already become habituated. Only the lines of sleepless-
ness around her eyes and the grim set of her mouth
showed that she was clenching herself.

When she was ready to go, he gave himself a deliberate VSE, then forced his shoulders into the straps
of his pack and followed her down the file as if her
stiff back were a demand he could not refuse.

Before the day was done, he was an expert on that
back. It never compromised; it never admitted a
doubt about its authority, never offered the merest
commiseration. Though his muscles tightened until
they became as inarticulate as bone—though the
aching rictus of his shoulders made him hunch in his
pack like a cripple—though the leagues aggravated
his sore feet until he hobbled along like a man harried
by vultures—her back compelled him like an ulti-
matum: keep moving or go mad; I permit no other
alternatives. And he could not deny her. She stalked

ahead of him like a nightmare figure, and he followed as if she held the key to his existence.

Late in the morning, they left the end of the file, and found themselves on a heathered hillside almost directly north of the high, grim finger of Kevin's Watch. They could see the South Plains off to the west; and as soon as the file ended, the stream turned that way, flowing to some distant union with the Mithil. But Atiaran led Covenant still northward, weaving her way along fragmentary tracks and across unpathed leas which bordered the hills on her right.

To the west, the grasslands of the plains were stiff with bracken, purplish in the sunlight. And to the east, the hills rose calmly, cresting a few hundred feet higher than the path which Atiaran chose along their sides. In this middle ground, the heather alternated with broad swaths of bluegrass. The hillsides wore flowers and butterflies around thick copses of wattle and clusters of taller trees—oaks and sycamores, a few elms, and some gold-leaved trees—Atiaran called them "Gilden"—which looked like maples. All the colors—the trees, the heather, and bracken, the *aliantha*, the flowers, and the infinite azure sky—were vibrant with the eagerness of spring, lush and exuberant rebirth of the world.

But Covenant had no strength to take in such things. He was blind and deaf with exhaustion, pain, incomprehension. Like a penitent, he plodded on through the afternoon at Atiaran's behest.

At last the day came to an end. Covenant covered the final league staggering numbly, though he did not pass out on his feet as he had the previous day; and when Atiaran halted and dropped her pack, he toppled to the grass like a felled tree. But his overstrained muscles twitched as if they were appalled; he could not hold them still without clenching. In involuntary restlessness, he helped Atiaran by unpacking the blankets while she cooked supper. During their meal, the sun set across the plains, streaking the grasslands with shadows and lavender; and when the stars came out he lay and watched them, trying with the help of springwine to make himself relax.

At last he faded into sleep. But his slumbers were troubled. He dreamed that he was trudging through a desert hour after hour, while a sardonic voice urged him to enjoy the freshness of the grass. The pattern ran obsessively in his mind until he felt that he was sweating anger. When the dawn came to wake him, he met it as if it were an affront to his sanity.

He found that his feet were already growing tougher, and his cut hand had healed almost completely. His overt pain was fading. But his nerves were no less alive. He could feel the ends of his socks with his toes, could feel the breeze on his fingers. Now the immediacy of these inexplicable sensations began to infuriate him. They were evidence of health, vitality—a wholeness he had spent long, miserable months of his life learning to live without—and they seemed to inundate him with terrifying implications. They seemed to deny the reality of his disease.

But that was impossible. It's one or the other, he panted fiercely. Not both. Either I'm a leper or I'm not. Either Joan divorced me or she never existed. There's no middle ground.

With an effort that made him grind his teeth, he averred, I'm a leper. I'm dreaming. That's a fact.

He could not bear the alternative. If he were dreaming, he might still be able to save his sanity, survive, endure. But if the Land were real, actual— ah, then the long anguish of his leprosy was a dream, and he was mad already, beyond hope.

Any belief was better than that. Better to struggle for a sanity he could at least recognize than to submit to a "health" which surpassed all explanation.

He chewed the gristle of such thoughts for leagues as he trudged along behind Atiaran, but each argument brought him back to the same position. The mystery of his leprosy was all the mystery he could tolerate, accept as fact. It determined his response to every other question of credibility.

It made him stalk along at Atiaran's back as if he were ready to attack her at any provocation.

Nevertheless, he did receive one benefit from his dilemma. Its immediate presence and tangibility built a kind of wall between him and the particular fears and actions which had threatened him earlier. Certain memories of violence and blood did not recur. And without shame to goad it, his anger remained manageable, discrete. It did not impel him to rebel against Atiaran's uncompromising lead.

Throughout that third day, her erect, relentless form did not relax its compulsion. Up slopes and down hillsides, across glens, around thickets—along the western margin of the hills—she drew him onward against his fuming mind and recalcitrant flesh. But early in the afternoon she stopped suddenly, looked about her as if she had heard a distant cry of fear. Her unexpected anxiety startled Covenant, but before he could ask her what was the matter, she started grimly forward again.

Some time later she repeated her performance. This time, Covenant saw that she was smelling the air as if the breeze carried an erratic scent of evil. He sniffed, but smelled nothing. "What is it?" he asked. "Are we being followed again?"

She did not look at him. "Would that Trell were here," she breathed distractedly. "Perhaps he would know why the Land is so unquiet." Without explanation she swung hastening away northward once more.

That evening she halted earlier than usual. Late in the afternoon, he noticed that she was looking for something, a sign of some kind in the grass and trees; but she said nothing to explain herself, and so he could do nothing but watch and follow. Then without warning she turned sharply to the right, moved into a shallow valley between two hills. They had to skirt the edge of the valley to avoid a large patch of brambles which covered most of its bottom; and in a few hundred yards they came to a wide, thick copse in the northern hill. Atiaran walked around the copse, then unexpectedly vanished into it.

Dimly wondering, Covenant went to the spot where she had disappeared. There he was able to pick out a thin sliver of a path leading into the copse. He had to turn sideways to follow this path around some of the trees, but in twenty feet he came to an open space like a chamber grown into the center of the woods.

The space was lit by light filtering through the walls, which were formed of saplings standing closely side by side in a rude rectangle; and a faint rustling breeze blew through them. But interwoven branches and leaves made a tight roof for the chamber. It was comfortably large enough for three or four people, and along each of its walls were grassy mounds like beds. In one corner stood a larger tree with a hollow center, into which shelves had been built, and these were laden with pots and flasks made of both wood and stone. The whole place seemed deliberately welcoming and cozy.

As Covenant looked around, Atiaran set her pack on one of the beds, and said abruptly, "This is a Waymeet." When he turned a face full of questions toward her, she sighed and went on, "A resting place for travelers. Here is food and drink and sleep for any who pass this way."

She moved away to inspect the contents of the shelves, and her busyness forced Covenant to hold onto his questions until a time when she might be more accessible. But while she replenished the supplies in her pack and prepared a meal, he sat and reflected that she was not ever likely to be accessible to him; and he was in no mood to be kept in ignorance. So after they had eaten, and Atiaran had settled herself for the night, he said with as much gentleness as he could manage, "Tell me more about this place. Maybe I'll need to know sometime."

She kept her face away from him, and lay silent in the gathering darkness for a while. She seemed to be waiting for courage, and when at last she spoke, she sighed only, "Ask."

Her delay made him abrupt. "Are there many places like this?"

"There are many throughout the Land."

"Why? Who sets them up?"

"The Lords caused them to be made. Revelstone is only one place, and the people live in many—therefore the Lords sought a way to help travelers, so that people might come to Revelstone and to each other more easily."

"Well, who takes care of them? There's fresh food here."

Atiaran sighed again, as if she found talking to him arduous. The night had deepened; he could see nothing of her but a shadow as she explained tiredly, "Among the Demondim-spawn that survived the Desolation, there were some who recalled Loric Vilesilencer with gratitude. They turned against the ur-viles, and asked the Lords to give them a service to perform, as expiation for the sins of their kindred. These creatures, the Waynhim, care for the Waymeets —helping the trees to grow, providing food and drink. But the bond between men and Waynhim is fragile, and you will not see one. They serve for their own reasons, not for love of us—performing simple tasks to redeem the evil of their mighty lore."

The darkness in the chamber was now complete. In spite of his irritation, Covenant felt ready to sleep. He asked only one more question. "How did you find this place? Is there a map?"

"There is no map. A Waymeet is a blessing which one who travels accepts wherever it is found—a token of the health and hospitality of the Land. They may be found when they are needed. The Waynhim leave signs in the surrounding land."

Covenant thought he could hear a note of appreciation in her voice which clashed with her reluctance. The sound reminded him of her constant burden of conflicts—her sense of personal weakness in the face of the Land's strong need, her desires to both punish and preserve him. But he soon forgot such things as the image of Waymeets filled his reverie. Enfolded by the smell of the fresh grass on which he lay, he swung easily into sleep.

During the night, the weather changed. The morning came glowering under heavy clouds on a ragged wind out of the north, and Covenant met it with a massive frown that seemed to weigh down his forehead. He awoke before Atiaran called him. Though he had slept soundly in the security of the

Waymeet, he felt as tired as if he had spent the whole night shouting at himself.

While Atiaran was preparing breakfast, he took out Triock's knife, then scanned the shelves and found a basin for water and a small mirror. He could not locate any soap—apparently the Waynhim relied on the same fine sand which he had used in Atiaran's home. So he braced himself to shave without lather. Triock's knife felt clumsy in his right hand, and he could not shake lurid visions of slitting his throat.

To marshal his courage, he studied himself in the mirror. His hair was tousled wildly; with his stubbled beard he looked like a rude prophet. His lips were thin and tight, like the chiseled mouth of an oracle, and there was grit in his gaunt eyes. All he needed to complete the picture was a touch of frenzy. Muttering silently, All in good time, he brought the knife to his cheek.

To his surprise, the blade felt slick on his skin, and it cut his whiskers without having to be scraped over them repeatedly. In a short time, he had given himself a shave which appeared adequate, at least by contrast, and he had not damaged himself. With a sardonic nod toward his reflection, he put the blade away in his pack and began eating his breakfast.

Soon he and Atiaran were ready to leave the Waymeet. She motioned for him to precede her; he went ahead a few steps along the path, then stopped to see what she was doing. As she left the chamber, she raised her head to the leafy ceiling, and said softly, "We give thanks for the Waymeet. The giving of this gift honors us, and in accepting it we return honor to the giver. We leave in Peace." Then she followed Covenant out of the copse.

When they reached the open valley, they found dark clouds piling over them out of the north. Tensely, Atiaran looked at the sky, smelled the air; she seemed distraught by the coming rain. Her reaction made the boiling thunderheads appear ominous to Covenant, and when she turned sharply down the valley to resume her northward path, he hurried after her, calling out, "What's the matter?"

"Ill upon evil," she replied. "Do you not smell it? The Land is unquiet."

"What's wrong?"

"I do not know," she murmured so quietly that he could barely hear her. "There is a shadow in the air. And this rain—! Ah, the Land!"

"What's wrong with rain? Don't you get rain in the spring?"

"Not from the north," she answered over her shoulder. "The spring of the Land arises from the southwest. No, this rain comes straight from Gravin Threndor. The Cavewight Staff wrong-wielder tests his power—I feel it. We are too late."

She stiffened her pace into the claws of the wind, and Covenant pressed on behind her. As the first raindrops struck his forehead, he asked, "Does this Staff really run the weather?"

"The Old Lords did not use it so—they had no wish to violate the Land. But who can say what such power may accomplish?"

Then the full clouts of the storm hit them. The wind scourged the rain southward as if the sky were lashing out at them, at every defenseless living thing. Soon the hillsides were drenched with ferocity. The wind rent at the trees, tore, battered the grass; it struck daylight from the hills, buried the earth in preternatural night. In moments, Atiaran and Covenant were soaked, gasping through the torrent. They kept their direction by facing the dark fury, but they could see nothing of the terrain; they staggered down rough slopes, wandered helplessly into hip-deep streams, lurched headlong through thickets; they forced against the wind as if it were the current of some stinging limbo, some abyss running from nowhere mercilessly into nowhere. Yet Atiaran lunged onward erect, with careless determination, and the fear of losing her kept Covenant lumbering at her heels.

But he was wearying rapidly. With an extra effort that made his chest ache, he caught up to Atiaran, grabbed her shoulder, shouted in her ear, "Stop! We've got to stop!"

"No!" she screamed back. "We are too late! I do not dare!"

Her voice barely reached him through the howl of the wind. She started to pull away, and he tightened his grip on her robe, yelling, "No choice! We'll kill ourselves!" The rain thrashed brutally; for an instant he almost lost his hold. He got his other arm around her, tugged her streaming face close to his. "Shelter!" he cried. "We've got to stop!"

Through the water, her face had a drowning look as she answered, "Never! No time!" With a quick thrust of her weight and a swing of her arms, she broke his grip, tripped him to the ground. Before he could recover, she snatched up his right hand and began dragging him on through the grass and mud, hauling him like an unsupportable burden against the opposition of the storm. Her pull was so desperate that she had taken him several yards before he could heave upward and get his feet under him.

As he braced himself, her hold slipped off his hand, and she fell away from him. Shouting, "By hell, we're going to stop!" he leaped after her. But she eluded his grasp, ran unevenly away from him into the spite of the storm.

He stumbled along behind her. For several long moments, he slipped and scrambled through the flailing rain after her untouchable back, furious to get his hands on her. But some inner resource galvanized her strength beyond anything he could match; soon he failed at the pace. The rain hampered him as if he were trying to run on the bottom of a breaking wave.

Then a vicious skid sent him sledding down the hill with his face full of mud. When he looked up again through the rain and dirt, Atiaran had vanished into the dark storm as if she were in terror of him, dreaded his touch.

Fighting his way to his feet, Covenant roared at the rampant clouds, "Hellfire! You can't do this to me!"

Without warning, just as his fury peaked, a huge white flash exploded beside him. He felt that a bolt of lightning had struck his left hand.

The blast threw him up the hill to his right. For uncounted moments, he lay dazed, conscious only of the power of the detonation and the flaming pain in his hand. His wedding ring seemed to be on fire. But when he recovered enough to look, he could see no mark on his fingers, and the pain faded away while he was still hunting for its source.

He shook his head, thrust himself into a sitting position. There were no signs of the blast anywhere around him. He was numbly aware that something had changed, but in his confusion he could not identify what it was.

He climbed painfully to his feet. After only a moment, he spotted Atiaran lying on the hillside twenty yards ahead of him. His head felt unbalanced with bewilderment, but he moved cautiously toward her, concentrating on his equilibrium. She lay on her back, apparently unhurt, and stared at him as he approached. When he reached her, she said in wonderment, "What have you done?"

The sound of her voice helped focus his attention. He was able to say without slurring, "Me? I didn't —nothing."

Atiaran came slowly to her feet. Standing in front of him, she studied him gravely, uncertainly, as she said, "Something has aided us. See, the storm is less. And the wind is changed—it blows now as it should. Gravin Threndor no longer threatens. Praise the Earth, Unbeliever, if this is not your doing."

"Of course it's not my doing," murmured Covenant. "I don't run the weather." There was no asperity in his tone. He was taken aback by his failure to recognize the change in the storm for himself.

Atiaran had told the simple truth. The wind had shifted and dropped considerably. The rain fell steadily, but without fury; now it was just a good, solid, spring rain.

Covenant shook his head again. He felt strangely unable to understand. But when Atiaran said gently, "Shall we go?" he heard a note of unwilling respect in her voice. She seemed to believe that he had in fact done something to the storm.

Numbly, he mumbled, "Sure," and followed her onward again.

They walked in clean rain for the rest of the day. Covenant's sense of mental dullness persisted, and the only outside influences that penetrated him were wetness and cold. Most of the day passed without his notice in one long, drenched push against the cold. Toward evening, he had regained enough of himself to be glad when Atiaran found a Waymeet, and he checked over his body carefully for any hidden injuries while his clothes dried by the graveling. But he still felt dazed by what had happened. He could not shake the odd impression that whatever force had changed the fury of the storm had altered him also.

The next day broke clear, crisp, and glorious, and he and Atiaran left the Waymeet early in the new spring dawn. After the strain of the previous day, Covenant felt keenly alert to the joyous freshness of the air and the sparkle of dampness on the grass, the sheen on the heather and the bursting flavor of the treasure-berries. The Land around him struck him as if he had never noticed its beauty before. Its vitality seemed curiously tangible to his senses. He felt that he could see spring fructifying within the trees, the grass, the flowers, hear the excitement of the calling birds, smell the newness of the buds and the cleanliness of the air.

Then abruptly Atiaran stopped and looked about her. A grimace of distaste and concern tightened her features as she sampled the breeze. She moved her head around intently, as if she were trying to locate the source of a threat.

Covenant followed her example, and as he did so, a thrill of recognition ran through him. He could tell that there was indeed something wrong in the air, something false. It did not arise in his immediate vicinity—the scents of the trees and turf and flowers, the lush afterward of rain, were all as they should be—but it lurked behind those smells like something uneasy, out of place, unnatural in the distance. He understood instinctively that it was the odor of ill—the odor of premeditated disease.

A moment later, the breeze shifted; the odor vanished. But that ill smell had heightened his perceptions; the contrast vivified his sense of the vitality of his surroundings. With an intuitive leap, he grasped the change which had taken place within him or for him. In some way that completely amazed him, his senses had gained a new dimension. He looked at the grass, smelled its freshness—and *saw* its verdancy, its springing life, its fitness. Jerking his eyes to a nearby *aliantha,* he received an impression of potency, health, that dumbfounded him.

His thoughts reeled, groped, then suddenly clarified around the image of *health.* He was seeing health, smelling natural fitness and vitality, hearing the true exuberance of spring. *Health* was as vivid around him as if the spirit of the Land's life had become palpable, incarnate. It was as if he had stepped without warning into an altogether different universe. Even Atiaran— she was gazing at his entrancement with puzzled surprise—was manifestly healthy, though her life was complicated by uneasiness, fatigue, pain, resolution.

By hell, he mumbled. Is my leprosy this obvious to her? Then why doesn't she understand—? He turned away from her stare, hunted for some way to test both his eyes and hers. After a moment, he spotted near the top of a hill a Gilden tree that seemed to have something wrong with it. In every respect that he could identify, specify, the tree appeared normal, healthy, yet it conveyed a sense of inner rot, an unexpected pang of sorrow, to his gaze. Pointing at it, he asked Atiaran what she saw.

Soberly, she replied, "I am not one of the *lillianrill,* but I can see that the Gilden dies. Some blight has stricken its heart. Did you not see such things before?"

He shook his head.

"Then how does the world from which you come live?" She sounded dismayed by the prospect of a place in which *health* itself was invisible.

He shrugged off her question. He wanted to challenge her, find out what she saw in him. But then he remembered her saying, *You are closed to me.* Now he understood her comment, and the comprehension gave him a feeling of relief. The privacy of his own illness was intact, safe. He motioned her northward again, and when after a moment she started on her way, he followed her with pleasure. For a long time he forgot himself in the sight of so much healthiness.

Gradually, as the day moved through afternoon into gloaming and the onset of night, he adjusted to seeing health behind the colors and forms which met his eyes. Twice more his nostrils had caught the elusive odor of wrongness, but he could not find it anywhere near the creek by which Atiaran chose to make camp. In its absence he thought that he would sleep peacefully.

But somehow a rosy dream of soul health and beauty became a nightmare in which spirits threw off their bodies and revealed themselves to be ugly, rotten, contemptuous. He was glad to wake up, glad even to take the risk of shaving without the aid of a mirror.

On the sixth day, the smell of wrong became persistent, and it grew stronger as Atiaran and Covenant worked their way north along the hills. A brief spring shower dampened their clothes in the middle of the morning, but it did not wash the odor from the air. That smell made Covenant uneasy, whetted his anxiety until he seemed to have a cold blade of dread poised over his heart.

Still he could not locate, specify, the odor. It keened in him behind the bouquet of the grass and the tangy bracken and the *aliantha,* behind the loveliness of the vital hills, like the reek of a rotting corpse just beyond the range of his nostrils.

Finally he could not endure it any longer in silence. He drew abreast of Atiaran, and asked, "Do you smell it?"

Without a glance at him, she returned heavily, "Yes, Unbeliever. I smell it. It becomes clear to me."

"What does it mean?"

"It means that we are walking into peril. Did you not expect it?"

Thinking, Hellfire! Covenant rephrased his question. "But what does it come from? What's causing it?"

"How can I say?" she countered. "I am no oracle."

Covenant caught himself on the edge of an angry retort. With an effort, he kept his temper. "Then what *is* it?"

"It is murder," Atiaran replied flatly, and quickened her pace to pull away from him. Do not ask me to forget, her back seemed to say, and he stumped fuming after it. Cold anxiety inched closer to his heart.

By midafternoon, he felt that his perception of wrongness was sharpening at almost every step. His eyes winced up and down the hills, as though he expected at any moment to see the source of the smell. His sinuses ached from constantly tasting the odor. But there was nothing for him to perceive—nothing but Atiaran's roaming path through the dips and hollows and valleys and outcroppings of the hills—nothing but healthy trees and thickets and flowers and verdant grass, the blazonry of the Earth's spring and nothing but the intensifying threat of something ill in the air. It was a poignant threat, and he felt obscurely that the cause would be worth bewailing.

The sensation of it increased without resolution for some time. But then a sudden change in the tension of Atiaran's back warned Covenant to brace himself scant instants before she hissed at him to stop. She had just rounded the side of a hill far enough to see into the hollow beyond it. For a moment she froze, crouching slightly and peering into the hollow. Then she began running down the hill.

At once, Covenant followed. In three strides, he reached the spot where she had halted. Beyond him, in the bottom of the hollow, stood a single copse like an eyot in a broad glade. He could see nothing amiss. But his sense of smell jabbered at him urgently, and Atiaran was dashing straight toward the copse. He sprinted after her.

She stopped short just on the east side of the trees. Quivering feverishly, she glared about her with an expression of terror and hatred, as if she wanted to enter the copse and did not have the courage. Then she cried out, aghast, "Waynhim? *Melenkurion!* Ah, by the Seven, what evil!"

When Covenant reached her side, she was staring a silent scream at the trees. She held her hands clasped together at her mouth, and her shoulders shook.

As soon as he looked at the copse, he saw a thin path leading into it. Impulsively, he moved forward, plunged between the trees. In five steps, he was in an open space much like the other Waymeets he had seen. This chamber was round, but it had the same tree walls, branch-woven roof, beds, and shelves.

But the walls were spattered with blood, and a figure lay in the center of the floor.

Covenant gasped as he saw that the figure was not human.

Its outlines were generally manlike, though the torso was inordinately long, and the limbs were short, matched in length, indicating that the creature could both stand erect and run on its hands and feet. But the face was entirely alien to Covenant. A long, flexible neck joined the hairless head to the body; two pointed ears perched near the top of the skull on either side; the mouth was as thin as a mere slit in the flesh. And there were no eyes. Two gaping nostrils surrounded by a thick, fleshy membrane filled the center of the face. The head had no other features.

Driven through the center of the creature's chest —pinning it to the ground—was a long iron spike.

The chamber stank of violence so badly that in a few breaths Covenant felt about to suffocate. He wanted to flee. He was a leper; even dead things were dangerous to him. But he forced himself to remain still while he sorted out one impression. On seeing the creature, his first thought had been that the Land was rid of something loathsome. But as he gritted himself, his eyes and nose corrected him. The wrongness which assailed his senses came from the killing—from the spike—not from the creature. Its flesh had a hue of ravaged health; it had been natural, right—a proper part of the life of the Land.

Gagging on the stench of the crime, Covenant turned and fled.

As he broke out into the sunlight, he saw Atiaran already moving away to the north, almost out of the hollow. He needed no urging to hurry after her; his bones ached to put as much distance as possible between himself and the desecrated Waymeet. He hastened in her direction as if there were fangs snapping at his heels.

For the rest of the day, he found relief in putting leagues behind him. The edge of the unnatural smell was slowly blunted as they hurried onward. But it did not fade below a certain level. When he and Atiaran were forced by fatigue and darkness to stop for the night, he felt sure that there was uneasiness still ahead—that the killer of the Waynhim was moving invidiously to the north of them. Atiaran seemed to share his conviction; she asked him if he knew how to use the knife he carried.

After sleep had eluded him for some time, he made himself ask her, "Shouldn't we have—buried it?"

She answered softly from her shadowed bed across the low light of the graveling, "They would not thank our interference. They will take care of their own. But the fear is on me that they may break their bond with the Lords—because of this."

That thought gave Covenant a chill he could not explain, and he lay sleepless for half the night under the cold mockery of the stars.

The next day dawned on short rations for the travelers. Atiaran had been planning to replenish her supplies at a Waymeet the previous day, so now she had no springwine left and little bread or staples. However, they were in no danger of going hungry —treasure-berries were plentiful along their path. But they had to start without warm food to steady them after the cold, uncomforting night. And they had to travel in the same direction that the killer of the Waynhim had taken. Covenant found himself stamping angrily into the dawn as if he sensed that the murder had been intended for him. For the first time in several days, he allowed himself to think of Drool and Lord Foul. He knew that either of them was capable of killing a Waynhim, even of killing it gratuitously. And the Despiser, at least, might easily know where he was.

But the day passed without mishap. The dim, constant uneasiness in the air grew no worse and *aliantha* abounded. As the leagues passed, Covenant's anger lost its edge. He relaxed into contemplation of the health around him, looked with undiminished wonder at the trees, the magisterial oaks and dignified elms, the comforting spread of the Gilden, the fine filigree of the mimosas, the spry saplings of wattle —and at the calm old contours of the hills, lying like slumberous heads to the reclining earth of the western plains. Such things gave him a new sense of the pulse and pause, the climbing sap and the still rock of the Land. In contrast, the trailing ordure of death seemed both petty—insignificant beside the vast abundant vitality of the hills—and vile, like an act of cruelty done to a child.

The next morning, Atiaran changed her course, veering somewhat eastward, so that she and Covenant climbed more and more into the heart of the hills. They took a crooked trail, keeping primarily to valleys that wandered generally northward between the hills. And when the sun was low enough to cast the eastern hillsides into shadow, the travelers came in sight of Soaring Woodhelven.

Their approach gave Covenant a good view of the tree village from some distance away across a wide glade. He judged the tree to be nearly four hundred feet high, and a good thirty broad at the base. There were no branches on the trunk until forty or fifty feet above the ground, then abruptly huge limbs spread out horizontally from the stem, forming in outline a half-oval with a flattened tip. The whole tree was so thickly branched and leaved that most of the village was hidden; but Covenant could see a few ladders between the branches and along the trunk; and in some tight knots on the limbs he thought he could make out the shapes of dwellings. If any people were moving through the foliage,

they were so well camouflaged that he could not
discern them.

"That is Soaring Woodhelven," said Atiaran, "a
home for the people of the *lillianrill,* as Mithil Stonedown is a home for those of the *rhadhamaerl.* I
have been here once, on my returning from the
Loresraat. The Woodhelvennin are a comely folk,
though I do not understand their wood-lore. They
will give us rest and food, and perhaps help as well.
It is said, 'Go to the *rhadhamaerl* for truth, and the
lillianrill for counsel.' My need for counsel is sore
upon me. Come."

She led Covenant across the glade to the base of
the great tree. They had to pass around the rough-
barked trunk to the northwest curve, and there they
found a large natural opening in the hollow stem.
The inner cavity was not deep; it was only large
enough to hold a spiral stairway. Above the first thick
limb was another opening, from which ladders began
their way upward.

The sight gave Covenant a quiver of his old fear
of heights, almost forgotten since his ordeal on the
stairs of Kevin's Watch. He did not want to have to
climb those ladders.

But it appeared that he would not have to climb.
The opening to the trunk was barred with a heavy
wooden gate, and there was no one to open it. In
fact, the whole place seemed too quiet and dark for
a human habitation. Dusk was gathering, but no
home glimmers broke through the overhanging shadow,
and no gloaming calls between families interrupted
the silence.

Covenant glanced at Atiaran, and saw that she
was puzzled. Resting her hands on the bars of the
gate, she said, "This is not well, Thomas Covenant.
When last I came here, there were children in the
glade, people on the stair, and no gate at the door.
Something is amiss. And yet I sense no great evil.
There is no more ill here than elsewhere along our
path."

Stepping back from the gate, she raised her head
and called, "Hail! Soaring Woodhelven! We are trav-

elers, people of the Land! Our way is long—our future dark! What has become of you?" When no answering shout came, she went on in exasperation, "I have been here before! In those days, it was said that Woodhelvennin hospitality had no equal! Is this your friendship to the Land?"

Suddenly, they heard a light scattering fall behind them. Spinning around, they found themselves encircled by seven or eight men gripping smooth wooden daggers. Instinctively, Atiaran and Covenant backed away. As the men advanced, one of them said, "The meaning of friendship changes with the times. We have seen darkness, and heard dark tidings. We will be sure of strangers."

A torch flared in the hands of the man who had spoken. Through the glare, Covenant got his first look at the Woodhelvennin. They were all tall, slim, and lithe, with fair hair and light eyes. They dressed in cloaks of woodland colors, and the fabric seemed to cling to their limbs, as if to avoid snagging on branches. Each man held a pointed dagger of polished wood which gleamed dully in the torchlight.

Covenant was at a loss, but Atiaran gathered her robe about her and answered with stern pride, "Then be sure. I am Atiaran Trell-mate of Mithil Stonedown. This is Thomas Covenant, Unbeliever and message-bearer to the Lords. We come in friendship and need, seeking safety and help. I did not know that it is your custom to make strangers prisoner."

The man who held the torch stepped forward and bowed seriously. "When we are sure, we will ask your pardon. Until that time, you must come with me to a place where you may be examined. We have seen strange tokens, and see more now." He nodded at Covenant. "'We would make no mistake, either in trust or in doubt. Will you accompany me?"

"Very well," Atiaran sighed. "But you would not be treated so in Mithil Stonedown."

The man replied, "Let the Stonedownors taste our troubles before they despise our caution. Now, come behind me." He moved forward to open the gate.

At the command, Covenant balked. He was not

prepared to go climbing around a tall tree in the dark. It would have been bad enough in the light, when he could have seen what he was doing, but the very thought of taking the risk at night made his pulse hammer in his forehead. Stepping away from Atiaran, he said with a quaver he could not repress, "Forget it."

Before he could react, two of the men grabbed his arms. He tried to twist away, but they held him, pulled his hands up into the torchlight. For one stark moment, the Woodhelvennin stared at his hands—at the ring on his left and the scar on his right—as if he were some kind of ghoul. Then the man with the torch snapped, "Bring him."

"No!" Covenant clamored. "You don't understand. I'm not good at heights. I'll fall." As they wrestled him toward the gate, he shouted, "Hellfire! You're trying to kill me!"

His captors halted momentarily. He heard a series of shouts, but in his confused, angry panic he did not understand. Then the leader said, "If you do not climb well, you will not be asked to climb."

The next moment, the end of a rope fell beside Covenant. Instantly, two more men lashed his wrists to the line. Before he realized what was happening, the rope sprang taut. He was hauled into the air like a sack of miscellaneous helplessness.

He thought he heard a shout of protest from Atiaran, but he could not be sure. Crying silently, Bloody hell! he tensed his shoulders against the strain and stared wildly up into the darkness. He could not see anyone drawing up the rope—in the last glimmering of the torch, the line seemed to stretch up into an abyss—and that made him doubly afraid.

Then the light below him vanished.

The next moment, a low rustling of leaves told him that he had reached the level of the first branches. He saw a yellow glow through the upper opening of the tree's stairwell. But the rope hauled him on upward into the heights of the village.

His own movements made him swing slightly, so that at odd intervals he brushed against the leaves.

But that was his only contact with the tree. He saw
no lights, heard no voices; the deep black weights
of the mighty limbs slid smoothly past him as if he
were being dragged into the sky.

Soon both his shoulders throbbed sharply, and his
arms went numb. With his head craned upward, he
gaped into a lightless terror and moaned as if he
were drowning, Hellfire! Ahh!

Then without warning his movement stopped.
Before he could brace himself, a torch flared, and
he found himself level with three men who were
standing on a limb. In the sudden light, they looked
identical to the men who had captured him, but one
of them had a small circlet of leaves about his head.
The other two considered Covenant for a moment,
then reached out and gripped his shirt, pulling him
toward their limb. As the solid branch struck his feet,
the rope slackened, letting his arms drop.

His wrists were still tied together, but he tried to
get a hold on one of the men, keep himself from
falling off the limb. His arms were dead; he could
not move them. The darkness stretched below him
like a hungry beast. With a gasp, he lunged toward
the men, striving to make them save him. They grappled him roughly. He refused to bear his own weight,
forced them to carry and drag him down the limb
until they came to a wide gap in the trunk. There
the center of the stem was hollowed out to form a
large chamber, and Covenant dropped heavily to the
floor, shuddering with relief.

Shortly, a rising current of activity began around
him. He paid no attention to it; he kept his eyes
shut to concentrate on the hard stability of the floor,
and on the pain of blood returning to his hands and
arms. The hurt was excruciating, but he endured it
in clenched silence. Soon his hands were tingling,
and his fingers felt thick, hot. He flexed them, curled
them into claws. Through his teeth, he muttered to
the fierce rhythm of his heart, Hellfire. Hell and
blood.

He opened his eyes.

He was lying on polished wood at the center of

the myriad concentric circles of the tree trunk. The age rings made the rest of the room seem to focus toward him as if he were sprawled on a target. His arms felt unnaturally inarticulate, but he forced them to thrust him into a sitting position. Then he looked at his hands. His wrists were raw from the cut of the rope, but they were not bleeding.

Bastards!

He raised his head and glowered around him.

The chamber was about twenty feet wide, and seemed to fill the whole inside diameter of the trunk. The only opening was the one through which he had stumbled, and he could see darkness outside; but the room was brightly lit by torches set into the walls—torches which burned smokelessly, and did not appear to be consumed. The polished walls gleamed as if they were burnished, but the ceiling, high above the floor, was rough, untouched wood.

Five Woodhelvennin stood around Covenant in the hollow—three men, including the one wearing the circlet of leaves, and two women. They all were dressed in similar cloaks which clung to their outlines, though the colors varied, and all were taller than Covenant. Their tallness seemed threatening, so he got slowly to his feet, lowering the pack from his shoulders as he stood.

A moment later, the man who had led Covenant's captors on the ground entered the chamber, followed by Atiaran. She appeared unharmed, but weary and depressed, as though the climb and the distrust had sapped her strength. When she saw Covenant, she moved to take her stand beside him.

One of the women said, "Only two, Soranal?"

"Yes," Atiaran's guard answered. "We watched, and there were no others as they crossed the south glade. And our scouts have not reported any other strangers in the hills."

"Scouts?" asked Atiaran. "I did not know that scouts were needed among the people of the Land."

The woman took a step forward and replied, "Atiaran Trell-mate, the folk of Mithil Stonedown have been known to us since our return to the Land in the new age. And there are those among us who remember your visit here. We know our friends, and the value of friendship."

"Then in what way have we deserved this treatment?" Atiaran demanded. "We came in search of friends."

The woman did not answer Atiaran's question directly. "Because we are all people of the Land," she said, "and because our peril is a peril for all, I will attempt to ease the sting of our discourtesy by explaining our actions. We in this heartwood chamber are the Heers of Soaring Woodhelven, the leaders of our people. I am Llaura daughter of Annamar. Here also"—she indicated each individual with a nod— "are Omournil daughter of Mournil, Soranal son of Thiller, Padrias son of Mill, Malliner son of Veinnin, and Baradakas, Hirebrand of the *lillianrill*." This last was the man wearing the circlet of leaves. "We made the decision of distrust, and will give our reasons.

"I see that you are impatient." A taste of bitterness roughened her voice. "Well, I will not tire you with the full tale of the blighting wind which has blown over us from time to time from Gravin Threndor. I will not describe the angry storms, or show you the body of the three-winged bird that died atop our Woodhelven, or discuss the truth of the rumors of murder which have reached our ears. By the Seven! There are angry songs that should be sung—but I will not sing them now. This I will tell you: all servants of the Gray Slayer are not dead. It is our belief that a Raver has been among us."

That name carried a pang of danger that made Covenant look rapidly about him, trying to locate the peril. For an instant, he did not comprehend. But then he noticed how Atiaran stiffened at Llaura's words—saw the jumping knot at the corner of her jaw, felt the heightened fear in her, though she said nothing—and he understood. The Woodhelvennin feared that he and she might be Ravers.

Without thinking, he snapped, "That's ridiculous."

The Heers ignored him. After a short pause, Soranal continued Llaura's explanation. "Two days past, in the high sun of afternoon, when our people were busy at their crafts and labors, and the children were playing in the upper branches of the Tree, a stranger came to Soaring Woodhelven. Two days earlier, the last ill storm out of Mount Thunder had broken suddenly and turned into good—and on the day the stranger came our hearts were glad, thinking that a battle we knew not of had been won for the Land. He wore the appearance of a Stonedownor, and said his name was Jehannum. We welcomed him with the hospitality which is the joy of the Land. We saw no reason to doubt him, though the children shrank from him with unwonted cries and fears. Alas for us—the young saw more clearly than the old.

"He passed among us with dark hints and spite in his mouth, casting sly ridicule on our crafts and customs. And we could not answer him. But we remembered Peace, and did nothing for a day.

"In that time, Jehannum's hints turned to open foretelling of doom. So at last we called him to the heartwood chamber and the meeting of the Heers. We heard the words he chose to speak, words full of glee and the reviling of the Land. Then our eyes saw more deeply, and we offered him the test of the *lomillialor*."

"You know of the High Wood, *lomillialor*—do you not, Atiaran?" Baradakas spoke for the first time. "There is much in it like the *orcrest* of the *rhadhamaerl*. It is an offspring of the One Tree, from which the Staff of Law itself was made."

"But we had no chance to make the test," Soranal resumed. "When Jehannum saw the High Wood, he sprang away from us and escaped. We gave pursuit, but he had taken us by surprise—we were too full of quiet, not ready for such evils—and his fleetness far surpassed ours. He eluded us, and made his way toward the east."

He sighed as he concluded, "In the one day which has passed since that time, we have begun relearning the defense of the Land."

After a moment, Atiaran said quietly, "I hear you. Pardon my anger—I spoke in haste and ignorance.

But surely now you can see that we are no friends of the Gray Slayer."

"We see much in you, Atiaran Trell-mate," said Llaura, her eyes fixed keenly on the Stonedownor, "much sorrow and much courage. But your companion is closed to us. It may be that we will need to emprison this Thomas Covenant."

"Melenkurion!" hissed Atiaran. "Do not dare! Do you not know? Have you not looked at him?"

At this, a murmur of relief passed among the Heers, a murmur which accented their tension. Stepping toward Atiaran, Soranal extended his right hand, palm forward, in the salute of welcome, and said, "We have looked—looked and heard. We trust you, Atiaran Trell-mate. You have spoken a name which no Raver would call upon to save a companion." He took her by the arm and drew her away from Covenant, out of the center of the chamber.

Without her at his shoulder, Covenant felt suddenly exposed, vulnerable. For the first time, he sensed how much he had come to depend upon her presence, her guidance, if not her support. But he was in no mood to meet threats passively. He poised himself on the balls of his feet, ready to move in any direction; and his eyes shifted quickly among the faces that stared at him from the gleaming walls of the chamber.

"Jehannum predicted many things," said Llaura, "but one especially you should be told. He said that a great evil in the semblance of Berek Halfhand walked the hills toward us out of the south. And here—" She pointed a pale arm at Covenant, her voice rising sternly as she spoke. "Here is an utter stranger to the Land—half unhanded on his right, and on his left bearing a ring of white gold. Beyond doubt carrying messages to the Lords—messages of doom!"

With a pleading intensity, Atiaran said, "Do not presume to judge. Remember the Oath. You are not Lords. And dark words may be warnings as well as prophecies. Will you trust the word of a Raver?"

Baradakas shrugged slightly. "It is not the message we judge. Our test is for the man." Reaching behind him, he lifted up a smooth wooden rod three feet long from which all the bark had been stripped. He held it by the middle gently, reverently. "This is *lomillialor.*" As he said the name, the wood glistened as if its clear grain were moist with dew.

What the hell is this? Covenant tried to balance himself for whatever was coming.

But the Hirebrand's next move caught him by surprise. Baradakas swung his rod and lofted it toward the Unbeliever.

He jerked aside and clutched at the *lomillialor* with his right hand. But he did not have enough fingers to get a quick grip on it; it slipped away from him, dropped to the floor with a wooden click that seemed unnaturally loud in the hush of the chamber.

For an instant, everyone remained still, frozen while they absorbed the meaning of what they had seen. Then, in unison, the Heers uttered their verdict with all the finality of a death sentence.

"The High Wood rejects him. He is a wrong in the Land."

TEN: The Celebration of Spring

In one fluid motion, Baradakas drew a club from his cloak and raised it as he moved toward Covenant.

Covenant reacted instinctively, defensively. Before the Hirebrand could reach him, he stooped and snatched up the *lomillialor* rod with his left hand. As Baradakas swung the club at his head, he slashed the Hirebrand's arm with the rod.

In a shower of white sparks, the club sprang into

splinters. Baradakas was flung back as if he had been blasted away by an explosion.

The force of the hit vibrated through Covenant's hand to his elbow, and his fingers were struck momentarily numb. The rod started to slip from his hand. He gaped at it, thinking, What the hell—?

But then the mute astonishment of the Heers, and the Hirebrand's crumpled form, steadied him. Test me? he rasped. Bastards. He took the rod in his right hand, holding it by the middle as Baradakas had done. Its glistening wood felt slick; it gave him a sensation of slippage, as if it were oozing from his grasp, though the wood did not actually move. As he gripped it, he glared around at the Heers, put all the anger their treatment had sparked in him into his gaze. "Now why don't you tell me one more time about how this thing rejects me."

Soranal and Llaura stood on either side of Atiaran, with Malliner opposite them against the wall. Omournil and Padrias were bent over the fallen Hirebrand. As Covenant surveyed them, Atiaran faced him grimly. "In the older age," she said, "when High Lord Kevin trusted the Gray Slayer, he was given priceless gifts of *orcrest* and *lomillialor*. The tale says that these gifts were soon lost—but while the Gray Slayer possessed them they did not reject him. It is possible for Despite to wear the guise of truth. Perhaps the wild magic surpasses truth."

Thanks a lot! Covenant glowered at her. What're you trying to do to me?

In a pale voice, Llaura replied, "That is the tale. But we are only Woodhelvennin—not Lords. Such matters are beyond us. Never in the memory of our people has a test of truth struck down a Hirebrand of the *lillianrill*. What is the song?—'he will save or damn the Earth.' Let us pray that we will not find damnation for our distrust." Extending an unsteady hand toward Covenant in the salute of welcome, she said, "Hail, Unbeliever! Pardon our doubts, and be welcome in Soaring Woodhelven."

For an instant, Covenant faced her with a bitter retort twisting his lips. But he found when he met her eyes that he could see the sincerity of her apology. The perception abashed his vehemence. With conflicting intentions, he muttered, "Forget it."

Llaura and Soranal both bowed as if he had accepted her apology. Then they turned to watch as Baradakas climbed dazedly to his feet. His hands pulled at his face as if it were covered with cobwebs, but he assured Omournil and Padrias that he was unharmed. With a mixture of wonder and dismay in his eyes, he also saluted Covenant.

Covenant responded with a dour nod. He did not wait for the Hirebrand to ask; he handed the *lomillialor* to Baradakas, and was glad to be rid of its disquieting, insecure touch.

Baradakas received the rod and smiled at it crookedly, as if it had witnessed his defeat. Then he slipped it away into his cloak. Turning his smile toward Covenant, he said, "Unbeliever, our presences are no longer needed here. You have not eaten, and the weariness of your journey lies heavily upon you. Will you accept the hospitality of my house?"

The invitation surprised Covenant; for a moment he hesitated, trying to decide whether or not he could trust the Hirebrand. Baradakas appeared calm, unhostile, but his smile was more complex than Llaura's apology. But then Covenant reflected that if the question were one of trust, he would be safer with Baradakas alone than with all the Heers together. Stiffly, he said, "You honor me."

The Hirebrand bowed. "In accepting a gift you honor the giver." He looked around at the other Woodhelvennin, and when they nodded their approval, he turned and moved out of the heartwood chamber.

Covenant glanced toward Atiaran, but she was already talking softly to Soranal. Without further delay, he stepped out onto the broad limb beside Baradakas.

The night over the great tree was now scattered with lights—the home fires of the Woodhelvennin. They illuminated the fall far down through the branches, but did not reach to the ground. Involuntarily, Covenant clutched at Baradakas' shoulder.

"It is not far," the Hirebrand said softly. "Only up

to the next limb. I will come behind you—you will
not fall."

Cursing silently through his teeth, Covenant gripped
the rungs of the ladder. He wanted to retreat, go
back to the solidity of the heartwood chamber, but
pride and anger prevented him. And the rungs
felt secure, almost adhesive, to his fingers. When
Baradakas placed a reassuring hand on his back, he
started awkwardly upward.

As Baradakas had promised, the next limb was not
far away. Soon Covenant reached another broad
branch. A few steps out from the trunk, it forked,
and in the fork sat the Hirebrand's home. Holding
Baradakas' shoulders for support, he gained the doorway, crossed the threshold as if he were being blown
in by a gust of relief.

He was in a neat, two-roomed dwelling formed
entirely from the branches of the tree. Interwoven
limbs made part of the floor and all the walls, including the partition between the rooms. And the ceiling
was a dome of twigs and leaves. Along one wall of
the first room, broad knees of wood grew into the
chamber like chairs, and a bunk hung opposite them.
The place had a warm, clean atmosphere, an ambience
of devotion to lore, that Covenant found faintly
disturbing, like a reminder that the Hirebrand could
be a dangerous man.

While Covenant scanned the room, Baradakas set
torches in each of the outer walls and lit them by
rubbing his hands over their ends and murmuring
softly. Then he rummaged around in the far room for
a moment, and returned carrying a tray laden with
slabs of bread and cheese, a large bunch of grapes,
and a wooden jug. He set a small, three-legged table
between two of the chairs, put the tray on it, and
motioned for Covenant to sit down.

At the sight of the food, Covenant discovered that
he was hungry; he had eaten nothing but *aliantha* for
the past two days. He watched while Baradakas bowed
momentarily over the food. Then he seated himself.
Following his host's example, he made sandwiches
with cheese and grapes between slices of fresh bread,

and helped himself liberally to the jug of springwine. In the first rush of eating, he said nothing, saving his attention for the food.

But he did not forget who his host was, what had happened between them.

Leaving the springwine with Covenant, Baradakas cleared away the remains of the meal. When he returned after storing his food in the far room, he said, "Now, Unbeliever. In what other way may I give you comfort?"

Covenant took a deep draft of springwine, then replied as casually as he could, "Give an answer. You were ready to split my head open—back there. And it looked as if you got quite a jolt from that—from that High Wood. Why did you invite me here?"

For a moment, Baradakas hesitated, as if pondering how much he should say. Then he reached into his back room, picked up a smooth staff nearly six feet long, and sat down on the bed across from Covenant. As he spoke, he began polishing the white wood of the staff with a soft cloth. "There are many reasons, Thomas Covenant. You required a place to sleep, and my home is nearer to the heartwood chamber than any other—for one who dislikes heights. And neither you nor I are necessary for the consideration of counsel and help which will be done this night. Atiaran knows the Land—she will say all that need be said concerning your journey. And both Soranal and Llaura are able to give any help she may ask."

As he looked across the room at the Hirebrand's working hands and light, penetrating eyes, Covenant had the odd feeling that his test had been resumed— that the encounter of the *lomillialor* had only begun Baradakas' examining. But the springwine unknotted his fears and tensions; he was not anxious. Steadily, he said, "Tell me more."

"I also intended that my offer of hospitality should be an apology. I was prepared to injure you, and that violation of my Oath of Peace needs reparation. Had you shown yourself to be a servant of the Gray Slayer, it would have sufficed to capture you. And injury might have deprived the Lords of a chance to examine you. So in that way I was wrong. And became more wrong still when you lifted the *lomillialor,* and its fire struck me. I hope to amend my folly."

Covenant recognized the Hirebrand's frankness, but his sense of being probed sharpened rather than faded. He held his host's eyes as he said, "You still haven't answered my question."

In an unsurprised tone, Baradakas countered, "Are there other reasons? What do you see in me?"

"You're still testing me," Covenant growled.

The Hirebrand nodded slowly. "Perhaps. Perhaps I am." He got to his feet and braced one end of the staff against the floor as he gave a last touch to its polish. Then he said, "See, Thomas Covenant—I have made a staff for you. When I began it, I believed it was for myself. But now I know otherwise. Take it. It may serve you when help and counsel fail." To the brief question in Covenant's eyes, he replied, "No, this is not High Wood. But it is good nonetheless. Let me give it to you."

Covenant shook his head. "Finish your testing."

Suddenly, Baradakas raised the staff and struck the wood under his feet a hard blow. For an instant, the entire limb shook as if a gale had come up; the smaller branches thrashed, and the dwelling tossed like a chip on an angry wave. Covenant feared that the tree was falling, and he gripped his chair in apprehension. But almost immediately the violence passed. Baradakas leveled his pale eyes at Covenant and whispered, "Then hear me, Unbeliever. Any test of truth is no greater than the one who gives it. And I have felt your power. In all the memory of the *lillianrill,* no Hirebrand has ever been struck by the High Wood. We are the friends of the One Tree, not its foes. But beside you I am as weak as a child. I cannot force the truth from you. In spite of my testing, you might be the Gray Slayer himself, come to turn all the life of the Land to ashes."

Incensed by the suggestion, Covenant spat, "That's ridiculous."

Baradakas stepped closer, drove his probing gaze

deep into Covenant's eyes. Covenant squirmed; he could feel the Hirebrand exploring parts of him that he wanted to protect, keep hidden. What has that bastard Foul to do with me? he demanded bitterly. I didn't exactly choose to be his errand boy.

Abruptly, Baradakas' eyes widened, and he fell back across the room as if he had seen something of astonishing power. He caught himself on the bed, sat there for a moment while he watched his hands tremble on the staff. Then he said carefully, "True. One day I may be wise enough to know what can be relied upon. Now I need time to understand. I trust you, my friend. At the last trial, you will not abandon us to death.

"Here." He proffered the staff again. "Will you not accept my gift?"

Covenant did not reply at once. He was trembling also, and he had to clench himself before he could say without a tremor, "Why? Why do you trust me?"

The Hirebrand's eyes gleamed as if he were on the verge of tears, but he was smiling as he said, "You are a man who knows the value of beauty."

Covenant stared at that answer for a moment, then looked away. A complex shame came over him; he felt unclean, tainted, in the face of Baradakas' trust. But then he stiffened. Keep moving. Survive. What does trust have to do with it? Brusquely, he reached out and accepted the staff.

It felt pure in his hands, as if it had been shaped from the healthiest wood by the most loving devotion. He gripped it, scrutinized it, as if it could provide him with the innocence he lacked.

A short time later, he surprised himself with a wide yawn. He had not realized that he was so tired. He tried to suppress his weariness, but the effort only produced another yawn.

Baradakas responded with a kindly smile. He left the bed and motioned for Covenant to lie down.

Covenant had no intention of going to sleep, but as soon as he was horizontal, all the springwine he had consumed seemed to rush to his head, and he

felt himself drifting on the high tree breeze. Soon he
was fast in slumber.

He slept soundly, disturbed only by the memory of
the Hirebrand's intense, questioning eyes, and by the
sensation that the *lomillialor* was slipping through his
fingers, no matter how hard he clenched it. When he
awoke the next morning, his arms ached as if he had
been grappling with an angel all night.

Opening his eyes, he found Atiaran sitting across
the room from him, waiting. As soon as she saw that
he was awake, she stood and moved closer to him.
"Come, Thomas Covenant," she said. "Already we
have lost the dawn of this day."

Covenant studied her for a moment. The
background of her face held a deepening shadow of
fatigue, and he guessed that she had spent much of
the night talking with the Heers. But she seemed
somehow comforted by what she had shared and
heard, and the brightness of her glance was almost
optimistic. Perhaps she now had some sort of hope.

He approved of anything that might reduce her
hostility toward him, and he swung out of bed as if
he shared her optimism. Despite the soreness of his
arms, he felt remarkably refreshed, as if the ambience
of the Woodhelven had been exerting its hospitality,
its beneficence, to help him rest. Moving briskly, he
washed his face, dried himself on a thick towel of
leaves, then checked himself for injuries and adjusted his clothing. A loaf lay on the three-
legged table, and when he broke off a hunk for his
breakfast, he found that it was made of bread and
meat baked together. Munching it, he went to look
out one of the windows.

Atiaran joined him, and together they gazed
through the branches northward. In the far distance,
they saw a river running almost directly east, and beyond it the hills spread on to the horizon. But
something more than the river separated these
northern hills from those beside which the travelers
had been walking since they had left Mithil Stonedown. The land beyond the river seemed to ripple in
the morning sunshine, as if the quiet earth were flow-

ing over shoals—as if there the secret rock of the Land ruffled the surface, revealing itself to those who could read it. From his high Woodhelven vantage, Covenant felt he was seeing something that surpassed even his new perceptions.

"There," said Atiaran softly, as if she were speaking of a holy place, "there is Andelain. The Hirebrand has chosen his home well for such a view. Here the Mithil River runs east before turning north again toward Gravin Threndor and the Soulsease. And beyond are the Andelainian Hills, the heart-healing richness of the Land. Ah, Covenant, the seeing of them gives me courage. And Soranal has taught me a path which may make possible my fondest dream— With good fortune and good speed, we may see that which will turn much of my folly to wisdom. We must go. Are you prepared?"

No, Covenant thought. Not to go climbing around this tree. But he nodded. Atiaran had brought his pack to him, and while she stepped out of the Hirebrand's home onto the broad branch, he pulled the straps onto his shoulders, ignoring the ache of his arms. Then he took up the staff Baradakas had given him, and braced himself to risk his neck on the descent of the Woodhelven.

The trunk was only three or four steps away, but the two-hundred-foot drop to the ground made him freeze, hesitate apprehensively while the first reels of vertigo gnawed at his resolve. But as he stood in the Hirebrand's doorway, he heard the shouting of young voices, and saw children scampering through the branches overhead. Some of them pursued others, and in the chase they sprang from limb to limb as blithely as if the fall were helpless to hurt them.

The next instant, two children, a boy and a girl, dropped onto the limb before Covenant from a branch nearly twenty feet above. The girl was in merry pursuit of the boy, but he eluded her touch and darted around behind Covenant. From this covert, he shouted gleefully, "Safe! Chase another! I am safe!"

Without thinking, Covenant said, "He's safe."

The girl laughed, faked a lunge forward, and sprang away after someone else. At once, the boy dashed to the trunk and scurried up the ladder toward higher playgrounds.

Covenant took a deep breath, clutched the staff for balance, and stepped away from the door. Teetering awkwardly, he struggled to the relative safety of the trunk.

After that, he felt better. When he slid the staff through his pack straps, he could grip the ladder with both hands, and then the secure touch of the rungs reassured him. Before he had covered half the distance, his heart was no longer pounding, and he was able to trust his hold enough to look about him at the dwellings and people he passed.

Finally, he reached the lowest branches, and followed Atiaran down the stair to the ground. There the Heers were gathered to say their farewells. When he saw Baradakas, Covenant took the staff in his hands to show that he had not forgotten it, and grimaced in response to the Hirebrand's smile.

"Well, message-bearers," said Llaura after a pause, "you have told us that the fate of the Land is on your shoulders, and we believe. It sorrows us that we cannot ease the burden—but we judge that no one can take your place in this matter. What little help we can give we have given. All which remains for us is to defend our homes, and to pray for you. We wish you good speed for the sake of all the Land. And for your own sake we urge you to be in time for the Celebration. There are great omens of hope for any who view that festival.

"Atiaran Trell-mate, go in Peace and fealty. Remember the path Soranal taught you, and do not turn aside.

"Thomas Covenant, Unbeliever and stranger to the Land—be true. In the hour of darkness, remember the Hirebrand's staff. Now be on your way."

Atiaran replied as formally as if she were completing a ritual. "We go, remembering Soaring Woodhelven for home and help and hope." She bowed, touching her palms to her forehead and then spreading her arms wide. Uncertainly, Covenant followed her example. The Heers returned the heart-opening gesture of farewell with ceremonial deliberateness. Then Atiaran strode off northward, and Covenant scudded along behind her like a leaf in the wake of her determination.

Neither of them looked back. The rest and restoration of the fair tree village made them brisk, gave them a forward air. They were both in their separate ways eager for Andelain, and they knew that Jehannum had left Soaring Woodhelven toward the east, not the north. They hastened ahead among the richening hills, and reached the banks of the Mithil River early that afternoon.

They crossed by wading a wide shallows. Before she entered the water, Atiaran removed her sandals, and some half-conscious insight urged Covenant to take off his boots and socks, roll up his pant legs. As he smelled the first lush scents of the Hills, he felt somehow that he needed to wade the Mithil barefoot in order to be ready, that the foot-washing of the stream was necessary to transubstantiate his flesh into the keener essence of Andelain. And when he stepped onto the north bank, he found that he could feel its vitality through his feet; now even his soles were sensitive to the Land's health.

He so liked the strong sensation of the Hills under his toes that he was loath to put his boots back on, but he denied himself that pleasure so that he would be able to keep up with Atiaran's pace. Then he followed her along the path which Soranal had taught her—an easy way through the center of Andelain— walked and wondered at the change that had come over the Earth since they had crossed the river.

He felt the change distinctly, but it seemed to go beyond the details which composed it. The trees were generally taller and broader than their southern relations; abundant and prodigal *aliantha* sometimes covered whole hillsides with viridian; the rises and vales luxuriated in deep aromatic grass; flowers bobbed in the breeze as spontaneously as if just moments before they had gaily burst from the nurture of the soil; small woodland animals—rabbits, squirrels, badgers, and the like—scampered around, only vaguely remembering that they were wary of humans. But the real difference was transcendent. The Andelainian Hills carried a purer impression of health to all Covenant's senses than anything else he had experienced. The aura of rightness here was so powerful that he began to regret he belonged in a world where health was impalpable, indefinite, discernible only by implication. For a time, he wondered how he would be able to endure going back, waking up. But the beauty of Andelain soon made him forget such concerns. It was a dangerous loveliness—not because it was treacherous or harmful, but because it could seduce. Before long, disease, VSE, Despite, anger, all were forgotten, lost in the flow of health from one vista to another around him.

Enclosed in the Hills, surrounded by such tangible and specific vitality, he became more and more surprised that Atiaran did not wish to linger. As they hiked over the lambent terrain, penetrating league after league deeper into Andelain, he wanted to stop at each new revelation, each new valley or avenue or dale, to savor what he saw—grip it with his eyes until it was a part of him, indelible, secure against any coming bereavement. But Atiaran pushed on—arising early, stopping little, hurrying late. Her eyes were focused far away, and the fatigue mounting behind her features seemed unable to reach the surface. Clearly, even these Hills paled for her beside her anticipation of the unexplained "Celebration." Covenant had no choice but to urge himself after her; her will tolerated no delay.

Their second night away from Soaring Woodhelven was so bright and clear that they did not have to stop with the setting of the sun, and Atiaran kept going until nearly midnight. After supper, Covenant sat for a while looking at the sky and the piquant stars. The aging crescent of the moon stood high in the heavens, and its white sliver sent down only a suggestion of the eldritch light which had illuminated his first night in the Land. Casually, he remarked, "The moon'll be dark in a few days."

At that, Atiaran looked at him sharply, as if she suspected that he had discovered some secret of hers. But she said nothing, and he did not know whether she reacted to a memory or to an anticipation.

The next day began as splendidly as the previous one. Sunshine begemmed the dew, sparkled like diamonds among the grass and leaves; air as fresh as the Earth's first breath carried the tang of *aliantha* and larch, the fragrance of Gilden and peony, across the Hills. Covenant beheld such things with something like bliss in his heart, and followed Atiaran northward as if he were content. But early in the afternoon something happened which darkened all his joy, offended him to the marrow of his bones. As he traveled down a natural lane between tree-thick hills, walking with a fine sense of the springy grass under his feet, he stepped without warning on a patch of turf that felt as dangerous as a pit of quicksand.

Instinctively, he recoiled, jerked back three steps. At once, the threatening sensation vanished. But his nerves remembered it from the sole of his foot up the whole length of his leg.

He was so surprised, so insulted, that he did not think to call Atiaran. Instead, he cautiously approached the spot on which he had felt the danger, and touched it with one tentative toe. This time, however, he felt nothing but the lush grass of Andelain. Bending down, he went over the grass for a yard in all directions with his hands. But whatever had fired his sense of wrongness was gone now, and after a moment of perplexity he started forward again. At first he took each step gingerly, expecting another jolt. But the earth seemed as full of pure, resonant vitality as before. Shortly, he broke into a trot to catch up with Atiaran.

Toward evening, he felt the sting of wrong again, as if he had stepped in acid. This time, he reacted in violent revulsion; he pitched forward as if diving away from a blast of lightning, and a yell ripped past his teeth before he could stop himself. Atiaran came back to him at a run, and found him pawing over the grass, tearing up the blades in handfuls of outrage.

"Here!" he gritted, thumping the turf with his fist. "By hell! It was here."

Atiaran blinked at him blankly. He jumped to his feet, pointed an accusing finger at the ground. "Didn't you feel it? It was there. Hellfire!" His finger quivered. "How did you miss it?"

"I felt nothing," she replied evenly.

He shuddered and dropped his hand. "It felt as if I—as if I stepped in quicksand—or acid—or"— he remembered the slain Waynhim—"or murder."

Slowly, Atiaran knelt beside the spot he indicated. For a moment, she studied it, then touched it with her hands. When she stood up, she said, "I feel nothing—"

"It's gone," he interrupted.

"—but I have not the touch of a *rhadhamaerl*," she went on. "Have you felt this before?"

"Once. Earlier."

"Ah," she sighed, "would that I were a Lord, and knew what to do. There must be an evil working deep in the Earth—a great evil, indeed, if the Andelainian Hills are not altogether safe. But the ill is new yet, or timid. It does not remain. We must hope to outrun it. Ah, weak! Our speed becomes less sufficient with each passing day."

She pulled her robe tightly about her, strode away into the evening. She and Covenant traveled on without a halt until night was thick around them, and the waning moon was high in its path among the stars.

The next day, Covenant felt convulsions of ill through the grass more often. Twice during the morning, and four times during the afternoon and evening, one foot or the other recoiled with sudden ferocity from the turf, and by the time Atiaran stopped for the night, his nerves from his legs to the roots of his teeth were raw and jangling. He felt intensely that such sore spots were an affront to, even a betrayal of, Andelain, where every other touch and line and hue of sky and tree and grass and hill was redolent with richness. Those attacks, pangs, stings made him involuntarily wary of the ground itself, as if the very foundation of the Earth had been cast into doubt.

On the fifth day since Soaring Woodhelven, he felt the wrongness in the grass less often, but the attacks showed an increase in virulence. Shortly after noon, he found a spot of ill that did not vanish after he first touched it. When he set his foot on it again, he felt a quiver as if he had stepped on an ache in the ground. The vibration rapidly numbed his foot, and his jaws hurt from clenching his teeth, but he did not back away. Calling to Atiaran, he knelt on the grass and touched the earth's sore with his hands.

To his surprise, he felt nothing.

Atiaran explored the ground herself, then considered him with a frown in her eyes. She also felt nothing.

But when he probed the spot with his foot, he found that the pain was still there. It scraped his brain, made sweat bead on his forehead, drew a snarl from his throat. As the ache spread through his bones, sending cold numbness up his leg, he bent to slide his fingers under the sole of his boot. But his hands still felt nothing; only his feet were sensitive to the peril.

On an impulse, he threw off one boot, removed his sock, and placed his bare foot on the spot of ill. This time, the discrepancy was even more surprising. He could feel the pain with his booted foot, but not with his bare one. And yet his sensations were perfectly clear; the wrong arose from the ground, not from his boot.

Before he could stop himself, he snatched off his other boot and sock, and cast them away from him. Then he dropped heavily to sit on the grass, and clutched his throbbing head in both hands.

"I have no sandals for you," Atiaran said stiffly. "You will need footwear before this journey has reached its end."

Covenant hardly heard her. He felt acutely that

he had recognized a danger, identified a threat which had been warping him for days without his knowledge.

Is that how you're going to do it, Foul? he snarled. First my nerves come back to life. Then Andelain makes me forget— Then I throw away my boots. Is that it? Break down all my defenses one at a time so that I won't be able to protect myself? Is that how you're going to destroy me?

"We must go on," Atiaran said. "Decide what you will do."

Decide? Bloody hell! Covenant jerked himself to his feet. Fuming, he grated through his teeth, "It's not that easy." Then he stalked over to retrieve his boots and socks.

Survive.

He laced his feet into his boots as if they were a kind of armor.

For the rest of the day, he shied away from every hint of pain in the ground, and followed Atiaran grimly, with a clenched look in his eyes, striving against the stinging wrong to preserve his sovereignty, his sense of himself. And toward evening his struggle seemed to find success. After a particularly vicious attack late in the afternoon, the ill pangs stopped. He did not know whether or not they would return, but for a while at least he was free of them.

That night was dark with clouds, and Atiaran was forced to make camp earlier than usual. Yet she and Covenant got little rest. A light, steady rain soaked their blankets, and kept them awake most of the night, huddling for shelter under the deeper shadow of an enshrouding willow.

But the next morning—the sixth of their journey from Soaring Woodhelven—dawned bright and full of Andelainian cheer. Atiaran met it with haste and anticipation in her every move; and the way she urged Covenant along seemed to express more friendliness, more companionship, than anything she had done since the beginning of their sojourn. Her desire for speed was infectious; Covenant was glad to share it because it rescued him from thinking about the possibility of further attacks of wrong. They began the day's travel at a lope.

The day was made for traveling. The air was cool, the sun clean and encouraging; the path led straight and level; springy grass carried Atiaran and Covenant forward at every stride. And her contagious eagerness kept him trotting behind her league after league. Toward midday, she slowed her pace to eat treasure-berries along the way; but even then she made good speed, and as evening neared she pushed their pace into a lope again.

Then the untracked path which the Woodhelvennin had taught her brought them to the end of a broad valley. After a brief halt while she verified her bearings, she started straight up a long, slow hillside that seemed to carry on away eastward for a great distance. She chose a plumb-line direction which took her directly between two matched Gilden trees a hundred yards above the valley, and Covenant followed her toiling lope up the hill without question. He was too tired and out of breath to ask questions.

So they ascended that hillside—Atiaran trotting upward with her head held high and her hair fluttering, as if she saw fixed before her the starry gates of heaven, and Covenant plodding, pumping behind her. At their backs, the sun sank in a deep exhalation like the release of a long-pent sigh. And ahead of them the slope seemed to stretch on into the sky.

Covenant was dumbfounded when Atiaran reached the crest of the hill, stopped abruptly, grabbed his shoulders, and spun him around in a circle, crying joyfully, "We are here! We are in time!"

He lost his balance and fell to the turf. For a moment he lay panting, with hardly enough energy to stare at her. But she was not aware of him. Her eyes were fixed down the eastern slope of the hill as she called in a voice short-breathed by fatigue and exultation and reverence, *"Banas Nimoram!* Ah, glad heart! Glad heart of Andelain. I have lived to this time."

Caught by the witchery of her voice, Covenant

levered himself to his feet and followed her gaze as
if he expected to behold the soul of Andelain incarnate.

He could not refrain from groaning in the first
sag of his disappointment. He could see nothing
to account for Atiaran's rapture, nothing that was
more healthy or precious than the myriad vistas of
Andelain past which she had rushed unheeding. Below him, the grass dipped into a smooth wide bowl
set into the hills like a drinking cup for the night
sky. With the sun gone, the outlines of the bowl were
not clear, but starlight was enough to show that there
were no trees, no bushes, no interruptions to the
smoothness of the bowl. It looked as regular as if
the surface of the grass had been sanded and burnished. On this night, the stars seemed especially gay,
as if the darkness of the moon challenged them to
new brightness. But Covenant felt that such things
were not enough to reward his bone-deep fatigue.

However, Atiaran did not ignore his groan. Taking his arm, she said, "Do not judge me yet," and
drew him forward. Under the branches of the last
tree on the bowl's lip, she dropped her pack and sat
against the trunk, facing down the hill. When Covenant had joined her, she said softly, "Control your mad
heart, Unbeliever. We are here in time. This is *Banas
Nimoram,* the dark of the moon on the middle night
of spring. Not in my generation has there been
such a night, such a time of rareness and beauty.
Do not measure the Land by the standard of yourself. Wait. This is *Banas Nimoram,* the Celebration
of Spring—finest rite of all the treasures of the Earth.
If you do not disturb the air with anger, we will see
the Dance of the Wraiths of Andelain." As she
spoke, her voice echoed with rich harmonics as if
she were singing; and Covenant felt the force of
what she promised, though he did not understand.
It was not a time for questions, and he set himself
to wait for the visitation.

Waiting was not difficult. First Atiaran passed bread
and the last of her springwine to him, and eating
and drinking eased some of his weariness. Then, as

the night deepened, he found that the air which flowed
up to them from the bowl had a lush, restful effect.
When he took it far into his lungs, it seemed to un-
wind his cares and dreads, setting everything but itself behind him and lifting him into a state of calm
suspense. He relaxed in the gentle breeze, settled
himself more comfortably against the tree. Atiaran's
shoulder touched his with warmth, as if she had for-
given him. The night deepened, and the stars
gleamed expectantly, and the breeze sifted the cobwebs and dust from Covenant's heart—and waiting
was not difficult.

The first flickering light came like a twist of resolution which brought the whole night into focus. Across
the width of the bowl, he saw a flame like the burn of
a candle—tiny in the distance, and yet vivid, swaying
yellow and orange as clearly as if he held the candle-
stick in his hands. He felt strangely sure that the distance was meaningless; if the flame were before him
on the grass, it would be no larger than his palm.

As the Wraith appeared, Atiaran's breath hissed intently between her teeth, and Covenant sat up
straighter to concentrate more keenly.

With a lucid, cycling movement, the flame moved
down into the bowl. It was not halfway to the bottom
when a second fire arrived on the northern rim. Then
two more Wraiths entered from the south—and then,
too suddenly to be counted, a host of flames began
tracing their private ways into the bowl from all directions. Some passed within ten feet of Atiaran and
Covenant on either side, but they seemed unconscious
of the observers; they followed their slow cycles as if
each were alone in the Hills, independent of every
gleam but its own. Yet their lights poured together,
casting a dome of gold through which the stars could
barely be seen; and at moments particular Wraiths
seemed to bow and revolve around each other, as if
sharing a welcome on their way toward the center.

Covenant watched the great movement that brought
thousands of the flames, bobbing at shoulder height,
into the bowl, and he hardly dared to breathe. In the
excess of his wonder, he felt like an unpermitted spec-

tator beholding some occult enactment which was not meant for human eyes. He clutched his chest as if his chance to see the Celebration to its end rode on the utter silence of his respiration, as if he feared that any sound might violate the fiery conclave, scare the Wraiths away.

Then a change came over the gathered flames. Up into the sky rose a high, scintillating, wordless song, an arching melody. From the center of the bowl, the private rotations of the Wraiths resolved themselves into a radiating, circling Dance. Each Wraith seemed finally to have found its place in a large, wheel-like pattern which filled half the bowl, and the wheel began to turn on its center. But there were no lights in the center; the wheel turned on a hub of stark blackness which refused the glow of the Wraiths.

As the song spread through the night, the great circle revolved—each flame dancing a secret, independent dance, various in moves and sways—each flame keeping its place in the whole pattern as it turned. And in the space between the inner hub and the outer rim, more circles rolled, so that the whole wheel was filled with many wheels, all turning. And no Wraith kept one position long. The flames flowed continuously through their moving pattern, so that as the wheel turned, the individual Wraiths danced from place to place, now swinging along the outer rim, now gyring through the middle circles, now circling the hub. Every Wraith moved and changed places constantly, but the pattern was never broken—no hiatus of misstep gapped the wheel, even for an instant—and every flame seemed both perfectly alone, wandering mysteriously after some personal destiny through the Dance, and perfectly a part of the whole. While they danced, their light grew stronger, until the stars were paled out of the sky, and the night was withdrawn, like a distant spectator of the Celebration.

And the beauty and wonder of the Dance made of Covenant's suspense a yearning ache.

Then a new change entered the festival. Covenant did not realize it until Atiaran touched his arm; her signal sent a thrill of awareness through him, and he saw that the wheel of the Wraiths was slowly bending. The rest of the wheel retained its shape, and the black core did not move. Gradually, the turning circle became lopsided as the outer Wraiths moved closer to the onlookers. Soon the growing bulge pointed unmistakably at Covenant.

In response, he seemed to feel their song more intensely—a keening, ecstatic lament, a threnody as throbbingly passionate as a dirge and as dispassionate as a sublime, impersonal affirmation. Their nearing flames filled him with awe and fascination, so that he shrank within himself but could not move. Cycle after cycle, the Wraiths reached out toward him, and he clasped his hands over his knees and held himself still, taut-hearted and utterless before the fiery Dancers.

In moments, the tip of this long extension from the circle stood above him, and he could see each flame bowing to him as it danced by. Then the rim of the extension dipped, and the pace of the Dance slowed, as though to give each Wraith a chance to linger in his company. Soon the fires were passing within reach of his hand. Then the long arm of the Dance flared, as if a decision had run through the Dancers. The nearest Wraith moved forward to settle on his wedding band.

He flinched, expecting the fire to burn him, but there was no pain. The flame attached itself to the ring as to a wick, and he felt faintly the harmonies of the Celebration song through his finger. As the Wraith held to his ring, it danced and jumped as if it were feeding excitedly there. And slowly its color turned from flaming yellow-orange to silver-white.

When the transformation was complete, that Wraith flashed away, and the next took its place. A succession of fires followed, each dancing on his ring until it became argent; and as his anxiety relaxed, the succession grew faster. In a short time, the line of glistening white Wraiths had almost reached back to the rest of the Dance. Each new flame presented itself swiftly, as if eager for some apotheosis, some culmination of its being, in the white gold of Covenant's ring.

Before long, his emotion became too strong to let him remain seated. He surged to his feet, holding out his ring so that the Wraiths could light on it without lowering themselves.

Atiaran stood beside him. He had eyes only for the transformation which his ring somehow made possible, but she looked away across the Dance.

What she saw made her dig her fingers like claws of despair into his arm. "No! By the Seven! This must not be!"

Her cry snatched at his attention; his gaze jumped across the bowl.

"There! That is the meaning of the ill your feet have felt!"

What he saw staggered him like a blow to the heart.

Coming over the northeast rim of the bowl into the golden light was an intruding wedge of blackness, as pitch-dark and unilluminable as the spawning ground of night. The wedge cut its narrow way down toward the Dance, and through the song of the flames, it carried a sound like a host of bloody feet rushing over clean grass. Deliberately, agonizingly, it reached inward without breaking its formation. In moments, the tip of the darkness sliced into the Dance and began plunging toward its center.

In horror, Covenant saw that the Dance did not halt or pause. At the wedge's first touch, the song of the Wraiths dropped from the air as if it had been ripped away by sacrilege, leaving no sound behind it but a noise like running murder. But the Dance did not stop. The flames went on revolving as if they were unconscious of what was happening to them, helpless. They followed their cycles into the wedge's path and vanished as if they had fallen into an abyss. No Wraith emerged from that darkness.

Swallowing every light that touched it, the black wedge gouged its way into the Celebration.

"They will all die!" Atiaran groaned. "They cannot stop—cannot escape. They must dance until the Dance is done. All dead—every Wraith, every bright light of the Land! This must not be. Help them! Covenant, help them!"

But Covenant did not know how to help. He was paralyzed. The sight of the black wedge made him

feel as nauseated as if he were observing across a gulf
of numbness his fingers being eaten by a madman—
nauseated and enraged and impotent, as if he had
waited too long to defend himself, and now had no
hands with which to fight back. The knife of Triock
slipped from his numb fingers and disappeared in
darkness.

How—?

For an instant, Atiaran dragged furiously at him.
"Covenant! Help them!" she shrieked into his face.
Then she turned and raced down into the valley to
meet the wedge.

The Wraiths—!

Her movement broke the freeze of his horror.
Snatching up the staff of Baradakas, he ducked under
the flames and sped after her, holding himself bent over
to stay below the path of the Wraiths. A madness
seemed to hasten his feet; he caught Atiaran before she
was halfway to the hub. Thrusting her behind him, he
dashed on toward the penetrating wedge, spurred by
a blind conviction that he had to reach the center before the blackness did.

Atiaran followed, shouting after him, "Ware and
ward! They are ur-viles! Demondim corruption!"

He scarcely heard her. He was focused on the furious need to gain the center of the Dance. For better
speed, he ran more upright, flicking his head aside
whenever a Wraith flashed near the level of his eyes.

With a last burst, he broke into the empty core of
the wheel.

He halted. Now he was close enough to see that the
wedge was composed of tall, crowded figures, so black-
fleshed that no light could gleam or glisten on their
skin. As the helpless Wraiths swung into the wedge,
the attackers ate them.

The ur-viles drew nearer. The tip of their wedge
was a single figure, larger than the rest. Covenant
could see it clearly. It looked like one of the Waynhim
grown tall and evil—long torso, short limbs of equal
length, pointed ears high on its head, eyeless face almost filled by gaping nostrils. Its slit mouth snapped
like a trap whenever a Wraith came near. Mucus

trailed from its nostrils back along either side of its head. When Covenant faced it, its nose twitched as if it smelled new game, and it snarled out a cadenced bark like an exhortation to the other creatures. The whole wedge thrust eagerly forward.

Atiaran caught up with Covenant and shouted in his ear, "Your hand! Look at your hand!"

He jerked up his left hand. A Wraith still clung to his ring—burning whitely—obliviously dancing.

The next instant, the leading ur-vile breached the core of the Dance and stopped. The attackers stood packed against each other's shoulders behind their leader. Dark, roynish, and cruel, they slavered together and bit at the helpless Wraiths.

Covenant quailed as if his heart had turned to sand. But Atiaran raged, "Now! Strike them now!"

Trembling, he stepped forward. He had no idea what to do.

At once, the first ur-vile brandished a long knife with a seething, blood-red blade. Fell power radiated from the blade; in spite of themselves, Covenant and Atiaran recoiled.

The ur-vile raised its hand to strike.

Impulsively, Covenant shoved the white, burning Wraith at the ur-vile's face. With a snarl of pain, the creature jumped back.

A sudden intuition gripped Covenant. Instantly, he touched the end of his staff to the burning Wraith. With a flash, bold white flame bloomed from the staff, shading the gold of the Dance and challenging the force of the ur-viles. Their leader retreated again.

But at once it regained its determination. Springing forward, it stabbed into the heart of the white fire with its blood-red blade.

Power clashed in the core of the Dance. The ur-vile's blade seethed like hot hate, and the staff blazed wildly. Their conflict threw sparks as if the air were aflame in blood and lightning.

But the ur-vile was a master. Its might filled the bowl with a deep, crumbling sound, like the crushing of a boulder under huge pressure. In one abrupt exertion, Covenant's fire was stamped out.

The force of the extinguishing threw him and Atiaran to their backs on the grass. With a growl of triumph, the ur-viles poised to leap for the kill.

Covenant saw the red knife coming, and cowered with a pall of death over his mind.

But Atiaran scrambled back to her feet, crying, *"Melenkurion! Melenkurion abatha!"* Her voice sounded frail against the victory of the ur-viles, but she met them squarely, grappled with the leader's knife-hand. Momentarily, she withheld its stroke.

Then, from behind her to the west, her cry was answered. An iron voice full of fury shouted, *"Melenkurion abatha! Binas mill Banas Nimoram khabaal! Melenkurion abatha! Abatha Nimoram!"* The sound broke through Covenant's panic, and he lurched up to Atiaran's aid. But together they could not hold back the ur-vile; it flung them to the ground again. At once, it pounced at them.

It was stopped halfway by a hulking form that leaped over them to tackle it. For a moment, the two wrestled savagely. Then the newcomer took the blood-red blade and drove it into the heart of the creature.

A burst of snarls broke from the ur-viles. Covenant heard a sweeping noise like the sound of many children running. Looking up, he saw a stream of small animals pour into the bowl—rabbits, badgers, weasels, moles, foxes, a few dogs. With silent determination, they hurled themselves at the ur-viles.

The Wraiths were scattering. While Covenant and Atiaran stumbled to their feet, the last flame passed from the bowl.

But the ur-viles remained, and their size made the animals' attack look like a mere annoyance. In the sudden darkness, the creatures seemed to expand, as if the light had hindered them, forced them to keep their close ranks. Now they broke away from each other. Dozens of blades that boiled like lava leaped out as one, and in horrible unison began to slaughter the animals.

Before Covenant could take in all that was happening, the hulking figure who had saved them turned and hissed, "Go! North to the river. I have released the Wraiths. Now we will make time for your escape. Go!"

"No!" Atiaran panted. "You are the only man. The animals are not enough. We must help you fight."

"Together we are not enough!" he cried. "Do you forget your task? You must reach the Lords—must! Drool must pay for this Desecration! Go! I cannot give you much time!" Shouting, "*Melenkurion abatha!*" he whirled and jumped into the thick of the fray, felling ur-viles with his mighty fists.

Pausing only to pick up the staff of Baradakas, Atiaran fled northward. And Covenant followed her, running as if the ur-vile blades were striking at his back. The stars gave them enough light. They drove themselves up the slope, not looking to see if they were pursued, not caring about the packs they left behind—afraid to think of anything except their need for distance. As they passed over the rim of the bowl, the sounds of slaughter were abruptly dimmed. They heard no pursuit. But they ran on—ran, and still ran, and did not stop until they were caught in midstride by a short scream, full of agony and failed strength.

At the sound, Atiaran fell to her knees and dropped her forehead to the earth, weeping openly. "He is dead!" she wailed. "The Unfettered One, dead! Alas for the Land! All my paths are ill, and destruction fills all my choices. From the first, I have brought wrong upon us. Now there will be no more Celebrations, and the blame is mine." Raising her face to Covenant, she sobbed, "Take your staff and strike me, Unbeliever!"

Blankly, Covenant stared into the pooled hurt of her eyes. He felt benumbed with pain and grief and wasted rage, and did not understand why she castigated herself. He stooped for the staff, then took her arm and lifted her to her feet. Stunned and empty, he led her onward into the night until she had cried out her anguish and could stand on her own again. He wanted to weep himself, but in his long struggle with the misery of being a leper he had forgotten how, and now he could only keep on walking. He was

aware as Atiaran regained control of herself and
pulled away from him that she accused him of something. Throughout the sleepless night of their northward trek, he could do nothing about it.

ELEVEN: The Unhomed

GRADUALLY, night stumbled as if stunned and
wandering aimlessly into an overcast day—limped
through the wilderland of transition as though there
were no knowing where the waste of darkness ended
and the ashes of light began. The low clouds seemed
full of grief—tense and uneasy with accumulated woe
—and yet affectless, unable to rain, as if the air
clenched itself too hard for tears. And through the
dawn, Atiaran and Covenant moved heavily, unevenly, like pieces of a broken lament.

The coming of one day made no difference to them,
did not alter the way they fled—terrorless because
their capacity for fear was exhausted—into the north.
Day and night were nothing but disguises, motley
raiment, for the constant shadow on the Land's heart.
To that heart they could not guess how much damage
had been done. They could only judge by their own
hurt—and so throughout the long, dismal night and
day which followed the defilement of the Celebration,
they walked on haunted by what they had witnessed and numb to everything else, as though even
hunger and thirst and fatigue were extinguished in
them.

That night, their flesh reached the end of its endurance, and they pitched blindly into sleep, no longer
able to care what pursuit was on their trail. While they

slept, the sky found some release for its tension. Blue lightning flailed the Hills; thunder groaned in long-suppressed pain. When the travelers awoke, the sun stood over them, and their clothes were drenched with the night's rain. But sunshine and morning could not unscar their wounded memories. They clambered like corpses to their feet—ate *aliantha,* drank from a stream—set off again walking as if they were stiff with death.

Yet time and *aliantha* and Andelainian air slowly worked their resuscitations. Slowly, Covenant's weary thoughts shifted; the trudging horror of slaughter receded, allowed a more familiar pain to ache in him. He could hear Atiaran crying, *Covenant, help them!* and the sound made his blood run cold with impotence.

The Wraiths, the Wraiths! he moaned dimly, distantly, to himself. They had been so beautiful—and he had been so unable to save them.

Yet Atiaran had believed him capable of saving them; she had expected some putting forth of power — Like Lena and Baradakas and everyone else he met, she saw him as Berek Halfhand reborn, the master of wild magic. *You have might,* the Despiser had said. *You will never know what it is.* He did not know; how could he? What did magic, or even dreams, have to do with him?

And yet the Wraiths had paid homage to his ring as if they recognized his lost humanity. They had been changed by it.

After a time, he said without meaning to speak aloud, "I would have saved them if I could."

"You have the power." Atiaran's voice was dull, inert, as if she were no longer capable of grief or anger.

"What power?" he asked painfully.

"Do you wear the white gold for nothing?"

"It's just a ring. I wear it—I wear it because I'm a leper. I don't know anything about power."

She did not look at him. "I cannot see. You are closed to me."

At that, he wanted to protest, cry out, grab her by

the shoulders and shout into her face, Closed? Look
—look at me! I'm no Berek! No hero. I'm too sick for
that. But he lacked the strength. And he had been too
badly hurt—hurt as much by Atiaran's impossible demand as by his powerlessness.

How—?

The Wraiths!

How can this happen to me?

A moment passed while he groaned over the question. Then he sighed to himself, I should have known
— He should have heard his danger in Atiaran's singing of the Berek legend, seen it in Andelain, felt it in
the revulsion in his boots. But he had been deaf,
blind, numb. He had been so busy moving ahead,
putting madness behind him, that he had ignored the
madness toward which the path of his dream tended.
This dream wanted him to be a hero, a savior; therefore it seduced him, swept him along—urging him
forward so that he would run heedless of himself to
risk his life for the sake of Wraiths, the Land, illusion.
The only difference in this between Atiaran and Lord
Foul was that the Despiser wanted him to fail.

You will never know what it is. Of course he would
never know. A visceral anger writhed under his
fatigue. He was dreaming—that was the answer to
everything, to the Land's impossible expectations of
him as well as to the Land's impossibility. He knew
the difference between reality and dream; he was sane.

He was a leper.

And yet the Wraiths had been so beautiful. They
had been slaughtered—

I'm a leper!

Trembling, he began to give himself a VSE. Hellfire! What do Wraiths and wild magic and Berek
bloody Halfhand have to do with me? His body
appeared whole—he could see no injuries, his clothing was rumpled but unrent—but the end of the
Hirebrand's staff had been blackened by the power
of the ur-viles. By hell! They can't do this to me.

Fuming against his weariness, he shambled along
at Atiaran's side. She did not look at him, did not seem
to recognize his presence at all; and during that day

he left her alone as if he feared how he would respond
if he gave her an opportunity to accuse him. But when
they halted that evening, the cold night and the brittle
stars made him regret the loss of their blankets and
graveling. To distract himself from his hollow discomfort, he resumed his half-forgotten efforts to learn
about the Land. Stiffly, he said, "Tell me about that
—whoever saved us. Back there."

A long silence passed before she said, "Tomorrow." Her voice was lightless, unillumined by anything
expect torpor or defeat. "Let me be. Until tomorrow."

Covenant nodded in the darkness. It felt thick with
cold and beating wings, but he could answer it better
than he could reply to Atiaran's tone. For a long time
he shivered as if he were prepared to resent every
dream that afflicted a miserable mankind, and at last
he fell into fitful slumber.

The next day, the ninth from Soaring Woodhelven,
Atiaran told Covenant about the Unfettered One in a
voice as flat as crushed rock, as if she had reached
the point where what she said, how she exposed herself, no longer mattered to her. "There are those from
the Loresraat," she said, "who find that they cannot
work for the Land or the Lore of the Old Lords in the
company of their fellows—Lords or Lorewardens,
the followers of Sword or Staff. Those have some private vision which compels them to seek it in isolation.
But their need for aloneness does not divide them
from the people. They are given the Rites of Unfettering, and freed from all common demands, to quest
after their own lore with the blessing of the Lords
and the respect of all who love the Land. For the
Lords learned long ago that the desire for aloneness
need not be a selfish desire, if it is not made so by
those who do not feel it.

"Many of the Unfettered have never returned into
knowledge. But stories have grown up around those
Ones who have not vanished utterly. Some are said
to know the secrets of dreams, others to practice deep
mysteries in the arts of healing, still others to be the
friends of the animals, speaking their language and
calling on their help in times of great need.

"Such a One saved us"—her voice thickened momentarily—"a learner of the Wraiths and a friend to the small beasts of the woods. He knew more of the Seven Words than my ears have ever heard." She groaned softly. "A mighty man, to have been so slain. He released the Wraiths, and saved our lives. Would that I were worth so much. By the Seven! No evil has ever before been aimed at the Wraiths of Andelain. The Gray Slayer himself never dared— And it is said that the Ritual of Desecration itself had no power to touch them. Now it is in my heart that they will not dance again."

After a heavy pause, she went on: "No matter. All things end, in perversion and death. Sorrow belongs to those who also hope. But that Unfettered One gave his life so that you and your message and your ring might reach the Lords. This we will accomplish, so that such sacrifices may have meaning."

She fell silent again for a moment, and Covenant asked himself, Is that why? Is that what living is for? To vindicate the deaths of others? But he said nothing, and shortly Atiaran's thoughts limped back to her subject. "But the Unfettered. Some are dreamers, some healers, some share the life of the animals. Some delve the earth to uncover the secrets of the Cavewights, others learn the lore of the Demondim— whatever knowledge guides the One's private prophecy. I have even heard it whispered that some Unfettered follow the legend of Caerroil Wildwood of Garroting Deep, and become Forestals. But that is a perilous thought, even when whispered.

"Never before have I seen one of the Unfettered. But I have heard the Rites of Unfettering. A hymn is sung." Dully, she recited:

> Free
> Unfettered
> Shriven
> Free—
> Dream that what is dreamed will be:
> Hold eyes clasped shut until they see,
> And sing the silent prophecy—

And be
Unfettered
Shriven
Free.

There is more, but my weakness will not recall— It may be that I will not sing any song again." She pulled her robe tight around her shoulders as if a wind were chilling through her, and said nothing more for the rest of the day.

That night, when they had camped, Covenant again could not sleep. Unwillingly he lay awake and watched for the sliver of the new moon. When it finally rose over the Hills, he was appalled to see that it was no longer silver-white, but red—the color of blood and Drool's laval eyes.

It hued the Hills with wrongness, gave the night a tinge of crimson like blood sweat sheening the shrubs and trees and grass and slopes, as if the whole of Andelain were in torment. Under it, the violated ground shimmered as if it were shuddering.

Covenant stared at it, could not close his eyes. Though he badly wanted company, he clamped his teeth together, refused to awaken Atiaran. Alone and shivering, with the staff of Baradakas clutched in his sweating hands, he sat up until moonset, then slept on the edge of consternation until dawn.

And on the fourth day after the night of the Dance, it was he who set the pace of their traveling. He pushed their speed more and more as the day passed, as though he feared that the bloody moon were gaining on them.

When they halted for the night, he gave Atiaran his staff and made her sit awake to see the moon. It came over the horizon in a crimson haze, rising like a sickle of blood in the heavens. Its crescent was noticeably fuller than it had been the previous night. She stared at it rigidly, clenched the staff, but did not cry out. When she had tasted all its wrong, she said tonelessly, "There is no time," and turned her face away.

But when morning came, she once more took charge of their pace. Under the pall of the despoiled moon she seemed to have reached a resolution, and now she drove herself forward as if she were spurred by some self-curse or flagellation which rejected through naked determination the logic of defeat. She seemed to believe that she had lost everything for herself and for the Land, yet the way she walked showed that pain could be as sharp a goad as any. Again Covenant found himself hurrying as hard as he could to keep up with her fierce back.

He accepted her pace in the name of his complex dread; he did not want to be caught by the forces that could attack Wraiths and render moons incarnadine. But he was scrupulous about his VSE and other self-protections. If he could have found a blade other than his penknife, he would have shaved with it.

They spent that day, part of the night, and the morning of the next day stumbling forward on the verge of a run. Covenant sustained their rate as best he could, but long days and restless nights had drained his stamina, made his stride ragged and his muscles irresilient. He came to lean more and more on his staff, unable to keep his balance without it. And even with it he might have fallen if he had been pursuing such a pace in some other region. But the keen essence of Andelain supported him. Healthy air salved his lungs, thick grass cushioned his sore joints, Gilden shaded him, treasure-berries burst with energy in his mouth. And at last, near noon on the sixth day, he and Atiaran staggered over the crest of a hill and saw at the bottom of the slope beyond them the Soulsease River.

Blue under the azure sky, it meandered broad, quiet and slow almost directly eastward across their path like a demarcation or boundary of achievement. As it turned and ran among the Hills, it had a glitter of youth, a sparkle of contained exuberance which could burst into laughter the moment it was tickled by any shoals. And its water was as clean, clear and fresh as an offer of baptism. At the sight of it, Covenant felt a rushing desire to plunge in, as if the stream had the power to wash away his mortality.

But he was distracted from it almost immediately.

Some distance away to the west, and moving upstream in the center of the river, was a boat like a skiff with a tall figure in the stern. The instant she saw it, Atiaran cried out sharply, waved her arms, then began pelting down the slope, calling with a frantic edge to her voice, "Hail! Help! Come back! Come back!"

Covenant followed less urgently. His gaze was fixed on the boat.

With a swing of its prow, it turned in their direction.

Atiaran threw her arms into the air again, gave one more call, then dropped to the ground. When Covenant reached her, she was sitting with her knees clasped to her chest, and her lips trembled as if her face were about to break. She stared feverishly at the approaching boat.

As it drew nearer, Covenant began to see with growing surprise just how tall the steering figure was. Before the boat was within a hundred feet of them, he was sure that the steersman was twice his own height. And he could see no means of propulsion. The craft appeared to be nothing more than an enormous rowboat, but there were no oarlocks, no oars, no poles. He gaped widely at the boat as it glided closer.

When it was within thirty feet of them, Atiaran thrust herself to her feet and called out, "Hail, Rockbrother! The Giants of Seareach are another name for friendship! Help us!" The boat kept gliding toward the bank, but its steersman did not speak; and shortly Atiaran added in a whisper that only Covenant could hear, "I beg you."

The Giant kept his silence as he approached. For the last distance, he swung the tiller over so that the boat's prow aimed squarely at the riverbank. Then, just before the craft struck, he drove his weight down in the stern. The prow lifted out of the water and grounded itself securely a few yards from Atiaran and Covenant. In a moment, the Giant stood before them on the grass, offering them the salute of welcome.

Covenant shook his head in wonder. He felt that it was impossible for anyone to be so big; the Giant was at least twelve feet tall. But the rocky concreteness of the Giant's presence contradicted him. The Giant struck his perceptions as tangibly as stumbling on rough stone.

Even for a being twelve feet tall, he appeared gnarled with muscles, like an oak come to life. He was dressed in a heavy leather jerkin and leggings, and carried no weapons. A short beard, as stiff as iron, jutted from his face. And his eyes were small, deep-set and enthusiastic. From under his brows, massed over his sockets like the wall of a fortress, his glances flashed piercingly, like gleams from his cavernous thoughts. Yet, in spite of his imposing appearance, he gave an impression of incongruous geniality, of immense good humor.

"Hail, Rocksister," he said in a soft, bubbling tenor voice which sounded too light and gentle to come from his bemuscled throat. "What is your need? My help is willing, but I am a legate, and my embassy brooks little delay."

Covenant expected Atiaran to blurt out her plea; the hesitation with which she met the Giant's offer disturbed him. For a long moment, she gnawed her lips as if she were chewing over her rebellious flesh, searching for an utterance which would give direction, one way or another, to a choice she hated. Then, with her eyes downcast as if in shame, she murmured uncertainly, "Where do you go?"

At her question, the Giant's eyes flashed, and his voice bubbled like a spring of water from a rock as he said, "My destination? Who is wise enough to know his own goal? But I am bound for— No, that name is too long a story for such a time as this. I go to Lord's Keep, as you humans call it."

Still hesitating, Atiaran asked, "What is your name?"

"That is another long story," the Giant returned, and repeated, "What is your need?"

But Atiaran insisted dully, "Your name."

Again a gleam sprang from under the Giant's massive brows. "There is power in names. I do not wish to be invoked by any but friends."

"Your name!" Atiaran groaned.

For an instant, the Giant paused, indecisive. Then

he said, "Very well. Though my embassy is not a
light one, I will answer for the sake of the loyalty between my people and yours. To speak shortly, I am
called Saltheart Foamfollower."

Abruptly, some resistance, some hatred of her decision, crumbled in Atiaran as if it had been defeated
at last by the Giant's trust. She raised her head, showing Covenant and Foamfollower the crushed landscape behind her eyes. With grave deliberation, she
gave the salute of welcome. "Let it be so. Saltheart
Foamfollower, Rockbrother and Giants' legate, I
charge you by the power of your name, and by the
great Keep of faith which was made between
Damelon Giantfriend and your people, to take this
man, Thomas Covenant, Unbeliever and stranger to
the Land, in safety to the Council of Lords. He bears
messages to the Council from Kevin's Watch. Ward
him well, Rockbrother. I can go no farther."

What? Covenant gaped. In his surprise, he almost
protested aloud, And give up your revenge? But he
held himself still with his thoughts reeling, and waited
for her to take a stance he could comprehend.

"Ah, you are too quick to call on such bold names,"
the Giant said softly. "I would have accepted your
charge without them. But I urge you to join us. There
are rare healings at Lord's Keep. Will you not come?
Those who await you would not begrudge such a
sojourn—not if they could see you as I do now."

Bitterness twisted Atiaran's lips. "Have you seen
the new moon? That comes of the last healing I
looked for." As she went on, her voice grew gray with
self-despite. "It is a futile charge I give you. I have already caused it to fail. There has been murder in all
my choices since I became this man's guide, such
murder—" She choked on the bile of what she had
seen, and had to swallow violently before she could
continue. "Because my path took us too close to
Mount Thunder. You passed around that place. You
must have seen the evil working there."

Distantly, the Giant said, "I saw."

"We went into the knowledge of that wrong, rather
than make our way across the Center Plains. And

now it is too late for anyone. He— The Gray Slayer has returned. I chose that path because I desired healing for myself. What will happen to the Lords if I ask them to help me now?"

And give up your revenge? Covenant wondered. He could not comprehend. He turned completely toward her and studied her face, trying to see her health, her spirit.

She looked as if she were in the grip of a ravaging illness. Her mien had thinned and sharpened; her spacious eyes were shadowed, veiled in darkness; her lips were drained of blood. And vertically down the center of her forehead lay a deep line like a rift in her skull—the tool work of unblinkable despair. Etched there was the vastness of the personal hurt which she contained by sheer force of will, and the damage she did herself by containing it.

At last Covenant saw clearly the moral struggle that wasted her, the triple conflict between her abhorrence of him, her fear for the Land, and her dismay at her own weakness—a struggle whose expense exhausted her resources, reduced her to penury. The sight shamed his heart, made him drop his gaze. Without thinking, he reached toward her and said in a voice full of self-contradicting pleas, "Don't give up."

"Give up?" she gasped in virulence, backing away from him. "If I gave up, I would stab you where you stand!" Suddenly, she thrust a hand into her robe and snatched out a stone knife like the one Covenant had lost. Brandishing it, she spat, "Since the Celebration—since you permitted Wraiths to die—this blade has cried out for your blood. Other crimes I could set aside. I speak for my own. But that—! To countenance such desecration—!"

She hurled the knife savagely to the ground, so that it stuck hilt-deep in the turf by Covenant's feet. "Behold!" she cried, and in that instant her voice became abruptly gelid, calm. "I wound the Earth instead of you. It is fitting. I have done little else since you entered the Land.

"Now hear my last word, Unbeliever. I let you go because these decisions surpass me. Delivering chil-

dren in the Stonedown does not fit me for such choices.
But I will not intrude my desires on the one hope of
the Land—barren as that hope is. Remember that I
have withheld my hand—I have kept my Oath."

"Have you?" he asked, moved by a complex impulse of sympathy and nameless ire.

She pointed a trembling finger at her knife. "I have
not harmed you. I have brought you here."

"You've hurt yourself."

"That is my Oath," she breathed stiffly. "Now,
farewell. When you have returned in safety to your
own world, remember what evil is."

He wanted to protest, argue, but her emotion
mastered him, and he held himself silent before the
force of her resolve. Under the duress of her eyes, he
bent, and drew her knife out of the grass. It came up
easily. He half expected to see blood ooze from the
slash it had made in the turf, but the thick grass
closed over the cut, hiding it as completely as an absolution. Unconsciously, he tested the blade with his
thumb, felt its acuteness.

When he looked up again, he saw that Atiaran was
climbing up the hill and away, moving with the un-
equal stride of a cripple.

This isn't right! he shouted at her back. Have mercy!
—pity! But his tongue felt too thick with the pain of
her renunciation; he could not speak. At least forgive
yourself. The tightness of his face gave him a nasty
impression that he was grinning. Atiaran! he groaned.
Why are we so unable?

Into his aching, the Giant's voice came gently.
"Shall we go?"

Dumbly, Covenant nodded. He tore his eyes from
Atiaran's toiling back, and shoved her knife under his
belt.

Saltheart Foamfollower motioned for him to climb
into the boat. When Covenant had vaulted over the
gunwale and taken a seat on a thwart in the prow—
the only seat in the thirty-foot craft small enough for
him—the Giant stepped aboard, pushing off from the
bank at the same time. Then he went to the broad,
shallow stern. Standing there, he grasped the tiller. A

surge of power flowed through the keel. He swung his craft away from the riverbank into midstream, and shortly it was moving westward among the Hills.

As soon as he had taken his seat, Covenant had turned with failure in his throat to watch Atiaran's progress up the hillside. But the surge of power which moved the boat gave it a brisk pace as fast as running, and in moments distance had reduced her to a brown mite in the lush, oblivious green of Andelain. With a harsh effort, he forced his eyes to let her go, compelled himself to look instead for the source of the boat's power.

But he could locate no power source. The boat ran smoothly up against the current as if it were being towed by fish. It had no propulsion that he could discern. Yet his nerves were sensitive to the energy flowing through the keel. Dimly, he asked, "What makes this thing move? I don't see any engine."

Foamfollower stood in the stern, facing upstream, with the high tiller under his left arm and his right held up to the river breezes; and he was chanting something, some plainsong in a language Covenant could not understand—a song with a wave-breaking, salty timbre like the taste of the sea. For a moment after Covenant's question, he kept up his rolling chant. But soon its language changed, and Covenant heard him sing:

Stone and Sea are deep in life,
two unalterable symbols of the world:
permanence at rest, and permanence in motion;
participants in the Power that remains.

Then Foamfollower stopped, and looked down at Covenant with humor sparkling under his unbreachable brows. "A stranger to the Land," he said. "Did that woman teach you nothing?"

Covenant stiffened in his seat. The Giant's tone seemed to demean Atiaran, denigrate the cost she had borne; his bland, impregnable forehead and humorous glance appeared impervious to sympathy. But her pain was vivid to Covenant. She had been dispossessed of so much normal human love and warmth. In a voice rigid with anger, he retorted, "She is Atiaran Trell-mate, of Mithil Stonedown, and she did better than teach me. She brought me safely past Ravers, murdered Waynhim, a bloody moon, ur-viles— Could you have done it?"

Foamfollower did not reply, but a grin spread gaily over his face, raising the end of his beard like a mock salute.

"By hell!" Covenant flared. "Do you think I'm lying? I wouldn't condescend to lie to you."

At that, the Giant's humor burst into high, headback, bubbling laughter.

Covenant watched, stifling with rage, while Foamfollower laughed. Briefly, he bore the affront. Then he jumped from his seat and raised his staff to strike the Giant.

Foamfollower stopped him with a placating gesture. "Softly, Unbeliever," he said. "Will you feel taller if I sit down?"

"Hell and blood!" Covenant howled. Swinging his arms savagely, he struck the floorboards with the urvile-blackened end of his staff.

The boat pitched as if his blow had sent the river into convulsions. Staggering, he clutched a thwart to save himself from being thrown overboard. In a moment, the spasm passed, leaving the sun-glittered stream as calm as before. But he remained gripping the thwart for several long heartbeats, while his nerves jangled and his ring throbbed heavily.

Covenant, he snarled to steady himself, you would be ridiculous if you weren't so—ridiculous. He drew himself erect, and stood with his feet braced until he had a stranglehold on his emotions. Then he bent his gaze toward Foamfollower, probed the Giant's aura. But he could perceive no ill; Foamfollower seemed as hale as native granite. Ridiculous! Covenant repeated. "She deserves respect."

"Ah, forgive me," said the Giant. With a twist, he lowered the tiller so that he could hold it under his arm in a sitting position. "I meant no disrespect. Your loyalty relieves me. And I know how to value what

she has achieved." He seated himself in the stern and
leaned back against the tiller so that his eyes were
only a foot above Covenant's. "Yes, and how to grieve
for her as well. There are none in the Land, not men
or Giants or Ranyhyn, who would bear you to—to
Lord's Keep faster than I will."

Then his smile returned. "But you, Thomas Covenant, Unbeliever and stranger in the Land—you burn
yourself too freely. I laughed when I saw you because
you seemed like a rooster threatening one of the
Ranyhyn. You waste yourself, Thomas Covenant."

Covenant took a double grip on his anger, and said
quietly, "Is that a fact? You judge too quickly,
Giant."

Another fountain of laughter bubbled out of Foamfollower's chest. "Bravely said! Here is a new thing in
the Land—a man accusing a Giant of haste. Well, you
are right. But did you not know that men consider us
a"—he laughed again—"a deliberate people? I was
chosen as legate because short human names, which
bereave their bearers of so much history and power
and meaning, are easier for me than for most of my
people. But now it appears that they are too easy."
Once more he threw back his head and let out a
stream of deep gaiety.

Covenant glared at the Giant as if all this humor
were incomprehensible to him. Then with an effort he
pulled himself away, dropped his staff into the bottom
of the boat, and sat down on the thwart facing forward, into the west and the afternoon sun. Foamfollower's laughter had a contagious sound, a
coloration of uncomplicated joy, but he resisted it. He
could not afford to be the victim of any more seductions. Already he had lost more of himself than he
could hope to regain.

Nerves don't regenerate. He tolled the words as if
they were a private litany, icons of his embattled self.
Giants don't exist. I know the difference.

Keep moving, survive.

He chewed his lips as if that pain could help him
keep his balance, keep his rage under command.

At his back, Saltheart Foamfollower softly began to

chant again. His song rolled through its channel like a long inlet to the sea, rising and falling like a condensation of the tides, and the winds of distance blew through the archaic words. At intervals, they returned to their refrain—

Stone and Sea are deep in life—

then voyaged away again. The sound of long sojourning reminded Covenant of his fatigue, and he slumped in the prow to rest.

Foamfollower's question caught him wandering. "Are you a storyteller, Thomas Covenant?"

Absently, he replied, "I was, once."

"And you gave it up? Ah, that is as sad a tale in three words as any you might have told me. But a life without a tale is like a sea without salt. How do you live?"

Covenant folded his arms across the gunwales and rested his chin on them. As the boat moved, Andelain opened constantly in front of him like a bud; but he ignored it, concentrated instead on the plaint of water past the prow. Unconsciously, he clenched his fist over his ring. "I live."

"Another?" Foamfollower returned. "In two words, a story sadder than the first. Say no more—with one word you will make me weep."

If the Giant intended any umbrage, Covenant could not hear it. Foamfollower sounded half teasing, half sympathetic. Covenant shrugged his shoulders, and remained silent.

In a moment, the Giant went on: "Well, this is a bad pass for me. Our journeying will not be easy, and I had hoped that you could lighten the leagues with a story. But no matter. I judge that you will tell no happy tales in any case. Ravers. Waynhim and Andelainian Wraiths slain. Well, some of this does not surprise me—our old ones have often guessed that Soulcrusher would not die as easily as poor Kevin hoped. Stone and Sea! All that Desecration—ravage and rapine—for a false hope. But we have a saying, and it comforts our children—few as they are—when

they weep for the nation, the homes, and company
of our people, which we lost—we say, Joy is in the
ears that hear, not in the mouth that speaks. The
world has few stories glad in themselves, and we must
have gay ears to defy Despite. Praise the Creator! Old
Lord Damelon Giantfriend knew the value of a good
laugh. When we reached the Land, we were too
grieved to fight for the right to live."

A good laugh, Covenant sighed morosely. Did I do
a whole life's laughing in that little time?

"You humans are an impatient lot, Thomas Covenant. Do you think that I ramble? Not a bit—I have
come hastening to the point. Since you have given
up the telling of stories, and since it appears that
neither of us is happy enough to withstand the recital
of your adventures—why, I must do the telling myself.
There is strength in stories—heart rebirth and thew
binding—and even Giants need strength when they
face such tasks as mine."

He paused, and Covenant, not wishing him to stop
—the Giant's voice seemed to weave the rush of water
past the boat into a soothing tapestry—said into the
silence, "Tell."

"Ah," Foamfollower responded, "that was not so
bad. You recover despite yourself, Thomas Covenant.
Now, then. Gladden your ears, and listen gaily, for I
am no purveyor of sorrows—though in times of action
we do not wince from facts. If you asked me to resail
your path here, I would require every detail of your
journey before I took three steps into the Hills. Re-
sailing is perilous, and too often return is impossible—
the path is lost, or the traveler changed, beyond hope
of recovery.

"But you must understand, Unbeliever, that select-
ing a tale is usually a matter for deliberation. The old
Giantish is a wealth of stories, and some take days in
the telling. Once, as a child, I heard three times in
succession the tale of Bahgoon the Unbearable and
Thelma Twofist, who tamed him—now that was a
story worth the laughter—but nine days were gone
before I knew it. However, you do not speak Giantish,
and translation is a long task, even for Giants, so

the problem of selection is simplified. But the lore of
our life in Seareach since our ships found the Land
contains many times many stories—tales of the reigns
of Damelon Giantfriend and Loric Vilesilencer and
Kevin, who is now called Landwaster—tales of
the building, the carving out of the mountain, of
Revelstone, revered rock, 'a handmark of allegiance
and fealty in the eternal stone of time,' as Kevin once
sang it, the mightiest making that the Giants have
done in the Land, a temple for our people to look
upon and remember what can be achieved—tales of
the voyage which saved us from the Desecration,
and of the many healings of the new Lords. But again
selection is made easy because you are a stranger. I
will tell you the first story of the Seareach Giants—
the Song of the Unhomed."

Covenant looked about him at the shining blue
tranquility of the Soulsease, and settled himself to
hear Foamfollower's story. But the narration did not
begin right away. Instead of starting his tale, the
Giant went back to his antique plainsong, spinning
the melody meditatively so that it unrolled like the
sea path of the river. For a long time, he sang, and
under the spell of his voice Covenant began to drowse.
He had too much exhaustion dripping through his
bones to keep his attention ready. While he waited,
he rested against the prow like a tired swimmer.

But then a modulation sharpened the Giant's chant.
The melody took on keener edges, and turned itself to
the angle of a lament. Soon Foamfollower was singing
words that Covenant could understand.

We are the Unhomed—
    lost voyagers of the world.
In the land beyond the Sunbirth Sea
    we lived and had our homes and grew—
    and set our sails to the wind,
    unheeding of the peril of the lost.

We are the Unhomed.
From home and hearth,

stone sacred dwellings crafted by our reverent
   hands,
we set our sails to the wind of the stars,
and carried life to lands across the earth,
careless of the peril of our loss.

We are the Unhomed—
   lost voyagers of the world.
From desert shore to high cliff crag,
   home of men and sylvan sea-edge faery
     lands—
   from dream to dream we set our sails,
   and smiled at the rainbow of our loss.

Now we are Unhomed,
   bereft of root and kith and kin.
From other mysteries of delight,
   we set our sails to resail our track;
   but the winds of life blew not the way we
     chose,
   and the land beyond the Sea was lost.

"Ah, Stone and Sea! Do you know the old lore-
legend of the Wounded Rainbow, Thomas Covenant?
It is said that in the dimmest past of the Earth, there
were no stars in our sky. The heavens were a blankness
which separated us from the eternal universe of the
Creator. There he lived with his people and his myriad bright children, and they moved to the music of
play and joy.

"Now, as the ages spired from forever to forever,
the Creator was moved to make a new thing for the
happy hearts of his children. He descended to the
great forges and cauldrons of his power, and brewed
and hammered and cast rare theurgies. And when he
was done, he turned to the heavens, and threw his
mystic creation to the sky—and, behold! A rainbow
spread its arms across the universe.

"For a moment, the Creator was glad. But then he
looked closely at the rainbow—and there, high in the
shimmering span, he saw a wound, a breach in the
beauty he had made. He did not know that his Enemy,

the demon spirit of murk and mire that crawled through the bowels of even his universe, had seen him at work, and had cast spite into the mortar of his creating. So now, as the rainbow stood across the heavens, it was marred.

"In vexation, the Creator returned to his works, to find a cure for his creation. But while he labored, his children, his myriad bright children, found the rainbow, and were filled with rejoicing at its beauty. Together, they climbed into the heavens and scampered happily up the bow, dancing gay dances across its colors. High on the span, they discovered the wound. But they did not understand it. Chorusing joy, they danced through the wound, and found themselves in our sky. This new unlighted world only gladdened them the more, and they spun through the sky until it sparkled with the glee of play.

"When they tired of this sport, they sought to return to their universe of light. But their door was shut. For the Creator had discovered his Enemy's handiwork—the cause of the wound—and in his anger his mind had been clouded. Thoughtless, he had torn the rainbow from the heavens. Not until his anger was done did he realize that he had trapped his children in our sky. And there they remain, stars to guide the sojourners of our nights, until the Creator can rid his universe of his Enemy, and find a way to bring his children Home.

"So it was with us, the Unhomed. In our long-lost rocky land, we lived and flourished among our own kind, and when we learned to travel the seas we only prospered the more. But in the eagerness of our glee and our health and our wandering, we betrayed ourselves into folly. We built twenty fine ships, each large enough to be a castle for you humans, and we made a vow among ourselves to set sail and discover the whole Earth. Ah, the whole Earth! In twenty ships, two thousand Giants said high farewells to their kindred, promising to bring back in stories every face of the multitudinous world—and they launched themselves into their dream.

"Then from sea to sea, through tempest and calm,

drought and famine and plenty, between reef and landfall, the Giants sailed, glorying in the bite of the salt air, and the stretch of sailors' thews, and the perpetual contest with the ocean, 'permanence in motion'—and in the exaltation of binding together new peoples in the web of their wandering.

"Three ships they lost in half a generation. One hundred Giants chose to remain and live out their lot with the sylvan faery *Elohim*. Two hundred died in the war service of the *Bhrathair*, who were nearly destroyed by the Sandgorgons of the great Desert. Two ships were reefed and wrecked. And when the first children born on the voyage were old enough to be sailors themselves, the fifteen vessels held council, and turned their thoughts toward Home—for they had learned the folly of their vow, and were worn from wrestling with the seas.

"So they set their sails by the stars, and sought for Home. But they were prevented. Familiar paths led them to unknown oceans and unencountered perils. Tempests drove them beyond their reckoning until their hands were stripped to the bone by the flailing ropes, and the waves rose up against them as if in hatred. Five more ships were lost—though the wreckage of one was found, and the sailors of another were rescued from the island on which they had been cast. Through ice that held them in its clutch for many seasons, killing scores of them—through calms that made them close comrades of starvation—they endured, struggling for their lives and Home. But disasters erased every vestige of knowledge from their bearings, until they knew not where they were or where to go. When they reached the Land, they cast their anchors. Less than a thousand Giants stepped down to the rocky shore of Seareach. In disconsolation, they gave up their hope of Home.

"But the friendship of High Lord Damelon Heartthew-son renewed them. He saw omens of promise in his mighty Lore, and at his word the Giants lifted up their hearts. They made Seareach their place, and swore fealty to the Lords—and sent three vessels out in quest of Home. Since that time—for more than three times a thousand years—there have always been three Giant ships at sea, seeking our land turn by turn, three new standing out when the old return, their hands empty of success. Still we are Unhomed, lost in the labyrinth of a foolish dream.

"Stone and Sea! We are a long-lived people, compared to your humans—I was born on shipboard during the short voyage which saved us from the Desecration, and my great-grandparents were among the first wanderers. And we have so few children. Rarely does any woman bear more than one child. So now there are only five hundred of us, and our vitality narrows with each generation.

"We cannot forget.

"But in the old lore-legend, the children of the Creator had hope. He put rainbows in our sky after cleansing rains, as a promise to the stars that somehow, someday, he would find a way to bring them home.

"If we are to survive, we must find the Home that we have lost, the heartland beyond the Sunbirth Sea."

During Foamfollower's tale the sun had declined into late afternoon; and as he finished, sunset began on the horizon. Then the Soulsease ran out of the west with fiery, orange-gold glory reflected flame for flame in its burnished countenance. In the fathomless heavens the fire radiated both loss and prophecy, coming night and promised day, darkness which would pass; for when the true end of day and light came, there would be no blazonry to make it admirable, no spectacle or fine fire or joy, nothing for the heart to behold but decay and gray ashes.

In splendor, Foamfollower lifted up his voice again, and sang with a plummeting ache:

We set our sails to resail our track;
but the winds of life blew not the way we chose,
and the land beyond the Sea was lost.

Covenant pushed himself around to look at the Giant. Foamfollower's head was held high, with wet streaks of gleaming gold-orange fire drawn delicately down his cheeks. As Covenant watched, the reflected light took on a reddish-shade and began to fade.

Softly, the Giant said, "Laugh, Thomas Covenant— laugh for me. Joy is in the ears that hear."

Covenant heard the subdued, undemanding throb and supplication in Foamfollower's voice, and his own choked pain groaned in answer. But he could not laugh; he had no laughter of any kind in him. With a spasm of disgust for the limitations that crippled him, he made a rough effort in another direction. "I'm hungry."

For an instant, Foamfollower's shadowed eyes flared as if he had been stung. But then he put back his head and laughed for himself. His humor seemed to spring straight from his heart, and soon it had banished all tension and tears from his visage.

When he had relaxed into quiet chuckling, he said, "Thomas Covenant, I do not like to be hasty—but I believe you are my friend. You have toppled my pride, and that would be fair service even had I not laughed at you earlier.

"Hungry? Of course you are hungry. Bravely said. I should have offered you food earlier—you have the transparent look of a man who has eaten only *aliantha* for days. Some old seers say that privation refines the soul—but I say it is soon enough to refine the soul when the body has no other choice.

"Happily, I am well supplied with food." He pushed a prodigious leather sack toward Covenant with his foot, and motioned for him to open it. When Covenant loosened its drawstrings, he found salt beef, cheese, old bread, and more than a dozen tangerines as big as his two fists, as well as a leather jug which he could hardly lift. To postpone this difficulty, he tackled the staples first, washing the salt out of his throat with sections of a tangerine. Then he turned his attention to the jug.

"That is *diamondraught*," said Foamfollower. "It is a vital brew. Perhaps I should— No, the more I look at you, my friend, the more weariness I see. Just drink from the jug. It will aid your rest."

Tilting the jug, Covenant sipped the *diamon-*

draught. It tasted like light whiskey, and he could smell its potency; but it was so smooth that it did not bite or burn. He took several relishing swallows, and at once felt deeply refreshed.

Carefully, he closed the jug, replaced the food in the sack, then with an effort pushed the sack back into Foamfollower's reach. The *diamondraught* glowed in his belly, and he felt that in a little while he would be ready for another story. But as he lay down under the thwarts in the bow, the twilight turned into crystal darkness in the sky, and the stars came out lornly, like scattered children. Before he knew that he was drowsing, he was asleep.

It was an uneasy slumber. He staggered numbly through plague-ridden visions full of dying moons and slaughter and helpless ravaged flesh, and found himself lying in the street near the front bumper of the police car. A circle of townspeople had gathered around him. They had eyes of flint, and their mouths were stretched in one uniform rictus of denunciation. Without exception, they were pointing at his hands. When he lifted his hands to look at them, he saw that they were rife with purple, leprous bruises.

Then two white-clad, brawny men came up to him and manhandled him into a stretcher. He could see the ambulance nearby. But the men did not carry him to it immediately. They stood still, holding him at waist-level like a display to the crowd.

A policeman stepped into the circle. His eyes were the color of contempt. He bent over Covenant and said sternly, "You got in my way. That was wrong. You ought to be ashamed." His breath covered Covenant with the smell of attar.

Behind the policeman, someone raised his voice. It was as full of unction as that of Joan's lawyer. It said, "That was wrong."

In perfect unison, all the townspeople vomited gouts of blood onto the pavement.

I don't believe this, Covenant thought.

At once, the unctuous voice purred, "He doesn't believe us." A silent howl of reality, a rabid assertion of fact, sprang up from the crowd. It battered Covenant until he cowered under it, abject and answerless.

Then the townspeople chorused, "You are dead. Without the community, you can't live. Life is in the community, and you have no community. You can't live if no one cares." The unison of their voices made a sound like crumbling, crushing. When they stopped, Covenant felt that the air in his lungs had been turned to rubble.

With a sigh of satisfaction, the unctuous voice said, "Take him to the hospital. Heal him. There is only one good answer to death. Heal him and throw him out."

The two men swung him into the ambulance. Before the door slammed shut, he saw the townspeople shaking hands with each other, beaming their congratulations. After that, the ambulance started to move. He raised his hands, and saw that the purple spots were spreading up his forearms. He stared at himself in horror, moaning, Hellfire hellfire hellfire!

But then a bubbling tenor voice said kindly, "Do not fear. It is a dream." The reassurance spread over him like a blanket. But he could not feel it with his hands, and the ambulance kept on moving. Needing the blanket, he clenched at the empty air until his knuckles were white with loneliness.

When he felt that he could not ache anymore, the ambulance rolled over, and he fell out of the stretcher into blankness.

TWELVE: Revelstone

THE pressure against his left cheek began slowly to wear his skin raw, and the pain nagged him up off the bottom of his slumber. Turbulence rushed under his head, as if he were pillowed on shoals. He

labored his way out of sleep. Then his cheek was
jolted twice in rapid succession, and his resting place
heaved. Pushing himself up, he smacked his head on
a thwart of the boat. Pain throbbed in his skull. He
gripped the thwart, swung himself away from the rib
which had been rubbing his cheek, and sat up to look
over the gunwales.

He found that the situation of the boat had changed
radically. No shade or line or resonance of Andelainian
richness remained in the surrounding terrain. On the
northeast, the river was edged by a high, bluff rock
wall. And to the west spread a gray and barren plain,
a crippled wilderness like a vast battleground where
more than men had been slain, where the fire that
scorched and the blood that drenched had blighted
the ground's ability to revitalize itself, bloom again—
an uneven despoiled lowland marked only by the
scrub trees clinging to life along the river which
poured into the Soulsease a few hundred yards ahead
of the boat. The eastering wind carried an old burnt
odor, and behind it lay the fetid memory of a crime.

Already, the river joining ahead troubled the
Soulsease—knotted its current, stained its clarity
with flinty mud—and Covenant had to grip the
gunwales to keep his balance as the pitching of the
boat increased.

Foamfollower held the boat in the center of the
river, away from the turmoil against the northeast
rock wall. Covenant glanced back at the Giant. He
was standing in the stern—feet widely braced, tiller
clamped under his right arm. At Covenant's glance,
he called over the mounting clash of the rivers,
"Trothgard lies ahead! Here we turn north—the
White River! The Gray comes from the west!" His
voice had a strident edge to it, as if he had been singing as strongly as he could all night; but after a moment he sang out a fragment of a different song:

> For we will not rest—
>   not turn aside,
>   lost faith,
>   or fail—

until the Gray flows Blue,
and Rill and Maerl are as new and clean
    as ancient Llurallin.

The heaving of the river mounted steadily. Covenant stood in the bottom of the boat—bracing himself against one of the thwarts, gripping the gunwale—and watched the forced commingling of the clean and tainted waters. Then Foamfollower shouted, "One hundred leagues to the Westron Mountains—Guards Gap and the high spring of the Llurallin—and one hundred fifty southwest to the Last Hills and Garroting Deep! We are seventy from Lord's Keep!"

Abruptly, the river's moiling growl sprang louder, smothered the Giant's voice. An unexpected lash of the current caught the boat and tore its prow to the right, bringing it broadside to the stream. Spray slapped Covenant as the boat heeled over; instinctively, he threw his weight onto the left gunwale.

The next instant, he heard a snatch of Foamfollower's plainsong, and felt power thrumming deeply along the keel. Slowly, the boat righted itself, swung into the current again.

But the near-disaster had carried them dangerously close to the northeast wall. The boat trembled with energy as Foamfollower worked it gradually back into the steadier water flowing below the main force of the Gray's current. Then the sensation of power faded from the keel.

"Your pardon!" the Giant shouted. "I am losing my seamanship!" His voice was raw with strain.

Covenant's knuckles were white from clenching the gunwales. As he bounced with the pitch of the boat, he remembered, *There is only one good answer to death.*

One good answer, he thought. This isn't it.

Perhaps it would be better if the boat capsized, better if he drowned—better if he did not carry Lord Foul's message halfhanded and beringed to Revelstone. He was not a hero. He could not satisfy such expectations.

"Now the crossing!" Foamfollower called. "We

must pass the Gray to go on north. There is no great danger—except that I am weary. And the rivers are high."

This time, Covenant turned and looked closely at the Giant. He saw now that Saltheart Foamfollower was suffering. His cheeks were sunken, hollowed as if something had gouged the geniality out of his face; and his cavernous eyes burned with taut, febrile volition. Weary? Covenant thought. More like exhausted. He lurched awkwardly from thwart to thwart until he reached the Giant. His eyes were no higher than Foamfollower's waist. He tipped his head back to shout, "I'll steer! You rest!"

A smile flickered on the Giant's lips. "I thank you. But no—you are not ready. I am strong enough. But please lift the *diamondraught* to me."

Covenant opened the food sack and put his hands on the leather jug. Its weight and suppleness made it unwieldy for him, and the tossing of the boat unbalanced him. He simply could not lift the jug. But after a moment he got his arms under it. With a groan of exertion, he heaved it upward.

Foamfollower caught the neck of the jug neatly in his left hand. "Thank you, my friend," he said with a ragged grin. Raising the jug to his mouth, he disregarded the perils of the current for a moment to drink deeply. Then he put down the jug and swung the boat toward the mouth of the Gray River.

Another surge of power throbbed through the craft. As it hit the main force of the Gray, Foamfollower turned downstream and angled across the flow. Energy quivered in the floorboards. In a smooth maneuver, Foamfollower reached the north side of the current, pivoted upstream with the backwash along the wall, and let it sling him into the untroubled White. Once he had rounded the northward curve, the roar of the joining began to drop swiftly behind the boat.

A moment later, the throb of power faded again. Sighing heavily, Foamfollower wiped the sweat from his face. His shoulders sagged, and his head bowed. With labored slowness, he lowered the tiller, and at last dropped into the stern of the boat. "Ah, my friend," he groaned, "even Giants are not made to do such things."

Covenant moved to the center of the boat and took a seat in the bottom, leaning against one of the sides. From that position, he could not see over the gunwales, but he was not at present curious about the terrain. He had other concerns. One of them was Foamfollower's condition. He did not know how the Giant had become so exhausted.

He tried to approach the question indirectly by saying, "That was neatly done. How did you do it? You didn't tell me what powers this thing." And he frowned at the tactless sound of his voice.

"Ask for some other story," Foamfollower sighed wearily. "That one is nearly as long as the history of the Land. I have no heart to teach you the meaning of life here."

"You don't know any short stories," responded Covenant.

At this, the Giant managed a wan smile. "Ah, that is true enough. Well, I will make it brief for you. But then you must promise to tell a story for me—something rare, that I will never guess for myself. I will need that, my friend."

Covenant agreed with a nod, and Foamfollower said, "Well. Eat, and I will talk."

Vaguely surprised at how hungry he was, Covenant tackled the contents of Foamfollower's sack. He munched meat and cheese rapidly, satisfied his thirst with tangerines. And while he ate, the Giant began in a voice flat with fatigue: "The time of Damelon Giantfriend came to an end in the Land before my people had finished the making of *Coercri,* their home in Seareach. They carved Lord's Keep, as men call it, out of the mountain's heart before they labored on their own Lord-given land, and Loric was High Lord when *Coercri* was done. Then my forebearers turned their attention outward—to the Sunbirth Sea, and to the friendship of the Land.

"Now, both *lillianrill* and *rhadhamaerl* desired to study the lore of the Giants, and the time of High Lord Loric Vilesilencer was one of great growth for

the *lillianrill*. To help in this growth, it was necessary
for the Giants to make many sojourns to Lord's Keep"
—he broke into a quiet chant, singing for a while as
if in invocation of the old grandeur of Giantish reverence—"to mighty Revelstone. This was well, for it
kept Revelstone bright in their eyes.

"But the Giants are not great lovers of walking—
no more so then than now. So my forebearers be-
thought them of the rivers which flow from the
Westron Mountains to the Sea, and decided to build
boats. Well, boats cannot come here from the Sea, as
you may know—Landsdrop, on which stands Gravin
Threndor, blocks the way. And no one, Giant or
otherwise, would willingly sail the Defiles Course from
Lifeswallower, the Great Swamp. So the Giants built
docks on the Soulsease, upriver from Gravin Threndor
and the narrows now called Treacher's Gorge. There
they kept such boats as this—there, and at Lord's
Keep at the foot of Furl Falls, so that at least two
hundred leagues of the journey might be on the water
which we love.

"In this journeying, Loric and the *lillianrill* desired
to be of aid to the Giants. Out of their power they
crafted Gildenlode—a strong wood which they named
lor-liarill—and from this wood they made rudders
and keels for our riverboats. And it was the promise
of the Old Lords that, when their omens of hope for
us came to pass, then Gildenlode would help us.

"Ah, enough," Foamfollower sighed abruptly. "In
short, it is I who impel this craft." He lifted his hand
from the tiller, and immediately the boat began to
lose headway. "Or rather it is I who call out the power
of the Gildenlode. There is life and power in the
Earth—in stone and wood and water and earth. But
life in them is somewhat hidden—somewhat slumberous. Both knowledge and strength are needed—
yes, and potent vital songs—to awaken them." He
grasped the tiller again, and the boat moved forward
once more.

"So I am weary," he breathed. "I have not rested
since the night before we met." His tone reminded
Covenant of Trell's fatigue after the Gravelingas had

healed the broken pot. "For two days and two nights I have not allowed the Gildenlode to stop or slow, though my bones are weak with the expense." To the surprise in Covenant's face, he added, "Yes, my friend—you slept for two nights and a day. From the west of Andelain across the Center Plains to the marge of Trothgard, more than a hundred leagues." After a pause, he concluded, *"Diamondraught* does such things to humans. But you had need of rest."

For a moment, Covenant sat silent, staring at the floorboards as if he were looking for a place to hit them. His mouth twisted sourly when he raised his head and said, "So now I'm rested. Can I help?"

Foamfollower did not reply immediately. Behind the buttress of his forehead, he seemed to weigh his various uncertainties before he muttered, "Stone and Sea! Of course you can. And yet the very fact of asking shows that you cannot. Some unwillingness or ignorance prevents."

Covenant understood. He could hear dark wings, see slaughtered Wraiths. Wild magic! he groaned. Heroism! This is unsufferable. With a jerk of his head, he knocked transitions aside and asked roughly, "Do you want my ring?"

"Want?" Foamfollower croaked, looking as if he felt he should laugh but did not have the heart for it. "Want?" His voice quavered painfully, as if he were confessing to some kind of aberration. "Do not use such a word, my friend. *Wanting* is natural, and may succeed or fail without wrong. Say *covet*, rather. To covet is to desire something which should not be given. Yes, I covet your un-Earth, wild magic, peace-ending white gold:

There is wild magic graven in every rock,
contained for white gold to unleash or control—

I admit the desire. But do not tempt me. Power has a way of revenging itself upon its usurpers. I would not accept this ring if you offered it to me."

"But you do know how to use it?" Covenant inquired dully, half dazed by his inchoate fear of the answer.

This time Foamfollower did laugh. His humor was emaciated, a mere wisp of its former self, but it was clean and gay. "Ah, bravely said, my friend. So covetousness collapses of its own folly. No, I do not know. If the wild magic may not be called up by the simple decision of use, then I do not understand it at all. Giants do not have such lore. We have always acted for ourselves—though we gladly use such tools as Gildenlode. Well, I am rewarded for unworthy thoughts. Your pardon, Thomas Covenant."

Covenant nodded mutely, as if he had been given an unexpected reprieve. He did not want to know how wild magic worked; he did not want to believe in it in any way. Simply carrying it around was dangerous. He covered it with his right hand and gazed dumbly, helplessly, at the Giant.

After a moment, Foamfollower's fatigue quenched his humor. His eyes dimmed, and his respiration sighed wearily between his slack lips. He sagged on the tiller as if laughing had cost him vital energy. "Now, my friend," he breathed. "My courage is nearly spent. I need your story."

Story? Covenant thought. I don't have any stories. I burned them.

He had burned them—both his new novel and his best-seller. They had been so complacent, so abjectly blind to the perils of leprosy, which lurked secretive and unpredictable behind every physical or moral existence—and so unaware of their own sightlessness. They were carrion—like himself, like himself—fit only for flames. What story could he tell now?

But he had to keep moving, act, survive. Surely he had known that before he had become the victim of dreams. Had he not learned it at the leprosarium, in putrefaction and vomit? Yes, yes! Survive! And yet this dream expected power of him, expected him to put an end to slaughter— Images flashed through him like splinters of vertigo, mirror shards: Joan, police car, Drool's laval eyes. He reeled as if he were falling.

To conceal his sudden distress, he moved away from Foamfollower, went to sit in the prow facing north. "A story," he said thickly. In fact, he did know one story—one story in all its grim and motley disguises. He sorted quickly, vividly, until he found one which suited the other things he need to articulate. "I'll tell you a story. A true story."

He gripped the gunwales, fought down his dizziness. "It's a story about culture shock. Do you know what culture shock is?" Foamfollower did not reply. "Never mind. I'll tell you about it. Culture shock is what happens when you take a man out of his own world and put him down in a place where the assumptions, the— the standards of being a person—are so different that he can't possibly understand them. He isn't built that way. If he's—facile—he can pretend to be someone else until he gets back to his own world. Or he can just collapse and let himself be rebuilt—however. There's no other way.

"I'll give you an example. While I was at the leprosarium, the doctors talked about a man—a leper—like me. Outcast. He was a classic case. He came from another country—where leprosy is a lot more common—he must have picked up the bacillus there as a child, and years later when he had a wife and three kids of his own and was living in another country, he suddenly lost the nerves in his toes and started to go blind.

"Well, if he had stayed in his own country, he would have been— The disease is common—it would have been recognized early. As soon as it was recognized, he—and his wife—and his kids—and everything he owned—and his house—and his animals—and his close relatives—they would have all been declared *unclean*. His property and house and animals would have been burned to the ground. And he and his wife and his kids and his close relatives would have been sent away to live in the most abject poverty in a village with other people who had the same disease. He would have spent the rest of his life there—without treatment—without hope—while hideous deformity gnawed his arms and legs and face—until he and his wife and his kids and his close relatives all died of gangrene.

"Do you think that's cruel? Let me tell you what did happen to the man. As soon as he recognized his disease, he went to his doctor. His doctor sent him to the leprosarium—alone—without his family—where the spread of the disease was arrested. He was treated, given medicine and training—rehabilitated. Then he was sent home to live a 'normal' life with his wife and kids. How nice. There was only one problem. He couldn't handle it.

"To start with, his neighbors gave him a hard time. Oh, at first they didn't know he was sick—they weren't familiar with leprosy, didn't recognize it—but the local newspaper printed a story on him, so that everyone in town knew he was *the leper*. They shunned him, hated him because they didn't know what to do about him. Then he began to have trouble keeping up his self-treatments. His home country didn't have medicine and leper's therapy—in his bones he believed that such things were magic, that once his disease was arrested he was *cured,* pardoned—given a stay of something worse than execution. But, lo and behold! When he stops taking care of himself, the numbness starts to spread again. Then comes the clincher. Suddenly he finds that behind his back—while he wasn't even looking, much less alert—he has been cut off from his family. They don't share his trouble—far from it. They want to get rid of him, go back to living the way they were before.

"So they pack him off to the leprosarium again. But after getting on the plane—they didn't have planes in his home country, either—he goes into the bathroom as if he had been disinherited without anyone ever telling him why and slits his wrists."

He gaped wide-eyed at his own narration. He would have been willing, eager, to weep for the man if he had been able to do so without sacrificing his own defenses. But he could not weep. Instead, he swallowed thickly, and let his momentum carry him on again.

"And I'll tell you something else about culture shock. Every world has its own ways of committing suicide, and it is a lot easier to kill yourself using methods that you're not accustomed to. I could never slit my wrists. I've read too much about it—talked about it too much. It's too vivid. I would throw up. But I could go to that man's world and sip belladonna tea without nausea. Because I don't know enough about it. There's something vague about it, something obscure—something not quite fatal.

"So that poor man in the bathroom sat there for over an hour, just letting his lifeblood run into the sink. He didn't try to get help until all of a sudden, finally, he realized that he was going to die just as dead as if he had sipped belladonna tea. Then he tried to open the door—but he was too weak. And he didn't know how to push the button to get help. They eventually found him in this grotesque position on the floor with his fingers broken, as if he—as if he had tried to crawl under the door. He—"

He could not go on. Grief choked him into silence, and he sat still for a time, while water lamented dimly past the prow. He felt sick, desperate for survival; he could not submit to these seductions. Then Foamfollower's voice reached him. Softly, the Giant said, "Is this why you abandoned the telling of stories?"

Covenant sprang up, whirled in instant rage. "This Land of yours is trying to kill me!" he spat fiercely. "It—you're pressuring me into suicide! White gold!—Bcrck!—Wraiths! You're doing things to me that I can't handle. I'm not that kind of person—I don't live in that kind of world. All these—seductions! Hell and blood! I'm a leper! Don't you understand that?"

For a long moment, Foamfollower met Covenant's hot gaze, and the sympathy in the Giant's eyes stopped his outburst. He stood glaring with his fingers clawed while Foamfollower regarded him sadly, wearily. He could see that the Giant did not understand; *leprosy* was a word that seemed to have no meaning in the Land. "Come on," he said with an ache. "Laugh about it. Joy is in the ears that hear."

But then Foamfollower showed that he did understand something. He reached into his jerkin and drew out a leather packet, which he unfolded to produce a

large sheet of supple hide. "Here," he said, "you will
see much of this before you are done with the Land.
It is *clingor*. The Giants brought it to the Land long
ages ago—but I will spare us both the effort of telling." He tore a small square from the corner of the
sheet and handed the piece to Covenant. It was sticky
on both sides, but transferred easily from hand to
hand, and left no residue of glue behind. "Trust it.
Place your ring upon that piece and hide it under your
raiment. No one will know that you bear a talisman
of wild magic."

Covenant grasped at the idea. Tugging his ring
from his finger, he placed it on the square of *clingor*.
It stuck firmly; he could not shake the ring loose, but
he could peel the *clingor* away without difficulty.
Nodding sharply to himself, he placed his ring on the
leather, then opened his shirt and pressed the *clingor*
to the center of his chest. It held there, gave him no
discomfort. Rapidly, as if to seize an opportunity before it passed, he rebuttoned his shirt. To his surprise,
he seemed to feel the weight of the ring on his heart,
but he resolved to ignore it.

Carefully, Foamfollower refolded the *clingor*, replaced it within his jerkin. Then he studied Covenant
again briefly. Covenant tried to smile in response, express his gratitude, but his face seemed only capable
of snarls. At last, he turned away, reseated himself in
the prow to watch the boat's progress and absorb
what Foamfollower had done for him.

After musing for a time, he remembered Atiaran's
stone knife. It made possible a self-discipline that he
sorely needed. He leaned over the side of the boat to
wet his face, then took up the knife and painstakingly
shaved his whiskers. The beard was eight days old,
but the keen, slick blade slid smoothly over his cheeks
and down his neck, and he did a passable job of
shaving without cutting himself. But he was out of
practice, no longer accustomed to the risk; the prospect of blood made his heart tremble. Then he began
to see how urgently he needed to return to his real
world, needed to recover himself before he altogether
lost his ability to survive as a leper.

Later that day came rain, a light drizzle which spattered the surface of the river, whorling the sky mirror into myriad pieces. The drops brushed his face like spray, seeped slowly into his clothes until he was as soaked and uncomfortable as if he had been drenched. But he endured it in a gray, dull reverie, thinking about what he gained and lost by hiding his ring.

At last, the day ended. Darkness dripped into the air as if the rain were simply becoming blacker, and in the twilight Covenant and Foamfollower ate their supper glumly. The Giant was almost too weak to feed himself, but with Covenant's help he managed a decent meal, drank a great quantity of *diamondraught*. Then they returned to their respective silences. Covenant was glad for the dusk; it spared him the sight of Foamfollower's exhaustion. Unwilling to lie down on the damp floorboards, he huddled cold and wet against the side of the boat and tried to relax, sleep.

After a time, Foamfollower began to chant faintly:

Stone and Sea are deep in life,
two unalterable symbols of the world:
permanence at rest, and permanence in motion;
participants in the Power that remains.

He seemed to gather strength from the song, and with it he impelled the boat steadily against the current, drove northward as if there were no fatigue that could make him falter.

Finally, the rain stopped; the cloud cover slowly broke open. But Covenant and Foamfollower found no relief in the clear sky. Over the horizon, the red moon stood like a blot, an imputation of evil, on the outraged background of the stars. It turned the surrounding terrain into a dank bloodscape, full of crimson and evanescent forms like uncomprehended murders. And from the light came a putrid emanation, as if the Land were illumined by a bane. Then Foamfollower's plainsong sounded dishearteningly frail, futile, and the stars themselves seemed to shrink away from the moon's course.

But dawn brought a sunlight-washed day unriven by any taint or memory of taint. When Covenant raised himself to look around, he saw mountains directly to the north. They spread away westward, where the tallest of them were still snow-crested; but the range ended abruptly at a point in line with the White River. Already the mountains seemed near at hand.

"Ten leagues," Foamfollower whispered hoarsely. "Half a day against this current."

The Giant's appearance filled Covenant with sharp dismay. Dull-eyed and slack-lipped, Foamfollower looked like a corpse of himself. His beard seemed grayer, as if he had aged several years overnight, and a trail of spittle he was helpless to control ran from the corner of his mouth. The pulse in his temples limped raggedly. But his grip on the tiller was as hard as a gnarled knot of wood, and the boat plowed stiffly up the briskening river.

Covenant moved to the stern to try to be of help. He wiped the Giant's lips, then held up the jug of *diamondraught* so that Foamfollower could drink. The fragments of a smile cracked the Giant's lips, and he breathed, "Stone and Sea. It is no easy thing to be your friend. Tell your next ferryman to take you downstream. Destinations are for stronger souls than mine."

"Nonsense," said Covenant gruffly. "They're going to make up songs about you for this. Don't you think it's worth it?"

Foamfollower tried to respond, but the effort made him cough violently, and he had to retreat into himself, concentrate the fading fire of his spirit on the clench of his fist and the progress of the boat.

"That's all right," Covenant said softly. "Everyone who helps me ends up exhausted—one way or another. If I were a poet, I would make up your song myself." Cursing silently at his helplessness, he fed the Giant sections of tangerine until there was no fruit left. As he looked at Foamfollower, the tall being shriven of everything except the power to endure, self-divested, for reasons Covenant could not comprehend, of every quality of humor or even dignity as if they were mere appurtenances, he felt irrationally in debt to Foamfollower, as if he had been sold—behind his back and with blithe unregard for his consent—into the usury of his only friend. "Everyone who helps me," he muttered again. He found the prices the people of the Land were willing to pay for him appalling.

Finally he was no longer able to stand the sight. He returned to the bow, where he stared at the looming mountains with deserted eyes and grumbled, I didn't ask for this.

Do I hate myself so much? he demanded. But his only answer was the rattle of Foamfollower's breathing.

Half the morning passed that way, measured in butchered hunks out of the impenetrable circumstance of time by the rasp of Foamfollower's respiration. Around the boat the terrain stiffened, as if preparing itself for a leap into the sky. The hills grew higher and more ragged, gradually leaving behind the heather and banyan trees of the plains for a stiffer scrub grass and a few scattered cedars. And ahead the mountains stood taller beyond the hills with every curve of the river. Now Covenant could see that the east end of the range dropped steeply to a plateau like a stair into the mountains—a plateau perhaps two or three thousand feet high that ended in a straight cliff to the foothills. From the plateau came a waterfall, and some effect of the light on the rock made the cascade gleam pale blue as it tumbled. Furl Falls, Covenant said to himself. In spite of the rattle of Foamfollower's breathing, he felt a stirring in his heart, as if he were drawing near to something grand.

But the drawing near lost its swiftness steadily. As the White wound between the hills, it narrowed; and as a result, the current grew increasingly stiff. The Giant seemed to have passed the end of his endurance. His respiration sounded stertorous enough to strangle him at any time; he moved the boat hardly faster than a walk. Covenant did not see how they could cover the last leagues.

He studied the riverbanks for a place to land the

boat; he intended somehow to make the Giant take
the boat to shore. But while he was still looking, he
heard a low rumble in the air like the running of
horses. What the hell—? A vision of ur-viles flared in
his mind. He snatched up his staff from the bottom
of the boat and clenched it, trying to control the sudden drum of his trepidation.

The next moment, like a breaking wave over the
crest of a hill upstream and east from the boat, came
cantering a score of horses bearing riders. The riders
were human, men and women. The instant they saw
the boat, one of them shouted, and the group broke
into a gallop, sweeping down the hill to rein in at the
edge of the river.

The riders looked like warriors. They wore high,
soft-soled boots over black leggings, black sleeveless
shirts covered by breastplates molded of a yellow
metal, and yellow headbands. A short sword hung
from each belt, a bow and quiver of arrows from
each back. Scanning them rapidly, Covenant saw the
characteristic features of both Woodhelvennin and
Stonedownor; some were tall and fair, light-eyed and
slim, and others, square, dark, and muscular.

As soon as their horses were stopped, the riders
slapped their right fists in unison to their hearts, then
extended their arms, palms forward, in the gesture of
welcome. A man distinguished by a black diagonal line
across his breastplate shouted over the water, "Hail,
Rockbrother! Welcome and honor and fealty to you
and to your people! I am Quaan, Warhaft of the
Third Eoman of the Warward of Lord's Keep!" He
paused for a reply, and when Covenant said nothing,
he went on in a more cautious tone, "Lord Mhoram
sent us. He saw that important matters were moving
on the river today. We are come as escort."

Covenant looked at Foamfollower, but what he saw
only convinced him that the Giant was past knowing
what happened around him. He slumped in the stern,
deaf and blind to everything except his failing effort
to drive the boat. Covenant turned back toward the
Eoman and called out, "Help us! He's dying!"

Quaan stiffened, then sprang into action. He

snapped an order, and the next instant he and two other riders plunged their horses into the river. The two others headed directly for the west bank, but Quaan guided his horse to intercept the boat. The mustang swam powerfully, as if such work were part of its training. Quaan soon neared the boat. At the last moment, he stood up on his mount's back and vaulted easily over the gunwales. On command, his horse started back toward the east bank.

Momentarily, Quaan measured Covenant with his eyes, and Covenant saw in his thick black hair, broad shoulders, and transparent face that he was a Stonedownor. Then the Warhaft moved toward Foamfollower. He gripped the Giant's shoulders and shook them, barking words which Covenant could not understand.

At first, Foamfollower did not respond. He sat sightless, transfixed, with his hand clamped like a death-grip onto the tiller. But slowly Quaan's voice seemed to penetrate him. The cords of his neck trembled as he lifted his head, tortuously brought his eyes into focus on Quaan. Then, with a groan that seemed to spring from the very marrow of his bones, he released the tiller and fell over sideways.

The craft immediately lost headway, began drifting back downriver. But by this time the two other riders were ready on the west bank. Quaan stepped past Covenant into the bow of the boat, and when he was in position, one of the two riders threw the end of a long line to him. He caught it neatly and looped it over the prow. It stuck where he put it; it was not rope, but *clingor*. At once, he turned toward the east bank. Another line reached him, and he attached it also to the prow. The lines pulled taut; the boat stopped drifting. Then Quaan waved his arm, and the riders began moving along the banks, pulling the boat upstream.

As soon as he understood what was being done, Covenant turned back to Foamfollower. The Giant lay where he had fallen, and his breathing was shallow, irregular. Covenant groped momentarily for some way to help, then lifted the leather jug and poured a

quantity of *diamondraught* over Foamfollower's head.
The liquid ran into his mouth; he sputtered at it,
swallowed heavily. Then he took a deep, rattling
breath, and his eyes slitted open. Covenant held the
jug to his lips, and after drinking from it, he stretched
out flat in the bottom of the boat. At once, he fell
into deep sleep.

In relief, Covenant murmured over him, "Now
that's a fine way to end a song—'and then he went to
sleep.' What good is being a hero if you don't stay
awake until you get congratulated?"

He felt suddenly tired, as if the Giant's exhaustion
had drained his own strength, and sighing he sat down
on one of the thwarts to watch their progress up the
river, while Quaan went to the stern to take the
tiller. For a while, Covenant ignored Quaan's scrutiny.
But finally he gathered enough energy to say,
"He's Saltheart Foamfollower, a—a legate from the
Seareach Giants. He hasn't rested since he picked me
up in the center of Andelain—three days ago." He saw
comprehension of Foamfollower's plight spread across
Quaan's face. Then he turned his attention to the passing terrain.

The towing horses kept up a good pace against the
White's tightening current. Their riders deftly managed the variations of the riverbanks, trading haulers
and slackening one rope or the other whenever necessary. As they moved north, the soil became rockier,
and the scrub grass gave way to bracken. Gilden trees
spread their broad boughs and leaves more and more
thickly over the foothills, and the sunlight made the
gold foliage glow warmly. Ahead, the plateau now
appeared nearly a league wide, and on its west the
mountains stood erect as if they were upright in pride.

By noon, Covenant could hear the roar of the
great falls, and he guessed that they were close to
Revelstone, though the high foothills now blocked
most of his view. The roaring approached steadily.
Soon the boat passed under a wide bridge. And a short
time later, the riders rounded a last curve, drew the
boat into a lake at the foot of Furl Falls.

The lake was round and rough in shape, wide, edged

along its whole western side by Gilden and pine. It stood at the base of the cliff—more than two thousand feet of sheer precipice—and the blue water came thundering down into it from the plateau like the loud heart's-blood of the mountains. In the lake, the water was as clean and cool as rain-washed ether, and Covenant could see clearly the depths of its bouldered bottom.

Knotted jacarandas with delicate blue flowers clustered on the wet rocks at the base of the falls, but most of the lake's eastern shore was clear of trees. There stood two large piers and several smaller loading docks. At one pier rested a boat much like the one Covenant rode in, and smaller craft—skiffs and rafts—were tied to the docks. Under Quaan's guidance, the riders pulled the boat up to one of the piers, where two of the Eoman made it fast. Then the Warhaft gently awakened Foamfollower.

The Giant came out of his sleep with difficulty, but when he pried his eyes open they were calm, unhaggard, though he looked as weak as if his bones were made of sandstone. With help from Quaan and Covenant, he climbed into a sitting position. There he rested, looking dazedly about him as if he wondered where his strength had gone.

After a time, he said thinly to Quaan, "Your pardon, Warhaft. I am—a little tired."

"I see you," Quaan murmured. "Do not be concerned. Revelstone is near."

For a moment, Foamfollower frowned in perplexity as he tried to remember what had happened to him. Then a look of recollection tensed his face. "Send riders," he breathed urgently. "Gather the Lords. There must be a Council."

Quaan smiled. "Times change, Rockbrother. The newest Lord, Mhoram son of Variol, is a seer and oracle. Ten days ago he sent riders to the Loresraat, and to High Lord Prothall in the north. All will be at the Keep tonight."

"That is well," the Giant sighed. "These are shadowed times. Terrible purposes are abroad."

"So we have seen," responded Quaan grimly. "But

Saltheart Foamfollower has hastened enough. I will send the fame of your brave journey ahead to the Keep. They will provide a litter to bear you, if you desire it."

Foamfollower shook his head, and Quaan vaulted up to the pier to give orders to one of his Eoman. The Giant looked at Covenant and smiled faintly. "Stone and Sea, my friend," he said, "did I not say that I would bring you here swiftly?"

That smile touched Covenant's heart like a clasp of affection. Thickly, he replied, "Next time take it easier. I can't stand—watching— Do you always keep promises—this way?"

"Your messages are urgent. How could I do otherwise?"

From his leper's perspective, Covenant countered, "Nothing's *that* urgent. What good does anything do you if you kill yourself in the process?"

For a moment, Foamfollower did not respond. He braced a heavy hand on Covenant's shoulder, and heaved himself, tottering, to his feet. Then he said as if he were answering Covenant's question, "Come. We must see Revelstone."

Willing hands helped him onto the pier, and shortly he was standing on the shore of the lake. Despite the toll of his exertion, he dwarfed even the men and women on horseback. And as Covenant joined him, he introduced his passenger with a gesture like an according of dominion. "Eoman of the Warward, this is my friend, Thomas Covenant, Unbeliever and message-bearer to the Council of Lords. He partakes of many strange knowledges, but he does not know the Land. Ward him well, for the sake of friendship, and for the semblance which he bears of Berek Heartthew, Earthfriend and Lord-Fatherer."

In response, Quaan gave Covenant the salute of welcome. "I offer you the greetings of Lord's Keep, Giant-wrought Revelstone," he said. "Be welcome in the Land—welcome and true."

Covenant returned the gesture brusquely, but did not speak, and a moment later Foamfollower said to

Quaan, "Let us go. My eyes are hungry to behold the great work of my forebearers."

The Warhaft nodded, spoke to his command. At once, two riders galloped away to the east, and two more took positions on either side of the Giant so that he could support himself on the backs of their horses. Another warrior, a young, fair-haired Woodhelvennin woman, offered Covenant a ride behind her. For the first time, he noticed that the saddles of the Eoman were nothing but *clingor,* neither horned nor padded, forming broad seats and tapering on either side into stirrup loops. It would be like riding a blanket glued to both horse and rider. But though Joan had taught him the rudiments of riding, he had never overcome his essential distrust of horses. He refused the offer. He got his staff from the boat and took a place beside one of the horses supporting Foamfollower, and the Eoman started away from the lake with the two travelers.

They passed around one foothill on the south side, and joined the road from the bridge below the lake. Eastward, the road worked almost straight up the side of a traverse ridge. The steepness of the climb made Foamfollower stumble several times, and he was barely strong enough to catch himself on the horses. But when he had labored up the ridge, he stopped, lifted up his head, spread his arms wide, and began to laugh. "There, my friend. Does that not answer you?" His voice was weak, but gay with refreshed joy.

Ahead over a few lower hills was Lord's Keep.

The sight caught Covenant by surprise, almost took his breath away. Revelstone was a masterwork. It stood in granite permanence like an enactment of eternity, a timeless achievement formed of mere lasting rock by some pure, supreme Giantish participation in skill.

Covenant agreed that *Revelstone* was too short a name for it.

The eastern end of the plateau was finished by a broad shaft of rock, half as high as the plateau and separate from it except at the base, the first several hundred feet. This shaft had been hollowed into a tower which guarded the sole entrance to the Keep, and circles of windows rose up past the abutments to the fortified crown. But most of Lord's Keep was carved into the mountain gut-rock under the plateau.

A surprising distance from the tower, the entire cliff face had been worked by the old Giants—sheered and crafted into a vertical outer wall for the city, which, Covenant later learned, filled this whole, wedge-shaped promontory of the plateau. The wall was intricately labored—lined and coigned and serried with regular and irregular groups of windows, balconies, buttresses—orieled and parapeted—wrought in a prolific and seemingly spontaneous multitude of details which appeared to be on the verge of crystallizing into a pattern. But light flashed and danced on the polished cliff face, and the wealth of variation in the work overwhelmed Covenant's senses, so that he could not grasp whatever pattern might be there.

But with his new eyes he could see the thick, bustling, communal life of the city. It shone from behind the wall as if the rock were almost translucent, almost lit from within like a chiaroscuro by the life-force of its thousands of inhabitants. The sight made the whole Keep swirl before him. Though he looked at it from a distance, and could encompass it all— Furl Falls roaring on one side and the expanse of the plains reclining on the other—he felt that the old Giants had outdone him. Here was a work worthy of pilgrimages, ordeals. He was not surprised to hear Foamfollower whisper like a vestal, "Ah, Revelstone! Lord's Keep! Here the Unhomed surpass their loss."

The Eoman responded in litany:

> Giant-troth Revelstone, ancient ward—
> Heart and door of Earthfriend's main:
> Preserve the true with Power's sword,
> Thou ages-Keeper, mountain-reign!

Then the riders started forward again. Foamfollower and Covenant moved in wonder toward the looming walls, and the distance passed swiftly, unmarked except by the beat of their uplifted hearts.

The road ran parallel to the cliff to its eastern edge, then turned up toward the tall doors in the southeast base of the tower. The gates—a mighty slab of rock on either side—were open in the free welcome of peace; but they were notched and beveled and balanced so that they could swing shut and interlock, closing like teeth. The entrance they guarded was large enough for the whole Eoman to ride in abreast.

As they approached the gates, Covenant saw a blue flag flying high on the crown of the tower—an azure oriflamme only a shade lighter than the clear sky. Beneath it was a smaller flag, a red-pennant the color of the bloody moon and Drool's eyes. Seeing the direction of Covenant's gaze, the woman near him said, "Do you know the colors? The blue is High Lord's Furl, the standard of the Lords. It signifies their Oath and guidance to the peoples of the Land. And the red is the sign of our present peril. It will fly there while the danger lasts."

Covenant nodded without taking his eyes off the Keep. But after a moment he looked away from the flags down toward the entrance to Revelstone. The opening looked like a cave that plunged straight into the mountain, but he could see sunlight beyond it.

Three sentries stood in an abutment over the gates. Their appearance caught Covenant's attention; they did not resemble the riders of the Warward. They were like Stonedownors in size and build, but they were flat-faced and brown-skinned, with curly hair cropped short. They wore short ocher tunics belted in blue that appeared to be made of vellum, and their lower legs and feet were bare. Simply standing casual and unarmed on the abutment, they bore themselves with an almost feline balance and alertness; they seemed ready to do battle at an instant's notice.

When his Eoman was within call of the gate, Quaan shouted to the sentries, "Hail! First Mark Tuvor! How is it that the Bloodguard have become guest welcomers?"

The foremost of the sentries responded in a voice that sounded foreign, awkward, as if the speaker were accustomed to a language utterly unlike the speech of the Land. "Giants and message-bearers have come together to the Keep."

"Well, Bloodguard," Quaan returned in a tone of camaraderie, "learn your duties. The Giant is Saltheart Foamfollower, legate from Seareach to the Council of Lords. And the man, the message-bearer, is Thomas Covenant, Unbeliever and stranger to the Land. Are their places ready?"

"The orders are given. Bannor and Korik await."

Quaan waved in acknowledgment. With his warriors, he rode into the stone throat of Lord's Keep.

THIRTEEN: Vespers

As he stepped between the balanced jaws, Covenant gripped his staff tightly in his left hand. The entrance was like a tunnel leading under the tower to an open courtyard between the tower and the main Keep, and it was lit only by the dim, reflected sunlight from either end. There were no doors or windows in the stone. The only openings were dark shafts directly overhead, which appeared to serve some function in Revelstone's defenses. The hooves of the horses struck echoes off the smooth stone, filling the tunnel like a rumor of war, and even the light click of Covenant's staff pranced about him as if shadows of himself were walking one hesitation step behind him down the Keep's throat.

Then the Eoman entered the sunlit courtyard. Here the native stone had been hollowed down to the level of the entrance so that a space nearly as wide as the tower stood open to the sky between high sheer walls.

The court was flat and flagged, but in its center was a broad plot of soil out of which grew one old Gilden, and a small fountain sparkled on either side of the hoary tree. Beyond were more stone gates like those in the base of the tower, and they also were open. That was the only ground-level entrance to the Keep, but at intervals above the court, wooden crosswalks spanned the open space from the tower to crenellated coigns on the inner face of the Keep. In addition, two doors on either side of the tunnel provided access to the tower.

Covenant glanced up the main Keep. Shadows lay within the south and east walls of the court, but the heights still gleamed in the full shine of the afternoon sun, and from his angle, Revelstone seemed tall enough to provide a foundation for the heavens. For a moment as he gazed, his awe made him wish that he were, like Foamfollower, an inheritor of Lord's Keep —that he could in some way claim its grandeur for himself. He wanted to belong here. But as Revelstone's initial impact on him passed, he began to resist the desire. It was just another seduction, and he had already lost too much of his fragile, necessary independence. He shut down his awe with a hard frown, pressed his hand against his ring. The fact that it was hidden steadied him.

There lay the only hope that he could imagine, the only solution to his paradoxical dilemma. As long as he kept his ring secret, he could deliver his message to the Lords, satisfy his exigent need to keep moving, and still avoid dangerous expectations, demands of power that he could not meet. Foamfollower—and Atiaran, too, perhaps involuntarily—had given him a certain freedom of choice. Now he might be able to preserve himself—if he could avoid further seductions, and if the Giant did not reveal his secret.

"Foamfollower," he began, then stopped. Two men were approaching him and the Giant from the main Keep. They resembled the sentries. Their flat, unreadable faces showed no signs of youth or age, as if their relationship with time was somehow ambivalent; and they conveyed such an impression of solidity to

Covenant's eyes that he was distracted from the
Giant. They moved evenly across the courtyard as if
they were personified rock. One of them greeted
Foamfollower, and the other strode toward Covenant.

When he reached Covenant, he bowed fractionally
and said, "I am Bannor of the Bloodguard. You are
in my charge. I will guide you to the place prepared."
His voice was awkward, as if his tongue could not relax in the language of the Land, but through his tone
Covenant heard a stiffness that sounded like distrust.

It and the Bloodguard's hard, imposing aura made
him abruptly uneasy. He looked toward Foamfollower,
saw him give the other Bloodguard a salute full of
respect and old comradeship. "Hail, Korik!" Foamfollower said. "To the Bloodguard I bring honor and
fealty from the Giants of Seareach. These are conse-
quential times, and in them we are proud to name
the Bloodguard among our friends."

Flatly, Korik responded, "We are the Bloodguard.
Your chambers have been made ready, so that you
may rest. Come."

Foamfollower smiled. "That is well. My friend, I
am very weary." With Korik, he walked toward the
gates.

Covenant started after them, but Bannor barred his
way with one strong arm. "You will accompany me,"
the Bloodguard said without inflection.

"Foamfollower!" Covenant called uncertainly.
"Foamfollower! Wait for me."

Over his shoulder, the Giant replied, "Go with
Bannor. Be at Peace." He seemed to have no awareness of Covenant's misapprehension; his tone expressed only grateful relief, as if rest and Revelstone
were his only thoughts. "We will meet again—tomorrow." Moving as if he trusted the Bloodguard
implicitly, he went with Korik into the main Keep.

"Your place is in the tower," Bannor said.

"In the tower? Why?"

The Bloodguard shrugged. "If you question this, you
will be answered. But now you must accompany
me."

For a moment, Covenant met Bannor's level eyes, and read there the Bloodguard's competence, his ability and willingness to enforce his commands. The sight sharpened Covenant's anxiety still further. Even the eyes of Soranal and Baradakas when they had first captured him, thinking him a Raver, had not held such a calm and committed promise of coercion, violence. The Woodhelvennin had been harsh because of their habitual gentleness, but Bannor's gaze gave no hint of any Oath of Peace. Daunted, Covenant looked away. When Bannor started toward one of the tower doors, he followed in uncertainty and trepidation.

The door opened as they approached, and closed behind them, though Covenant could not see who or what moved it. It gave into an open-centered, spiral stairwell, up which Bannor climbed steadily until after a hundred feet or more he reached another door. Beyond it, Covenant found himself in a jumbled maze of passageways, stairs, doors that soon confused his sense of direction completely. Bannor led him this way and that at irregular intervals, up and down unmeasured flights of steps, along broad and then narrow corridors, until he feared that he would not be able to make his way out again without a guide. From time to time, he caught glimpses of other people, primarily Bloodguard and warriors, but he did not encounter any of them. At last, however, Bannor stopped in the middle of what appeared to be a blank corridor. With a short gesture, he opened a hidden door. Covenant followed him into a large living chamber with a balcony beyond it.

Bannor waited while Covenant gave the room a brief look, then said, "Call if there is anything you require," and left, pulling the door shut behind him.

For a moment, Covenant continued to glance around him; he took a mental inventory of the furnishings so that he would know where all the dangerous corners, projections, edges were. The room contained a bed, a bath, a table arrayed with food, chairs—one of which was draped with a variety of apparel—and an arras on one wall. But none of these presented any urgent threat, and shortly his gaze returned to the door.

It had no handle, knob, latch, draw-line—no means by which he could open it.

What the hell—?

He shoved at it with his shoulder, tried to grip it by the edges and pull; he could not budge the heavy stone.

"Bannor!" With a wrench, his mounting fear turned to anger. "Bloody damnation! Bannor. Open this door!"

Almost immediately, the stone swung inward. Bannor stood impassively in the doorway. His flat eyes were expressionless.

"I can't open the door," Covenant snapped. "What is this? Some kind of prison?"

Bannor's shoulders lifted fractionally. "Call it what you choose. You must remain here until the Lords are prepared to send for you."

" 'Until the Lords are prepared.' What am I supposed to do in the meantime? Just sit here and *think?*"

"Eat. Rest. Do whatever you will."

"I'll tell you what I will. I will not stay here and go crazy waiting for the good pleasure of those Lords of yours. I came here all the way from Kevin's Watch to talk to them. I risked my—" With an effort, he caught himself. He could see that his fuming made no impression on the Bloodguard. He gripped his anger with both hands, and said stiffly, "Why am I a prisoner?"

"Message-bearers may be friends or foes," Bannor replied. "Perhaps you are a servant of Corruption. The safety of the Lords is in our care. The Bloodguard will not permit you to endanger them. We will be sure of you before we allow you to move freely."

Hellfire! Covenant swore. Just what I need. The room behind him seemed suddenly full of the dark, vulturine thoughts on which he had striven so hard to turn his back. How could he defend against them if he did not keep moving? But he could not bear to stand where he was with all his fears exposed to Bannor's dispassionate scrutiny. He forced himself to turn around. "Tell them I don't like to wait." Trem-

bling, he moved to the table and picked up a stoneware flask of springwine.

When he heard the door close, he took a long draft
like a gesture of defiance. Then, with his teeth
clenched on the fine beery flavor of the springwine,
he looked around the room again, glared about him
as if he were daring dark specters to come out of
hiding and attack.

This time, the arras caught his attention. It was
a thick, varicolored weaving, dominated by stark reds
and sky blues, and after a moment's incomprehension
he realized that it depicted the legend of Berek Halfhand.

Prominent in the center stood the figure of Berek in
a stylized stance which combined striving and beatitude. And around this foreground were worked scenes
encapsulating the Lord-Fatherer's history—his pure
loyalty to his Queen, the King's greedy pursuit of
power, the Queen's repudiation of her husband,
Berek's exertions in the war, the cleaving of his hand,
his despair on Mount Thunder, the victory of the
Fire-Lions. The effect of the whole was one of salva-
tion, of redemption purchased on the very brink of
ruin by rectitude—as if the Earth itself had intervened, could be trusted to intervene, to right the moral
imbalance of the war.

Oh, bloody hell! Covenant groaned. Do I have to
put up with this?

Clutching the stoneware flask as if it were the only
solid thing in the room, he went toward the balcony.

He stopped in the entryway, braced himself against
the stone. Beyond the railing of the balcony was a fall
of three or four hundred feet to the foothills. He did
not dare step out to the railing; already a premonition
of giddiness gnawed like nausea in his guts. But he
made himself look outward long enough to identify
his surroundings.

The balcony was in the eastern face of the tower,
overlooking a broad reach of plains. The late afternoon sun cast the shadow of the promontory eastward
like an aegis, and in the subdued light beyond the
shadow the plains appeared various and colorful.

Bluish grasslands and plowed brown fields and new-green crops intervaled each other into the distance, and between them sun-silvered threads of streams ran east and south; the clustered spots of villages spread a frail web of habitation over the fields; purple heather and gray bracken lay in broadening swaths toward the north. To his right, Covenant could see far away the White River winding in the direction of Trothgard.

The sight reminded him of how he had come to this place—of Foamfollower, Atiaran, Wraiths, Baradakas, a murdered Waynhim— A vertigo of memories gyred up out of the foothills at him. Atiaran had blamed him for the slaughter of the Wraiths. And yet she had forsworn her own just desire for retribution, her just rage. He had done her so much harm—

He recoiled back into the chamber, stumbled to sit down at the table. His hands shook so badly that he could not drink from the flask. He set it down, clenched both fists, and pressed his knuckles against the hard ring hidden over his heart.

I will not think about it.

A scowl like a contortion of the skull gripped his forehead.

I am not Berek.

He locked himself there until the sound of dangerous wings began to recede, and the giddy pain in his stomach eased. Then he unclawed his stiff fingers. Ignoring their impossible sensitivity, he started to eat.

On the table he found a variety of cold meats, cheeses, and fruits, with plenty of brown bread. He ate deliberately, woodenly, like a puppet acting out the commands of his will, until he was no longer hungry. Then he stripped off his clothes and bathed, scrubbing himself thoroughly and scrutinizing his body to be sure he had no hidden wounds. He sorted through the clothing provided for him, finally donned a pale blue robe which he could tie closed securely to conceal his ring. Using Atiaran's knife, he shaved meticulously. Then, with the same wooden deliberateness, he washed his own clothes in the bath and hung them on

chair backs to dry. All the time, his thoughts ran to
the rhythm of,

I will not—

I am not—

While he worked, evening drifted westward over
Revelstone, and when he was done he set a chair in
the entrance to the balcony so that he could sit and
watch the twilight without confronting the height of
his perch. But darkness appeared to spread outward
from the unlit room behind him into the wide world,
as if his chamber were the source of night. Before
long, the empty space at his back seemed to throng
with carrion eaters.

He felt in the depths of his heart that he was becoming frantic to escape this dream.

The knock at his door jolted him, but he yanked
his way through the darkness to answer it. "Come—
come in." In momentary confusion, he groped for a
handle which was not there. Then the door opened to
a brightness that dazzled him.

At first, all he could see were three figures, one
back against the wall of the outer corridor and two
directly in the doorway. One of them held a flaming
wooden rod in either hand, and the other had each
arm wrapped around a pot of graveling. The dazzle
made them appear to loom toward him out of a penumbra, and he stepped back, blinking rapidly.

As if his retreat were a welcome, the two men entered his room. From behind them a voice curiously
rough and gentle said, "May we come in? I am Lord
Mhoram—"

"Of course," the taller of the two men interrupted
in a voice veined and knuckled with old age. "He requires light, does he not? Darkness withers the heart.
How can he receive light if we do not come in? Now
if he knew anything, he could fend for himself. Of
course. And he will not see much of us. Too busy.
There is yet Vespers to attend to. The High Lord may
have special instructions. We are late as it is. Because
he knows nothing. Of course. But we are swift. Darkness withers the heart. Pay attention, young man. We

cannot afford to return merely to redeem your ignorance."

While the man spoke, jerking the words like lazy servants up off the floor of his chest, Covenant's eyes cleared. Before him, the taller man resolved into an erect but ancient figure, with a narrow face and a beard that hung like a tattered flag almost to his waist. He wore a Woodhelvennin cloak bordered in blue, and a circlet of leaves about his head.

His immediate companion appeared hardly older than a boy. The youth was clad in a brown Stonedownor tunic with blue woven like epaulets into the shoulders, and he had a clean, merry face. He was grinning at the old man in amusement and affection.

As Covenant studied the pair, the man behind them said admonishingly, "He is a guest, Birinair." The old man paused as if he were remembering his manners, and Covenant looked past him at Lord Mhoram. The Lord was a lean man about Covenant's height. He wore a long robe the color of High Lord's Furl, with a pitch-black sash, and held a long staff in his right hand.

Then the old man cleared his throat. "Ah, very well," he fussed. "But this uses time, and we are late. There is Vespers to be made ready. Preparations for the Council. Of course. You are a guest. Be welcome. I am Birinair, Hirebrand of the *lillianrill* and Hearthrall of Lord's Keep. This grinning whelp is Tohrm, Gravelingas of the *rhadhamaerl* and likewise Hearthrall of Lord's Keep. Now harken. Attend." In high dignity, he moved toward the bed. Above it in the wall was a torch socket. Birinair said, "These are made for ignorant young men like yourself," and set the burning end of one rod in the socket. The flame died; but when he removed the rod, its fire returned almost at once. He placed the unlit end in the socket, then moved across the chamber to fix his other rod in the opposite wall.

While the Hirebrand was busy, Tohrm set one of his graveling pots down on the table and the other on the stand by the washbasin. "Cover them when you wish to sleep," he said in a light voice.

When he was done, Birinair said, "Darkness withers the heart. Beware of it, guest."

"But courtesy is like a drink at a mountain stream," murmured Tohrm, grinning as if at a secret joke.

"It is so." Birinair turned and left the room. Tohrm paused to wink at Covenant and whisper, "He is not as hard a taskmaster as you might think." Then he, too, was gone, leaving Covenant alone with Lord Mhoram.

Mhoram closed the door behind him, and Covenant got his first good look at one of the Lords. Mhoram had a crooked, humane mouth, and a fond smile for the Hearthralls lingered on his lips. But the effect of the smile was counterbalanced by his eyes. They were dangerous eyes—gray-blue irises flecked with gold—that seemed to pierce through subterfuge to the secret marrow of premeditation in what they beheld—eyes that seemed themselves to conceal something potent and unknown, as if Mhoram were capable of surprising fate itself if he were driven to his last throw. And between his perilous eyes and kind mouth, the square blade of his nose mediated like a rudder, steering his thoughts.

Then Covenant noticed Mhoram's staff. It was metal-shod like the Staff of Law, which he had glimpsed in Drool's spatulate fingers, but it was innocent of the carving that articulated the Staff. Mhoram held it in his left hand while he gave Covenant the salute of welcome with his right. Then he folded his arms on his chest, holding the staff in the crook of his elbow.

His lips twisted through a combination of amusement, diffidence, and watchfulness as he spoke. "Let me begin anew. I am Lord Mhoram son of Variol. Be welcome in Revelstone, Thomas Covenant, Unbeliever and message-bearer. Birinair is Hearthrall and chief *lillianrill* of Lord's Keep—but nevertheless there is time before Vespers. So I have come for several reasons. First to bid you welcome, second to answer the questions of a stranger in the Land—and last to inquire after the purpose which brings you to the

Council. Pardon me if I seem formal. You are a stranger, and I know not how to honor you."

Covenant wanted to respond. But he still felt confused by darkness; he needed time to clear his head. He blinked at the Lord for a moment, then said to fill the silence, "That Bloodguard of yours doesn't trust me."

Mhoram smiled wryly. "Bannor told me that you believe you have been emprisoned. That is also why I determined to speak with you this evening. It is not our custom to examine guests before they have rested. But I must say a word or two concerning the Bloodguard. Shall we be seated?" He took a chair for himself, sitting with his staff across his knees as naturally as if it were a part of him.

Covenant sat down by the table without taking his eyes off Mhoram. When he was settled, the Lord continued: "Thomas Covenant, I tell you openly—I assume that you are a friend—or at least not an enemy —until you are proven. You are a guest, and should be shown courtesy. And we have sworn the Oath of Peace. But you are as strange to us as we to you. And the Bloodguard have spoken a Vow which is not in any way like our Oath. They have sworn to serve the Lords and Revelstone—to preserve us against any threat by the strength of their fidelity." He sighed distantly. "Ah, it is humbling to be so served—in defiance of time and death. But let that pass. I must tell you two things. Left to the dictates of their Vow, the Bloodguard would slay you instantly if you raised your hand against any Lord—yes, against any inhabitant of Revelstone. But the Council of Lords has commanded you to their care. Rather than break that command—rather than permit any harm to befall you —Bannor or any Bloodguard would lay down his life in your defense."

When Covenant's face reflected his doubt, the Lord said, "I assure you. Perhaps it would be well for you to question Bannor concerning the Bloodguard. His distrust may not distress you—when you have come to understand it. His people are the *Haruchai,* who live high in the Westron Mountains beyond the passes which we now name Guards Gap. In the first years of Kevin Loric-son's High Lordship they came to the Land—came, and remained to make a Vow like that swearing which binds even the gods." For a moment, he seemed lost in contemplation of the Bloodguard. "They were a hot-blooded people, strong-loined and prolific, bred to tempest and battle—and now made by their pledged loyalty ascetic, womanless and old. I tell you, Thomas Covenant—their devotion has had such unforeseen prices— Such one-mindedness does not come easily to them, and their only reward is the pride of unbroken, pure service. And then to learn the bitterness of doubt—" Mhoram sighed again, then smiled diffidently. "Inquire of Bannor. I am too young to tell the tale aright."

Too young? Covenant wondered. How old are they? But he did not ask the question; he feared that the story Mhoram could tell would be as seductive as Foamfollower's tale of the Unhomed. After a moment, he pulled the loose ends of his attention together, and said, "I've got to talk to the Council."

Mhoram's gaze met him squarely. "The Lords will meet tomorrow to hear both you and Saltheart Foamfollower. Do you wish to speak now?" The Lord's gold-flecked eyes seemed to flame with concentration. Unexpectedly, he asked, "Are you an enemy, Unbeliever?"

Covenant winced inwardly. He could feel Mhoram's scrutiny as if its heat burned his mind. But he was determined to resist. Stiffly, he countered, "You're the seer and oracle. You tell me."

"Did Quaan call me that?" Mhoram's smile was disarming. "Well, I showed prophetic astuteness when I let a mere red moon disquiet me. Perhaps my oracular powers amaze you." Then he set aside his quiet self-deprecation, and repeated intently, "Are you an enemy?"

Covenant returned the Lord's gaze, hoping that his own eyes were hard, uncompromising. I will not— he thought. Am not— "I'm not anything to you by choice. I've got—a message for you. One way or another, I've been pressured into bringing it here. And some things happened along the way that might interest you."

"Tell me," Mhoram said in soft urgency.

But his look reminded Covenant of Baradakas—of Atiaran—of the times they had said, *You are closed*— He could see Mhoram's health, his dangerous courage, his vital love for the Land. "People keep asking me that," he murmured. "Can't you tell?"

An instant later, he answered himself, Of course not. What do they know about leprosy? Then he grasped the reason behind Mhoram's question. The Lord wanted to hear him talk, wanted his voice to reveal his truth or falsehood. Mhoram's ears could discern the honesty or irrectitude of the answer.

Covenant glanced at the memory of Foul's message, then turned away in self-defense. "No—I'll save it for the Council. Once is enough for such things. My tongue'll turn to sand if I have to say it twice."

Mhoram nodded as if in acceptance. But almost immediately he asked, "Does your message account for the befouling of the moon?"

Instinctively, Covenant looked out over his balcony.

There, sailing tortuously over the horizon like a plague ship, was the bloodstained moon. Its glow rode the plains like an incarnadine phantasm. He could not keep the shudder out of his voice as he replied. "He's showing off—that's all. Just showing us what he can do." Deep in his throat, he cried, Hellfire! Foul! The Wraiths were helpless! What do you do for an encore, rape children?

"Ah," Lord Mhoram groaned, "this comes at a bad time." He stepped away from his seat and pulled a wooden partition shut across the entrance to the balcony. "The Warward numbers less than two thousand. The Bloodguard are only five hundred—a pittance for any task but the defense of Revelstone. And there are only five Lords. Of those, two are old, at the limit of their strength, and none have mastered more than the smallest part of Kevin's First Ward. We are weaker than any other Earthfriends in all the ages of the Land. Together we can hardly make scrub grass grow in Kurash Plenethor.

"There have been more," he explained, returning to his seat, "but in the last generation nearly all the best at the Loresraat have chosen the Rites of Unfettering. I am the first to pass the tests in fifteen years. Alas, it is in my heart that we will want other power now." He clenched his staff until his knuckles whitened, and for a moment his eyes did not conceal his sense of need.

Gruffly, Covenant said, "Then tell your friends to brace themselves. You're not going to like what I've got to say."

But Mhoram relaxed slowly, as if he had not heard Covenant's warning. One finger at a time, he released his grip until the staff lay untouched in his lap. Then he smiled softly. "Thomas Covenant, I am not altogether reasonless when I assume that you are not an enemy. You have a *lillianrill* staff and a *rhadhamaerl* knife—yes, and the staff has seen struggle against a strong foe. And I have already spoken with Saltheart Foamfollower. You have been trusted by others. I do not think you would have won your way here without trust."

"Hellfire!" retorted Covenant. "You've got it backward." He threw his words like stones at a false image of himself. "They coerced me into coming. It wasn't my idea. I haven't had a choice since this thing started." With his fingers he touched his chest to remind himself of the one choice he did have.

"Unwilling," Mhoram replied gently. "So there is good reason for calling you 'Unbeliever.' Well, let it pass. We will hear your tale at the Council tomorrow.

"Now. I fear I have given your questions little opportunity. But the time for Vespers has come. Will you accompany me? If you wish we will speak along the way."

Covenant nodded at once. In spite of his weariness, he was eager for a chance to be active, keep his thoughts busy. The discomfort of being interrogated was only a little less than the distress of the questions he wanted to ask about white gold. To escape his

complicated vulnerabilities, he stood up and said,
"Lead the way."

The Lord bowed in acknowledgment, and at once
preceded Covenant into the corridor outside his room.
There they found Bannor. He stood against the wall
near the door with his arms folded stolidly across his
chest, but he moved to join them as Mhoram and
Covenant entered the passageway. On an impulse,
Covenant intercepted him. He met Bannor's gaze,
touched the Bloodguard's chest with one rigid finger,
and said, "I don't trust you either." Then he turned
in angry satisfaction back to the Lord.

Mhoram paused while Bannor went into Covenant's
room to pick up one of the torches. Then the Bloodguard took a position a step behind Covenant's left
shoulder, and Lord Mhoram led them down the corridor. Soon Covenant was lost again; the complexities
of the tower confused him as quickly as a maze. But
in a short time they reached a hall which seemed to
end in a dead wall of stone. Mhoram touched the
stone with an end of his staff, and it swung inward,
opening over the courtyard between the tower and
the main Keep. From this doorway, a crosswalk
stretched over to a buttressed coign.

Covenant took one look at the yawning gulf of the
courtyard, and backed away. "No," he muttered,
"forget it. I'll just stay here if you don't mind." Blood
rushed like shame into his face, and a rivulet of sweat
ran coldly down his back. "I'm no good at heights."

The Lord regarded him curiously for a moment,
but did not challenge his reaction. "Very well," he
said simply. "We will go another way."

Sweating half in relief, Covenant followed as
Mhoram retraced part of their way, then led a complex descent to one of the doors at the base of the
tower. There they crossed the courtyard.

Then for the first time Covenant was in the main
body of Revelstone.

Around him, the Keep was brightly lit with torches
and graveling. Its walls were high and broad enough
for Giants, and their spaciousness contrasted strongly
with the convolution of the tower. In the presence of

so much wrought, grand and magisterial granite, such
a weight of mountain rock spanning such open, illuminated halls, he felt acutely his own meagerness, his
mere frail mortality. Once again, he sensed that the
makers of Revelstone had surpassed him.

But Mhoram and Bannor did not appear meager to
him. The Lord strode forward as if these halls were
his natural element, as if his humble flesh flourished
in the service of this old grandeur. And Bannor's
personal solidity seemed to increase, as if he bore
within him something that almost equaled Revelstone's
permanence. Between them, Covenant felt half dis-
incarnate, void of some essential actuality.

A snarl jumped across his teeth, and his shoulders
hunched as he strangled such thoughts. With a grim
effort, he forced himself to concentrate on the superficial details around him.

They turned down a hallway which went straight
but for gradual undulations, as if it were carved to suit
the grain of the rock—into the heart of the mountain.
From it, connecting corridors branched out at various
intervals, some cutting directly across between cliff and
cliff, and some only joining the central hall with
the outer passages. Through these corridors, a steadily growing number of men and women entered the
central hall, all, Covenant guessed, going toward
Vespers. Some wore the breastplates and headbands
of warriors; others, Woodhelvennin and Stonedownor
garb with which Covenant was familiar. Several
struck him as being related in some way to the
lillianrill or *rhadhamaerl;* but many more seemed to
belong to the more prosaic occupations of running a
city—cooking, cleaning, building, repairing, harvest-
ing. Scattered through the crowd were a few Bloodguard. Many of the people nodded and beamed
respectfully at Lord Mhoram, and he returned saluta-
tions in all directions, often hailing his greeters by
name. But behind him, Bannor carried the torch and
walked as inflexibly as if he were alone in the Keep.

As the throng thickened, Mhoram moved toward
the wall on one side, then stopped at a door. Opening
it, he turned to Bannor and said, "I must join the

High Lord. Take Thomas Covenant to a place among
the people in the sacred enclosure." To Covenant, he
added, "Bannor will bring you to the Close at the
proper time tomorrow." With a salute, he left Covenant with the Bloodguard.

Now Bannor led Covenant ahead through Revelstone. After some distance, the hall ended, split at
right angles to arc left and right around a wide wall,
and into this girdling corridor the people poured from
all directions. Doors large enough to admit Giants
marked the curved wall at regular intervals; through
them the people passed briskly, but without confusion
or jostling.

On either side of each door stood a Gravelingas
and a Hirebrand; and as Covenant neared one of the
doors, he heard the door wardens intoning, "If there
is ill in your heart, leave it here. There is no room for
it within." Occasionally one of the people reached out
and touched a warder as if handing over a burden.

When he reached the door, Bannor gave his torch
to the Hirebrand. The Hirebrand quenched it by humming a snatch of song and closing his hand over the
flame. Then he returned the rod to Bannor, and
the Bloodguard entered the enclosure with Covenant
behind him.

Covenant found himself on a balcony circling the
inside of an enormous cavity. It held no lights, but
illumination streamed into it from all the open doors,
and there were six more balconies above the one on
which Covenant stood, all accessed by many open
doors. He could see clearly. The balconies stood in vertical tiers, and below them, more than a hundred feet
down, was the flat bottom of the cavity. A dais occupied one side, but the rest of the bottom was full of
people. The balconies also were full, but relatively
uncrowded; everyone had a full view of the dais below.

Sudden dizziness beat out of the air at Covenant's
head. He clutched at the chest-high railing, braced
his laboring heart against it. Revelstone seemed full
of vertigoes; everywhere he went, he had to contend
with cliffs, gulfs, abysms. But the rail was reassuring

granite. Hugging it, he fought down his fear, looked up to take his eyes away from the enclosure bottom.

He was dimly surprised to find that the cavity was not open to the sky; it ended in a vaulted dome several hundred feet above the highest balcony. The details of the ceiling were obscure, but he thought he could make out figures carved in the stone, giant forms vaguely dancing.

Then the light began to fail. One by one, the doors were being shut; as they closed, darkness filled the cavity like re-created night. Soon the enclosure was sealed free of light, and into the void the soft moving noises and breathing of the people spread like a restless spirit. The blackness seemed to isolate Covenant. He felt as anchorless as if he had been cast adrift in deep space, and the massive stone of the Keep impended over him as if its sheer brute tonnage bore personally on the back of his neck. Involuntarily, he leaned toward Bannor, touched the solid Bloodguard with his shoulder.

Then a flame flared up on the dais—two flames, a *lillianrill* torch and a pot of graveling. Their lights were tiny in the huge cavity, but they revealed Birinair and Tohrm standing on either side of the dais, holding their respective fires. Behind each Hearthrall were two blue-robed figures—Lord Mhoram with an ancient woman on his arm behind Birinair, and a woman and an old man behind Tohrm. And between these two groups stood another man robed in blue. His erect carriage denied the age of his white hair and beard. Intuitively, Covenant guessed, That's him—High Lord Prothall.

The man raised his staff and struck its metal three times on the stone dais. He held his head high as he spoke, but his voice remembered that he was old. In spite of bold carriage and upright spirit, there was a rheumy ache of age in his tone as he said, "This is the Vespers of Lord's Keep—ancient Revelstone, Giant-wrought bourne of all that we believe. Be welcome, strong heart and weak, light and dark, blood and bone and thew and mind and soul, for good and all. Set Peace about you and within you. This time is consecrate to the services of the Earth."

His companions responded, "Let there be healing and hope, heart and home, for the Land, and for all people in the services of the Earth—for you before us, you direct participants in Earthpower and Lore, *lillianrill* and *rhadhamaerl*, learners, Lorewardens, and warriors—and for you above us, you people and daily carers of the hearth and harvest of life—and for you among us, you Giants, Bloodguard, strangers—and for you absent Ranyhyn and Ramen and Stone-downors and Woodhelvennin, all brothers and sisters of the common troth. We are the Lords of the Land. Be welcome and true."

Then the Lords sang into the darkness of the sacred enclosure. The Hearthrall fires were small in the huge, high, thronged sanctuary—small, and yet for all their smallness distinct, cynosural, like uncorrupt courage. And in that light the Lords sang their hymn.

Seven Wards of ancient Lore
For Land's protection, wall and door:
And one High Lord to wield the Law
To keep all uncorrupt Earth's Power's core.

Seven Words for ill's despite—
Banes for evil's dooming wight:
And one pure Lord to hold the Staff
To bar the Land from Foul's betraying sight.

Seven hells for failed faith,
For Land's betrayers, man and wraith:
And one brave Lord to deal the doom
To keep the blacking blight from Beauty's bloom.

As the echo of their voices faded, High Lord Prothall spoke again. "We are the new preservers of the Land—votaries and handservants of the Earth-power; sworn and dedicated to the retrieval of Kevin's Lore, and to the healing of the Earth from all that is barren or unnatural, ravaged, foundationless, or per-verse. And sworn and dedicated as well, in equal bal-

ance with all other consecrations and promises—
sworn despite any urging of the importunate self—to
the Oath of Peace. For serenity is the only promise
we can give that we will not desecrate the Land
again."

The people standing before the dais replied in unison, "We will not redesecrate the Land, though the
effort of self-mastery wither us on the vine of our
lives. Nor will we rest until the shadow of our former
folly is lifted from the Land's heart, and the darkness
is whelmed in growth and life."

And Prothall returned, "But there is no withering
in the service of the Land. Service enables service, just
as servility perpetuates debasement. We may go from
knowledge to knowledge, and to still braver knowledge,
if courage holds, and commitment holds, and wisdom
does not fall under the shadow. We are the new
preservers of the Land—votaries and handservants to
the Earthpower.

> For we will not rest—
>   not turn aside,
>   lose faith,
>   or fail—
> until the Gray flows Blue,
> and Rill and Maerl are as new and clean
>   as ancient Llurallin."

To this the entire assembly responded by singing
the same words, line by line, after the High Lord;
and the massed communal voice reverberated in the
sacred enclosure as if his rheumy tone had tapped
some pent, subterranean passion. While the mighty
sound lasted, Prothall bowed his head in humility.

But when it was over, he threw back his head and
flung his arms wide as if baring his breast to a denunciation. "Ah, my friends!" he cried. "Handservants, votaries of the Land—why have we so failed
to comprehend Kevin's Lore? Which of us has in
any way advanced the knowledge of our predecessors?
We hold the First Ward in our hands—we read the
script, and in much we understand the words—and

yet we do not penetrate the secrets. Some failure in
us, some false inflection, some mistaken action, some
base alloy in our intention, prevents. I do not doubt
that our purpose is pure—it is High Lord Kevin's
purpose—and before him Loric's and Damelon's and
Heartthew's—but wiser, for we will never lift our
hands against the Land in mad despair. But what,
then? Where are we wrong, that we cannot grasp
what is given to us?"

For a moment after his voice faltered and fell,
the sanctuary was silent, and the void throbbed like
weeping, as if in his words the people recognized themselves, recognized the failure he described as their own.
But then a new voice arose. Saltheart Foamfollower
said boldly, "My Lord, we have not reached our end.
True, the work of our lifetime has been to comprehend and consolidate the gains of our forebearers.
But our labor will open the doors of the future. Our
children and their children will gain because we have
not lost heart, for faith and courage are the greatest
gift that we can give to our descendants. And the
Land holds mysteries of which we know nothing—
mysteries of hope as well as of peril. Be of good heart,
Rockbrothers. Your faith is precious above all things."

But you don't have time! Covenant groaned. Faith!
Children! Foul is going to destroy you. Within him,
his conception of the Lords whirled, altered. They
were not superior beings, fate-shapers; they were mortals like himself, familiar with impotence. Foul would
reave them—

For an instant, he released the railing as if he
meant to cry out his message of doom to the gathered
people. But at once vertigo broke through his resistance, pounced at him out of the void. Reeling, he
stumbled against the rail, then fell back to clutch at
Bannor's shoulder.

—that the uttermost limit of their span of days
upon the Land—

He would have to read them their death warrant.

"Get me out of here," he breathed hoarsely. "I
can't stand it."

Bannor held him, guided him. Abruptly, a door

opened into the brilliance of the outer corridor. Covenant half fell through the doorway. Without a word, Bannor relit his torch at one of the flaming brands set into the wall. Then he took Covenant's arm to support him.

Covenant threw off his hand. "Don't touch me," he panted inchoately. "Can't you see I'm sick?"

No flicker of expression shaded Bannor's flat countenance. Dispassionately, he turned and led Covenant away from the sacred enclosure.

Covenant followed, bent forward and holding his stomach as if he were nauseated. *—that the uttermost limit—* How could he help them? He could not even help himself. In confusion and heart distress, he shambled back to his room in the tower, stood dumbly in the chamber while Bannor replaced his torch and left, closing the door like a judgment behind him. Then he gripped his temples as if his mind were being torn in two.

None of this is happening, he moaned. How are they doing this to me?

Reeling inwardly, he turned to look at the arras as if it might contain some answer. But it only aggravated his distress, incensed him like a sudden affront. Bloody hell! Berek, he groaned. Do you think it's that easy? Do you think that ordinary human despair is enough, that if you just feel bad enough something cosmic or at least miraculous is bound to come along and rescue you? Damn you! he's going to destroy them! You're just another leper outcast unclean, and you don't even know it!

His fingers curled like feral claws, and he sprang forward, ripping at the arras as if he were trying to rend a black lie off the stone of the world. The heavy fabric refused to tear in his half-unfingered grasp, but he got it down from the wall. Throwing open the balcony, he wrestled the arras out into the crimson-tainted night and heaved it over the railing. It fell like a dead leaf of winter.

I am not Berek!

Panting at his effort, he returned to the room, slammed the partition shut against the bloody light.

He threw off his robe, put on his own underwear, then extinguished the fires and climbed into bed. But the soft, clean touch of the sheets on his skin gave him no consolation.

FOURTEEN: The Council of Lords

HE awoke in a dull haze which felt like the presage of some thunderhead, some black boil and white fire blaring. Mechanically he went through the motions of readying himself for the Council—washed, inspected himself, dressed in his own clothes, shaved again. When Bannor brought him a tray of food, he ate as if the provender were made of dust and gravel. Then he slipped Atiaran's knife into his belt, gripped the staff of Baradakas in his left hand, and sat down facing the door to await the summons.

Finally, Bannor returned to tell him that the time had come. For a few moments, Covenant sat still, holding the Bloodguard in his half-unseeing gaze, and wondering where he could get the courage to go on with this dream. He felt that his face was twisted, but he could not be sure.

—*that the uttermost limit*—

Get it over with.

He touched the hard, hidden metal of his ring to steady himself, then levered his reluctant bones erect. Glaring at the doorway as if it were a threshold into peril, he lumbered through it and started down the corridor. At Bannor's commanding back, he moved out of the tower, across the courtyard, then inward and down through the raveled and curiously wrought passages of Revelstone.

Eventually they came through bright-lit halls deep in the mountain to a pair of arching wooden doors. These were closed, sentried by Bloodguard; and lining both walls were stone chairs, some man-sized and others large enough for Giants. Bannor nodded to the sentries. One of them pulled open a door while the other motioned for Bannor and Covenant to enter. Bannor guided Covenant into the council chamber of the Lords.

The Close was a huge, sunken, circular room with a ceiling high and groined, and tiers of seats set around three-quarters of the space. The door through which Covenant entered was nearly level with the highest seats, as were the only two other doors—both of them small—at the opposite side of the chamber. Below the lowest tier of seats were three levels: on the first, several feet below the gallery, stood a curved stone table, three-quarters round, with its gap toward the large doors and many chairs around its outer edge; below this, contained within the *C* of the table, was the flat floor of the Close; and finally, in the center of the floor, lay a broad, round pit of graveling. The yellow glow of the fire stones was supported by four huge *lillianrill* torches, burning without smoke or consumption in their sockets around the upper wall.

As Bannor took him down the steps toward the open end of the table, Covenant observed the people in the chamber. Saltheart Foamfollower lounged nearby at the table in a massive stone chair; he watched Covenant's progress down the steps and grinned a welcome for his former passenger. Beyond him, the only people at the table were the Lords. Directly opposite Covenant, at the head of the table, sat High Lord Prothall. His staff lay on the stone before him. An ancient man and woman were several feet away on either side of him; an equal distance from the woman on her left was Lord Mhoram; and opposite Mhoram, down the table from the old man, sat a middle-aged woman. Four Bloodguard had positioned themselves behind each of the Lords.

There were only four other people in the Close. Beyond the High Lord near the top of the gallery sat the

Hearthralls, Birinair and Tohrm, side by side as if they complemented each other. And just behind them were two more men, one a warrior with a double black diagonal on his breastplate, and the other Tuvor, First Mark of the Bloodguard. With so few people in it, the Close seemed large, hollow, and cryptic.

Bannor steered Covenant to the lone chair below the level of the Lords' table and across the pit of graveling from the High Lord. Covenant seated himself stiffly and looked around. He felt that he was uncomfortably far from the Lords; he feared he would have to shout his message. So he was surprised when Prothall stood and said softly, "Thomas Covenant, be welcome to the Council of Lords." His rheumy voice reached Covenant as clearly as if they had been standing side by side.

Covenant did not know how to respond; uncertainly, he touched his right fist to his chest, then extended his arm with his palm open and forward. As his senses adjusted to the Close, he began to perceive the presence, the emanating personality and adjudication, of the Lords. They gave him an impression of stern vows gladly kept, of wide-ranging and yet single-minded devotion. Prothall stood alone, meeting Covenant's gaze. The High Lord's appearance of white age was modified by the stiffness of his beard and the erectness of his carriage; clearly, he was strong yet. But his eyes were worn with the experience of an asceticism, an abnegation, carried so far that it seemed to abrogate his flesh—as if he had been old for so long that now only the power to which he devoted himself preserved him from decrepitude.

The two Lords who flanked him were not so preserved. They had dull, age-marked skin and wispy hair; and they bowed at the table as if striving against the antiquity of their bones to distinguish between meditation and sleep. Lord Mhoram Covenant already knew, though now Mhoram appeared more incisive and dangerous, as if the companionship of his fellow Lords whetted his capacities. But the fifth Lord Covenant did not know; she sat squarely and factually at the table, with her blunt, forthright face fixed on him like a defiance.

"Let me make introduction before we begin," the High Lord murmured. "I am Prothall son of Dwillian, High Lord by the choice of the Council. At my right are Variol Tamarantha-mate and Pentil-son, once High Lord"—as he said this, the two ancient Lords raised their time-latticed faces and smiled privately at each other—"and Osondrea daughter of Sondrea. At my left, Tamarantha Variol-mate and Enesta-daughter, and Mhoram son of Variol. You know the Scarcach Giant, Saltheart Foamfollower, and have met the Hearthralls of Lord's Keep. Behind me also are Tuvor, First Mark of the Bloodguard, and Garth, Warmark of the Warward of Lord's Keep. All have the right of presence at the Council of Lords. Do you protest?"

Protest? Covenant shook his head dumbly.

"Then we shall begin. It is our custom to honor those who come before us. How may we honor you?"

Again, Covenant shook his head. *I don't want any honor. I made that mistake once already.*

After an inquiring pause, the High Lord said, "Very well." Turning toward the Giant, he raised his voice. "Hail and welcome, Giant of Seareach, Saltheart Foamfollower, Rockbrother and inheritor of Land's loyalty. The Unhomed are a blessing to the Land.

Stone and Sea are deep in life.

Welcome whole or hurt, in boon or bane—ask or give. To any requiring name we will not fail while we have life or power to meet the need. I am High Lord Prothall; I speak in the presence of Revelstone itself."

Foamfollower stood to return the salutation. "Hail, Lord and Earthfriend. I am Saltheart Foamfollower, legate from the Giants of Seareach to the Council of Lords. The truth of my people is in my mouth, and I hear the approval of the ancient sacred ancestral stone—

raw Earth rock—
pure friendship—
a handmark of allegiance and fealty in the
eternal stone of time.

Now is the time for proof and power of troth. Through
Giant Woods and Sarangrave Flat and Andelain, I
bear the name of the ancient promises." Then some
of the formality dropped from his manner, and he
added with a gay glance at Covenant, "And bearing
other things as well. My friend Thomas Covenant has
promised that a song will be made of my journey."
He laughed gently. "I am a Giant of Seareach. Make
no short songs for me."

His humor drew a chuckle from Lord Mhoram,
and Prothall smiled softly; but Osondrea's dour face
seemed incapable of laughter, and neither Variol nor
Tamarantha appeared to have heard the Giant. Foamfollower took his seat, and almost at once Osondrea
said as if she were impatient, "What is your embassy?"

Foamfollower sat erect in his chair, and his hands
stroked the stone of the table intently. "My Lords—
Stone and Sea! I am a Giant. These matters do not
come easily, though easier to me than to any of my
kindred—and for that reason I was chosen. But I will
endeavor to speak hastily.

"Please understand me. I was given my embassy in
a Giantclave lasting ten days. There was no waste of
time. When comprehension is needed, all tales must
be told in full. Haste is for the hopeless, we say—and
hardly a day has passed since I learned that there is
truth in sayings. So it is that my embassy contains
much that you would not choose to hear at present.
You must know the history of my people—all the sojourn and the loss which brought us ashore here, all
the interactions of our peoples since that age—if you
are to hear me. But I will forgo it. We are the Unhomed, adrift in soul and lessened by an unreplenish-
ing seed. We are hungry for our native land. Yet
since the time of Damelon Giantfriend we have not
surrendered hope, though Soulcrusher himself con-

trives against us. We have searched the seas, and have waited for the omens to come to pass."

Foamfollower paused to look thoughtfully at Covenant, then went on: "Ah, my Lords, omening is curious. So much is said—and so little made clear. It was not Home that Damelon foretold for us, but rather an end, a resolution, to our loss. Yet that sufficed for us—sufficed.

"Well. One hope we have found for ourselves. When spring came to Seareach, our questing ships returned, and told that at the very limit of their search they came upon an isle that borders the ancient oceans on which we once roamed. The matter is not sure, but our next questers can go directly to this isle and look beyond it for surer signs. Thus across the labyrinth of the seas we unamaze ourselves."

Prothall nodded, and through the perfect acoustics of the Close, Covenant could hear the faint rustle of the High Lord's robe.

With an air of nearing the crux of his embassy, Foamfollower continued, "Yet another hope we received from Damelon Giantfriend, High Lord and Heartthew's son. At the heart of his omening was this word: our exile would end when our seed regained its potency, and the decline of our offspring was reversed. Thus hope is born of hope, for without any foretelling we would gain heart and courage from any increase in our rare, beloved children. And behold! On the night that our ships returned, Wavenhair Haleall, wived to Sparlimb Keelsetter, was taken to her bed and delivered—ah, Stone and Sea, my Lords! It cripples my tongue to tell this without its full measure of long Giantish gratitude. How can there be joy for people who say everything briefly? Proud-wife, clean-limbed Wavenhair gave birth to three sons." No longer able to restrain himself, he broke into a chant full of the brave crash of breakers and the tang of salt.

To his surprise, Covenant saw that Lord Osondrea was smiling, and her eyes caught the golden glow of the graveling damply—eloquent witness to the gladness of the Giant's news.

But Foamfollower abruptly stopped himself. With

a gesture toward Covenant, he said, "Your pardon—
you have other matters in your hands. I must bring
myself to the bone of my embassy. Ah, my friend,"
he said to Covenant, "will you still not laugh for
me? I must remember that Damelon promised us an
end, not a return Home—though I cannot envision
any end but Home. It may be that I stand in the
gloaming of the Giants."

"Hush, Rockbrother," Lord Tamarantha interrupted. "Do not make evil for your people by uttering such things."

Foamfollower responded with a hearty laugh. "Ah,
my thanks, Lord Tamarantha. So the wise old Giants
are admonished by young women. My entire people
will laugh when I tell them of this."

Tamarantha and Variol exchanged a smile, and
returned to their semblance of meditation or dozing.

When he was done laughing, the Giant said, "Well,
my Lords. To the bone, then. Stone and Sea! Such
haste makes me giddy. I have come to ask the fulfill-
ment of the ancient offers. High Lord Loric Vilesilencer promised that the Lords would give us a gift
when our hope was ready—a gift to better the chances
of our Homeward way."

"Birinair," said Lord Osondrea.

High in the gallery behind Prothall, old Birinair
stood and replied, "Of course. I am not asleep. Not as
old as I look, you know. I hear you."

With a broad grin, Foamfollower called, "Hail,
Birinair! Hearthrall of Lord's Keep and Hirebrand of
the *lillianrill*. We are old friends, Giants and
lillianrill."

"No need to shout," Birinair returned. "I hear you.
Old friends from the time of High Lord Damelon.
Never otherwise."

"Birinair," Osondrea cut in, "does your lore recall
the gift promised by Loric to the Giants?"

"Gift? Why not? Nothing amiss with my memory.
Where is that whelp my apprentice? Of course. *Lor-
liarill*. Gildenlode, they call it. There. Keels and rudders for ships. True course—never becalmed. And

strong as stone," he said to Tohrm, "you grinning *rhadhamaerl* to the contrary. I remember."

"Can you accomplish this?" Osondrea asked quietly.

"Accomplish?" Birinair echoed, apparently puzzled.

"Can you make Gildenlode keels and rudders for the Giants? Has that lore been lost?" Turning to Foamfollower, Lord Osondrea asked, "How many ships will you need?"

With a glance at Birinair's upright dignity, Foamfollower contained his humor, and replied simply, "Seven. Perhaps five."

"Can this be done?" Osondrea asked Birinair again, distinctly but without irritation. Covenant's blank gaze followed from speaker to speaker as if they were talking in a foreign language.

The Hearthrall pulled a small tablet and stylus from his robe and began to calculate, muttering to himself. The scrape of his stylus could be heard throughout the Close until he raised his head and said stiffly, "The lore remains. But not easily. The best we can do. Of course. And time—it will need time. *Bodach glas,* it will need time."

"How much time?"

"The best we can do. If we are left alone. Not my fault. I did not lose all the proudest lore of the *lillianrill*. Forty years." In a sudden whisper, he added to Foamfollower, "I am sorry."

"Forty years?" Foamfollower laughed gently. "Ah, bravely said, Birinair, my friend. Forty years? That does not seem a long time to me." Turning to High Lord Prothall, he said, "My people cannot thank you. Even in Giantish, there are no words long enough. Three millenia of our loyalty have not been enough to repay seven Gildenlode keels and rudders."

"No," protested Prothall. "Seventy times seven Gildenlode gifts are nothing compared to the great friendship of the Seareach Giants. Only the thought that we have aided your return Home can fill the emptiness your departure will leave. And our help is forty years distant. But we will begin at once, and it may be that some new understanding of Kevin's Lore will shorten the time."

Echoing, "At once," Birinair reseated himself.

Forty years? Covenant breathed. You don't have forty years.

Then Osondrea said, "Done?" She looked first at Foamfollower, then at High Lord Prothall. When they both nodded to her, she turned on Covenant and said, "Then let us get to the matter of this Thomas Covenant." Her voice seemed to whet the atmosphere like a distant thunderclap.

Smiling to ameliorate Osondrea's forthrightness, Mhoram said, "A stranger called the Unbeliever."

"And for good reason," Foamfollower added.

The Giant's words rang an alarm in Covenant's clouded trepidations, and he looked sharply at Foamfollower. In the Giant's cavernous eyes and buttressed forehead, he saw the import of the comment. As clearly as if he were pleading outright, Foamfollower said, *Acknowledge the white gold and use it to aid the Land*. Impossible, Covenant replied. The backs of his eyes felt hot with helplessness and belligerence, but his face was as stiff as a marble slab.

Abruptly, Lord Osondrea demanded, "The tapestry from your room was found. Why did you cast it down?"

Without looking at her, Covenant answered, "It offended me."

"Offended?" Her voice quivered with disbelief and indignation.

"Osondrea," Prothall admonished gently. "He is a stranger."

She kept the defiance of her face on Covenant, but fell silent. For a moment, no one moved or spoke; Covenant received the unsettling impression that the Lords were debating mentally with each other about how to treat him. Then Mhoram stood, walked around the end of the stone table, and moved back inside the circle until he was again opposite Osondrea. There he seated himself on the edge of the table with his staff across his lap, and fixed his eyes down on Covenant.

Covenant felt more exposed than ever to Mhoram's scrutiny. At the same time, he sensed that Bannor had stepped closer to him, as if anticipating an attack on Mhoram.

Wryly, Lord Mhoram said, "Thomas Covenant, you must pardon our caution. The desecrated moon signifies an evil in the Land which we hardly suspected. Without warning, the sternest test of our age appears in the sky, and we are utterly threatened. Yet we do not prejudge you. You must prove your ill—if ill you are." He looked to Covenant for some response, some acknowledgment, but Covenant only stared back emptily. With a slight shrug, the Lord went on, "Now. Perhaps it would be well if you began with your message."

Covenant winced, ducked his head like a man harried by vultures. He did not want to recite that message, did not want to remember Kevin's Watch, Mithil Stonedown, anything. His guts ached at visions of vertigo. Everything was impossible. How could he retain his outraged sanity if he thought about such things?

But Foul's message had a power of compulsion. He had borne it like a wound in his mind too long to repudiate it now. Before he could muster any defense, it came over him like a convulsion. In a tone of irremediable contempt, he said, "These are the words of Lord Foul the Despiser.

"'Say to the Council of Lords, and to the High Lord Prothall son of Dwillian, that the uttermost limit of their span of days upon the Land is seven times seven years from this present time. Before the end of those days are numbered, I will have the command of life and death in my hand. And as a token that what I say is the one word of truth, tell them this: Drool Rockworm, Cavewight of Mount Thunder, has found the Staff of Law, which was lost ten times a hundred years ago by Kevin at the Ritual of Desecration. Say to them that the task appointed to their generation is to regain the Staff. Without it, they will not be able to resist me for seven years, and my complete victory

will be achieved six times seven years earlier than it
would be else.

"'As for you, groveler: do not fail with this message. If you do not bring it before the Council, then
every human in the Land will be dead before ten seasons have passed. You do not understand—but I tell
you Drool Rockworm has the Staff, and that is a cause
for terror. He will be enthroned at Lord's Keep in two
years if the message fails. Already, the Cavewights
are marching to his call; and wolves, and ur-viles of
the Demondim, answer the power of the Staff. But war
is not the worst peril. Drool delves ever deeper into
the dark roots of Mount Thunder—Gravin Threndor,
Peak of the Fire-Lions. And there are banes buried in
the deeps of the Earth too potent and terrible for any
mortal to control. They would make of the universe a
hell forever. But such a bane Drool seeks. He
searches for the Illearth Stone. If he becomes its master, there will be woe for low and high alike until
Time itself falls.

"'Do not fail with my message, groveler. You have
met Drool. Do you relish dying in his hands?'" Covenant's heart lurched with the force of his loathing for
the words, the tone. But he was not done. "'One word
more, a final caution. Do not forget whom to fear at
the last. I have had to be content with killing and torment. But now my plans are laid, and I have begun. I
shall not rest until I have eradicated hope from the
Earth. Think on that, and be dismayed!'"

As he finished, he heard fear and abhorrence flare
in the Close as if ignited by his involuntary peroration.
Hellfire hellfire! he moaned, trying to clear his gaze
of the darkness from which Foul's contempt had
sprung. Unclean!

Prothall's head was bowed, and he clenched his
staff as if he were trying to wring courage from it. Behind him, Tuvor and Warmark Garth stood in
attitudes of martial readiness. Oddly, Variol and
Tamarantha doddered in their seats as if dozing, unaware of what had been said. But Osondrea gaped at
Covenant as if he had stabbed her in the heart. Opposite her, Mhoram stood erect, head high and eyes

closed, with his staff braced hard against the floor; and where his metal met the stone, a hot blue flame burned. Foamfollower hunched in his seat; his huge hands clutched a stone chair. His shoulders quivered, and suddenly the chair snapped.

At the noise, Osondrea covered her face with her hands, gave one stricken cry, *"Melenkurion abatha!"* The next instant, she dropped her hands and resumed her stony, amazed stare at Covenant. And he shouted, *Unclean!* as if he were agreeing with her.

"Laugh, Covenant," Foamfollower whispered hoarsely. "You have told us the end of all things. Now help us. Laugh."

Covenant replied dully, "You laugh. 'Joy is in the ears that hear.' I can't do it."

To his astonishment, Foamfollower did laugh. He lifted his head and made a strangled, garish noise in his throat that sounded like sobbing; but in a moment the sound loosened, clarified, slowly took on the tone of indomitable humor. The terrible exertion appalled Covenant.

As Foamfollower laughed, the first shock of dismay passed from the Council. Gradually, Prothall raised his head. "The Unhomed are a blessing to the Land," he murmured. Mhoram sagged, and the fire between his staff and the floor went out. Osondrea shook her head, sighed, passed her hands through her hair. Again, Covenant sensed a kind of mental melding from the Lords; without words, they seemed to join hands, share strength with each other.

Sitting alone and miserable, Covenant waited for them to question him. And as he waited, he struggled to recapture all the refusals on which his survival depended.

Finally, the Lords returned their attention to him. The flesh of Prothall's face seemed to droop with weariness, but his eyes remained steady, resolute. "Now, Unbeliever," he said softly. "You must tell us all that has happened to you. We must know how Lord Foul's threats are embodied."

Now, Covenant echoed, twisting in his chair. He could hardly resist a desire to clutch at his ring. Dark

memories beat at his ears, trying to break down his
defenses. Shortly, everyone in the Close was looking
at him. Tossing his words down as if he were discard-
ing flawed bricks, he began.

"I come from—someplace else. I was brought to
Kevin's Watch—I don't know how. First I got a look
at Drool—then Foul left me on the Watch. They
seemed to know each other."

"And the Staff of Law?" Prothall asked.

"Drool had a staff—all carved up, with metal ends
like yours. I don't know what it was."

Prothall shrugged the doubt away; and grimly Covenant forced himself to describe without any personal
mention of himself, any reference to Lena or Triock
or Baradakas, the events of his journey. When he spoke
of the murdered Waynhim, Osondrea's breath hissed
between her teeth, but the Lords made no other response.

Then, after he mentioned the visit to Soaring
Woodhelven of a malicious stranger, possibly a Raver,
Mhoram asked intently, "Did the stranger use a
name?"

"He said his name was Jehannum."

"Ah. And what was his purpose?"

"How should I know?" Covenant rasped, trying to
conceal his falsehood with belligerence. "I don't know
any Ravers."

Mhoram nodded noncommittally, and Covenant
went on to relate his and Atiaran's progress through
Andelain. He avoided gruffly any reference to the
wrong which had attacked him through his boots. But
when he came to the Celebration of Spring, he faltered.

The Wraiths—! he ached silently. The rage and
horror of that night were still in him, still vivid to his
raw heart. *Covenant, help them!* How could I? It's
madness! I'm not—I am not Berek.

With an effort that made his throat hurt as if his
words were too sharp to pass through it, he said, "The
Celebration was attacked by ur-viles. We escaped.
Some of the Wraiths were saved by—by one of the
Unfettered, Atiaran said. Then the moon turned red.

Then we got to the river and met Foamfollower. Atiaran decided to go back home. How the hell much longer do I have to put up with this?"

Unexpectedly, Lord Tamarantha raised her nodding head. "Who will go?" she asked toward the ceiling of the Close.

"It has not yet been determined that anyone will go," Prothall replied in a gentle voice.

"Nonsense," she sniffed. Tugging at a thin wisp of hair behind her ear, she coaxed her old bones erect. "This is too high a matter for caution. We must act. Of course I trust him. He has a Hirebrand's staff, does he not? What Hirebrand would give a staff without sure reason? And look at it—one end blackened. He has fought with it—at the Celebration, if I do not mistake. Ah, the poor Wraiths. That was ill, ill." Looking across at Variol, she said, "Come. We must prepare."

Variol worked himself to his feet. Taking Tamarantha's arm, he left the Close through one of the doors behind the High Lord.

After a respectful pause for the old Lords, Osondrea leveled her stare at Covenant and demanded, "How did you gain that staff?"

"Baradakas—the Hirebrand—gave it to me."

"Why?"

Her tone sparked his anger. He said distinctly, "He wanted to apologize for distrusting me."

"How did you teach him to trust you?"

Damnation! "I passed his bloody test of truth."

Carefully, Lord Mhoram asked, "Unbeliever—why did the Hirebrand of Soaring Woodhelven desire to test you?"

Again, Covenant felt compelled to lie. "Jehannum made him nervous. He tested everyone."

"Did he also test Atiaran?"

"What do you think?"

"I think," Foamfollower interposed firmly, "that Atiaran Trell-mate of Mithil Stonedown would not require any test of truth to demonstrate her fidelity."

This affirmation produced a pause, during which the Lords looked at each other as if they had reached an impasse. Then High Lord Prothall said sternly,

"Thomas Covenant, you are a stranger, and we have had no time to learn your ways. But we will not surrender our sense of what is right to you. It is clear that you have spoken falsehood. For the sake of the Land, you must answer our questions. Please tell us why the Hirebrand Baradakas gave to you the test of truth, but not to Atiaran your companion."

"No."

"Then tell us why Atiaran Trell-mate chose not to accompany you here. It is rare for a person born of the Land to stop short of Revelstone."

"No."

"Why do you refuse?"

Covenant glared seething up at his interrogators. They sat above him like judges with the power of outcasting in their hands. He wanted to defend himself with shouts, curses; but the Lords' intent eyes stopped him. He could see no contempt in their faces. They regarded him with anger, fear, disquietude, with offended love for the Land, but no contempt. Very softly, he said, "Don't you understand? I'm trying to get out of telling you an even bigger lie. If you keep pushing me—we'll all suffer."

The High Lord met his irate, supplicating gaze for a moment, then sighed catarrhally, "Very well. You make matters difficult for us. Now we must deliberate. Please leave the Close. We will call for you in a short time."

Covenant stood, turned on his heel, started up the steps toward the big doors. Only the sound of his boots against the stone marked the silence until he had almost reached the doors. Then he heard Foamfollower say as clearly as if his own heart uttered the words, "Atiaran Trell-mate blamed you for the slaughter of the Wraiths."

He froze, waiting in blank dread for the Giant to continue. But Foamfollower said nothing more. Trembling, Covenant passed through the doors and moved awkwardly to sit in one of the chairs along the wall. His secret felt so fragile within him that he could hardly believe it was still intact.

I am not—

When he looked up, he found Bannor standing before him. The Bloodguard's face was devoid of expression, but it did not seem uncontemptuous. Its flat ambiguity appeared capable of any response, and now it implied a judgment of Covenant's weakness, his disease.

Impelled by anger and frustration, Covenant muttered to himself, Keep moving. Survive. "Bannor," he growled, "Mhoram seems to think we should get to know each other. He told me to ask you about the Bloodguard."

Bannor shrugged as if he were impervious to any question.

"Your people—the *Haruchai*"—Bannor nodded—"live up in the mountains. You came to the Land when Kevin was High Lord. How long ago was that?"

"Centuries before the Desecration." The Bloodguard's alien tone seemed to suggest that units of time like years and decades had no significance. "Two thousand years."

Two thousand years. Thinking of the Giants, Covenant said, "That's why there's only five hundred of you left. Since you came to the Land you've been dying off."

"The Bloodguard have always numbered five hundred. That is the Vow. The *Haruchai*—are more." He gave the name a tonal lilt that suited his voice.

"More?"

"They live in the mountains as before."

"Then how do you—You say that as if you haven't been back there for a long time." Again Bannor nodded slightly. "How do you maintain your five hundred here? I haven't seen any—"

Bannor interrupted dispassionately. "When one of the Bloodguard is slain, his body is sent into the mountains through Guards Gap, and another of the *Haruchai* comes to take his place in the Vow."

Is slain? Covenant wondered. "Haven't you been home since? Don't you visit your— Do you have a wife?"

"At one time."

Bannor's tone did not vary, but something in his inflectionlessness made Covenant feel that the question was important. "At one time?" he pursued. "What happened to her?"

"She has been dead."

An instinct warned Covenant, but he went on, spurred by the fascination of Bannor's alien, inflexible solidity. "How—how long ago did she die?"

Without a flicker of hesitation, the Bloodguard replied, "Two thousand years."

What! For a long moment, Covenant gaped in astonishment, whispering to himself as if he feared that Bannor could hear him, *That's impossible. That's impossible.* In an effort to control himself, he blinked dumbly. *Two—? What is this?*

Yet in spite of his amazement, Bannor's claim carried conviction. That flat tone sounded incapable of dishonesty, of even misrepresentation. It filled Covenant with horror, with nauseated sympathy. In sudden vision he glimpsed the import of Mhoram's description, *made by their pledged loyalty ascetic, womanless, and old.* Barren—how could there be any limit to a barrenness which had already lasted for two thousand years? "How," he croaked, "how old are you?"

"I came to the Land with the first *Haruchai,* when Kevin was young in High Lordship. Together we first uttered the Vow of service. Together we called upon the Earthpower to witness our commitment. Now we do not return home until we have been slain."

Two thousand years, Covenant mumbled. *Until we have been slain.* That's impossible. None of this is happening. In his confusion, he tried to tell himself that what he heard was like the sensitivity of his nerves, further proof of the Land's impossibility. But it did not feel like proof. It moved him as if he had learned that Bannor suffered from a rare form of leprosy. With an effort, he breathed, "Why?"

Flatly, Bannor said, "When we came to the Land, we saw wonders—Giants, Ranyhyn, Revelstone— Lords of such power that they declined to wage war with us lest we be destroyed. In answer to our chal-

lenge, they gave to the *Haruchai* gifts so precious—"
He paused, appeared to muse for a moment over
private memories. "Therefore we swore the Vow. We
could not equal that generosity in any other way."

"Is that your answer to death?" Covenant struggled
with his sympathy, tried to reduce what Bannor said
to manageable proportions. "Is that how things are
done in the Land? Whenever you're in trouble you
just do the impossible? Like Berek?"

"We have sworn the Vow. The Vow is life. Corruption is death."

"But for two thousand years?" Covenant protested.
"Damnation! It isn't even decent. Don't you think
you've done enough?"

Without expression, the Bloodguard replied, "You
cannot corrupt us."

"Corrupt you? I don't want to corrupt you. You
can go on serving those Lords until you wither for all
I care. I'm talking about your life, Bannor! How long
do you go on serving without just once asking yourself
if it's worth it? Pride or at least sanity requires that.
Hellfire!" He could not conceive how even a healthy
man remained unsuicidal in the face of so much existence. "It isn't like salad dressing—you can't just spoon
it around. You're human. You weren't born to be
immortal."

Bannor shrugged impassively. "What does immor-
tality signify? We are the Bloodguard. We know only
life or death—the Vow or Corruption."

An instant passed before Covenant remembered that
Corruption was the Bloodguard name for Lord Foul.
Then he groaned, "Well of course I understand. You
live forever because your pure, sinless service is utterly
and indomitably unballasted by any weight or dross
of mere human weakness. Ah, the advantages of clean
living."

"We do not know." Bannor's awkward tone echoed
strangely. "Kevin saved us. How could we guess what
was in his heart? He sent us all into the mountains—
into the mountains. We questioned, but he gave the
order. He charged us by our Vow. We knew no
reason to disobey. How could we know? We would

have stood by him at the Desecration—stood by or prevented. But he saved us—the Bloodguard. We who swore to preserve his life at any cost."

Saved, Covenant breathed painfully. He could feel the unintended cruelty of Kevin's act. "So now you don't know whether all these years of living are right or wrong," he said distantly. How do you stand it? "Maybe your Vow is mocking you."

"There is no accusation which can raise its finger against us," Bannor averred. But for an instant his dispassion sounded a shade less immaculate.

"No, you do all that yourself."

In response, Bannor blinked slowly, as if neither blame nor exculpation carried meaning to the ancient perspective of his devotion.

A moment later, one of the sentries beckoned Covenant toward the Close. Trepidation constricted his heart. His horrified sympathy for Bannor drained his courage; he did not feel able to face the Lords, answer their demands. He climbed to his feet as if he were tottering, then hesitated. When Bannor motioned him forward, he said in a rush, "Tell me one more thing. If your wife were still alive, would you go to visit her and then come back here? Could you—" He faltered. "Could you bear it?"

The Bloodguard met his imploring gaze squarely, but thoughts seemed to pass like shadows behind his countenance before he said softly, "No."

Breathing heavily as if he were nauseated, Covenant shambled through the door and down the steps toward the yellow immolation of the graveling pit.

Prothall, Mhoram, and Osondrea, Foamfollower, the four Bloodguard, the four spectators—all remained as he had left them. Under the ominous expectancy of their eyes, he seated himself in the lone chair below the Lords' table. He was shivering as if the fire-stones radiated cold rather than heat.

When the High Lord spoke, the age rattle in his voice seemed worse than before. "Thomas Covenant, if we have treated you wrongly we will beg your pardon at the proper time. But we must resolve our doubt of you. You have concealed much that we must know. However, on one matter we have been able to agree. We see your presence in the Land in this way.

"While delving under Mount Thunder, Drool Rockworm found the lost Staff of Law. Without aid, he would require many years to master it. But Lord Foul the Despiser learned of Drool's discovery, and agreed for his own purposes to teach the Cavewight the uses of the Staff. Clearly he did not wrest the Staff from Drool. Perhaps he was too weak. Or perhaps he feared to use a tool not made for his hand. Or perhaps he has some terrible purpose which we do not grasp. But again it is clear that Lord Foul induced Drool to use the Staff to summon you to the Land—only the Staff of Law has such might. And Drool could not have conceived or executed that task without deep-lored aid. You were brought to the Land at Lord Foul's behest. We can only pray that there were other powers at work as well."

"But that does not tell us why," said Mhoram intently. "If the carrying of messages were Lord Foul's only purpose, he had no need of someone from beyond the Land—and no need to protect you from Drool, as he did when he bore you to Kevin's Watch, and as I believe he attempted to do by sending his Raver to turn you from your path toward Andelain. No, you are our sole guide to the Despiser's true intent. Why did he call someone from beyond the Land? And why you? In what way do you serve his designs?"

Panting, Covenant locked his jaws and said nothing.

"Let me put the matter another way," Prothall urged. "The tale you have told us contains evidence of truth. Few living know that the Ravers were at one time named Herem, Sheol, and Jehannum. And we know that one of the Unfettered has been studying the Wraiths of Andelain for many years."

Unwillingly, Covenant remembered the hopeless courage of the animals that had helped the Unfettered One to save him in Andelain. They had hurled themselves into their own slaughter with desperate and futile ferocity. He gritted his teeth, tried to close his ears to the memory of their dying.

Prothall went on without a pause, "And we know

that the *lomillialor* test of truth is sure—if the one
tested does not surpass the tester."

"But the Despiser also knows," snapped Osondrea.
"He could know that an Unfettered One lived and
studied in Andelain. He could have prepared this tale
and taught it to you. If he did," she enunciated
darkly, "then the matters on which you have refused
to speak are precisely those on which your story
would fail. Why did the Hirebrand of Soaring
Woodhelven test you? How was the testing done?
Who have you battled with that staff? What instinct
turned Atiaran Trell-mate against you? You fear to
reply because then we will see the Despiser's handiwork."

Authoritatively, High Lord Prothall rattled,
"Thomas Covenant, you must give us some token that
your tale is true."

"Token?" Covenant groaned.

"Give us proof that we should trust you. You have
uttered a doom upon our lives. That we believe. But
perhaps it is your purpose to lead us from the true
defense of the Land. Give us some token, Unbeliever."

Through his quavering, Covenant felt the impenetrable circumstance of his dream clamp shut on him,
deny every desire for hope or independence. He
climbed to his feet, strove to meet the crisis erect. As
a last resort, he grated to Foamfollower, "Tell them.
Atiaran blamed herself for what happened to the Celebration. Because she ignored the warnings. Tell them."

He burned at Foamfollower, willing the Giant to
support his last chance for autonomy, and after a
grave moment the Giant said, "My friend Thomas
Covenant speaks truth, in his way. Atiaran Trell-mate
believed the worst of herself."

"Nevertheless!" Osondrea snapped. "Perhaps she
blamed herself for guiding him to the Celebration—
for enabling— Her pain does not approve him." And
Prothall insisted in a low voice, "Your token, Covenant. The necessity for judgment is upon us. You must
choose between the Land and the Land's Despiser."

Covenant, help them!

"No!" he gasped hoarsely, whirling to face the High

Lord. "It wasn't my fault. Don't you see that this is just what Foul wants you to do?"

Prothall stood, braced his weight on his staff. His stature seemed to expand in power as he spoke. "No, I do not see. You are closed to me. You ask to be trusted, but you refuse to show trustworthiness. No. I demand the token by which you refuse us. I am Prothall son of Dwillian, High Lord by the choice of the Council. I demand."

For one long instant, Covenant remained suspended in decision. His eyes fell to the graveling pit. *Covenant, help them!* With a groan, he remembered how much Atiaran had paid to place him where he stood now. *Her pain does not approve.* In counterpoint he heard Bannor saying, *Two thousand years. Life or death. We do not know.* But the face he saw in the fire-stones was his wife's. *Joan!* he cried. Was one sick body more important than everything?

He tore open his shirt as if he were trying to bare his heart. From the patch of *clingor* on his chest, he snatched his wedding band, jammed it onto his ring finger, raised his left fist like a defiance. But he was not defiant. "I can't use it!" he shouted lornly, as if the ring were still a symbol of marriage, not a talisman of wild magic. "I'm a leper!"

Astonishment rang in the Close, clanging changes in the air. The Hearthralls and Garth were stunned. Prothall shook his head as if he were trying to wake up for the first time in his life. Intuitive comprehension broke like a bow wave on Mhoram's face, and he snapped to his feet in stiff attention. Grinning gratefully, Foamfollower stood as well. Lord Osondrea also joined Mhoram, but there was no relief in her eyes. Covenant could see her shouldering her way through a throng of confusions to the crux of the situation— could see her thinking, *Save or damn, save or damn.* She alone among the Lords appeared to realize that even this token did not suffice.

Finally the High Lord mastered himself. "Now at last we know how to honor you," he breathed. "Ur-Lord Thomas Covenant, Unbeliever and white gold wielder, be welcome and true. Forgive us, for we did

not know. Yours is the wild magic that destroys
peace. And power is at all times a dreadful thing."

The Lords saluted Covenant as if they wished to
both invoke and ward against him, then together began to sing:

> There is wild magic graven in every rock,
> contained for white gold to unleash or control—
> gold, rare metal, not born of the Land,
> nor ruled, limited, subdued
> by the Law with which the Land was created
> (for the Land is beautiful,
> as if it were a strong soul's dream of peace and
>   harmony,
> and Beauty is not possible without discipline—
> and the Law which gave birth to Time
> is the Land's Creator's self-control)—
> but keystone rather, pivot, crux
> for the anarchy out of which Time was made,
> and with Time Earth,
> and with Earth those who people it:
> wild magic restrained in every particle of life,
> and unleashed or controlled by gold
> (not born of the Land)
> because that power is the anchor of the arch of
>   life
> that spans and masters Time:
> and white—white gold,
> not ebon, ichor, incarnadine, viridian—
> because white is the hue of bone:
> structure of flesh,
> discipline of life.
>
> This power is a paradox,
> because Power does not exist without Law,
> and wild magic has no Law;
> and white gold is a paradox,
> because it speaks for the bone of life,
> but has no part of the Land.
> And he who wields white wild magic gold
> is a paradox—
> for he is everything and nothing,

hero and fool,
potent, helpless—
and with the one word of truth or treachery
he will save or damn the Earth
because he is mad and sane,
cold and passionate,
lost and found.

It was an involuted song, curiously harmonized, with no resolving cadences to set the hearers at rest. And in it Covenant could hear the vulture wings of Foul's voice saying, *You have might, but you will never know what it is. You will not be able to fight me at the last.* As the song ended, he wondered if his struggling served or defied the Despiser's manipulations. He could not tell. But he hated and feared the truth in Foul's words. He cut into the silence which followed the Lords' hymning. "I don't know how to use it. I don't want to know. That's not why I wear it. If you think I'm some kind of personified redemption—it's a lie. I'm a leper."

"Ah, ur-Lord Covenant," Prothall sighed as the Lords and Foamfollower reseated themselves, "let me say again, please forgive us. We understand much now—why you were summoned—why the Hirebrand Baradakas treated you as he did—why Drool Rockworm attempted to ensnare you at the Celebration of Spring. Please understand in turn that knowledge of the ring is necessary to us. Your semblance to Berek Halfhand is not gratuitous. But, sadly, we cannot tell you how to use the white gold. Alas, we know little enough of the Lore we already possess. And I fear that if we held and comprehended all Seven Wards and Words, the wild magic would still be beyond us. Knowledge of white gold has come down to us through the ancient prophecies—foretellings, as Saltheart Foamfollower has observed, which say much but clarify little—but we comprehend nothing of the wild magic. Still, the prophecies are clear about your importance. So I name you 'ur-Lord,' a sharer of all the matters of the Council until you depart from us. We must trust you."

Pacing back and forth now on the spur of his conflicting needs, Covenant growled, "Baradakas said just about the same thing. By hell! You people terrify me. When I try to be responsible, you pressure me—and when I collapse you— You're not asking the right questions. You don't have the vaguest notion of what a leper is, and it doesn't even occur to you to inquire. *That's* why Foul chose me for this. Because I can't— Damnation! Why don't you ask me about where I come from? I've got to tell you. The world I come from doesn't allow anyone to live except on its own terms. Those terms—those terms contradict yours."

"What are its terms?" the High Lord asked carefully.

"That your world is a dream."

In the startled stillness of the Close, Covenant grimaced, winced as images flashed at him—courthouse columns, an old beggar, the muzzle of the police car. A dream! he panted feverishly. A dream! None of this is happening—!

Then Osondrea shot out, "What? A dream? Do you mean to say that you are dreaming? Do you believe that you are asleep?"

"Yes!" He felt weak with fear; his revelation bereft him of a shield, exposed him to attack. But he could not recant it. He needed it to regain some kind of honesty. "Yes."

"Indeed!" she snapped. "No doubt that explains the slaughter of the Celebration. Tell me, Unbeliever —do you consider that a nightmare, or does your world relish such dreams?"

Before Covenant could retort, Lord Mhoram said, "Enough, sister Osondrea. He torments himself—sufficently."

Glaring, she fell silent, and after a moment Prothall said, "It may be that gods have such dreams as this. But we are mortals. We can only resist ill or surrender. Either way, we perish. Were you sent to mock us for this?"

"Mock you?" Covenant could not find the words to respond. He chopped dumbly at the thought with his halfhand. "It's the other way around. He's mocking me." When all the Lords looked at him in incomprehension, he cried abruptly, "I can feel the pulse in my fingertips! But that's impossible. I've got a disease. An incurable disease. I've—I've got to figure out a way to keep from going crazy. Hell and blood! I don't want to lose my mind just because some perfectly decent character in a dream needs something from me that I can't produce."

"Well, that may be." Prothall's voice held a note of sadness and sympathy, as if he were listening to some abrogation or repudiation of sanity from a revered seer. "But we will trust you nonetheless. You are bitter, and bitterness is a sign of concern. I trust that. And what you say also meets the old prophecy. I fear the time is coming when you will be the Land's last hope."

"Don't you understand?" Covenant groaned, unable to silence the ache in his voice. "That's what Foul wants you to think."

"Perhaps," Mhoram said thoughtfully. "Perhaps." Then, as if he had reached a decision, he turned the peril of his gaze straight at Covenant. "Unbeliever, I must ask you if you have resisted Lord Foul. I do not speak of the Celebration. When he bore you from Drool Rockworm to Kevin's Watch—did you oppose him?"

The question made Covenant feel abruptly frail, as if it had snapped a cord of his resistance. "I didn't know how." Wearily, he reseated himself in the loneliness of his chair. "I didn't know what was happening."

"You are ur-Lord now," murmured Mhoram. "There is no more need for you to sit there."

"No need to sit at all," amended Prothall, with sudden briskness. "There is much work to be done. We must think and probe and plan—whatever action we will take in this trial must be chosen quickly. We will meet again tonight. Tuvor, Garth, Birinair, Tohrm —prepare yourselves and those in your command. Bring whatever thoughts of strategy you have to the Council tonight. And tell all the Keep that Thomas

Covenant has been named ur-Lord. He is a stranger and a guest. Birinair—begin your work for the Giants at once. Bannor, I think the ur-Lord need no longer stay in the tower." He paused and looked about him, giving everyone a chance to speak. Then he turned and left the Close. Osondrea followed him, and after giving Covenant another formal salute, Mhoram also departed.

Numbly, Covenant moved behind Bannor up through the high passages and stairways until they reached his new quarters. The Bloodguard ushered him into a suite of rooms. They were high-ceilinged, lit by reflected sunlight through several broad windows, abundantly supplied with food and springwine, and unadorned. When Bannor had left, Covenant looked out one of the windows, and found that his rooms were perched in the north wall of Revelstone, with a view of the rough plains and the northward-curving cliff of the plateau. The sun was overhead, but a bit south of the Keep, so that the windows were in shadow.

He left the window, moved to the tray of food, and ate a light meal. Then he poured out a flask of springwine, which he carried into the bedroom. There he found one orieled window. It had an air of privacy, of peace.

Where did he go from here? He did not need to be self-wise or prophetic to know that he could not remain in Revelstone. He was too vulnerable here.

He sat down in the stone alcove to brood over the Land below and wonder what he had done to himself.

FIFTEEN: The Great
Challenge

THAT night, when Bannor entered the suite to call Thomas Covenant to the evening meeting of the Lords, he found Covenant still sitting within the oriel of his bedroom window. By the light of Bannor's torch, Covenant appeared gaunt and spectral, as if half seen through shadows. The sockets of his eyes were dark with exhausted emotion; his lips were gray, bloodless; and the skin of his forehead had an ashen undertone. He held his arms across his chest as if he were trying to comfort a pain in his heart—watched the plains as if he were waiting for moonrise. Then he noticed the Bloodguard, and his lips pulled back, bared his teeth.

"You still don't trust me," he said in a spent voice.

Bannor shrugged. "We are the Bloodguard. We have no use for white gold."

"No use?"

"It is a knowledge—a weapon. We have no use for weapons."

"No use?" Covenant repeated dully. "How do you defend the Lords without weapons?"

"We"—Bannor paused as if searching the language of the Land for a word to match his thought—"suffice."

Covenant brooded for a moment, then swung himself out of the oriel. Standing in front of Bannor, he said softly, "Bravo." Then he picked up his staff and left the rooms.

This time, he paid more attention to the route Bannor chose, and did not lose his sense of direction.

Eventually, he might be able to dispense with Bannor's guidance. When they reached the huge wooden doors of the Close, they met Foamfollower and Korik. The Giant greeted Covenant with a salute and a broad grin, but when he spoke his voice was serious. "Stone and Sea, ur-Lord Covenant! I am glad you did not choose to make me wrong. Perhaps I do not comprehend all your dilemma. But I believe you have taken the better risk—for the sake of all the Land."

"You're a fine one to talk," replied Covenant wanly. His sarcasm was a defensive reflex; he had lost so much other armor. "How long have you Giants been lost? I don't think you would know a good risk if it kicked you."

Foamfollower chuckled. "Bravely said, my friend. It may be that the Giants are not good advisers—all our years notwithstanding. Still you have lightened my fear for the Land."

Grimacing uselessly, Covenant went on into the Close.

The council chamber was as brightly lit and acoustically perfect as before, but the number of people in it had changed. Tamarantha and Variol were absent, and scattered through the gallery were a number of spectators—*rhadhamaerl, lillianrill,* warriors, Lorewardens. Bloodguard sat behind Mhoram and Osondrea; and Tuvor, Garth, Birinair, and Tohrm were in their places behind the High Lord.

Foamfollower took his former seat, gesturing Covenant into a chair near him at the Lords' table. Behind them, Bannor and Korik sat down in the lower tier of the gallery. The spectators fell silent almost at once; even the rustle of their clothing grew still. Shortly, everyone was waiting for the High Lord to begin.

Prothall sat as if wandering in thought for some time before he climbed tiredly to his feet. He held himself up by leaning on his staff, and when he spoke his voice rattled agedly in his chest. But he went without omission through the ceremonies of honoring Foamfollower and Covenant. The Giant responded with a gaiety which disguised the effort he made to be concise. But Covenant rejected the formality with a scowl and a shake of his head.

When he was done, Prothall said without meeting the eyes of his fellow Lords, "There is a custom among the new Lords—a custom which began in the days of High Lord Vailant, a hundred years ago. It is this: when a High Lord doubts his ability to meet the needs of the Land, he may come to the Council and surrender his High Lordship. Then any Lord who so chooses may claim the place for himself." With an effort, Prothall continued firmly, "I now surrender my leadership. Rock and root, the trial of these times is too great for me. Ur-Lord Thomas Covenant, you are permitted to claim the High Lordship if you wish."

Covenant held Prothall's eyes, trying to measure the High Lord's intentions. But he could find no duplicity in Prothall's offer. Softly, he replied, "You know I don't want it."

"Yet I ask you to accept it. You bear the white gold."

"Forget it," Covenant said. "It isn't that easy."

After a moment, Prothall nodded slowly. "I see." He turned to the other Lords. "Do you claim the High Lordship?"

"You are the High Lord," Mhoram averred. And Osondrea added, "Who else? Do not waste more time in foolishness."

"Very well." Prothall squared his shoulders. "The trial and the doom of this time are on my head. I am High Lord Prothall, and by the consent of the Council my will prevails. Let none fear to follow me, or blame another if my choices fail."

An involuntary twitch passed across Covenant's face, but he said nothing; and shortly Prothall sat down, saying, "Now let us consider what we must do."

In silence the Lords communed mentally with each other. Then Osondrea turned to Foamfollower. "Rockbrother, it is said, 'When many matters press you, consider friendship first.' For the sake of your people, you should return to Seareach as swiftly as may be. The Giants must be told all that has transpired here. But I judge that the waterway of Andelain will no longer be safe for you. We will provide an escort to accompany you through Grimmerdhore Forest and the North Plains until you are past Landsdrop and Sarangrave Flat."

"Thank you, my Lords," replied Foamfollower formally, "but that will not be needed. I have given some thought myself to this matter. In their wandering, my people learned a saying from the *Bhrathair:* 'He who waits for the sword to fall upon his neck will surely lose his head.' I believe that the best service which I can do for my people is to assist whatever course you undertake. Please permit me to join you."

High Lord Prothall smiled and bowed his head in acknowledgement. "My heart hoped for this. Be welcome in our trial. Peril or plight, the Giants of Seareach strengthen us, and we cannot sing our gratitude enough. But your people must not be left unwarned. We will send other messengers."

Foamfollower bowed in turn, and then Lord Osondrea resumed by calling on Warmark Garth.

Garth stood and reported, "Lord, I have done as you requested. Furl's Fire now burns atop Revelstone. All who see it will warn their folk, and will spread the warning of war south and east and north. By morning, all who live north of the Soulsease and west of Grimmerdhore will be forearmed, and those who live near the river will send runners into the Center Plains. Beyond that, the warning will carry more slowly.

"I have sent scouts in relays toward Grimmerdhore and Andelain. But six days will pass before we receive clear word of the Forest. And though you did not request it, I have begun preparations for a siege. In all, one thousand three hundred of my warriors are now at work. Twenty Eoman remain ready."

"That is well," said Osondrea. "The warning which must be taken to Seareach we entrust to you. Send as many warriors as you deem necessary to ensure the embassy."

Garth bowed and sat down.

"Now." She nodded her head as if to clear it of other considerations. "I have given my time to the study of ur-Lord Covenant's tale of his journey. The presence of white gold explains much. But still many things require thought—south-running storms, a three-winged bird, an abominable attack on the Wraiths of Andelain, the bloodying of the moon. To my mind, the meaning of these signs is clear."

Abruptly, she slapped the table with her palm as if she needed the sound and the pain to help her speak. "Drool Rockworm has already found his bane —the Illearth Stone or some other deadly evil. With the Staff of Law, he has might enough to blast the seasons in their course!"

A low groan arose from the gallery, but Prothall and Mhoram did not appear surprised. Still, a dangerous glitter intensified in Mhoram's eyes as he said softly, "Please explain."

"The evidence of power is unmistakable. We know that Drool has the Staff of Law. But the Staff is not a neutral tool. It was carved from the One Tree as a servant of the Earth and the Earth's Law. Yet all that has occurred is unnatural, wrong. Can you conceive the strength of will which could corrupt the Staff even enough to warp one bird? Well, perhaps madness gives Drool that will. Or perhaps the Despiser now controls the Staff. But consider—birthing a three-winged bird is the smallest of these ill feats. At his peak in the former age, Lord Foul did not dare attack the Wraiths. And as for the desecrated moon—only the darkest and most terrible of ancient prophecies bespeak such matters.

"Do you call this proof conclusive that Lord Foul indeed possesses the Staff? But consider—for less exertion than corrupting the moon requires, he could surely stamp us into death. We could not fight such might. And yet he spends himself so—so vainly. Would he employ his strength to so little purpose— against the Wraiths first when he could easily destroy us? And if he would, could he corrupt the moon using the Staff of Law—a tool not made for his hand, resisting his mastery at every touch?

"I judge that if Lord Foul controlled the Staff, he would not and perhaps could not do what has been done—not until we were destroyed. But if Drool still holds the Staff, then it alone does not suffice. No Cavewight is large enough to perform such crimes without the power of both Staff and Stone. The Cavewights are weak-willed creatures, as you know. They are easily swayed, easily enslaved. And they have no heaven-challenging lore. Therefore they have always been the fodder of Lord Foul's armies.

"If I judge truly, then the Despiser himself is as much at Drool's mercy as we are. The doom of this time rides on the mad whim of a Cavewight.

"This I conclude because we have not been attacked."

Prothall nodded glumly to Osondrea, and Mhoram took up the line of her reasoning. "So Lord Foul relies upon us to save him and damn ourselves. In some way, he intends that our response to ur-Lord Covenant's message will spring upon ourselves a trap which holds both us and him. He has pretended friendship to Drool to preserve himself until his plans are ripe. And he has taught Drool to use this new-found power in ways which will satisfy the Cavewight's lust for mastery without threatening us directly. Thus he attempts to ensure that we will make trial to wrest the Staff of Law from Drool."

"And therefore," Osondrea barked, "it would be the utterest folly for us to make trial."

"How so?" Mhoram objected. "The message said, 'Without it, they will not be able to resist me for seven years.' He foretells a sooner end for us if we do not make the attempt, or if we attempt and fail, than if we succeed."

"What does he gain by such foretellings? What but our immediate deaths? His message is only a lure of false hope to lead us into folly."

But Mhoram replied by quoting, " 'Drool Rockworm has the Staff, and that is a cause for terror. He will be enthroned at Lord's Keep in two years if the message fails.' "

"The message has not failed!" Osondrea insisted. "We are forewarned. We can prepare. Drool is mad, and his attacks will be flawed by madness. It may be that we will find his weakness and prevail. By the Seven! Revelstone will never fall while the Bloodguard remain. And the Giants and Ranyhyn will come to our aid." Turning toward the High Lord, she urged, "Prothall, do not follow the lure of this quest. It is chimera. We will fall under the shadow, and the Land will surely die."

"But if we succeed," Mhoram countered, "if we gain the Staff, then our chance is prolonged. Lord Foul's prophecy notwithstanding, we may find enough Earthpower in the Staff to prevail in war. And if we do not, still we will have that much more time to search for other salvations."

"How can we succeed? Drool has both the Staff of Law and the Illearth Stone."

"And is master of neither."

"Master enough! Ask the Wraiths the extent of his might. Ask the moon."

"Ask me," growled Covenant, climbing slowly to his feet. For a moment he hesitated, torn between a fear of Drool and a dread of what would happen to him if the Lords did not go in search of the Staff. He had a vivid apprehension of the malice behind Drool's laval eyes. But the thought of the Staff decided him. He felt that he had gained an insight into the logic of his dream. The Staff had brought him to the Land; he would need the Staff to escape. "Ask me," he said again. "Don't you think I have a stake in this?"

The Lords did not respond, and Covenant was forced to carry the argument forward himself. In his brooding, he had been able to find only one frail hope. With an effort, he broached the subject. "According to you, Foul chose me. But he talked about me on Kevin's Watch as if I had been chosen by someone else—'my Enemy,' he said. Who was he talking about?"

Thoughtfully, the High Lord replied, "I do not know. We said earlier that we hoped there were other forces at work in your selection. Perhaps there were. A few of our oldest legends speak of a Creator —the Creator of the Earth—but we know nothing of such a being. We only know that we are mortal, but Lord Foul is not—in some way, he surpasses flesh."

"The Creator," Covenant muttered. "All right." A disturbing memory of the old beggar who had accosted him outside the courthouse flared momentarily. "Why did he choose me?"

Prothall's abnegate eyes did not waver. "Who can say? Perhaps for the very reasons that Lord Foul chooses you."

That paradox angered Covenant, but he went on as if inspired by the contradiction, "Then this— Creator—also wanted you to hear Foul's message. Take that into account."

"There!" Osondrea pounced. "There is the lie I sought—the final bait. By raising the hope of unknown help, Lord Foul seeks to ensure that we will accept this mad quest."

Covenant did not look away from the High Lord. He held Prothall's eyes, tried to see beyond the wear of long asceticisms into his mind. But Prothall returned the gaze unflinchingly. The lines at the corners of his eyes seemed etched there by self-abrogation. "Lord Osondrea," he said evenly, "does your study reveal any signs of hope?"

"Signs? Omens?" Her voice sounded reluctant in the Close. "I am not Mhoram. If I were, I would ask Covenant what dreams he has had in the Land. But I prefer practical hopes. I see but one: so little time has been lost. It is in my heart that no other combination of chance and choice could have brought Covenant here so swiftly."

"Very well," Prothall replied. His look, locked with Covenant's, sharpened momentarily, and in it Covenant at last saw that the High Lord had already made his decision. He only listened to the debate to give himself one last chance to find an alternative. Awkwardly, Covenant dropped his eyes, slumped in his chair. How does he do it? he murmured pointlessly to himself. Where does all this courage come from?

Am I the only coward——?

A moment later, the High Lord pulled his blue robe about him and rose to his feet. "My friends," he said, his voice thick with rheum, "the time has come for decision. I must choose a course to meet our need. If any have thoughts which must be uttered, speak now." No one spoke, and Prothall seemed to draw dignity and stature from the silence. "Hear then the will of Prothall son of Dwillian, High Lord by the choice of the Council—and may the Land forgive me if I mistake or fail. In this moment, I commit the future of the Earth.

"Lord Osondrea, to you and to the Lords Variol and Tamarantha I entrust the defenses of the Land. I charge you—do all which wisdom or vision suggest to preserve the life in our sworn care. Remember that there is always hope while Revelstone stands. But if Revelstone falls, then all the ages and works of the Lords, from Berek Heartthew to our generation, shall come to an end, and the Land will never know the like again.

"Lord Mhoram and I will go in search of Drool Rockworm and the Staff of Law. With us will go the Giant Saltheart Foamfollower, ur-Lord Thomas Covenant, as many of the Bloodguard as First Mark Tuvor deems proper to spare from the defense of Revelstone, and one Eoman of the Warward. Thus we will not go blithe or unguarded into doom—but the main might of Lord's Keep will be left for the defense of the Land if we fail.

"Hear and be ready. The Quest departs at first light."

"High Lord!" protested Garth, leaping to his feet. "Will you not wait for some word from my scouts? You must brave Grimmerdhore to pass toward Mount Thunder. If the Forest is infested by the servants of Drool or the Gray Slayer, you will have little safety until my scouts have found out the movements of the enemy."

"That is true, Warmark," said Prothall. "But how long will we be delayed?"

"Six days, High Lord. Then we will know how much force the crossing of Grimmerdhore requires."

For some time, Mhoram had been sitting with his chin in his hands, staring absently into the graveling pit. But now he roused himself and said, "One hundred Bloodguard. Or every warrior that Revelstone can provide. I have seen it. There are ur-viles in Grimmerdhore—and wolves by the thousands. They hunt in my dreams." His voice seemed to chill the air in the Close like a wind of loss.

But Prothall spoke at once, resisting the spell of Mhoram's words. "No, Garth. We cannot delay. And the peril of Grimmerdhore is too great. Even Drool Rockworm must understand that our best road to Mount Thunder leads through the Forest and along the north of Andelain. No, we will go south—around Andelain, then east through Morinmoss to the Plains of Ra, before moving north to Gravin Threndor. I know—that seems a long way, full of needless leagues, for a Quest which must rue the loss of each day. But this southward way will enable us to gain the help of the Ramen. Thus all the Despiser's olden foes will share in our Quest. And perhaps we will throw Drool out of his reckoning.

"No, my choice is clear. The Quest will depart tomorrow, riding south. That is my word. Let any who doubt speak now."

And Thomas Covenant, who doubted everything, felt Prothall's resolution and dignity so strongly that he said nothing.

Then Mhoram and Osondrea stood, followed immediately by Foamfollower; and behind them the assembly rushed to its feet. All turned toward High Lord Prothall, and Osondrea lifted up her voice to say, "*Melenkurion* Skyweir watch over you, High Lord. *Melenkurion abatha!* Preserve and prevail! Seed and rock, may your purpose flourish. Let no evil blind or ill assail—no fear or faint, no rest or joy or pain, assuage the grief of wrong. Cowardice is inexculpate, corruption unassoiled. Skyweir watch and Earthroot anneal. *Melenkurion abatha! Minas mill khabaal!*"

Prothall bowed his head, and the gallery and the Lords responded with one unanimous salute, one extending of arms in mute benediction.

Then in slow order the people began to leave the Close. At the same time, Prothall, Mhoram, and Osondrea departed through their private doors.

Once the Lords were gone, Foamfollower joined Covenant, and they moved together up the steps, followed by Bannor and Korik. Outside the Close, Foamfollower hesitated, considering something, then said, "My friend, will you answer a question for me?"

"You think I've got something left to hide?"

"As to that, who knows? The faery *Elohim* had a saying—'The heart cherishes secrets not worth the telling.' Ah, they were a laughing people. But—"

"No," Covenant cut in. "I've been scrutinized enough." He started away toward his rooms.

"But you have not heard my question."

He turned. "Why should I? You were going to ask what Atiaran had against me."

"No, my friend," replied Foamfollower, laughing softly. "Let your heart cherish that secret to the end of time. My question is this. What dreams have you had since you came to the Land? What did you dream that night in my boat?"

Impulsively, Covenant answered, "A crowd of my people—real people—were spitting blood at me. And one of them said, 'There is only one good answer to death.'"

"Only one? What answer is that?"

"Turn your back on it," Covenant snapped as he strode away down the corridor. "Outcast it." Foamfollower's good-natured humor echoed in his ears, but he marched on until he could no longer hear the Giant. Then he tried to remember the way to his rooms. With some help from Bannor, he found the suite and shut himself in, only bothering to light one torch before closing the door on the Bloodguard.

He found that in his absence someone had shuttered his windows against the fell light of the moon. Perversely, he yanked one of them open. But the bloodscape hurt his eyes like the stink of a corpse, and he slammed the shutter closed again. Then for a long time before he went to bed he paced the floor, arguing with himself until fatigue overcame him.

When morning neared, and Bannor began shaking him awake, he resisted. He wanted to go on sleeping as if in slumber he could find absolution. Dimly, he remembered that he was about to start on a journey far more dangerous than the one he had just completed, and his tired consciousness moaned in protest.

"Come," said Bannor. "If we delay, we will miss the call of the Ranyhyn."

"Go to hell," Covenant mumbled. "Don't you ever sleep?"

"The Bloodguard do not sleep."

"What?"

"No Bloodguard has slept since the *Haruchai* swore their Vow."

With an effort, Covenant pulled himself into a sitting position. He peered blearily at Bannor for a moment, then muttered, "You're already in hell."

The alien flatness of Bannor's voice did not waver as he replied, "You have no reason to mock us."

"Of course not," Covenant growled, climbing out of bed. "Naturally, I'm supposed to enjoy having my integrity judged by someone who doesn't even need sleep."

"We do not judge. We are cautious. The Lords are in our care."

"Like Kevin—who killed himself. And took just about everything else with him." But as he made this retort, he felt suddenly ashamed of himself. In the firelight, he remembered the costliness of the Bloodguard's fidelity. Wincing at the coldness of the stone floor, he said, "Forget it. I talk like that in self-defense. Ridicule seems to be—my only answer." Then he hurried away to wash, shave, and get dressed. After a quick meal, he made sure of his knife and staff, and at last nodded his readiness to the Bloodguard.

Bannor led him down to the courtyard of the old Gilden tree. A haze of night still dimmed the air, but the stars were gone, and sunrise was clearly imminent. Unexpectedly, he felt that he was taking part in something larger than himself. The sensation was an odd one, and he tried to reason it away as he followed Bannor through the tunnel, between the huge, knuckled tower gates, and out into the dawn.

There, near the wall a short distance to the right of the gate, was gathered the company of the Quest. The warriors of the Third Eoman sat astride their horses in a semicircle behind Warhaft Quaan, and to their left stood nine Bloodguard led by First Mark Tuvor. Within the semicircle were Prothall, Mhoram, and Saltheart Foamfollower. The Giant carried in his belt a quarterstaff as tall as a man, and wore a blue neckscarf that fluttered ebulliently in the morning breeze. Nearby were three men holding three horses saddled in *clingor*. Above them all, the face of Revelstone was crowded with people. The dwellers of the mountain city thronged every balcony and terrace, every window. And facing the gathered company was Lord Osondrea. She held her head high as if she defied her responsibility to make her stoop.

Then the sun crested the eastern horizon. It caught the upper rim of the plateau, where burned the blue flame of warning; it moved down the wall until it lifted High Lord's Furl out of the gloaming like the lighting of a torch. Next it revealed the red pennant, and then a new white flag.

Nodding up at the new flag, Bannor said, "That is for you, ur-Lord. The sign of white gold." Then he went to take his place among the Bloodguard.

Silence rested on the company until the sunlight touched the ground, casting its gold glow over the Questers. As soon as the light reached her feet, Osondrea began speaking as if she had been waiting impatiently for this moment, and she covered the ache in her heart with a scolding tone. "I am in no mood for the ceremony, Prothall. Call the Ranyhyn and go.

The folly of this undertaking will not be made less by delay and brave words. There is nothing more for you to say. I am well suited for my task, and the defense of the Land will not falter while I live. Go—call the Ranyhyn."

Prothall smiled gently, and Mhoram said with a grin, "We are fortunate in you, Osondrea. I could not entrust any other with Variol my father and Tamarantha my mother."

"Taunt me at your peril!" she snapped. "I am in no mood—no mood, do you hear?"

"I hear. You know that I do not taunt you. Sister Osondrea, be careful."

"I am always careful. Now go, before I lose patience altogether."

Prothall nodded to Tuvor; the ten Bloodguard turned and spread out, so that each faced into the rising sun with no one to obscure his view. One at a time, each Bloodguard raised a hand to his mouth and gave a piercing whistle which echoed off the wall of the Keep into the dawn air.

They whistled again, and then a third time, and each call sounded as fierce and lonely as a heart cry. But the last whistle was answered by a distant whinny and a low thunder of mighty hooves. All eyes turned expectantly eastward, squinted into the morning glory. For a long moment, nothing appeared, and the rumble of the earth came disembodied to the company, a mystic manifestation. But then the horses could be seen within the sun's orb, as if they had materialized in skyfire.

Soon the Ranyhyn passed out of the direct line of the sun. There were ten of them—wild and challenging animals. They were great craggy beasts, deep-chested, proud-necked, with some of the delicacy of pure-blooded stock and some of the rough angularity of mustangs. They had long flying manes and tails, gaits as straight as plumb lines, eyes full of restless intelligence. Chestnuts, bays, roans, they galloped toward the Bloodguard.

Covenant knew enough about horses to see that the Ranyhyn were as individual as people, but they shared one trait: a white star marked the center of each forehead. As they approached, with the dawn burning on their backs, they looked like the Land personified—the essence of health and power.

Nickering and tossing their heads, they halted before the Bloodguard. And the Bloodguard bowed deeply to them. The Ranyhyn stamped their feet and shook their manes as if they were laughing affectionately at a mere human show of respect. After a moment Tuvor spoke to them. "Hail, Ranyhyn! Land-riders and proud-bearers. Sun-flesh and sky-mane, we are glad that you have heard our call. We must go on a long journey of many days. Will you bear us?"

In response, a few of the horses nodded their heads, and several others pranced in circles like colts. Then they moved forward, each approaching a specific Bloodguard and nuzzling him as if urging him to mount. This the Bloodguard did, though the horses were without saddle or bridle. Riding bareback, the Bloodguard trotted the Ranyhyn in a circle around the company, and arrayed themselves beside the mounted warriors.

Covenant felt that the departure of the company was imminent, and he did not want to miss his chance. Stepping close to Osondrea, he asked, "What does it mean? Where did they come from?"

The Lord turned and answered almost eagerly, as if glad for any distraction, "Of course—you are a stranger. Now, how can I explain such a deep matter briefly? Consider—the Ranyhyn are free, untamed, and their home is in the Plains of Ra. They are tended by the Ramen, but they are never ridden unless they choose a rider for themselves. It is a free choice. And once a Ranyhyn selects a rider, it is faithful to that one though fire and death interdict.

"Few are chosen. Tamarantha is the only living Lord to be blessed with a Ranyhyn mount—Hynaril bears her proudly—though neither Prothall nor Mhoram have yet made the trial. Prothall has been unwilling. But I suspect that one of his reasons for journeying south is to give Mhoram a chance to be chosen.

"No matter. Since the age of High Lord Kevin, a bond has grown up between the Ranyhyn and the Bloodguard. For many reasons, only some of which I can guess, no Bloodguard has remained unchosen.

"As to the coming here of the Ranyhyn today—that surpasses my explaining. They are creatures of Earthpower. In some way, each Ranyhyn knows when its rider will call—yes, knows, and never fails to answer. Here are Huryn, Brabha, Marny, and others. Ten days ago they heard the call which only reached our ears this morning—and after more than four hundred leagues, they arrive as fresh as the dawn. If we could match them, the Land would not be in such peril."

As she had been speaking, Prothall and Mhoram had mounted their horses, and she finished while walking Covenant toward his mustang. Under the influence of her voice, he went up to the animal without hesitation. But when he put his foot in the stirrup of the *clingor* saddle he felt a spasm of reluctance. He did not like horses, did not trust them; their strength was too dangerous. He backed away, and found that his hands were trembling.

Osondrea regarded him curiously; but before she could say anything a bustle of surprise ran through the company. When he looked up, Covenant saw three old figures riding forward—the Lords Variol and Tamarantha, and Hearthrall Birinair. Tamarantha sat astride a great roan Ranyhyn mare with laughing eyes.

Bowing toward them from the back of his horse, High Lord Prothall said, "I am glad that you have come. We need your blessing before we depart, just as Osondrea needs your help."

Tamarantha bowed in return, but there was a sly half-smile on her wrinkled lips. She scanned the company briefly. "You have chosen well, Prothall." Then she brought her old eyes back to the High Lord. "But you mistake us. We go with you."

Prothall began to object, but Birinair put in stoutly,

"Of course. What else? A Quest without a Hirebrand, indeed!"

"Birinair," said Prothall reprovingly, "surely our work for the Seareach Giants requires you."

"Requires? Of course. As to that, why," the Hirebrand huffed, "as to that—no. Shames me to say it. I have given all the orders. No. The others are abler. Have been for years."

"Prothall," Tamarantha urged, "do not forbid. We are old—of course we are old. And the way will be long and hard. But this is the great challenge of our time—the only high and bold enterprise in which we will ever be able to share."

"Is the defense of Revelstone then such a little thing?"

Variol jerked up his head as if Prothall's question had been a gibe. "Revelstone remembers we have failed to retrieve any of Kevin's Lore. What possible help can we be here? Osondrea is more than enough. Without this Quest, our lives will be wasted."

"No, my Lords—no. Not wasted," Prothall murmured. With a baffled expression, he looked to Mhoram for support. Smiling crookedly, Mhoram said, "Life is well designed. Men and women grow old so that someone will be wise enough to teach the young. Let them come."

After another moment's hesitation, Prothall decided. "Come, then. You will teach us all."

Variol smiled up at Tamarantha, and she returned his gaze from the high back of the Ranyhyn. Their faces were full of satisfaction and calm expectancy, which they shared in the silent marriage of their eyes. Watching them, Covenant abruptly snatched up his horse's reins and climbed into the saddle. His heart thudded anxiously, but almost at once the *clingor* gave him a feeling of security which eased his trepidation. Following the example of Prothall and Mhoram, he slid the staff under his left thigh, where it was held by the *clingor*. Then he gripped the mustang with his knees and tried not to fret.

The man who had been holding the horse touched Covenant's knee to get his attention. "Her name is

Dura—Dura Fairflank. Horses are rare in the Land. I have trained her well. She is as good as a Ranyhyn," he boasted, then lowered his eyes as if embarrassed by his exaggeration.

Covenant replied gruffly, "I don't want a Ranyhyn."

The man took this as approval of Dura, and beamed with pleasure. As he moved away, he touched his palms to his forehead and spread his arms wide in salute.

From his new vantage, Covenant surveyed the company. There were no packhorses, but attached to every saddle were bags of provisions and tools, and Birinair had a thick bundle of *lillianrill* rods behind him. The Bloodguard were unencumbered, but Foamfollower carried his huge sack over his shoulder, and looked ready to travel as fast as any horse.

Shortly, Prothall rose in his stirrups and called out over the company, "My friends, we must depart. The Quest is urgent, and the time of our trial presses upon us. I will not try to stir your hearts with long words, or bind you with awesome oaths. But I give you two charges. Be true to the limit of your strength. And remember the Oath of Peace. We go into danger, and perhaps into war—we will fight if need be. But the Land will not be served by angry bloodshed. Remember the Code:

> Do not hurt where holding is enough;
> do not wound where hurting is enough;
> do not maim where wounding is enough;
> and kill not where maiming is enough;
> the greatest warrior is one who does not need to kill."

Then the High Lord wheeled his mount to face Revelstone. He drew out his staff, swung it three times about his head, and raised it to the sky. From its end, a blue incandescent flame burst. And he cried to the Keep:

"Hail, Revelstone!"

The entire population of the Keep responded with one mighty, heart-shaking shout:

"Hail!"

That myriad-throated paean sprang across the hills; the dawn air itself seemed to vibrate with praise and salutation. Several of the Ranyhyn nickered joyously. In answer, Covenant clenched his teeth against a sudden thickening in his throat. He felt unworthy.

Then Prothall turned his horse and urged it into a canter down the hillside. Swiftly, the company swung into place around him. Mhoram guided Covenant to a position behind Prothall, ahead of Variol and Tamarantha. Four Bloodguard flanked the Lords on either side, Quaan, Tuvor, and Korik rode ahead of Prothall, and behind came Birinair and the Eoman. With a long, loping stride, Foamfollower pulled abreast of Mhoram and Covenant, where he jogged as easily as if such traveling were natural to him.

Thus the Quest for the Staff of Law left Lord's Keep in the sunlight of a new day.

SIXTEEN: Blood-Bourne

THOMAS Covenant spent the next three days in one long, acute discovery of saddle soreness. Sitting on thin leather, he felt as if he were riding bareback; the hard, physical fact of Dura's spine threatened to saw him open. His knees felt as if they were being twisted out of joint; his thighs and calves ached and quivered with the strain of gripping his mount—a pain which slowly spread into and up his back; and his neck throbbed from the lash of Dura's sudden lurchings as she crossed the obstacles of the terrain. At times, he remained on her back only because the *clingor* saddle did not let him fall. And at night his clenched muscles hurt so badly that he could not sleep without the benefit of *diamondraught*.

As a result, he noticed little of the passing country-side, or the weather, or the mood of the company. He ignored or rebuffed every effort to draw him into conversation. He was consumed by the painful sensation of being broken in half. Once again, he was forced to recognize the suicidal nature of this dream, of what the subconscious darkness of his mind was doing to him.

But the Giant's *diamondraught* and the Land's impossible health worked in him regardless of his suffering. His flesh grew tougher to meet the demands of Dura's back. And without knowing it he had been improving as a rider. He was learning how to move with instead of resisting his mount. When he woke up after the third night, he found that physical hurting no longer dominated him.

By that time, the company had left behind the cultivated region around Revelstone, and had moved out into rough plains. They had camped in the middle of a rude flatland; and when Covenant began to look about him, the terrain that met his eyes was rocky and unpromising.

Nevertheless, the sense of moving forward reasserted itself in him, gave him once again the illusion of safety. Like so many other things, Revelstone was behind him. When Foamfollower addressed him, he was able to respond without violence.

At that, the Giant remarked to Mhoram, "Stone and Sea, my Lord! I believe that Thomas Covenant has chosen to rejoin the living. Surely this is the work of *diamondraught*. Hail, ur-Lord Covenant. Welcome to our company. Do you know, Lord Mhoram, there is an ancient Giantish tale about a war which was halted by *diamondraught?* Would you like to hear? I can tell it in half a day."

"Indeed?" Mhoram chuckled. "And will it take only half a day if you tell it on the run, while we ride?"

Foamfollower laughed broadly. "Then I can be done by sunset tomorrow. I, Saltheart Foamfollower, say it."

"I have heard that tale," High Lord Prothall said. "But the teller assured me that *diamondraught* did not in fact end the conflict. The actual rein was Giantish talk. When the Giants were done asking after the causes of the war, the combatants had been listening so long that they had forgotten the answer."

"Ah, High Lord," Foamfollower chortled, "you misunderstand. It was the Giants who drank the *diamondraught.*"

Laughter burst from the listening warriors, and Prothall smiled as he turned to mount his horse. Soon the Quest was on its way, and Covenant fell into place beside Mhoram.

Now as he rode, Covenant listened to the traveling noises of the company. The Lords and Bloodguard were almost entirely silent, preoccupied; but over the thud of hooves, he could hear talk and snatches of song from the warriors. In Quaan's leadership, they sounded confident and occasionally eager, as if they looked forward to putting their years of Sword training to the test.

Sometime later, Lord Mhoram surprised Covenant by saying without preamble, "Ur-Lord, as you know there were questions which the Council did not ask of you. May I ask them now? I should like to know more concerning your world."

"My world." Covenant swallowed roughly. He did not want to talk about it; he had no desire to repeat the ordeal of the Council. "Why?"

Mhoram shrugged. "Because the more I know of you, the better I will know what to expect from you in times of peril. Or because an understanding of your world may teach me to treat you rightly. Or because I have asked the question in simple friendship."

Covenant could hear the candor in Mhoram's voice, and it disarmed his refusals. He owed the Lords and himself some kind of honesty. But that debt was bitter to him, and he could not find any easy way to articulate all the things which needed saying. Instinctively, he began to make a list. We have cancer, heart failure, tuberculosis, multiple sclerosis, birth defects, leprosy—we have alcoholism, venereal disease, drug addiction, rape, robbery, murder, child beating, genocide—but he could not bear to utter a catalog of woes that might run on forever. After a moment, he stood in his stirrups and gestured out over the ruggedness of the plains.

"You probably see it better than I do—but even I can tell that this is beautiful. It's alive—it's alive the way it should be alive. This kind of grass is yellow and stiff and thin—but I can see that it's healthy. It belongs here, in this kind of soil. By hell! I can even see what time of year this is by looking at the dirt. I can see *spring*.

"Where I come from we don't see— If you don't know the annual cycles of the plants, you can't tell the difference between spring and summer. If you don't have a—have a standard of comparison, you can't recognize— But the world is beautiful—what's left of it, what we haven't damaged." Images of Haven Farm sprang irrefusably across his mind. He could not restrain the mordancy of his tone as he concluded, "We have beauty, too. We call it 'scenery.' "

" 'Scenery,' " Mhoram echoed. "The word is strange to me—but I do not like the sound."

Covenant felt oddly shaken, as if he had just looked over his shoulder and found himself standing too close to a precipice. "It means that beauty is something extra," he rasped. "It's nice, but we can live without it."

"Without?" Mhoram's gaze glittered dangerously.

And behind him Foamfollower breathed in astonishment, "Live without beauty? Ah, my friend! How do you resist despair?"

"I don't think we do," Covenant muttered. "Some of us are just stubborn." Then he fell silent. Mhoram asked him no more questions, and he rode on chewing the gristle of his thoughts until High Lord Prothall called a rest halt.

As the day progressed, Covenant's silence seemed slowly to infect the company. The traveling banter and singing of the Eoman faded gradually into stillness; Mhoram watched Covenant curiously askance, but made no effort to renew their conversation; and Prothall looked as night-faced as the Bloodguard. After a time, Covenant guessed the cause of their reticence. Tonight would be the first full of the bloody moon.

A shiver ran through him. That night would be a kind of test of Drool's power. If the Cavewight could maintain his red hold even when the moon was full, then the Lords would have to admit that his might had no discernible limit. And such might would be spawning armies, would almost certainly have already produced marauders to feed Drool's taste for pillage. Then the company would have to fight for passage. Covenant remembered with a shudder his brief meeting with Drool in the cavern of Kiril Threndor. Like his companions, he fell under the pall of what the night might reveal.

Only Variol and Tamarantha seemed untouched by the common mood. She appeared half-asleep, and rode casually, trusting the Ranyhn to keep her on its back. Her husband sat erect, with a steady hand on his reins, but his mouth was slack and his eyes unfocused. They looked frail; Covenant felt that he could see the brittleness of their bones. But they alone of all the company were blithe against the coming night—blithe or uncomprehending.

The riders camped before dusk on the north side of a rough hill, partially sheltered from the prevailing southwest breeze. The air had turned cold like a re-visitation of winter, and the wind carried a chill to the hearts of the travelers. In silence, some of the warriors fed and rubbed down the horses, while others cooked a spare meal over a fire that Birinair coaxed from one of his *lillianrill* rods and some scrub wood. The Ranyhn galloped away together to spend the night in some secret play or rite, leaving the horses hobbled and the Bloodguard standing sentinel and the rest of the company huddled in their cloaks around the fire. As the last of the sunlight scudded from the air, the breeze stiffened into a steady wind.

Covenant found himself wishing for some of the camaraderie that had begun the day. But he could not supply the lack himself; he had to wait until High Lord Prothall rose to meet the apprehension of the Quest.

Planting his staff firmly, he began to sing the
Vespers hymn of Revelstone. Mhoram joined him,
followed by Variol and Tamarantha, and soon the
whole Eoman was on its feet, adding its many-
throated voice to the song. There they stood under
the stern sky, twenty-five souls singing like witnesses:

Seven hells for failed faith,
For Land's betrayers, man and wraith:
And one brave Lord to deal the doom
To keep the blacking blight from Beauty's
    bloom.

They raised their voices bravely, and their melody
was counterpointed by the tenor roll of Foamfollower's plainsong. When they were done, they reseated
themselves and began to talk together in low voices, as
if the hymn were all they needed to restore their
courage.

Covenant sat staring at his knotted hands. Without taking his eyes off them, he knew when moonrise
came; he felt the sudden stiffening around him as the
first crimson glow appeared on the horizon. But he
gnawed on his lip and did not look up. His companions breathed tensely; a red cast slowly deepened
in the heart of the fire; but he clenched his gaze as if
he were studying the way his knuckles whitened.

Then he heard Lord Mhoram's agonized whisper,
"Melenkurion," and he knew that the moon was full
red, stained as if its defilement were complete—as
bloody as if the night sky had been cut to the heart.
He felt the light touch his face, and his cheek twitched
in revulsion.

The next moment, there came a distant wail like
a cry of protest. It throbbed like desolation in the
chill air. In spite of himself, Covenant looked over
the blood-hued plain; for an instant, he expected the
company to leap to the relief of that call. But no one
moved. The cry must have come from some animal.
Glancing briefly at the full violated moon, he changed
his grip and lowered his eyes again.

When his gaze reached his fingers, he saw in horror

that the moonlight gave his ring a reddish cast. The metal looked as if it had been dipped in blood. Its inner silver struggled to show through the crimson, but the bloodlight seemed to be soaking inward, slowly quenching, perverting the white gold.

He understood instinctively. For one staggering heartbeat, he sat still, howled silent and futile warnings at his unsuspecting self. Then he sprang to his feet, erect and rigid as if he had been yanked upright by the moon—arms tight at his sides, fists clenched.

Behind him, Bannor said, "Do not fear, ur-Lord. The Ranyhyn will warn us if the wolves are any danger."

Covenant turned his head. The Bloodguard reached a restraining hand toward him.

"Don't touch me!" Covenant hissed.

He jerked away from Bannor. For an instant while his heart labored, he observed how the crimson moon made Bannor's face look like old lava. Then a vicious sense of wrong exploded under his feet, and he pitched toward the fire.

As he struck the earth he flung himself onward, careless of everything but his intense visceral need to escape the attack. After one roll, his legs crashed among the flaming brands.

But as Covenant fell, Bannor sprang forward. When Covenant hit the fire, the Bloodguard was only a stride away. He caught Covenant's wrist in almost the same instant, heaved him child-light out of the flames and onto his feet.

Even before he had regained his balance, Covenant spun on Bannor and yelled into the Bloodguard's face, "Don't touch me!"

Bannor released Covenant's wrist, backed away a step.

Prothall, Mhoram, Foamfollower, and all the warriors were on their feet. They stared at Covenant in surprise, confusion, outrage.

He felt suddenly weak. His legs trembled; he dropped to his knees beside the fire. Thinking, Hellfire and bloody Foul has done it to me, he's taking

me over damnation! he pointed an unsteady finger at
the ground that had stung him. "There," he gasped.
"It was there. I felt it."

The Lords reacted immediately. While Mhoram
shouted for Birinair, Prothall hurried forward and
stooped over the spot Covenant indicated. Mumbling softly to himself, he touched the spot with the
tips of his fingers like a physician testing a wound.
Then he was joined by Mhoram and Birinair. Birinair
thrust the High Lord aside, took his *lillianrill* staff
and placed its end on the sore place. Rotating the
staff between his palms, he concentrated imperi-
ously on his beloved wood.

"For one moment," Prothall murmured, "for one
moment I felt something—some memory in the
Earth. Then it passed beyond my touch." He sighed.
"It was terrible."

Birinair echoed, "Terrible," talking to himself in
his concentration. Prothall and Mhoram watched
him as his hands trembled with either age or sensitivity. Abruptly, he cried, "Terrible! The hand of
the Slayer! He dares do this?" He snatched himself away so quickly that he stumbled, and would
have fallen if Prothall had not caught him.

Momentarily, Prothall and Birinair met each
other's eyes as if they were trying to exchange some
knowledge that could not be voiced. Then Birinair
shook himself free. Looking about him as if he could
see the shards of his dignity scattered around his
feet, he mumbled gruffly, "Stand on my own. Not
that old yet." After a glance at Covenant, he went
on more loudly, "You think I am old. Of course.
Old and foolish. Push himself into a Quest when he
should be resting his bones by the hearth. Like a
lump." Pointing toward the Unbeliever, he concluded,
"Ask him. Ask."

Covenant had climbed to his feet while the attention of the company was on the Hirebrand, and had
pushed his hands into his pockets to hide the hue
of his ring. As Birinair pointed at him, he raised his
eyes from the ground. A sick feeling of presage

twisted his stomach as he remembered his attacks in Andelain, and what had followed them.

Prothall said firmly, "Step there again, ur-Lord."

Grimacing, Covenant strode forward and stamped his foot on the spot. As his heel hit the ground, he winced in expectation, tried to brace himself for the sensation that at this one point the earth had become insecure, foundationless. But nothing stung him. As in Andelain, the ill had vanished, leaving him with the impression that a veneer of trustworthiness had been replaced over a pit.

In answer to the silent question of the Lords, he shook his head.

After a pause, Mhoram said evenly, "You have felt this before."

With an effort, Covenant forced himself to say, "Yes. Several times—in Andelain. Before that attack on the Celebration."

"The hand of the Gray Slayer touched you," Birinair spat. But he could not sustain his accusation. His bones seemed to remember their age, and he sagged tiredly, leaned on his staff. In an odd tone of self-reproach, as if he were apologizing, he mumbled, "Of course. Younger. If I were younger." He turned from the company and shuffled away to his bed beyond the circle.

"Why did you not tell us?" Mhoram asked severely.

The question made Covenant feel suddenly ashamed, as if his ring were visible through the fabric of his pants. His shoulders hunched, drove his hands deeper into his pockets. "I didn't—at first I didn't want you to know what—how important Foul and Drool think I am. After that"—he referred to his crisis in the Close with his eyes—"I was thinking about other things."

Mhoram accepted this with a nod, and after a moment Covenant went on: "I don't know what it is. But I only get it through my boots. I can't touch it—with my hands or my feet."

Mhoram and Prothall shared a glance of surprise. Shortly, the High Lord said, "Unbeliever, the cause of these attacks surpasses me. Why do your boots make you sensitive to this wrong? I do not know. But either Lord Mhoram or myself must remain by you at all times, so that we may respond without delay." Over his shoulder, he said, "First Mark Tuvor. Warhaft Quaan. Have you heard?"

Quaan came to attention and replied, "Yes, High Lord." And from behind the circle Tuvor's voice carried softly, "There will be an attack. We have heard."

"Readiness will be needed," said Mhoram grimly, "and stout hearts to face an onslaught of ur-viles and wolves and Cavewights without faltering."

"That is so," the High Lord said at last. "But such things will come in their own time. Now we must rest. We must gather strength."

Slowly, the company began the business of bedding down. Humming his Giantish plainsong, Foamfollower stretched out on the ground with his arm around his leather flask of *diamondraught*. While the Bloodguard set watches, the warriors spread blankets for themselves and the Lords. Covenant went to bed self-consciously, as if he felt the company studying him, and he was glad of the blankets that helped him hide his ring. Then he lay awake long into the night, feeling too cold to sleep; the blankets did not keep out the chill which emanated from his ring.

But until he finally fell asleep, he could hear Foamfollower's humming and see Prothall sitting by the embers of the fire. The Giant and the High Lord kept watch together, two old friends of the Land sharing some vigil against their impending doom.

The next day dawned gray and cheerless—overcast with clouds like ashes in the sky—and into it Covenant rode bent in his saddle as if he had a weight around his neck. His ring had lost its red stain with the setting of the moon; but the color remained in his mind, and the ring seemed to drag him down like a meaningless crime. Helplessly, he perceived that an allegiance he had not chosen, could not have chosen, was being forced upon him. The evidence seemed irrefutable. Like the moon, he was falling prey to Lord Foul's machinations. His volition was not required;

the strings which dangled him were strong enough to overbear any resistance.

He did not understand how it could happen to him. Was his death wish, his leper's weariness or despair, so strong? What had become of his obdurate instinct for survival? Where was his anger, his violence? Had he been victimized for so long that now he could only respond as a victim, even to himself?

He had no answers. He was sure of nothing but the fear which came over him when the company halted at noon. He found that he did not want to get down from Dura's back.

He distrusted the ground, dreaded contact with it. He had lost a fundamental confidence: his faith that the earth was stable—a faith so obvious and constant and necessary that it had been unconscious until now —had been shaken. Blind silent soil had become a dark hand malevolently seeking out him and him alone.

Nevertheless, he swung down from the saddle, forced himself—set foot on the ground and was stung. The virulence of the sensation made all his nerves cringe, and he could hardly stand as he watched Prothall and Mhoram and Birinair try to capture what he had felt. But they failed completely; the misery of that ill touch withdrew the instant he jumped away from it.

That evening during supper he was stung again. When he went to bed to hide his ring from the moon, he shivered as if he were feverish. On the morning of the sixth day, he arose with a gray face and a crippled look in his eyes. Before he could mount Dura he was stung again.

And again during one of the company's rest halts.

And again the instant he mustered enough despair to dismount at the end of the day's ride. The wrong felt like another spike in his coffin lid. This time, his nerves reacted so violently that he tumbled to the ground like a demonstration of futility. He had to lie still for a long time before he could coax his arms and legs under control again, and when he finally regained his feet, he jerked and winced with fear at every step.

Pathetic, pathetic, he panted to himself. But he could not find the rage to master it.

With keen concern in his eyes, Foamfollower asked him why he did not take off his boots. Covenant had to think for a moment before he could remember why. Then he murmured, "They're part of me—they're part of the way I have to live. I don't have—very many parts left. And besides," he added wanly, "if I don't keep having these fits, how is Prothall going to figure them out?"

"Do not do such a thing for us," Mhoram replied intently. "How could we ask it?"

But Covenant only shrugged and went to sit by the fire. He could not face food that night—the thought of eating made his raw nerves nauseous—but he tried a few *aliantha* from a bush near the camp, and found that they had a calming effect. He ate a handful of the berries, absentmindedly tossing away the seeds as Lena had taught him, and returned to the fire.

When the company had finished its meal, Mhoram seated himself beside Covenant. Without looking at him, the Lord asked, "How can we help you? Should we build a litter so that you will not have to touch the earth? Or are there other ways? Perhaps one of Foamfollower's tales would ease your heart. I have heard Giants boast that the Despiser himself would become an Earthfriend if he could be made to listen to the story of Bahgoon the Unbearable and Thelma Twofist —such healing there is in stories." Abruptly, Mhoram turned squarely toward Covenant, and Covenant saw that the Lord's face was full of sympathy. "I see your pain, ur-Lord."

Covenant hung his head to avoid Mhoram's gaze, made sure his left hand was securely in his pocket. After a moment, he said distantly, "Tell me about the Creator."

"Ah," Mhoram sighed, "we do not know that a Creator lives. Our only lore of such a being comes from the most shadowy reaches of our oldest legends. We know the Despiser. But the Creator we do not know."

Then Covenant was vaguely startled to hear Lord

Tamarantha cut in, "Of course we know. Ah, the folly of the young. Mhoram my son, you are not yet a prophet. You must learn that kind of courage." Slowly, she pulled her ancient limbs together and got to her feet, leaning on her staff for support. Her thin white hair hung in wisps about her face as she moved into the circle around the fire, muttering frailly, "Oracles and prophecy are incompatible. According to Kevin's Lore, only Heartthew the Lord-Fatherer was both seer and prophet. Lesser souls lose the paradox. Why, I do not know. But when Kevin Landwaster decided in his heart to invoke the Ritual of Desecration, he saved the Bloodguard and the Ranyhyn and the Giants because he was an oracle. And because he was no prophet he failed to see that Lord Foul would survive. A lesser man than Berek. Of course the Creator lives."

She looked over at Variol for confirmation, and he nodded, but Covenant could not tell whether he was approving or drowsing. But Tamarantha nodded in return as if Variol had supported her. Lifting her head to the night sky and the stars, she spoke in a voice fragile with age.

"Of course the Creator lives," she repeated. "How else? Opposites require each other. Otherwise the difference is lost, and only chaos remains. No, there can be no Despite without Creation. Better to ask how the Creator could have forgotten that when he made the Earth. For if he did not forget, then Creation and Despite existed together in his one being, and he did not know it.

"This the elder legends tell us: into the infinity before Time was made came the Creator like a worker into his workshop. And since it is the nature of creating to desire perfection, the Creator devoted all himself to the task. First he built the arch of Time, so that his creation would have a place in which to be— and for the keystone of that arch he forged the wild magic, so that Time would be able to resist chaos and endure. Then within the arch he formed the Earth. For ages he labored, formed and unformed, trialed and tested and rejected and trialed and tested again, so that when he was done his creation would have no cause to reproach him. And when the Earth was fair to his eye, he gave birth to the inhabitants of the Earth, beings to act out in their lives his reach for perfection—and he did not neglect to give them the means to strive for perfection themselves. When he was done, he was proud as only those who create can be.

"Alas, he did not understand Despite, or had forgotten it. He undertook his task thinking that perfect labor was all that he required to create perfection. But when he was done, and his pride had tasted its first satisfaction, he looked closely at the Earth, thinking to gratify himself with the sight—and he was dismayed. For, behold! Buried deep in the Earth through no will or forming of his were banes of destruction, powers virile enough to rip his masterwork into dust.

"Then he understood or remembered. Perhaps he found Despite itself beside him, misguiding his hand. Or perhaps he saw the harm in himself. It does not matter. He became outraged with grief and torn pride. In his fury he wrestled with Despite, either within him or without, and in his fury he cast the Despiser down, out of the infinity of the cosmos onto the Earth.

"Alas! thus the Despiser was emprisoned within Time. And thus the Creator's creation became the Despiser's world, to torment as he chose. For the very Law of Time, the principle of power which made the arch possible, worked to preserve Lord Foul, as we now call him. That Law requires that no act may be undone. Desecration may not be undone—defilement may not be recanted. It may be survived or healed, but not denied. Therefore Lord Foul has afflicted the Earth, and the Creator cannot stop him—for it was the Creator's act which placed Despite here.

"In sorrow and humility, the Creator saw what he had done. So that the plight of the Earth would not be utterly without hope, he sought to help his creation in indirect ways. He guided the Lord-Fatherer to the fashioning of the Staff of Law—a weapon against Despite. But the very Law of the Earth's creation permits nothing more. If the Creator were to silence

Lord Foul, that act would destroy Time—and then the Despiser would be free in infinity again, free to make whatever befoulments he desired."

Tamarantha paused. She had told her tale simply, without towering rhetoric or agitation or any sign of passion beyond her agedness. But for a moment, her thin old voice convinced Covenant that the universe was at stake—that his own struggle was only a microcosm of a far larger conflict. During that moment, he waited in suspense for what she would say next.

Shortly, she lowered her head and turned her wrinkled gaze full on him. Almost whispering, she said, "Thus we are come to the greatest test. The wild magic is here. With a word our world could be riven to the core. Do not mistake," she quavered. "If we cannot win this Unbeliever to our cause, then the Earth will end in rubble." But Covenant could not tell whether her voice shook because she was old, or because she was afraid.

Moonrise was near; he went to his bed to avoid exposing the alteration of his ring. With his head under the blankets, he stared into the blackness, saw when the moon came up by the bloody glow which grew in his wedding band. The metal seemed more deeply stained than it had two nights ago. It held his covered gaze like a fixation; and when he finally slept, he was as exhausted as if he had been worn out under an interrogation.

The next morning, he managed to reach Dura's back without being attacked—and he groaned in unashamed relief. Then Prothall broke his usual habit and did not call for a halt at noon. The reason became clear when the riders topped a rise and came in sight of the Soulsease River. They rode down out of the harsh plains and swam their horses across the river before stopping to rest. And there again Covenant was not attacked when he set foot on the ground.

But the rest of the day contrasted grimly with this inexplicable respite. A few leagues beyond the Soulsease, the Quest came upon a Waymeet for the first time. Remembering Covenant's tale of a murdered Waynhim, Prothall sent two Bloodguard, Korik and

Terrel (who warded Lord Mhoram), into the Way-meet. The investigation was only necessary for confirmation. Even Covenant in his straitened condition could see the neglect, smell the disuse; the green travelers' haven had gone brown and sour. When Korik and Terrel returned, they could only report what the company had already perceived: the Way-meet was untended.

The Lords met this discovery with stern faces. Clearly, they had feared that the murder Covenant had described would lead the Waynhim to end their service. But several of the warriors groaned in shock and dismay, and Foamfollower ground his teeth. Covenant glanced around at the Giant, and for a moment saw Foamfollower's face suffused with fury. The expression passed quickly, but it left Covenant feeling shaken. Unexpectedly, he sensed that the un-marred loyalty of the Giants to the Land was dangerous; it was quick to judge.

So there was a gloom on the company at the end of the seventh day, a gloom which could only be aggravated by the moon, incarnadine and corrupt, as it colored the night like a conviction of disaster. Only Covenant received any relief; once again, his private, stalking ill left him alone. But the next day brought the riders in sight of Andelain. Their path lay along the outskirts of the Hills on the southwest side, and even through the hanging gray weather, the richness of Andelain glistened like the proudest gem of the Earth. It made the company feel light-boned, affected the Quest like a living view of what the Land had been like before the Desecration.

Covenant needed that quiet consolation as much as anyone, but it was denied him. While eating breakfast, he had been bitten again by the wrong in the earth. The previous day's respite seemed only to multiply the virulence of the attack; it was compact with malevolence, as if that respite had frustrated it, intensified its spite. The sensation of wrong left him foundering.

During one of the rest halts, he was struck again.

And that evening, while he made himself a supper

of *aliantha*, he was struck again. This time the wrong lashed him so viciously that he passed out for some time. When he regained consciousness, he was lying in Foamfollower's arms like a child. He felt vaguely that he had had convulsions.

"Take off your boots," Foamfollower urged intently.

Numbness filled Covenant's head like mist, clouded his reactions. But he mustered the lucidity to ask, "Why?"

"Why? Stone and Sea, my friend! When you ask like that, how can I answer? Ask yourself. What do you gain by enduring such wrong?"

"Myself," he murmured faintly. He wanted simply to recline in the Giant's arms and sleep, but he fought the desire, pushed himself away from Foamfollower until the Giant set him on his feet by Birinair's *lillianrill* fire. For a moment, he had to cling decrepitly to Foamfollower's arm to support himself, but then one of the warriors gave him his staff, and he braced himself on it. "By resisting."

But he knew in his bones that he was not resisting. They felt weak, as if they were melting under the strain. His boots had become a hollow symbol for an intransigence he no longer felt.

Foamfollower started to object, but Mhoram stopped him. "It is his choice," the Lord said softly.

After a while, Covenant fell into feverish sleep. He did not know that he was carried tenderly to bed, did not know that Mhoram watched over him during the night, and saw the bloody stain on his wedding band.

He reached some sort of crisis while he slept, and awoke with the feeling that he had lost, that his ability to endure had reached the final either-or of a toss which had gone against him. His throat was parched like a battleground. When he forced his eyes open, he found himself again prostrated in Foamfollower's arms. Around him, the company was ready to mount for the day's ride.

When he saw Covenant's eyes open, Foamfollower bent over him and said quietly, "I would rather bear you in my arms than see you suffer. Our journey to

Lord's Keep was easier for me than watching you now."

Part of Covenant rallied to look at the Giant. Foamfollower's face showed strain, but it was not the strain of exhaustion. Rather, it seemed like a pressure building up in his mind—a pressure that made the fortress of his forehead appear to bulge. Covenant stared at it dumbly for a long moment before he realized that it was sympathy. The sight of his own pain made Foamfollower's pulse throb in his temples.

Giants? Covenant breathed to himself. Are they all like this? Watching that concentration of emotion, he murmured, "What's a 'foamfollower'?"

The Giant did not appear to notice the irrelevance of the question. "A 'follower' is a compass," he answered simply. "So 'foam-follower'—'sea-compass.' "

Covenant began weakly moving, trying to get out of the Giant's arms. But Foamfollower held him, forbade him in silence to set his feet on the ground.

Lord Mhoram intervened. With grim determination in his voice, he said, "Set him down."

"Down," Covenant echoed.

Several retorts passed under Foamfollower's heavy brows, but he only said, "Why?"

"I have decided," Mhoram replied. "We will not move from this place until we understand what is happening to ur-Lord Covenant. I have delayed this risk too long. Death gathers around us. Set him down." His eyes flashed dangerously.

Still Foamfollower hesitated until he saw High Lord Prothall nod support for Mhoram. Then he turned Covenant upright and lowered him gently to the ground. For an instant, his hands rested protectively on Covenant's shoulders. Then he stepped back.

"Now, ur-Lord," said Mhoram. "Give me your hand. We will stand together until you feel the ill, and I feel it through you."

At that, a coil of weak panic writhed in Covenant's heart. He saw himself reflected in Mhoram's eyes, saw himself standing lornly with what he had lost written in his face. That loss dismayed him. In that tiny, reflected face he perceived abruptly that if the attacks continued he would inevitably learn to enjoy the sense of horror and loathing which they gave him. He had discovered a frontier into the narcissism of revulsion, and Mhoram was asking him to risk crossing over.

"Come," the Lord urged, extending his right hand. "We must understand this wrong if we are to resist it."

In desperation or despair, Covenant thrust out his hand. The heels of their palms met; they gripped each other's thumbs. His two fingers felt weak, hopeless for Mhoram's purpose, but the Lord's grasp was sturdy. Hand to hand like combatants, they stood there as though they were about to wrestle with some bitter ghoul.

The attack came almost at once. Covenant cried out, shook as if his bones were gibbering, but he did not leap away. In the first instant, Mhoram's hard grip sustained him. Then the Lord threw his arm around Covenant, clasped him to his chest. The violence of Covenant's distress buffeted Mhoram, but he held his ground, gritted his embrace.

As suddenly as it had come, the attack passed. With a groan, Covenant sagged in Mhoram's arms.

Mhoram held him up until he moved and began to carry his own weight. Then, slowly, the Lord released him. For a moment, their faces appeared oddly similar; they had the same haunted expression, the same sweat-damp hollow gaze. But shortly Covenant gave a shuddering sigh, and Mhoram straightened his shoulders—and the similarity faded.

"I was a fool," Mhoram breathed. "I should have known—That ill is Drool Rockworm, reaching out with the power of the Staff to find you. He can sense your presence by the touch of your boots on the earth, because they are unlike anything made in the Land. Thus he knows where you are, and so where we are.

"It is my guess that you were untouched the day we crossed the Soulsease because Drool expected us to move toward him on the River, and was searching for us on water rather than on land. But he learned his mistake, and regained contact with you yesterday."

The Lord paused, gave what he was saying a chance to penetrate Covenant. Then he concluded, "Ur-Lord, for the sake of us all—for the sake of the Land—you must not wear your boots. Drool already knows too much of our movements. His servants are abroad."

Covenant did not respond. Mhoram's words seemed to sap the last of his strength. The trial had been too much for him; with a sigh he fainted into the Lord's arms. So he did not see how carefully his boots and clothes were removed and packed in Dura's saddlebags—how tenderly his limbs were washed by the Lords and dressed in a robe of white samite—how sadly his ring was taken from his finger and placed on a new patch of *clingor* over his heart—how gently he was cradled in Saltheart Foamfollower's arms throughout the long march of that day. He lay in darkness like a sacrifice; he could hear the teeth of his leprosy devouring his flesh. There was a smell of contempt around him, insisting on his impotence. But his lips were bowed in a placid smile, a look of fondness, as if he had come at last to approve his disintegration.

He continued to smile when he awoke late that night and found himself staring into the wide ghoul-grin of the moon. Slowly, his smile stretched into a taut grimace, a look of happiness or hatred. But then the moon was blocked out of his vision by Foamfollower's great bulk. The Giant's huge palms, each as large as Covenant's face, stroked his head tenderly, and in time the caress had its effect on him. His eyes lost their ghastly appearance, and his face relaxed, drifted away from torment into repose. Soon he was deep in a less perilous slumber.

The next day—the tenth of the Quest—he awoke calmly, as if he were held in numb truce or stasis between irreconcilable demands. A feeling of affectlessness pervaded him, as if he no longer had the heart to care about himself. Yet he was hungry. He ate a large breakfast, and remembered to thank the Woodhelvennin woman who seemed to have assigned herself the task of providing for him. His new apparel he accepted with a rueful shrug, noticing in silent, dim sarcasm how easily after all he was able to shed himself—and how the white robe flattered his gaunt form as if he were born to it. Then, dumbly, he mounted Dura.

His companions watched him as if they feared he would fall. He was weaker than he had realized; he needed most of his concentration to keep his seat, but he was equal to the task. Gradually the Questers began to believe that he was out of danger. Among them, he rode through the sunshine and the warm spring air along the flowered marge of Andelain—rode attenuated and careless, as if he were locked between impossibilities.

SEVENTEEN: End in Fire

THAT night, the company camped in a narrow valley between two rocky hillsides half a league from the thick grasses of Andelain. The warriors were cheery, recovering their natural spirits after the tensions of the past few days, and they told stories and sang songs to the quiet audience of the Lords and Bloodguard. Though the Lords did not participate, they seemed glad to listen, and several times Mhoram and Quaan could be heard chuckling together.

But Covenant did not share the ebullience of the Eoman. A heavy hand of blankness held shut the lid of his emotions, and he felt separate, untouchable. Finally he went to his bed before the warriors were done with their last song.

He was awakened some time later by a hand on his shoulder. Opening his eyes, he found Foamfollower stooping beside him. The moon had nearly set. "Arise," the Giant whispered. "The Ranyhyn have brought word. Wolves are hunting us. Ur-viles may not be far behind. We must go."

Covenant blinked sleepily at the Giant's be-nighted face for a moment. "Why? Won't they follow?"

"Make haste, ur-Lord. Terrel, Korik, and perhaps a third of Quaan's Eoman will remain here in am-bush. They will scatter the pack. Come."

But Covenant persisted. "So what? They'll just fall back and follow again. Let me sleep."

"My friend, you try my patience. Arise, and I will explain."

With a sigh, Covenant rolled from his blankets. While he tightened the sash of his robe, settled his sandals on his feet, and assured himself of his staff and knife, his Woodhelvennin helper snatched up his bedding and packed it away. Then she led Dura to-ward him.

Amid the silent urgency of the company, he mounted, then went with Foamfollower toward the center of the camp, where the Lords and Bloodguard were already mounted. When the warriors were ready, Birinair extinguished the last embers of the fire, and climbed stiffly onto his horse. A moment later, the riders turned and fled the narrow valley, picking their way across the rough terrain by the last red light of the moon.

The ground under Dura's hooves looked like blood slowly clotting, and Covenant clutched his ring to preserve it from the crimson light. Around him, the company moved in a tight suspense of silence; every low, metal clatter of sword was instantly muffled, every breath covered. The Ranyhyn were as noise-less as shadows, and on their broad backs the Blood-guard sat like statues, eternally alert and insentient.

Then the moon set. Darkness was a relief, though it seemed to increase the hazard of their escape. But the whole company was surrounded, guided, by the Ranyhyn, and the mighty horses chose a path which kept the other mounts safe between them.

After two or three leagues had passed, the mood

of the Quest relaxed somewhat. They heard no pursuit, sensed no danger. Finally Foamfollower gave Covenant the explanation he had promised.

"It is simple," the Giant whispered. "After scattering the wolves, Korik and Terrel will lead a trail away from ours. They will go straight into Andelain, east toward Mount Thunder, until pursuit has been confused. Then they will turn and rejoin us."

"Why?" Covenant asked softly.

Lord Mhoram took up the explanation. "We doubt that Drool can understand our purpose." Covenant could not feel the Lord's presence as strongly as Foamfollower's, so Mhoram's voice sounded disembodied in the darkness, as if the night were speaking. That impression seemed to belie his words, as if without the verification of physical presence what the Lord said was vain. "Much of our Quest may seem foolhardy or foolish to him. Since he holds the Staff, we are mad to approach him. But if we mean to approach nonetheless, then our southward path is folly, for it is long, and his power grows—daily. He will expect us to turn east toward him, or south toward Doom's Retreat and escape. Korik and Terrel will give Drool's scouts reason to believe that we have turned to attack. If he becomes unsure of where we are, he will not guess our true aim. He will search for us in Andelain, and will seek to strengthen his defenses in Mount Thunder. Believing that we have turned to attack him, he will also believe that we have mastered the power of your white gold."

Covenant considered momentarily before asking, "What's Foul going to be doing during all this?"

"Ah," Mhoram sighed, "that is a question. There hangs the fate of our Quest—and of the Land." He was silent for a long time. "In my dreams, I see him laughing."

Covenant winced at the memory of Foul's crushing laughter, and fell silent. So the riders crept on through the dark, trusting themselves to the instincts of the Ranyhyn. When dawn came, they had left their ambush for the wolves far behind.

It took the company four more days of hard

riding, fifteen leagues a day, to reach the Mithil River, the southern boundary of Andelain. For sixty leagues, the Quest drove to the southeast without a hint of what had befallen Korik's group. In all, only eight people had left the company. But somehow without them the Quest seemed shrunken and puny. The concern of the High Lord and his companions rumbled in the hoofbeats of their mounts, and echoed in the silence that lay between them like an empty bier.

Gone now was the gladness of eye with which the warriors had beheld Andelain never more than a league to their left. From dawn to dusk every glance studied the eastern horizons; they saw nothing but a void in which Korik's riders had not appeared. Time and again, Foamfollower broke away from the company to trot up the nearest hill and peer into the distance; time and again, he returned panting and comfortless, and the company was left to conceive nightmares to explain Korik's absence.

The unspoken consensus was that no number of wolves was large enough to conquer two Bloodguard, mounted as they were on Huryn and Brabha of the Ranyhyn. No, Korik's group must have fallen into the hands of a small army of ur-viles—so the company reasoned, though Prothall argued that Korik might have had to ride many leagues to find a river or other means to throw the wolves off his trail. The High Lord's words were sound, but somehow under the incarnadine moon they seemed hollow. In spite of them, Warhaft Quaan went about his duties with the deaths of six warriors in his face.

All the riders were shrouded in gloom when, near twilight on the fourth day, they reached the banks of the Mithil.

Immediately on their left as they neared the river stood a steep hill like a boundary of Andelain. It guarded the north bank; the company could only cross its base into Andelain by riding single file along the river edge. But Prothall chose that path in preference to swimming the stiff current of the Mithil. With only Tuvor before him, he led the way east along the scant bank. The Questers followed one by one. Soon the entire company was traversing the boundary of the hill.

Spread out as they were, they were vulnerable. As the hill rose beside them, its slope became almost sheer, and its rocky crown commanded the path along the river like a fortification. The riders moved with their heads craned upward; they were keenly conscious of the hazard of their position.

They were still in the traverse when they heard a hail from the hilltop. Among the rocks, a figure rose into view. It was Terrel.

The riders returned his hail joyfully. Hurrying, they crossed the base of the hill, and found themselves in a broad, grassy valley where horses—two Ranyhyn and five mustangs—grazed up away from the river.

The mustangs were exhausted. Their legs quivered weakly, and their necks drooped; they barely had strength enough to eat.

Five, Covenant repeated. He felt numbly sure that he had miscounted.

Korik was on his way down from the hilltop. He was accompanied by five warriors.

With an angry shout, Quaan leaped from his horse and ran toward the Bloodguard. "Irin!" he demanded. "Where is Irin? By the Seven! What has happened to her?"

Korik did not answer until he stood with his group before High Lord Prothall. They struck Covenant as a strange combination: five warriors full of conflicting excitement, courage, grief; and one Bloodguard as impassive as a patriarch. If Korik felt any satisfaction or pain, he did not show it.

He held a bulging pack in one hand, but did not refer to it immediately. Instead, he saluted Prothall, and said, "High Lord. You are well. Have you been pursued?"

"We have seen no pursuit," Prothall replied gravely.

"That is good. It appeared to us that we were successful."

Prothall nodded, and Korik began his tale. "We met the wolves and sought to scatter them. But

they were *kresh*"—he made a splitting sound—
"not easily turned aside. So we led them eastward.
They would not enter Andelain. They howled on
our track, but would not enter. We watched from
a distance until they turned away to the north. Then
we rode east.

"After a day and a night, we broke trail and
turned south. But we came upon marauders. They
were mightier than we knew. There were ur-viles
and Cavewights together, and with them a *griffin*."

Korik's audience murmured with surprise and
chagrin, and the Bloodguard paused to utter what
sounded like a long curse in the tonal native tongue
of the *Haruchai*. Then he continued: "Irin purchased
our escape. But we were driven far from our way.
We reached this place only a short time before you."

With a revolted flaring of his nostrils, he lifted
the pack. "This morning we saw a hawk over us.
It flew strangely. We shot it." Reaching into the pack,
he drew out the body of the bird. Above its vicious
beak, it had only one eye, a large mad orb centered
in its forehead.

It struck the company with radiated malice. The
hawk was ill, incondign, a thing created by wrong
for purposes of wrong—bent away from its birth by
a power that dared to warp nature. The sight stuck
in Covenant's throat, made him want to retch. He
could hardly hear Prothall say, "This is the work of
the Illearth Stone. How could the Staff of Law perform such a crime, such an outrage? Ah, my friends,
this is the outcome of our enemy. Look closely. It
is a mercy to take such creatures out of life." Abruptly, the High Lord turned away, burdened by his
new knowledge.

Quaan and Birinair cremated the ill-formed hawk.
Soon the warriors who had gone with Korik began
to talk, and a fuller picture of their past four days
emerged. Attention naturally centered on the fight
which had killed Irin of the Eoman.

The Ranyhyn Brabha had first smelled danger,
and had given the warning to Korik. At once, he
had hidden his group in a thick copse to await the

coming of the marauders. Listening with his ear
to the ground, he had judged that they were a mixed
force of unmounted ur-viles and Cavewights—Cavewights had not the ur-viles' ability to step softly—
totaling no more than fifteen. So Korik had asked
himself which way his service lay: to preserve his
companions as defenders of the Lords, or to damage
the Lords' enemies. The Bloodguard were sworn to
the protection of the Lords, not of the Land. He had
elected to fight because he judged that his force
was strong enough, considering the element of surprise, to meet both duties without loss of life.

His decision had saved them. They learned later
that if they had not attacked they would have been
trapped in the copse; the panic of the horses would
have given away their hiding.

It was a dark night after moonset, the second
night after Korik's group had left the company, and
the marauders were moving without lights. Even the
Bloodguard's keen eyes discerned nothing more than
the shadowy outlines of the enemy. And the wind
blew between the two forces, so that the Ranyhyn
were prevented from smelling the extent of their
peril.

When the marauders reached open ground, Korik
signaled to his group; the warriors swept out of the
copse behind him and Terrel. The Ranyhyn outdis-
tanced the others at once, so Korik and Terrel had
just engaged the enemy when they heard the terror
screams of the horses. Wheeling around, the Bloodguard saw all six warriors struggling with their pan-
icked steeds—and the *griffin* hovering over them.
The *griffin* was a lion-like creature with sturdy wings
that enabled it to fly for short distances. It terrified
the horses, swooped at the riders. Korik and Terrel
raced toward their comrades. And behind them came
the marauders.

The Bloodguard hurled themselves at the *griffin,*
but aloft, with its clawed feet downward, it had no
vulnerable spots that they could reach without weapons. Then the marauders fell on the group. The warriors rallied to defend their horses. In the melee,

Korik poised himself on Brabha's back to spring up at the *griffin* at the first opportunity. But when his chance came, Irin cut in front of him. Somehow, she had captured a long Cavewightish broadsword. The *griffin* snatched her up in its claws, and as it ripped her apart she beheaded it.

The next moment, another party of marauders charged forward. The warriors' horses were too terrified to do anything but run. So Korik's group fled, dashed east and north with the enemy on their heels. By the time they lost the pursuit, they had been driven so far into Andelain that they had not been able to rejoin Prothall until the fourth day.

Early in the evening, the reunited company set up camp. While they prepared supper, a cool wind slowly mounted out of the north. At first it felt refreshing, full of Andelainian scents. But as moonrise neared, it stiffened with a palpable wrench until it was scything straight through the valley. Covenant could taste its unnaturalness; he had felt something like it before. Like a whip, it drove dark cloudbanks southward.

As the evening wore on, no one seemed inclined toward sleep. Depression deepened in the company as if the wind were taut with dismay. On opposite sides of the camp, Foamfollower and Quaan paced out their uneasiness. Most of the warriors squatted around in dejected attitudes, fiddling aimlessly with their weapons. Birinair poked in unrelieved dissatisfaction at the fire. Prothall and Mhoram stood squarely in the wind as if they were trying to read it with the nerves of their faces. And Covenant sat with his head bowed under a flurry of memories.

Only Variol and Tamarantha remained ungloomed. Arm in arm, the two ancient Lords sat and stared with a dreaming, drowsy look into the fire, and the firelight flickered like writing on their foreheads.

Around the camp, the Bloodguard stood as stolid as stone.

Finally, Mhoram voiced the feeling of the company. "Something happens—something dire. This is no natural wind."

Under the clouds, the eastern horizon glowed red with moonlight. From time to time, Covenant thought he saw an orange flicker in the crimson, but he could not be sure. Covertly, he studied his ring, and found the same occasional orange cast under the dominating blood. But he said nothing. He was too ashamed of Drool's hold on him.

Still no storm came. The wind blew on, rife with red mutterings and old ice, but it brought nothing but clouds and discouragement to the company. At last, most of the warriors dozed fitfully, shivering against the cut of the wind as it bore its harvest of distress toward Doom's Retreat and the Southron Wastes.

There was no dawn; clouds choked the rising sun. But the company was roused by a change in the wind. It dropped and warmed, swung slowly toward the west. But it did not feel healthier—only more subtle. Several of the warriors rolled out of their blankets, clutching their swords.

The company ate in haste, impelled by the indefinite apprehension of the breeze. The old Hirebrand, Birinair, was the first to understand. While chewing a mouthful of bread, he suddenly jerked erect as if he had been slapped. Quivering with concentration, he glowered at the eastern horizon, then spat the bread to the ground. "Burning!" he hissed. "The wind. I smell it. Burning. What? I can smell— Burning—a tree!

"A tree!" he wailed. "Ah, they dare!"

For an instant, the company stared at him in silence. Then Mhoram ejaculated, "Soaring Woodhelven is in flames!"

His companions sprang into action. Shrilly, the Bloodguard whistled for the Ranyhyn. Prothall snapped orders which Quaan echoed in a raw shout. Some of the warriors sprinted to saddle the horses, while others broke camp. By the time Covenant was dressed and mounted on Dura, the Quest was ready to ride. At once, it galloped away eastward along the Mithil.

Before long, the horses began to give trouble. Even

the freshest ones could not keep pace with the
Ranyhyn, and the mustangs which had been with
Korik in Andelain had not recovered their strength.
The terrain did not allow for speed; it was too un-
even. Prothall sent two Bloodguard ahead as scouts.
But after that he was forced to move more slowly;
he could not afford to leave part of his force behind.
Still, he kept the pace as fast as possible. It was a
frustrating ride—Covenant seemed to hear Quaan
grinding his teeth—but it could not be helped. Grimly,
Prothall held the fresher horses back.

By noon, they reached the ford of the Mithil.
Now they could see smoke due south of them, and
the smell of burning was powerful in the air. Prothall
commanded a halt to water the horses. Then the
riders pushed on, urging their weakest mounts to find
somewhere new resources of strength and speed.

Within a few leagues, the High Lord had to slow
his pace still more; the scouts had not returned. The
possibility that they had been ambushed clenched his
brow, and his eyes glittered as if the orbs had facets
of granite. He held the riders to a walk while he
sent two more Bloodguard ahead.

These two returned before the company had covered a league. They reported that Soaring Woodhelven was dead. The area around it was deserted;
signs indicated that the first two scouts had ridden
away to the south.

Muttering, *"Melenkurion!"* under his breath,
Prothall led the riders forward at a canter until they
reached the remains of the tree village.

The destruction was a fiendish piece of work. Fire
had reduced the original tree to smoldering spars
less than a hundred feet tall, and the charred trunk
had been split from top to bottom, leaving the two
halves leaning slightly away from each other. Occasional flames still flickered near their tips. And all
around the base of the tree, corpses littered the
ground as if the earth were already too full of dead
to contain the population of the village. Other
Woodhelvennin bodies, unburned, were scattered
generally in a line to the south across the glade.

Along this southward line, a few dead Cavewights sprawled in battle contortion. But near the tree there was only one body which was not human—one dead ur-vile. It lay on its long back on the south of the tree, facing the split trunk; and its soot-black frame was as twisted as the iron stave still clutched in its hands. Nearby lay a heavy iron plate nearly ten feet across.

The stench of dead, burned flesh appalled the surrounding glade. A memory of Woodhelvennin children writhed in Covenant's guts. He felt like vomiting.

The Lords seemed stupefied by the sight, stunned to realize that people under their care could be so murdered. After a moment, First Mark Tuvor reconstructed the battle for them.

The folk of Soaring Woodhelven had not had a chance.

Late the previous day, Tuvor judged, a large party of Cavewights and ur-viles—the trampling of the glade attested that the party was very large—had surrounded the tree. They had kept out of effective arrow range. Instead of assaulting the Woodhelvennin directly, they sent a few of their number—almost certainly ur-viles—forward under cover of the iron plate. Thus protected, the ur-viles set flame to the tree.

"A poor fire," Birinair inserted. Approaching the tree, he tapped it with his staff. A patch of charcoal fell away, showing white wood underneath. "Strong fire consumes everything," he muttered. "Almost, they survived. This is good wood. Make the flame a little weaker—and the wood survives. Those who dared— only strong enough by a little. Numbers are nothing. Strength counts. Of course. A narrow chance. Or if the Hirebrand had known. Been ready. He could have prepared the tree—given it strength. They could have lived. Ah! I should have been here. They would not do this to wood in my care."

Once the fire began, Tuvor explained, the attackers simply shot arrows to prevent the flames from being put out—and waited for the desperate Woodhelvennin to attempt escape. Hence the line of unburned bodies running southward; that was the direction taken by the sortie. Then, when the fire was too great for the Woodhelvennin to resist further, the ur-vile loremaster split the tree to destroy it utterly, and to shake any survivors from its limbs.

Again Birinair spoke. "He learned. Retribution. The fool—not master of his own power. The tree struck him down. Good wood. Even burning, it was not dead. The Hirebrand—a brave man. Struck back. And—and before the Desecration the *lillianrill* could have saved what life is left." He scowled as if he dared anyone to criticize him. "No more. This I cannot." But a moment later his imperiousness faded, and he turned sadly back to gaze on the ruined tree as if silently asking it to forgive him.

Covenant did not question Tuvor's analysis; he felt too sickened by the blood-thick reek around him. But Foamfollower did not seem affected in that way. Dully, he asserted, "This is not Drool's doing. No Cavewight is the master of such strategy. Winds and clouds to disguise the signs of attack, should any help be near. Iron protection carried here from who knows what distance. An attack with so little waste of resource. No, the hand of Soulcrusher is here from first to last. Stone and Sea!" Without warning, his voice caught, and he turned away, groaning his Giantish plainsong to steady himself.

Into the silence, Quaan asked, "But why here?" There was an edge like panic in his voice. "Why attack this place?"

Something in Quaan's tone, some hint of hysteria among brave but inexperienced, appalled young warriors, called Prothall back from the wilderland where his thoughts wandered. Responding to Quaan's emotion rather than to his question, the High Lord said sternly, "Warhaft Quaan, there is much work to be done. The horses will rest, but we must work. Burial must be dug for the dead. After their last ordeal, it would be unfitting to set them to the pyre. Put your Eoman to the task. Dig graves in the south glade—there." He indicated a spread of grass about a hundred feet from the riven tree.

"We—" he referred to his fellow Lords. "We will carry the dead to their graves."

Foamfollower interrupted his plainsong. "No. I will carry. Let me show my respect."

"Very well," Prothall replied. "We will prepare food and consider our situation." With a nod, he sent Quaan to give orders to the Eoman. Then, turning to Tuvor, he asked that sentries be posted. Tuvor observed that eight Bloodguard were not enough to watch every possible approach to an open area as large as the glade, but if he sent the Ranyhyn roaming separately around the bordering hills, he might not need to call on the Eoman for assistance. After a momentary pause, the First Mark asked what should be done about the missing scouts.

"We will wait," Prothall responded heavily.

Tuvor nodded, and moved away to communicate with the Ranyhyn. They stood in a group nearby, looking with hot eyes at the burned bodies around the tree. When Tuvor joined them, they clustered about him as if eager to do whatever he asked, and a moment later they charged out of the glade, scattering in all directions.

The Lords dismounted, unpacked the sacks of food, and set about preparing a meal on a small *lillianrill* fire Birinair built for them. Warriors took all the horses upwind from the tree, unsaddled and tethered them. Then the Eoman went to begin digging.

Taking great care not to step on any of the dead, Foamfollower moved toward the tree, reached the iron plate. It was immensely heavy, but he lifted it and carried it beyond the ring of bodies. There he began gently placing corpses on the plate, using it as a sled to move the bodies to their graves. Knots of emotion jumped and bunched across his buttressed forehead, and his eyes flared with a dangerous enthusiasm.

For a while, Covenant was the only member of the company without an assigned task. The fact disturbed him. The stench of the dead—Baradakas included somewhere among them, he thought achingly, Baradakas and Llaura and children, children!—made him remember Soaring Woodhelven as he had left it days ago: tall and proud, lush with the life of a fair people.

He needed something to do to defend himself.

As he scanned the company, he noticed that the warriors lacked digging tools. They had brought few picks and shovels with them; most of them were trying to dig with their hands or their swords. He walked over to the tree. Scattered around the trunk were many burned branches, some of them still solid in the core. Though he had to pick his way among the dead—though the close sight of all that flesh smeared like moldering wax over charred bones hurt his guts —he gathered branches that he could not break across his knee. These he carried away from the tree, then used his Stonedownor knife to scrape them clean and cut them into stakes. The work blackened his hands, his white robe, and the knife twisted awkwardly in his half-fingered grip, but he persisted.

The stakes he gave to the warriors, and with them they were able to dig faster. Instead of individual graves, they dug trenches, each deep and long enough to hold a dozen or more of the dead. Using Covenant's stakes, the warriors began to finish their graves faster than Foamfollower could fill them.

Late in the afternoon, Prothall called the company to eat. By that time, nearly half the bodies had been buried. No one felt like consuming food with their lungs full of acrid air and their eyes sore of tormented flesh, but the High Lord insisted. Covenant found this strange until he tasted the food. The Lords had prepared a stew unlike anything he had eaten in the Land. Its savor quickened his hunger, and when he swallowed it, it soothed his distress. It was the first meal he had had since the previous day, and he surprised himself by eating ravenously.

Most of the warriors were done eating, and the sun was about to set, when their attention was snatched erect by a distant hail. The southmost sentry answered, and a moment later the two missing Bloodguard came galloping into the glade. Their Ranyhyn were soaked with sweat.

They brought two people with them: a woman, and

a boy-child the size of a four-year-old, both Woodhelvennin, both marked as if they had survived a battle.

The tale of the scouts was quickly told. They had reached the deserted glade, and had found the southward trail of the Woodhelvennin's attempted escape. And they had seen some evidence that all the people might not have been killed. Since the enemy had gone—so there was no compelling need to ride back to warn the Lords—they had decided to search for survivors. They had erased the signs, so that any returning marauders might not find them, and had ridden south.

Early in the afternoon, they found the woman and child fleeing madly without thought or caution. Both appeared injured; the child gave no sign of awareness at all, and the woman vacillated between lucidity and incoherence. She accepted the Bloodguard as friends, but was unable to tell them anything. However, in a lucid moment, she insisted that an Unfettered Healer lived a league or two away. Hoping to gain knowledge from the woman, the scouts took her to the cave of the Healer. But the cave was empty —and appeared to have been empty for many days. So the scouts brought the two survivors back to Soaring Woodhelven.

The two stood before the Lords, the woman clutching the child's unresponsive hand. The boy gazed incuriously about him, but did not notice faces or react to voices. When his hand slipped from the woman's, his arm fell limply to his side; he neither resisted nor complied when she snatched it up again. His unfocused eyes seemed preternaturally dark, as if they were full of black blood.

The sight of him jabbed Covenant. The boy could have been the future of his own son, Roger—the son of whom he had been dispossessed, reft as if even his fatherhood had been abrogated by leprosy. Children! Foul? he panted. Children?

As if in oblique answer to his thoughts, the woman suddenly said, "He is Pietten son of Soranal. He likes the horses."

"It is true," one of the scouts responded. "He rode before me and stroked the Ranyhyn's neck."

But Covenant was not listening. He was looking at the woman. Confusedly, he sorted through the battle wreckage of her face, the cuts and burns and grime and bruises. Then he said hesitantly, "Llaura?"

The sun was setting, but there was no sunset. Clouds blanked the horizon, and a short twilight was turning rapidly into night. But as the sun fell, the air became thicker and more sultry, as if the darkness were sweating in apprehension.

"Yes, I know you," the woman said in a flagellated voice. "You are Thomas Covenant, Unbeliever and white gold wielder. In the semblance of Berek Half-hand. Jehannum spoke truth. Great evil has come." She articulated with extreme care, as if she were trying to balance her words on the edge of a sword. "I am Llaura daughter of Annamar, of the Heers of Soaring Woodhelven. Our scouts must have been slain. We had no warning. Be——"

But as she tried to say the words, her balance failed, and she collapsed into a hoarse, repeating moan—— "Uhn, uhn, uhn, uhn"——as if the connection between her brain and her throat broke, leaving her struggling frantically with her inability to speak. Her eyes burned with furious concentration, and her head shook as she tried to form words. But nothing came between her juddering lips except, "Uhn, uhn, uhn."

The Bloodguard scout said, "So she was when we found her. At one moment, she can speak. A moment later, she cannot."

Hearing this, Llaura clenched herself violently and pushed down her hysteria, rejecting what the scout said. "I am Llaura," she repeated, "Llaura—— of the Heers of Soaring Woodhelven. Our scouts must have been slain. I am Llaura, I am Llaura," she insisted. "Beware——" Again her voice broke into moaning, "Uhn, uhn."

Her panic mounted. "Be——uhn, uhn, uhn. Be—— uhn, uhn. I am Llaura. You are the Lords. You must l——uhn, uhn. Amb——uhn, uhn, uhn." As she fought, Covenant glanced around the company. Everyone was staring intently at Llaura, and Variol and Tamarantha had tears in their eyes. "Somebody do something," he muttered painfully. "Somebody."

Abruptly, Llaura seemed to collapse. Clutching her throat with her free hand, she shrieked, "You must hear me!" and started to fall.

As her knees gave way, Prothall stepped forward and caught her. With fierce strength, he gripped her upper arms and held her erect before him. "Stop," he commanded. "Stop. Do not speak anymore. Listen, and use your head to answer me."

A look of hope flared across Llaura's eyes, and she relaxed until Prothall set her on her feet. Then she regained the child's hand.

"Now," the High Lord said levelly, staring deep into her ravaged eyes. "You are not mad. Your mind is clear. Something has been done to you."

Llaura nodded eagerly, *Yes.*

"When your people attempted to escape, you were captured."

She nodded, *Yes.*

"You and the child."

Yes.

"And something was done to him as well?"

Yes.

"Do you know what it was?"

She shook her head, *No.*

"Was the same done to you both?"

No.

"Well," Prothall sighed. "Both were captured instead of slain. And the ur-vile loremaster afflicted you."

Llaura nodded, *Yes,* shuddering.

"Damaged you."

Yes.

"Caused the difficulty that you now have when you speak."

Yes!

"Now your ability to speak comes and goes."

No!

"No?"

Prothall paused to consider for a moment, and

Covenant interjected, "Hellfire! Get her to write it down."

Llaura shook her head, raised her free hand. It trembled uncontrollably.

Abruptly, Prothall said, "Then there are certain things that you cannot say."

Yes!

"There is something that the attackers do not wish you to speak."

Yes!

"Then—" The High Lord hesitated as if he could hardly believe his thoughts. "Then the attackers knew that you would be found—by us or others who came too late to the aid of Soaring Woodhelven."

Yes!

"Therefore you fled south, toward Banyan Woodhelven and the Southron Stonedowns."

She nodded, but her manner seemed to indicate that he had missed the point.

Observing her, he muttered, "By the Seven! This cannot do. Such questioning requires time, and my heart tells me we have little. What has been done to the boy? How could the attackers know that we—or anyone—would come this way? What knowledge could she have? Knowledge that an ur-vile loremaster would fear to have told? No, we must find other means."

At the edge of his sight, Covenant saw Variol and Tamarantha setting out their blankets near the campfire. Their action startled him away from Llaura for a moment. Their eyes held a sad and curiously secret look. He could not fathom it, but for some reason it reminded him that they had known what Prothall's decision for the Quest would be before that decision was made.

"High Lord," said Birinair stiffly.

Concentrating on Llaura, Prothall replied, "Yes?"

"That young whelp of a Gravelingas, Tohrm, gave me a *rhadhamaerl* gift. I almost thought he mocked me. Laughed because I am not a puppy like himself. It was hurtloam."

"Hurtloam?" Prothall echoed in surprise. "You have some?"

"Have it? Of course. No fool, you know. I keep it moist. Tohrm tried to teach me. As if I knew nothing."

Mastering his impatience, Prothall said, "Please bring it."

A moment later, Birinair handed to the High Lord a small stoneware pot full of the damp, glittering clay —hurtloam. "Watch out," Covenant murmured with complex memories in his voice, "it'll put her to sleep." But Prothall did not hesitate. In darkness lit only by Birinair's *lillianrill* fire and the last coals of the riven tree, he scooped out some of the hurtloam. Its golden flecks caught the firelight and gleamed. Tenderly, he spread the mud across Llaura's forehead, cheeks, and throat.

Covenant was marginally aware that Lord Mhoram no longer attended Prothall and Llaura. He had joined Variol and Tamarantha, and appeared to be arguing with them. They lay side by side on their backs, holding hands, and he stood over them as if he were trying to ward off a shadow. But they were unmoved. Through his protests, Tamarantha said softly, "It is better thus, my son." And Variol murmured, "Poor Llaura. This is all we can do."

Covenant snapped a look around the company. The warriors seemed entranced by the questioning of the Heer, but Foamfollower's cavernous eyes flicked without specific focus over the glade as if they were weaving dangerous visions. Covenant turned back toward Llaura with an ominous chill scrabbling along his spine.

The first touch of the hurtloam only multiplied her distress. Her face tightened in torment, and a rictus like a foretaste of death stretched her lips into a soundless scream. But then a harsh convulsion shook her, and the crisis passed. She fell to her knees and wept with relief as if a knife had been removed from her mind.

Prothall knelt beside her and clasped her in the solace of his arms, waiting without a word for her self-control to return. She needed a moment to put aside her weeping. Then she snatched herself up, crying, "Flee! You must flee! This is an ambush! You are trapped!"

But her warning came too late. At the same moment, Tuvor returned from his lookout at a run, followed almost at once by the other Bloodguard. "Prepare for attack," the First Mark said flatly. "We are surrounded. The Ranyhyn were cut off, and could not warn us. There will be battle. We have only time to prepare."

Covenant could not grasp the immediacy of what he heard. Prothall barked orders; the camp began to clear. Warriors and Bloodguard dove into the still-empty trenches, hid themselves in the hollow base of the tree. "Leave the horses," Tuvor commanded. "The Ranyhyn will break through to protect them if it is possible." Prothall consigned Llaura and the child to Foamfollower, who placed them alone in a grave and covered them with the iron plate. Then Prothall and Mhoram jumped together into the southmost trench. But Covenant stood where he was. Vaguely, he watched Birinair reduce the campfire to its barest embers, then position himself against the burned trunk of the tree. Covenant needed time to comprehend what had been done to Llaura. Her plight numbed him.

First she had been given knowledge which might have saved the Lords—and then she had been made unable to communicate that knowledge. And her struggles to give the warning only ensured her failure by guaranteeing that the Lords would attempt to understand her rather than ride away. Yet what had been done to her was unnecessary, gratuitous; the trap would have succeeded without it. In every facet of her misery, Covenant could hear Lord Foul laughing.

Bannor's touch on his shoulder jarred him. The Bloodguard said as evenly as if he were announcing the time of day, "Come, ur-Lord. You must conceal yourself. It is necessary."

Necessary? Silently, Covenant began to shout, *Do you know what he did to her?*

But when he turned, he saw Variol and Tamarantha

still lying by the last embers of the fire, protected by only two Bloodguard. What—? he gaped. They'll be killed!

At the same time, another part of his brain insisted, He's doing the same thing to me. Exactly the same thing. To Bannor he groaned, "Don't touch me. Hellfire and bloody damnation. Aren't you ever going to learn?"

Without hesitation, Bannor lifted Covenant, swung him around, and dropped him into one of the trenches. There was hardly room for him; Foamfollower filled the rest of the grave, squatting to keep his head down. But Bannor squeezed into the trench after Covenant, positioned himself with his arms free over the Unbeliever.

Then a silence full of the aches and quavers of fear fell over the camp. At last, the apprehension of the attack caught up with Covenant. His heart lurched; sweat bled from his forehead; his nerves shrilled as if they had been laid bare. A gray nausea that filled his throat like dirt almost made him gag. He tried to swallow it away, and could not. No! he panted. Not like this. I will not!

Exactly the same, exactly what happened to Llaura.

A hungry shriek ripped the air. After it came the tramp of approach. Covenant risked a glance over the rim of the grave, and saw the glade surrounded by black forms and hot laval eyes. They moved slowly, giving the encamped figures a chance to taste their own end. And flapping heavily overhead just behind the advancing line was the dark shape of a beast.

Covenant recoiled. In fear, he watched the attack like an outcast, from a distance.

As the Cavewights and ur-viles contracted their ring around the glade—centered their attack on the helpless campsite—the wall of them thickened, reducing at every step the chance that the company might be able to break through their ranks. Slowly their approach became louder; they stamped the ground as if they were trying to crush the grass. And a low wind of mutterings became audible—soft snarls, hissings through clenched teeth, gurgling, gleeful salivations —blew over the graves like an exhalation littered with the wreckage of mangled lives. The Cavewights gasped like lunatics tortured into a love of killing; the nasal sensing of the ur-viles sibilated wetly. And behind the other sounds, terrible in their quietness, came the wings of a *griffin,* drumming a dirge.

The tethered horses began to scream. The stark terror of the sound pulled Covenant up, and he looked long enough to see that the mustangs were not harmed. The tightening ring parted to bypass them, and a few Cavewights dropped from the attack to unfetter them, lead them away. The horses fought hysterically, but the strength of the Cavewights mastered them.

Then the attackers were less than a hundred feet from the graves. Covenant cowered down as far as he could. He hardly dared to breathe. The whole company was helpless in the trenches.

The next moment, a howl went up among the attackers. Several Cavewights cried, "Only five?"

"All those horses?"

"Cheated!"

In rage at the puny number of their prey, nearly a third of them broke ranks and charged the campfire.

Instantly, the company seized its chance.

The Ranyhyn whinnied. Their combined call throbbed in the air like the shout of trumpets. Together they thundered out of the east toward the captured horses.

Birinair stepped away from the riven tree. With a full swing of his staff and a cry, he struck the burned wood. The tree erupted in flames, threw dazzling light at the attackers.

Prothall and Mhoram sprang together from the southmost trench. Their staffs flared with blue Lordsfire. Crying, *"Melenkurion!"* they drove their power against the creatures. The nearest Cavewights and ur-viles retreated in fear from the flames.

Warriors and Bloodguard leaped out of the graves, sprinted from the hollow of the tree.

And behind them came the towering form of Saltheart Foamfollower, shouting a rare Giantish war call.

With cries of fear and rage, fire, swift blows and clashing weapons, the battle began.

The company was outnumbered ten to one.

Jerking his gaze from scene to scene, Covenant saw how the fighting commenced. The Bloodguard deployed themselves instantly, two to defend each Lord, with one standing by Birinair and another, Bannor, warding the trench where Covenant stood. The warriors rapidly formed groups of five. Guarding each other's backs, they strove to cut their way in and out of the line of the attackers. Mhoram charged around the fight, trying to find the commanders or lorcmasters of the enemy. Prothall stood in the center of the battle to give the company a rallying point. He shouted warnings and orders about him.

But Foamfollower fought alone. He rampaged through the attack like a berserker, pounding with his fists, kicking, throwing anything within reach. His war call turned into one long, piercing snarl of fury; his huge strides kept him in the thick of the fighting. At first, he looked powerful enough to handle the entire host alone. But soon the great strength of the Cavewights made itself felt. They jumped at him in bunches; four of them were able to bring him down. He was up again in an instant, flinging bodies about him like dolls. But it was clear that, if enough Cavewights attacked him together, he would be lost.

Variol and Tamarantha were in no less danger. They lay motionless under the onslaught, and their four Bloodguard strove extravagantly to preserve them. Some of the attackers risked arrows; the Bloodguard knocked the shafts aside with the backs of their hands. Spears followed, and then the Cavewights charged with swords and staves. Weaponless and unaided, the Bloodguard fought back with speed, balance, skill, with perfectly placed kicks and blows. They seemed impossibly successful. Soon a small ring of dead and unconscious Cavewights encircled the two Lords. But like Foamfollower they were vulnerable, would have to be vulnerable, to a concerted assault.

At Prothall's order, one group of warriors moved to help the four Bloodguard.

Covenant looked away.

He found Mhoram waging a weird contest with thirty or forty ur-viles. All the ur-viles in the attack— they were few in proportion to the Cavewights—had formed a fighting wedge behind their tallest member, their loremaster—a wedge which allowed them to focus their whole power in the leader. The loremaster wielded a scimitar with a flaming blade, and against it Mhoram opposed his fiery staff. The clashing of power showered hot sparks that dazzled and singed the air.

Then a swirl of battle swept toward Covenant's trench. Figures leaped over him; Bannor fought like a dervish to ward off spears. A moment later, a warrior came to his aid. She was the Woodhelvennin who had assigned herself to Covenant. She and Bannor struggled to keep him alive.

He clutched his hands to his chest as if to protect his ring. His fingers unconsciously took hold of the metal.

Through the dark flash of legs, he caught a glimpse of Prothall, saw that the High Lord was under attack. Using his blazing staff like a lance, he strove with the *griffin*. The beast's wings almost buffeted him from his feet, but he kept his position and jabbed his blue fire upward. But astride the *griffin* sat another ur-vile loremaster. The creature used a black stave to block the High Lord's thrusts.

As Covenant watched, the desperation of the conflict mounted. Figures fell and rose and fell again. Blood spattered down on him. Across the glade, Foamfollower heaved to his feet from under a horde of Cavewights, and was instantly deluged. Prothall fell to one knee under the combined force of his assailants. The ur-vile wedge drove Mhoram steadily backward; the two Bloodguard with him were hard pressed to protect his back.

Covenant's throat felt choked with sand.

Already, two warriors had fallen among the Cave-wights around Variol and Tamarantha. At one instant, a Bloodguard found himself, and Tamarantha behind him, attacked simultaneously by three Cave-wights with spears. The Bloodguard broke the first spear with a chop of his hand, and leaped high over the second to kick its wielder in the face. But even his great speed was not swift enough. The third Cavewight caught him by the arm. Grappling at once, the first latched his long fingers onto the Bloodguard's ankle. The two stretched their captive between them, and their companion jabbed his spear at the Bloodguard's belly.

Covenant watched, transfixed with helplessness, as the Bloodguard strained against the Cavewights, pulled them close enough together to wrench himself out of the path of the spear. Its tip scored his back. The next instant, he groined both his captors. They dropped him, staggered back. He hit the ground and rolled. But the middle Cavewight caught him with a kick so hard that it flung him away from Tamarantha.

Yelling his triumph, the Cavewight lunged forward with his spear raised high in both hands to impale the recumbent Lord.

Tamarantha!

Her peril overwhelmed Covenant's fear. Without thinking, he vaulted from the safety of his trench and started toward her. She was so old and frail that he could not restrain himself.

The Woodhelvennin yelled, "Down!" His sudden appearance aboveground distracted her, gave her opponents a target. As a result, she missed a parry, and a sword thrust opened her side. But Covenant did not see her. He was already running toward Tamarantha—and already too late.

The Cavewight drove his spear downward.

At the last instant, the Bloodguard saved Tamarantha by diving across her and catching the spear in his own back.

Covenant hurled himself at the Cavewight and tried to stab it with his stone knife. The blade twisted in his halfhand; he only managed to scratch the creature's shoulder blade.

The knife fell from his wrenched fingers.

The Cavewight whirled and struck him to the ground with a slap. The blow stunned him for a moment, but Bannor rescued him by attacking the creature. The Cavewight countered as if elevated, inspired, by his success against the dead Bloodguard. He shrugged off Bannor's blows, caught him in his long strong arms and began to squeeze. Bannor struck at the Cavewight's ears and eyes, but the maddened creature only tightened his grip.

Inchoate rage roared in Covenant's ears. Still half dazed, he stumbled toward Tamarantha's still form and snatched her staff from her side. She made no movement, and he asked no permission. Turning, he wheeled the staff wildly about his head and brought it down with all his strength on the back of the Cavewight's skull.

White and crimson power flashed in a silent explosion. The Cavewight fell instantly dead.

The ignition blinded Covenant for a moment. But he recognized the sick red hue of the flare. As his eyes cleared, he gaped at his hands, at his ring. He could not remember having removed it from the *clingor* on his chest. But it hung on his wedding finger and throbbed redly under the influence of the cloud-locked moon.

Another Cavewight loomed out of the battle at him. Instinctively, he hacked with the staff at the creature. It collapsed in a bright flash that was entirely crimson.

At the sight, his old fury erupted. His mind went blank with violence. Howling, "Foul!" as if the Despiser were there before him, he charged into the thick of the fray. Flailing about him like madness, he struck down another Cavewight, and another, and another. But he did not watch where he was going. After the third blow he fell into one of the trenches. Then for a long time he lay in the grave like a dead man. When he finally climbed to his feet, he was trembling with revulsion.

Above him, the battle burned feverishly. He could not judge how many of the attackers had been killed or disabled. But some turning point had been reached; the company had changed its tactics. Prothall fled from the *griffin* to Foamfollower's aid. And when the Giant regained his feet, he turned, dripping blood, to fight the *griffin* while Prothall joined Mhoram against the ur-viles. Bannor held himself over Covenant; but Quaan marshaled the survivors of his Eoman to make a stand around Variol and Tamarantha.

A moment later, the Ranyhyn gave a ringing call. Having freed the horses, they charged into the battle. And as their hooves and teeth crashed among the Cavewights, Prothall and Mhoram together swung their flaming staffs to block the loremaster's downstroke. Its hot scimitar shattered into fragments of lava, and the backlash of power felled the ur-vile itself. Instantly, the creatures shifted their wedge to present a new leader. But their strongest had fallen, and they began to give way.

On the other side of the battle, Foamfollower caught the *griffin* by surprise. The beast was harrying the warriors around Variol and Tamarantha. With a roar, Foamfollower sprang into the air and wrapped his arms in a death hug around the body of the *griffin*. His weight bore it to the ground; they rolled and struggled on the blood-slick grass. The riding ur-vile was thrown off, and Quaan beheaded it before it could raise its stave.

The *griffin* yowled hideously with rage and pain, tried to twist in Foamfollower's grip to reach him with its claws and fangs. But he squeezed it with all his might, silently braced himself against its thrashings and strove to kill it before it was able to turn and rend him.

For the most part, he succeeded. He exerted a furious jerk of pressure, and heard bones retort loudly in the beast's back. The *griffin* spat a final scream, and died. For a moment, he rested beside its body, panting hoarsely. Then he lumbered to his feet. His forehead had been clawed open to the bone.

But he did not stop. Dashing blood from his eyes, he ran and threw himself full-length onto the tight wedge of the ur-viles. Their formation crumbled under the impact.

At once, the ur-viles chose to flee. Before Foamfollower could get to his feet, they were gone, vanished into the darkness.

Their defection seemed to drain the Cavewights' mad courage. The gangrel creatures were no longer able to brave the Lords-fire. Panic spread among them from the brandished staffs, flash-firing in the sudden tinder of their hearts.

A cry of failure broke through the attack. The Cavewights began to run.

Howling their dismay, they scattered away from the blazing tree. They ran with grotesque jerkings of their knuckled joints, but their strength and length of limb gave them speed. In moments, the last of them had fled the glade.

Foamfollower charged after them. Yelling Giantish curses, he chased the fleers as if he meant to crush them all underfoot. Swiftly, he disappeared into the darkness, and soon he could no longer be heard. But from time to time there came faint screams through the night, as he caught escaping Cavewights.

Tuvor asked Prothall if some of the Bloodguard should join Foamfollower, but the High Lord shook his head. "We have done enough," he panted. "Remember the Oath of Peace."

For a time of exhaustion and relief, the company stood in silence underscored by the gasp of their breathing and the groans of the disabled Cavewights. No one moved; to Covenant's ears, the silence sounded like a prayer. Unsteadily, he pulled himself out of the trench. Looking about him with glazed eyes, he took the toll of the battle.

Cavewights sprawled around the camp in twisted heaps—nearly a hundred of them, dead, dying, and unconscious—and their blood lay everywhere like a dew of death. There were ten ur-viles dead. Five warriors would not ride again with their Eoman, and none of Quaan's command had escaped injury. But of the Bloodguard only one had fallen.

With a groan that belied his words, High Lord Prothall said, "We are fortunate."

"Fortunate?" Covenant echoed in vague disbelief.

"We are fortunate." An accent of anger emphasized the old rheumy rattle of Prothall's voice. "Consider that we might all have died. Consider such an attack during the full of the moon. Consider that while Drool's thoughts are turned here, he is not multiplying defenses in Mount Thunder. We have paid"— his voice choked for a moment—"paid but little for our lives and hope."

Covenant did not reply for a moment. Images of violence dizzied him. All the Woodhelvennin were dead—Cavewights—ur-viles—the warrior who had chosen to watch over him. He did not even know her name. Foamfollower had killed—he himself had killed five—five—

He was trembling, but he needed to speak, needed to defend himself. He was sick with horror.

"Foamfollower's right," he rasped hoarsely. "This is Foul's doing."

No one appeared to hear him. The Bloodguard went to the Ranyhyn and brought their fallen comrade's mount close to the fire. Lifting the man gently, they set him on the Ranyhyn's back and bound him in place with *clingor* thongs. Then together they gave a silent salute, and the Ranyhyn galloped away, bearing its dead rider toward the Westron Mountains and Guards Gap—home.

"Foul planned the whole thing."

When the Ranyhyn had vanished into the night, some of the Bloodguard tended the injuries of their mounts, while others resumed their sentry duty.

Meanwhile, the warriors began moving among the Cavewights, finding the living among the dead. All that were not mortally wounded were dragged to their feet and chased away from the camp. The rest were piled on the north side of the tree for a pyre.

"It means two things." Covenant strove to master the quaver in his voice. "It's the same thing that he's doing to me. It's a lesson—like what happened to Llaura. Foul is telling us what he's doing to us because he's sure that knowing won't help. He wants to milk us for all the despair we're worth."

With the aid of two warriors, Prothall released Llaura and Pietten from their tomb. Llaura looked exhausted to the limit; she was practically prostrate on her feet. But little Pietten ran his hands over the blood-wet grass, then licked his fingers.

Covenant turned away with a groan. "The other thing is that Foul really wants us to get at Drool. To die or not. He tricked Drool into this attack so that he wouldn't be busy defending himself. So Foul must know what we're doing, even if Drool doesn't."

Prothall seemed troubled by the occasional distant screams, but Mhoram did not notice them. While the rest of the company set about their tasks, the Lord went and knelt beside Variol and Tamarantha. He bent over his parents, and under his red-stained robe his body was rigid.

"I tell you, this is all part of Foul's plan. Hellfire! Aren't you listening to me?"

Abruptly, Mhoram stood and faced Covenant. He moved as if he were about to hurl a curse at Covenant's head. But his eyes bled with tears, and his voice wept as he said, "They are dead. Variol and Tamarantha my parents—father and mother of me, body and soul."

Covenant could see the hue of death on their old skin.

"It cannot be!" one of the warriors cried. "I saw. No weapon touched them. They were kept by the Bloodguard."

Prothall hastened to examine the two Lords. He touched their hearts and heads, then sagged and sighed, "Nevertheless."

Both Variol and Tamarantha were smiling.

The warriors stopped what they were doing; in silence, the Eoman put aside its own fatigue and grief to stand bowed in respect before Mhoram and his dead. Stooping, Mhoram lifted both Variol and Tamarantha in his arms. Their thin bones were light in his embrace, as if they had lost the weight of mortality. On his cheeks, tears gleamed orangely, but his shoulders were steady, un-sob-shaken, to uphold his parents.

Covenant's mind was beclouded. He wandered in mist, and his words were wind-torn from him. "Do you mean to tell me that we—that I—we—? For a couple of corpses?"

Mhoram showed no sign of having heard. But a scowl passed like a spasm across Prothall's face, and Quaan stepped to the Unbeliever's side at once, gripped his elbow, whispered into his ear, "If you speak again, I will break your arm."

"Don't touch me," Covenant returned. But his voice was forceless. He submitted, swirling in lost fog.

Around him, the company took on an attitude of ritual. Leaving his staff with one of the warriors, High Lord Prothall retrieved the staffs of the dead Lords and held them like an offering across his arms. And Mhoram turned toward the blaze of the tree with Variol and Tamarantha clasped erect in his embrace. The silence quivered painfully. After a long moment, he began to sing. His rough song sighed like a river, and he sang hardly louder than the flow of water between quiet banks.

Death reaps the beauty of the world—
bundles old crops to hasten new.
Be still, heart:
hold peace.
Growing is better than decay:
I hear the blade which severs life from life.
Be still, peace:
hold heart.
Death is passing on—
the making way of life and time for life.
Hate dying and killing, not death.
Be still, heart:
make no expostulation.
Hold peace and grief
and be still.

As he finished, his shoulders lurched as if unable to bear their burden without giving at least one sob to the dead. "Ah, Creator!" he cried in a voice full of bereavement. "How can I honor them? I am stricken at heart, and consumed with the work that I must do. You must honor them—for they have honored you."

At the edge of the firelight, the Ranyhyn Hynaril gave a whinny like a cry of grief. The great roan mare reared and pawed the air with her forelegs, then whirled and galloped away eastward.

Then Mhoram murmured again,

Be still, heart:
make no expostulation.
Hold peace and grief
and be still.

Gently, he laid Variol on the grass and lifted Tamarantha in both arms. Calling hoarsely, "Hail!" he placed her into the cleft of the burning tree. And before the flames could blacken her age-etched skin, he lifted Variol and set him beside her, calling again, "Hail!" Their shared smile could be seen for a moment before the blaze obscured it. So they lay together in consummation.

Already dead, Covenant groaned. That Bloodguard was killed. Oh, Mhoram! In his confusion, he could not distinguish between grief and anger.

His eyes now dry, Mhoram turned to the company, and his gaze seemed to focus on Covenant. "My friends, be still at heart," he said comfortingly. "Hold peace for all your grief. Variol and Tamarantha are ended. Who could deny them? They knew the time of their death. They read the close of their lives in the ashes of Soaring Woodhelven, and were glad to serve us with their last sleep. They chose to draw the attack upon themselves so that we might live. Who will say that the challenge which they met was not great? Remember the Oath, and hold Peace."

Together, the Eoman made the heart-opening salute of farewell, arms spread wide as if uncovering their hearts to the dead. Then Quaan cried, "Hail!" and led his warriors back to the work of piling Cavewights and burying Woodhelvennin.

After the Eoman had left, High Lord Prothall said to Mhoram, "Lord Variol's staff. From father to son. Take it. If we survive this Quest to reach a time of peace, master it. It has been the staff of a High Lord."

Mhoram accepted it with a bow.

Prothall paused for a moment, irresolute, then turned to Covenant. "You have used Lord Tamarantha's staff. Take it for use again. You will find it readier to aid your ring than your Hirebrand's staff. The *lillianrill* work in other ways than the Lords, and you are ur-Lord, Thomas Covenant."

Remembering the red blaze which had raged out of that wood to kill and kill, Covenant said, "Burn it."

A touch of danger tightened Mhoram's glance. But Prothall shrugged gently, took Lord Tamarantha's staff to the fire, and placed it into the cleft of the tree.

For an instant, the metal ends of the staff shone as if they were made of verdigris. Then Mhoram cried, "Ware the tree!" Quickly, the company moved away from the fiery spars.

The staff gave a sharp report like the bursting of bonds. Blue flame detonated in the cleft; and the riven tree dropped straight to the ground in fragments, collapsing as if its core had been finally killed. The heap of wood burned furiously.

From a distance, Covenant heard Birinair snort, "The Unbeliever's doing," as if that were a calumny.

Don't touch me, he muttered to himself.

He was afraid to think. Around him, darkness lurked like vulture wings made of midnight. Horrors threatened; he felt ghoul-begotten. He could not bear the bloodiness of his ring, could not bear what he had become. He searched about him as if he were looking for a fight.

Unexpectedly, Saltheart Foamfollower returned.

He shambled out of the night like a massacre metaphored in flesh—an icon of slaughter. He was everywhere smeared in blood, and much of it was his own. The wound on his forehead covered his face with a dark, wet sheen, and through the stain his deep eyes looked sated and miserable. Shreds of Cavewight flesh still clung to his fingers.

Pietten pointed at the Giant, and twisted his lips in a grin that showed his teeth. At once, Llaura grabbed his hand, pulled him away to a bed which the warriors had made for them.

Prothall and Mhoram moved solicitously toward the Giant, but he pushed past them to the fire. He knelt near the blaze as if his soul needed warming, and his groan as he sank to his knees sounded like a rock cracking.

Covenant saw his chance, approached the Giant. Foamfollower's manifest pain brought his confused, angry grief to a pitch that demanded utterance. He himself had killed five Cavewights, five——! His ring was full of blood. "Well," he snarled, "that must've been fun. I hope you enjoyed it."

From the other side of the camp, Quaan hissed threateningly. Prothall moved to Covenant's side, said softly, "Do not torment him. Please. He is a Giant. This is the *caamora*—the fire of grief. Has there not been enough pain this night?"

I killed five Cavewights! Covenant cried in bereft fury.

But Foamfollower was speaking as if entranced by the fire and unable to hear them. His voice had a keening sound; he knelt before the fire in an attitude of lament.

"Ah, brothers and sisters, did you behold me? Did you see, my people? We have come to this. Giants, I am not alone. I feel you in me, your will in mine. You would not have done differently—not felt other than I felt, not grieved apart from my grief. This is the result. Stone and Sea! We are diminished. Lost Home and weak seed have made us less than we were. Do we remain faithful, even now? Ah, faithful? My people, my people, if steadfastness leads to this? Look upon me! Do you find me admirable? I stink of hate and unnecessary death." A chill blew through his words. Tilting back his head, he began a low chant.

His threnody went on until Covenant felt driven to the brink of screaming. He wanted to hug or kick the Giant to make him cease. His fingers itched with mounting frenzy. Stop! he moaned. I can't stand it!

A moment later, Foamfollower bowed his head and fell silent. He remained still for a long time as if he were preparing himself. Then he asked flatly, "Who has been lost?"

"Very few," Prothall answered. "We were fortunate. Your valor served us well."

"Who?" Foamfollower ached.

With a sigh, Prothall named the five warriors, the Bloodguard, Variol and Tamarantha.

"Stone and Sea!" the Giant cried. With a convulsion of his shoulders, he thrust his hands into the fire.

The warriors gasped; Prothall stiffened at Covenant's side. But this was the Giantish *caamora,* and no one dared interfere.

Foamfollower's face stretched in agony, but he held himself still. His eyes seemed to bulge in their sockets; yet he kept his hands in the fire as if the blaze could heal, or at least sear, the blood on them, cauterize if it could not assuage the stain of shed life. But his pain showed in his forehead. The hard heart-pulse of hurt broke the crust on his wound; new blood dripped around his eyes and down his cheeks into his beard.

Panting, Hellfire hellfire! Covenant pushed away from Prothall. Stiffly, he went close to the kneeling Giant. With a fierce effort that made him sound caustic in spite of his intent, he said, "Now somebody really ought to laugh at you." His jutting head was barely as high as the Giant's shoulder.

For a moment, Foamfollower gave no sign of having heard. But then his shoulders slumped. With a slow exertion almost as though he were reluctant to stop torturing himself, he withdrew his hands. They were unharmed—for some reason, his flesh was impervious to flame—but the blood was gone from them; they looked as clean as if they had been scrubbed by exoneration.

His fingers were still stiff with hurt, and he flexed them painfully before he turned his bloody face toward Covenant. As if he were appealing a condemnation, he met the Unbeliever's impacted gaze and asked, "Do you feel nothing?"

"Feel?" Covenant groaned. "I'm a leper."

"Not even for tiny Pietten? A child?"

His appeal made Covenant want to throw his arms around the Giant, accept this terrible sympathy as some kind of answer to his dilemma. But he knew it was not enough, knew in the deepest marrow of his leprosy that it did not suffice. "We killed them too," he croaked. "I killed— I'm no different than they are."

Abruptly he turned, walked away into the darkness to hide his shame. The battleground was a fit and proper place for him; his nostrils were numb to the stink of death. After a time, he stumbled, then lay down among the dead, on blood surrounded by graves and pyres.

Children! He was the cause of their screams and their agony. Foul had attacked the Woodhelven because of his white gold ring. Not again— I won't— His voice was empty of weeping.

I will not do any more killing.

EIGHTEEN: The Plains of Ra

DESPITE the battleground—despite the acrid smoke of flame and flesh and power—despite the nearby trenches, where the dead were graved like lumps of charred agony, piled wearily into the earth like accumulated pain for which only the ground could now find use or surcease—despite his own inner torn and trampled ground—Covenant slept. For what was left of the night, the other survivors of the battle labored to bury or burn the various dead, but Covenant slept. Restless unconsciousness arose from within him like a perpetually enumerated VSE, and he spent his repose telling in dreams that rigid round: left arm shoulder to wrist, left hand palm and back, each finger, right arm, shirt, chest, left leg—

He awoke to meet a dawn which wore the aspect of an uncomfortable tomb. Shuddering himself to his feet, he found that all the work of burying was done; each of the trenches was filled, covered with dirt, and planted with a sapling which Birinair had found somewhere. Now most of the warriors lay awkwardly on the ground, in fatigue searching themselves for some kind of strength. But Prothall and Mhoram were busy cooking a meal, and the Bloodguard were examining and readying the horses.

A spate of disgust crossed Covenant's face—disgust that he had not done his share of the work. He looked at his robe; the samite was stiff and black with encrusted blood. Fit apparel for a leper, he thought, an outcast.

He knew that it was past time for him to make a decision. He had to determine where he stood in his impossible dilemma. Propped on his staff in the sepulchral dawn, he felt that he had reached the end of his evasions. He had lost track of his self-protective habits, lost the choice of hiding his ring, lost even his tough boots—and he had shed blood. He had brought down doom on Soaring Woodhelven. He had been so preoccupied with his flight from madness that he had not faced the madness toward which his fleeing took him.

He had to keep moving; he had learned that. But going on posed the same impenetrable problem. Participate, and go mad. Or refuse to participate, and go mad. He had to make a decision, find bedrock somewhere and cling to it. He could not accept the

Land—and could not deny it. He needed an answer. Without it, he would be trapped like Llaura—forced to the tune of Foul's glee to lose himself in order to avoid losing himself.

Then Mhoram looked up from his stirring and saw the disgust and dismay on Covenant's face. Gently, the Lord said, "What troubles you, my friend?"

For a moment, Covenant stared at Mhoram. The Lord looked as if he had become old overnight. The smoke and dirt of battle marked his face, accentuating the lines on his forehead and around his eyes like a sudden aggravation of wear and decay. His eyes seemed dulled by fatigue. But his lips retained their kindness, and his movements, though draped in such a rent and bloodied robe, were steady.

Covenant flinched instinctively away from the tone in which Mhoram said, *my friend*. He could not afford to be anyone's friend. And he flinched away, too, from his impulse to ask what had caused Tamarantha's staff to become so violent in his hands. He feared the answer to that question. To cover his wincing, he turned roughly away, and went in search of Foamfollower.

The Giant was sitting with his back to the last standing, extinguished fragment of Soaring Woodhelven. Grime and blood darkened his face; his skin had the color of a flaw in the heart of a tree. But the wound on his forehead dominated his appearance. Ripped flesh hung over his brows like a foliage of pain, and through the wound, drops of new blood seeped as if red thoughts were making their way from a crack in his skull. He had his right arm wrapped around his great jug of *diamondraught,* and his eyes followed Llaura as she tended little Pietten.

Covenant approached the Giant; but before he could speak, Foamfollower said, "Have you considered them? Do you know what has been done to them?"

The question raised black echoes in Covenant's mind. "I know about her."

"And Pietten? Tiny Pietten? A child?"

Covenant shrugged awkwardly.

"Think, Unbeliever!" His voice was full of swirling mists. "I am lost. You can understand."

With an effort, Covenant replied, "The same thing. Just exactly what's been done to us. And to Llaura." A moment later he added mordantly, "And to the Cavewights." Foamfollower's eyes shied, and Covenant went on, "We're all going to destroy—whatever we want to preserve. The essence of Foul's method. Pietten is a present to us—an example of what we're going to do to the Land when we try to save it. Foul is that confident. And prophecies like that are self-fulfilling."

At this, Foamfollower stared at Covenant as if the Unbeliever had just laid a curse on him. Covenant tried to hold the Giant's eyes, but an unexpected shame made him drop his head. He looked at the power-scorched grass. The burning of the grass was curious. Some patches did not look as wrong as others—apparently Lords-fire did less essential damage than the might of the ur-viles.

After a moment, Foamfollower said, "You forget that there is a difference between a prophet and a seer. Seeing the future is not prophecy."

Covenant did not want to think about it. To get away from the subject, he demanded, "Why didn't you get some of that hurtloam for your forehead?"

This time, Foamfollower's eyes turned away. Distantly, he said, "There was none left." His hands opened and closed in a gesture of helplessness. "Others were dying. And others needed the hurtloam to save their arms or legs. And—" His voice stumbled momentarily. "And I thought tiny Pietten might be helped. He is only a child," he insisted, looking up suddenly with an appeal that Covenant could not understand. "But one of the Cavewights was dying slowly—in such pain." A new trickle of blood broke open in his forehead and began to drip from his brow. "Stone and Sea!" he moaned. "I could not endure it. Hearthrall Birinair kept aside a touch of hurtloam for me, from all the wounds to be treated. But I gave it to the Cavewight. Not to Pietten—to the Cavewight. Because of the pain."

Abruptly, he put back his head and took a long pull of *diamondraught*. With the heel of his palm he wiped roughly at the blood on his brows.

Covenant gazed intently at the Giant's wracked visage. Because he could find no other words for his sympathy, he asked, "How're your hands?"

"My hands?" Foamfollower seemed momentarily confused, but then he remembered. "Ah, the *caamora*. My friend, I am a Giant," he explained. "No ordinary fire can harm me. But the pain—the pain teaches many things." A flinch of self-disgust crossed his lips. "It is said that the Giants are made of granite," he mumbled. "Do not be concerned for me."

On an impulse, Covenant responded, "In parts of the world where I come from, there are little old ladies who sit by the side of the road pounding away all day on hunks of granite with little iron hammers. It takes a long time—but eventually they turn big pieces into little pieces."

Foamfollower considered briefly before asking, "Is that prophecy, ur-Lord Covenant?"

"Don't ask me. I wouldn't know a prophecy if it fell on me."

"Nor would I," said Foamfollower. A dim smile tinged his mouth.

Shortly, Lord Mhoram called the company to the meal he and Prothall had prepared. Through a haze of suppressed groans, the warriors pried themselves to their feet and moved toward the fire. Foamfollower lurched upright. He and Covenant followed Llaura and Pietten to get something to eat.

The sight and smell of food suddenly brought Covenant's need for decision to a head. He was empty, hollow with hunger, but when he reached out to take some bread, he saw how his arm was befouled with blood and ashes. He had killed— The bread dropped from his fingers. This is all wrong, he murmured. Eating was a form of acquiescence—a submission to the physical actuality of the Land. He could not afford it.

I've got to think.

The emptiness in him ached with demands, but he

refused them. He took a drink of springwine to clear his throat, then turned away from the fire with a gesture of rejection. The Lords and Foamfollower looked after him inquiringly, but made no comment.

He needed to put himself to the test, discover an answer that would restore his ability to survive. With a grimace, he resolved to go hungry until he found what he required. Perhaps in hunger he would become lucid enough to solve the fundamental contradiction of his dilemma.

All the abandoned weapons had been cleared from the glade, gathered into a pile. He went to it and searched until he found Atiaran's stone knife. Then, on an obscure impulse, he walked over to the horses to see if Dura had been injured. When he learned that she was unscathed, he felt a vague relief. He did not want under any circumstances to be forced to ride a Ranyhyn.

A short time later, the warriors finished their meal. Wearily, they moved to take up the Quest again.

As Covenant mounted Dura, he heard the Blood-guard whistle sharply for the Ranyhyn. The call seemed to hang in the air for a moment. Then, from various directions around the glade, the great horses came galloping—manes and tails flaring as if afire, hooves pounding in long, mighty, trip-rhythmed strides—nine star-browed chargers as swift and elemental as the life-pulse of the Land. Covenant could hear in their bold nickering the excitement of going home, toward the Plains of Ra.

But the Questers who left dead Soaring Woodhelven that morning had little of the bold or home-going in their attitudes. Quaan's Eoman was now six warriors short, and the survivors were gaunt with weariness and battle. They seemed to carry their shadows in their faces as they rode north toward the Mithil River. The riderless horses they took with them to provide relief for the weaker mounts. Among them, Saltheart Foamfollower trudged as if he were carrying the weight of all the dead. In the crook of one arm he cradled Pietten, who had fallen asleep as soon as the sun cleared the eastern horizon. Llaura rode behind Lord

Mhoram, gripping the sides of his robe. She appeared bent and frail behind his grim-set face and erect posture; but he shared with her an eroded expression, an air of inarticulate grief. Ahead of them moved Prothall, and his shoulders bespoke the same kind of inflexible will which Atiaran had used to make Covenant walk from Mithil Stonedown to the Soulsease River.

Vaguely, Covenant wondered how much farther he would have to follow other people's choices. But he let the thought go and looked at the Bloodguard. They were the only members of the company who did not appear damaged by the battle. Their short robes hung in tatters; they were as filthy as anyone; one of their number had been killed, and several were injured. They had defended the Lords, especially Variol and Tamarantha, to the utmost; but the Bloodguard were unworn and undaunted, free of rue. Bannor rode his prancing, reinless Ranyhyn beside Covenant, and gazed about him with an impervious eye.

The horses of the company could manage only a slow, stumbling walk, but even that frail pace brought the riders to the ford of the Mithil before noon. Leaving their mounts to drink or graze, all of them except the Bloodguard plunged into the stream. Scrubbing at themselves with fine sand from the river bottom, they washed the blood and grit and pain of death and long night into the wide current of the Mithil. Clear skin and eyes reappeared from under the smears of battle; minor un-hurtloamed wounds opened and bled clean; scraps of shredded clothing floated out of reach. Among them, Covenant beat his robe clean, rubbed and scratched stains from his flesh as if he were trying to rid himself of the effects of killing. And he drank quantities of water in an effort to appease the aching hollowness of his hunger.

Then, when the warriors were done, they went to their horses to get new clothing from their saddlebags. After they had dressed and regained command of their weapons, they posted themselves as sentries while First Mark Tuvor and the Bloodguard bathed. The Bloodguard managed to enter and leave the river without splashing, and they washed noiselessly. In a few moments, they were dressed in new robes and mounted on the Ranyhyn. The Ranyhyn had refreshed themselves by crossing into Andelain and rolling on the grass while their riders bathed. Now the company was ready to travel. High Lord Prothall gave the signal, and the company rode away eastward along the south bank of the river.

The rest of the day was easy for the riders and their mounts. There was soft grass underhoof, clean water at one side, a tang of vitality in the air, and a nearby view of Andelain itself, which seemed to pulse with robust sap. The people of the Land drew healing from the ambience of the Hills. But the day was hard for Covenant. He was hungry, and the vital presence of Andelain only made him hungrier.

He kept his gaze away from it as best he could, refusing the sight as he had refused food. His gaunt face was set in stern lines, and his eyes were hollow with determination. He followed a double path: his flesh rode Dura doggedly, keeping his position in the company; but in his mind, he wandered in chasms, and their dark, empty inanition hurt him.

I will not—

He wanted to survive.

I am not—

From time to time, *aliantha* lay directly in his path like a personal appeal from the Land, but he did not succumb.

Covenant, he thought. Thomas Covenant. Unbeliever. Leper outcast unclean. When a pang from his hunger made him waver, he remembered Drool's bloody grip on his ring, and his resolve steadied.

From time to time, Llaura looked at him with the death of Soaring Woodhelven in her eyes, but he only clenched himself harder and rode on.

I won't do any more killing.

He had to have some other answer.

That night, he found that a change had come over his ring. Now all evidence that it resisted red encroachments was gone. His wedding band burned completely crimson under the dominion of the moon, flaming coldly on his hand as if in greedy response to Drool's power. The next morning, he began the day's riding like a man torn between opposing poles of insanity.

But there was a foretaste of summer in the noon breeze. The air turned warm and redolent with the ripeness of the earth. The flowers had a confident bloom, and the birds sang languidly. Gradually, Covenant grew full of lassitude. Languor loosened the strings of his will. Only the habit of riding kept him on Dura's back; he became numb to such superficial considerations. He hardly noticed when the river began to curve northward away from the company, or when the hills began to climb higher. He moved blankly on the warm currents of the day. That night he slept deeply, dreamlessly, and the next day he rode on in numbness and unconcern.

Waking slumber held him. It was a wilderland that he wandered unaware; he was in danger without knowing it. Lassitude was the first step in an inexorable logic, the law of leprosy. The next was gangrene, a stink of rotting live flesh so terrible that even some physicians could not bear it—a stench which ratified the outcasting of lepers in a way no mere compassion or unprejudice could oppose. But Covenant traveled his dream with his mind full of sleep.

When he began to recover—early in the afternoon of the third day from Soaring Woodhelven, the eighteenth since the company had left Revelstone—he found himself looking over Morinmoss Forest. The company stood on the last hilltop before the land fell under the dark aegis of the trees.

Morinmoss lay at the foot of the hill like a lapping sea; its edges gripped the hillsides as if the trees had clenched their roots in the slopes and refused to be driven back. The dark, various green of the Forest spread to the horizon north and east and south. It had a forbidding look; it seemed to defy the Quest to pass through it. High Lord Prothall stopped on the crest of the hill, and gazed for a long time over the Forest, weighing the time needed to ride around Morinmoss against the obscure dangers of the trees.

Finally, he dismounted. He looked over the riders, and his eyes were full of potential anger as he spoke. "We will rest now. Then we will ride into Morinmoss, and will not stop until we have reached the far side —a journey of nearly a day and a night. During that ride, we must show neither blade nor spark. Hear you? All swords sheathed, all arrows quivered, all knives cloaked, all spear tips bound. And every spark or gleam of fire quenched. I will have no mistake. Morinmoss is wilder than Grimmerdhore—and none go unanxious into that wood. The trees have suffered for ages, and they do not forget their kinship with Garroting Deep. Pray that they do not crush us all, regardless." He paused, scanning the company until he was sure that all understood him. Then he added more gently, "It is possible that there is still a Forestal in Morinmoss—though that knowledge has been lost since the Desecration."

Several of the warriors tensed at the word *Forestal*. But Covenant, coming slowly out of his languor, felt none of the awe which seemed to be expected of him. He asked as he had once before, "Do you worship trees?"

"Worship?" Prothall seemed puzzled. "The word is obscure to me."

Covenant stared.

A moment later, the High Lord went on, "Do you ask if we reverence the forests? Of course. They are alive, and there is Earthpower in all living things, all stone and earth and water and wood. Surely you understand that we are the servants of that Power. We care for the life of the Land." He glanced back at the Forest, then continued, "The Earthpower takes many forms between wood and stone. Stone bedrocks the world, and to the best of our comprehension— weak as it is—that form of power does not know itself. But wood is otherwise.

"At one time, in the dimmest, lost distance of the past, nearly all the Land was One Forest—one mighty wood from Trothgard and *Melenkurion* Skyweir to Sarangrave Flat and Seareach. And the Forest was awake. It knew and welcomed the new life which people brought to the Land. It felt the pain when mere men—blind, foolish moments in the ancientness of the Land—cut down and burned out the trees to make space in which to breed their folly. Ah, it is hard to take pride in human history. Before the slow knowledge spread throughout the Forest, so that each tree knew its peril, hundreds of leagues of life had been decimated. By our reckoning, the deed took time —more than a thousand years. But it must have seemed a rapid murder to the trees. At the end of that time, there were only four places left in the Land where the soul of the Forest lingered—survived, and shuddered in its awesome pain—and took resolve to defend itself. Then for many ages Giant Woods and Grimmerdhore and Morinmoss and Garroting Deep lived, and their awareness endured in the care of the Forestals. They remembered, and no human or Vile or Cavewight who dared enter them survived.

"Now even those ages are past. We know not if the Forestals yet live—though only a fool would deny that Caerroil Wildwood still walks in Garroting Deep. But the awareness which enabled the trees to strike back is fading. The Lords have defended the Forests since Berek Halfhand first took up the Staff of Law—we have not let the trees diminish. Yet their spirit fails. Cut off from each other, the collective knowledge of the Forests dies. And the glory of the world becomes less than it was."

Prothall paused sadly for a moment before concluding, "It is in deference to the remaining spirit, and in reverence for the Earthpower, that we ask permission for so many to enter the Forest at one time. And it is in simple caution that we offer no offense. The spirit is not dead. And the power of Morinmoss could crush a thousand thousand men if the trees were pained into wakefulness."

"Are there other dangers?" Quaan asked. "Will we need our weapons?"

"No. Lord Foul's servants have done great harm to the Forests in ages past. Perhaps Grimmerdhore has lost its power, but Morinmoss remembers. And tonight is the dark of the moon. Even Drool Rockworm is not mad enough to order his forces into Morinmoss at such a time. And the Despiser has never been such a fool."

Quietly, the riders dismounted. Some of the Eoman fed the horses, while others prepared a quick meal. Soon all the company except Covenant had eaten. And after the meal, while the Bloodguard watched, the Questers laid themselves down to rest before the long passage of the Forest.

When they were roused again and ready to travel, Prothall strode up to the edge of the hillcrest. The breeze was stronger there; it fluttered his black-sashed blue robe as he raised his staff and cried loudly, "Hail, Morinmoss! Forest of the One Forest! Enemy of our enemies! Morinmoss, hail!" His voice fell into the expanse of the woods forlornly, without echo. "We are the Lords—foes to your enemies, and learners of the *lillianrill* lore! We must pass through!

"Harken, Morinmoss! We hate the ax and flame which hurt you! Your enemies are our enemies. Never have we brought edge of ax or flame of fire to touch you—nor ever shall. Morinmoss, harken! Let us pass!"

His call disappeared into the depths of the Forest. At last, he lowered his arms, then turned and came back to the company. He mounted his horse, looked once more sternly over the riders. At his signal, they rode down toward the knuckled edges of Morinmoss.

They seemed to fall like a stone into the Forest. One moment, they were still winding down the hillside above the trees; the next, they had penetrated the gloomy deep, and the sunlight closed behind them like an unregainable door. Birinair went at the head of the company, with his Hirebrand's staff held across his mount's neck; and behind him rode First Mark Tuvor on the Ranyhyn stallion Marny—for the Ranyhyn had nothing to fear from the old anger of Morinmoss, and Marny could guide Birinair if the aged Hearthrall went astray. Behind Tuvor came Prothall and Mhoram, with Llaura at Mhoram's back; and behind them came Covenant and Foamfollower. The Giant still carried the sleeping child. Then followed Quaan and his Eoman, bunched together among the Bloodguard.

There was room for them to pass. The trees with their dark-mingled ebony and russet trunks were widely placed, leaving space between them for undergrowth and animals; and the riders found their way without difficulty. But the trees were not tall. They rose for fifteen or twenty feet on squat trunks, then spread outward in gnarled, drooping branches heavy with foliage, so that the company was completely enshrouded in the gloom of Morinmoss. The branches interwove until each tree seemed to be standing with its arms braced heavily on the shoulders of its kindred. And from the limbs hung great curtains and strands of moss—dark, thick, damp moss falling from the branches like slow blood caught and frozen as it bled. The moss dangled before the riders as if it were trying to turn them aside, deflect them from their path. And on the deep, mossy ground the hooves of the horses made no sound. The riders went their way as silently as if they had been translated into an illusion.

Instinctively dodging away from the dark touch of the moss, Covenant peered into the Forest's perpetual gloaming. As far as he could see in all directions, he was surrounded by the grotesque ire of moss and branch and trunk. But beyond the limit of his explicit senses he could see more—see, and smell, and in the silence of the Forest hear, the brooding heart of the woods. There the trees contemplated their grim memories—the broad, budding burst of self-awareness, when the spirit of the wood lay grandly over hundreds of leagues of rich earth; and the raw plummet of pain and horror and disbelief, spreading like ripples on an ocean until the farthest leaves in the Land shivered, when the slaughter of the trees began, root and branch and all cut and consumed by ax and flame, and stumps dragged away; and the scurry and anguish of the animals, slaughtered too or bereft of home and health and hope; and the clear song of the Forestal, whose tune taught the secret, angry pleasure of crushing, of striking back at tiny men and tasting their blood at the roots; and the slow weakness which ended even that last fierce joy, and left the trees with nothing but their stiff memories and their despair as they watched their rage fall into slumber.

Covenant sensed that the trees knew nothing of Lords or friendship; the Lords were too recent in the Land to be remembered. No, it was weakness, the failure of spirit, that let the riders pass—weakness, sorrow, helpless sleep. Here and there, he could hear trees that were still awake and aching for blood. But they were too few, too few. Morinmoss could only brood, bereft of force by its own ancient mortality.

A hand of moss struck him, and left moisture on his face. He wiped the wet away as if it were acid.

Then the sun set beyond Morinmoss, and even that low light was gone. Covenant leaned forward in his saddle, alert now, and afraid that Birinair would lose his way, or stumble into a curtain of moss and be smothered. But as darkness seeped into the air as if it were dripping from the enshrouding branches, a change came over the wood. Gradually, a silver glow grew on the trunks—grew and strengthened as night filled the Forest, until each tree stood shimmering like a lost soul in the gloom. The silver light was bright enough to show the riders their way. Across the shifting patterns of the glow, the moss sheets hung like shadows of an abyss—black holes into emptiness—giving the wood a blotched, leprous look. But the company huddled together, and rode on through a night illumined only by the gleam of the trees, and by the red burn of Covenant's ring.

He felt that he could hear the trees muttering in horror at the offense of his wedding band. And its pulsing red glow appalled him. Moss fingers flicked his face with a wet, probing touch. He clenched his hands over his heart, trying to pull himself inward, reduce himself and pass unnoticed—rode as if he carried an ax under his robe, and was terrified lest the trees discover it.

That long ride passed like the hurt of a wound. Acute throbs finally blurred together, and at last the company was again riding through the dimness of day. Covenant shivered, looked about within himself. What he saw left him mute. He felt that the cistern of his rage was full of darkness.

But he was caught in toils of insoluble circumstance. The darkness was a cup which he could neither drink nor dash aside.

And he was trembling with hunger.

He could hardly restrain himself from striking back at the damp clutch of the moss.

Still the company traveled the perpetual twilight of Morinmoss. They were silent, stifled by the enshrouding branches; and in the cloying quiet, Covenant felt as lost as if he had missed his way in the old Forest which had covered all the Land. With vague fury, he ducked and dodged the grasping of the moss. Time passed, and he had a mounting desire to scream.

Then, finally, Birinair waved his staff over his head and gave a weak shout. The horses understood; they stumbled into a tired run beside the strong step of the Ranyhyn. For a moment, the trees seemed to stand back, as if drawing away from the company's madness. Then the riders broke out into sunshine. They found themselves under a noon sky on a slope which bent gradually down to a river lying squarely across their way. Birinair and Marny had brought them unerringly to Roamsedge Ford.

Hoarsely shouting their relief, the warriors set heels to their mounts, and the company swept down the slope at a brave gallop. Shortly, the horses splashed into the stream, showering themselves and their glad riders with the cool spray of the Roamsedge. On the southern bank, Prothall called a halt. The passage of Morinmoss was over.

Once halted, the company tasted the toll of the passage. Their foodless vigil had weakened the riders. But the horses were in worse condition. They quivered with exhaustion. Once their last run was over, their necks and backs sagged; they scarcely had the strength to eat or drink. Despite the nickering encouragement of the Ranyhyn, two of the Eoman mustangs collapsed on their sides on the grass, and the others stood around with unsteady knees like foals. "Rest—rest," Prothall said in rheumy anxiety. "We go no farther this day." He walked among the horses, touching them with his old hands and humming a strengthening song.

Only the Ranyhyn and the Bloodguard were unmarred by fatigue. Foamfollower lowered the child Pietten into Llaura's arms, then dropped himself wearily on his back on the stiff grass. Since the company had left Soaring Woodhelven, he had been unnaturally silent; he had avoided speaking as if he feared his voice would betray him. Now he appeared to feel the strain of traveling without the support of stories and laughter.

Covenant wondered if he would ever hear the Giant laugh again.

Sourly, he reached a hand up to get his staff from Dura's saddle, and noticed for the first time what Morinmoss had done to his white robe. It was spattered and latticed with dark green stains—the markings of the moss.

The stains offended him. With a scowl, he looked around the company. The other riders must have been more adept at dodging; they showed none of the green signature of the moss. Lord Mhoram was the only exception; each shoulder of his robe bore a dark stripe like an insignia.

Roughly, Covenant rubbed at the green. But it was dry and set. Darkness murmured in his ears like the distant rumor of an avalanche. His shoulders hunched like a strangler's. He turned away from the Questers, stamped back into the river. Knotting his fingers in his robe, he tried to scrub out the stains of the Forest.

But the marks had become part of the fabric, immitigable; they clung to his robe, signing it like a chart, a map to unknown regions. In a fit of frustration, he pounded the river with his fists. But its current erased his ripples as if they had never existed.

He stood erect and dripping in the stream. His heart labored in his chest. For a moment, he felt that his rage must either overflow or crack him to the bottom.

None of this is happening— His jaw quivered. I can't stand it.

Then he heard a low cry of surprise from the company. An instant later, Mhoram commanded quietly, "Covenant. Come."

Spitting protests against so many things that he could not name them all, he turned around. The Questers were all facing away from him, their attention bent on something which he could not see because of the water in his eyes.

Mhoram repeated, "Come."

Covenant wiped his eyes, waded to the bank, and climbed out of the river. He made his dripping way through the Eoman until he reached Mhoram and Prothall.

Before them stood a strange woman.

She was slim and slight—no taller than Covenant's shoulder—and dressed in a deep brown shift which left her legs and arms free. Her skin was sun-darkened to the color of earth. Her long black hair she wore tied into one strand by a heavy cord. The effect was severe, but this was relieved by a small necklace of yellow flowers. Despite her size, she stood proudly, with her arms folded and her legs slightly apart, as if she could deny the company entrance to the Plains of Ra if she chose. She watched Covenant's approach as if she had been waiting for him.

When he stopped, joining Mhoram and Prothall, she raised her hand and gave him the salute of welcome awkwardly, as if it were not a natural gesture for her. "Hail, Ringthane," she said in a clear, nickering voice. "White gold is known. We homage and serve. Be welcome."

He shook the water from his forehead and stared at her.

After greeting him, she turned with a ritual precision toward each of the others. "Hail, High Lord Prothall. Hail, Lord Mhoram. Hail, Saltheart Foamfollower. Hail, First Mark Tuvor. Hail, Warhaft

Quaan." In turn, they saluted her gravely, as if they recognized her as a potentate.

Then she said, "I am Manethrall Lithe. We see you. Speak. The Plains of Ra are not open to all."

Prothall stepped forward. Raising his staff, he held it in both hands level with his forehead and bowed deeply. At this, the woman smiled faintly. Holding her own palms beside her head, she matched his bow. This time, her movement was smooth, natural. "You know us," she said. "You come from afar, but you are not unknowing."

Prothall replied, "We know that the Manethralls are the first tenders of the Ranyhyn. Among the Ramen, you are most honored. And you know us."

He stood close to her now, and the slight stoop of his agedness inclined him over her. Her brown skin and his blue robe accentuated each other like earth and sky. But still she withheld her welcome. "No," she returned. "Not know. You come from afar. Unknown."

"Yet you speak our names."

She shrugged. "We are cautious. We have watched since you left Morinmoss. We heard your talk."

We? Covenant wondered blankly.

Slowly, her eyes moved over the company. "We know the sleepless ones—the Bloodguard." She did not appear pleased to see them. "They take the Ranyhyn into peril. But we serve. They are welcome." Then her gaze settled on the two collapsed horses, and her nostrils flared. "You have urgency?" she demanded, but her tone said that she would accept few justifications for the condition of the mustangs. At that, Covenant understood why she hesitated to welcome the Lords, though they must have been known to her, at least by legend or reputation; she wanted no one who mistreated horses to enter the Plains of Ra.

The High Lord answered with authority, "Yes. Fangthane lives."

Lithe faltered momentarily. When her eyes returned to Covenant, they swarmed with hints of distant fear. "Fangthane," she breathed. "Enemy of Earth and

Ranyhyn. Yes. White gold knows. The Ringthane is
here." Abruptly, her tone became hard. "To save
the Ranyhyn from rending." She looked at Covenant
as if demanding promises from him.

He had none to give her. He stood angrily dripping,
too soaked with hunger to respond in repudiation or
acquiescence or shame. Soon she retreated in baffle-
ment. To Prothall, she said, "Who is he? What manner of man?"

With an ambivalent smile, Prothall said, "He is ur-
Lord Thomas Covenant, Unbeliever and white gold
wielder. He is a stranger to the Land. Do not doubt
him. He turned the battle for us when we were
beset by the servants of Fangthane—Cavewights and
ur-viles, and a *griffin* spawned in some unknown pit
of malice."

Lithe nodded noncommittally, as if she did not
understand all his words. But then she said, "There
is urgency. No action against Fangthane must be
hindered or delayed. There have been other signs.
Rending beasts have sought to cross into the Plains.
High Lord Prothall, be welcome in the Plains of Ra.
Come with all speed to Manhome. We must take
counsel."

"Your welcome honors us," the High Lord responded. "We return honor in accepting. We will reach
Manhome the second day from today—if the horses
live."

His cautious speech made Lithe laugh lightly. "You
will rest in the hospitality of the Ramen before the
sun sets a second time from this moment. We have
not served the Ranyhyn knowledgeless from the beginning. Cords! Up! Here is a test for your Maneing."

At once, four figures appeared; they suddenly stood
up from the grass in a loose semicircle around the
company as if they had risen out of the ground. The
four, three men and a woman, were as slight as
Manethrall Lithe, and dressed like her in brown over
their tanned skin; but they wore no flowers, and had
short lengths of rope wrapped around their waists.

"Come, Cords," said Lithe. "Stalk these riders no
longer. You have heard me welcome them. Now

tend their horses and their safety. They must reach Manhome before nightfall of the next day." The four Ramen stepped forward, and Lithe said to Prothall, "Here are my Cords—Thew, Hurn, Grace, and Rustah. They are hunters. While they learn the ways of the Ranyhyn and the knowing of the Manethralls, they protect the Plains from dangerous beasts. I have spent much time with them—they can care for your mounts."

With courteous nods to the company, the Cords went straight to the horses and began examining them.

"Now," Lithe continued, "I must depart. The word of your coming must cross the Plains. The Winhomes must prepare for you. Follow Rustah. He is nearest to his Maneing. Hail, Lords! We will eat together at nightfall of the new day."

Without waiting for a reply, the Manethrall turned southward and sprinted away. She ran with surprising speed; in a few moments, she had crested a hill and vanished from sight.

Watching her go, Mhoram said to Covenant, "It is said that a Manethrall can run with the Ranyhyn —for a short time."

Behind them, Cord Hurn muttered, "It is said— and it is true."

Mhoram faced the Cord. He stood as if waiting to speak. His appearance was much like Lithe's, though his hair had not been permitted to grow as long as hers, and his features had a dour cast. When he had Mhoram's attention, he said, "There is a grass which will heal your horses. I must leave you to bring it."

Gently, the Lord responded, "The knowing is yours. Do what is best."

Hurn's eyes widened, as if he had not expected soft words from people who mistreated horses. Then, uncertain of his movements, he saluted Mhoram in Lords' fashion. Mhoram returned a Ramen bow. Hurn grinned, and was about to gallop away when Covenant abruptly asked, "Why don't you ride? You've got all those Ranyhyn."

Mhoram moved swiftly to restrain Covenant. But the damage was already done. Hurn stared as if he had heard blasphemy, and his strong fingers twitched the rope from about his waist, holding it between his fists like a garrote. "We do not ride."

"Have a care, Hurn," said Cord Rustah softly. "The Manethrall welcomed him."

Hurn glared at his companion, then roughly re-knotted his rope around his waist. He spun away from the company, and soon vanished as if he had disappeared into the earth.

Gripping Covenant's arm, Mhoram said sternly, "The Ramen serve the Ranyhyn. That is their reason for life. Do not affront them, Unbeliever. They are quick to anger—and the deadliest hunters in the Land. There might be a hundred of them within the range of my voice, and you would never know. If they chose to slay you, you would die ignorant."

Covenant felt the force of the warning. It seemed to invest the surrounding grass with eyes that peered balefully. He felt conspicuous, as if his green-mapped robe were a guide for deadly intentions hidden in the ground. He was trembling again.

While Hurn was away, the rest of the Cords worked on the horses—caressing, cajoling them into taking water and food. Under their hands, most of the mustangs grew steadier. Satisfied that their mounts were in good hands, the Lords went to talk with Quaan and Tuvor; and around them, the warriors began preparing food.

Covenant cursed the aroma. He lay on the stiff grass and tried to still his gnawing emptiness by staring at the sky. Fatigue caught up with him, and he dozed for a while. But soon he was roused by a new smell which made his hunger sting in his guts. It came from clumps of rich, ferny flowers that the horses were munching—the healing herbs which Cord Hurn had brought for them. All the horses were on their feet now, and they seemed to gain strength visibly as they ate. The piquant odor of the flowers gave Covenant a momentary vision of himself on his hands and knees, chewing like the horses, and he muttered in suppressed savagery, "Damn horses eat better than we do."

Cord Rustah smiled oddly, and said, "This grass is poison to humans. It is *amanibhavam,* the flower of health and madness. Horses it heals, but men and women—ah, they are not enough for it."

Covenant answered with a glare, and tried to stifle the groan of his hunger. He felt a perverse desire to taste the grass; it sang to his senses delectably. Yet the thought that he had been brought so low was bitter to him, and he savored its sourness instead of food.

Certainly, the plants worked wonders for the horses. Soon they were feeding and drinking normally—and looked sturdy enough to bear riders again. The Questers finished their meal, then packed away their supplies. The Cords pronounced the horses ready to travel. Shortly, the riders were on their way south over the swift hills of Ra, with the Ramen trotting easily beside them.

Under the hooves of the horses, the grasslands rolled and passed like mild billows, giving the company an impression of speed. They rode over the hardy grass up and down short low slopes, along shallow valleys between copses and small woods beside thin streams, across broad flats. It was a rough land. Except for the faithful *aliantha,* the terrain was unrefined by fruit trees or cultivation or any flowers other than *amanibhavam.* But still the Plains seemed full of elemental life, as if the low, quick hills were formed by the pulse of the soil, and the stiff grass were rich enough to feed anything strong enough to bear its nourishment. When the sun began to set, the bracken on the hillsides glowed purple. Herds of nilgai came out of the woods to drink at the streams, and ravens flocked clamorously to the broad chintz trees which dotted the flats.

But the riders gave most of their attention to the roaming Ranyhyn. Whether galloping by like triumphal banners or capering together in evening play, the great horses wore an aura of majesty, as if the very ground they thundered on were proud of their creation. They called in fierce joy to the bearers of the Bloodguard, and these chargers did little dances with their hooves, as if they could not restrain the exhilaration of their return home. Then the unmounted Ranyhyn dashed away, full of gay blood and unfetterable energy, whinnying as they ran. Their calls made the air tingle with vitality.

Soon the sun set in the west, bidding farewell to the Plains with a flare of orange. Covenant watched it go with dour satisfaction. He was tired of horses —tired of Ranyhyn and Ramen and Bloodguard and Lords and quests, tired of the unrest of life. He wanted darkness and sleep, despite the blood burn of his ring, the new-coming crescent of the moon, and the vulture wings of horror.

But when the sun was gone, Rustah told Prothall that the company would have to keep on riding. There was danger, he said. Warnings had been left in the grass by other Ramen. The company would have to ride until they were safe—a few leagues more. So they traveled onward. Later, the moon rose, and its defiled sliver turned the night to blood, calling up a lurid answer from Covenant's ring and his hungry soul.

Then Rustah slowed the riders, warned them to silence. With as much stealth as they could muster, they angled up the south side of a hill, and stopped just below its crest. The company dismounted, left a few of the Bloodguard to watch over the horses, and followed the Cords to the hilltop.

Low, flat ground lay to the north. The Cords peered across it for some time, then pointed. Covenant fought the fatigue of his eyes and the crimson dimness until he thought he saw a dark patch moving southward over the flat.

"*Kresh*," whispered Hurn. "Yellow wolves—Fangthane's brood. They have crossed Roamsedge."

"Wait for us," Rustah breathed. "You will be safe."

He and the other Cords faded into the night.

Instinctively, the company drew closer together, and stared with throbbing eyes through the thin red light which seemed to ooze like sweat from the moving darkness on the flat. In suspense, they stood hushed, hardly breathing.

Pietten sat in Llaura's arms, as wide awake as a vigil.

Covenant learned later that the pack numbered fifteen of the great yellow wolves. Their fore-shoulders were waist-high on a man; they had massive jaws lined with curved, ripping fangs, and yellow omnivorous eyes. They were drooling on the trail of two Ranyhyn foals protected only by a stallion and his mare. The legends of the Ramen said that the breath of such *kresh* was hot enough to scorch the ground, and they left a weal of pain across the grass wherever their plundering took them. But all Covenant saw now was an approaching darkness, growing larger moment by moment.

Then to his uncertain eyes the rear of the pack appeared to swirl in confusion briefly; and as the wolves moved on he thought he could see two or three black dots lying motionless on the flat.

The pack swirled again. This time, several short howls of surprise and fear broke the silence. One harsh snarl was suddenly choked off. The next instant, the pack started a straight dash toward the company, leaving five more dots behind. But now Covenant was sure that the dots were dead wolves.

Three more *kresh* dropped. Now he could see three figures leap away from the dead and sprint after the survivors.

They vanished into shadows at the foot of the hill. From the darkness came sounds of fighting—enraged snarls, the snap of jaws that missed their mark, bones cracking.

Then silence flooded back into the night. The apprehension of the company sharpened, for they could see nothing; the shadow reached almost to the crest of the hill where they stood.

Abruptly, they heard the sound of frantic running. It came directly toward them.

Prothall sprang forward. He raised his staff, and blue fire flared from its tip. The sudden light revealed a lone *kresh* with hatred in its eyes pelting at him.

Tuvor reached Prothall's side an instant before

Foamfollower. But the Giant went ahead to meet the wolf's charge.

Then, without warning, Cord Grace rose out of hiding squarely in front of the wolf. She executed her movement as smoothly as if she were dancing. As she stood, a swift jerk freed her rope. When the *kresh* sprang at her, she flipped a loop of the rope around its neck, and stepped neatly aside, turning as she did so to brace her feet. The force of the wolf's charge as it hit her noose broke its neck. The yank pulled her from her feet, but she rolled lightly to one side, keeping pressure on the rope, and came to her feet in a position to finish the *kresh* if it were still alive.

The Eoman met her performance with a low murmur of admiration. She glanced toward them and smiled diffidently in the blue light of Prothall's staff. Then she turned to greet the other Cords as they loped out of the shadow of the hill. They were uninjured. All the wolves were dead.

Lowering his staff, Prothall gave the Cords a Ramen bow. "Well done," he said. They bowed in acknowledgment.

When he extinguished his staff, red darkness returned to the hilltop. In the bloodlight, the riders began moving back to their horses. But Bannor stepped over to the dead wolf and pulled Grace's rope from around its neck. Holding the cord in a fighting grip, he stretched it taut.

"A good weapon," he said with his awkward inflectionlessness. "The Ramen did mighty work with it in the days when High Lord Kevin fought Corruption openly." Something in his tone reminded Covenant that the Bloodguard were lusty men who had gone unwived for more than two thousand years.

Then, on the spur of an obscure impulse, Bannor tightened his muscles, and the rope snapped. Shrugging slightly, he dropped the pieces on the dead *kresh*. His movement had the finality of a prophecy. Without a glance at Cord Grace, he left the hilltop to mount the Ranyhyn that had chosen him.

NINETEEN: Ringthane's Choice

CORD Rustah informed Prothall that, according to Ramen custom, dead renders of the Ranyhyn were left for the vultures. The Ramen had no desire to honor *kresh,* or to affront the earth, by burying them, and pyres raised the danger of fire on the Plains. So the riders could rest as soon as their horses were away from the smell of death. The Cord led the company on southward for nearly a league until he was satisfied that no night breeze would carry unrest to the animals. Then the Quest camped.

Covenant slept fitfully, as if he lay with the point of a spike against his stomach; and when the dawn came, he felt as ineffectual as if he had spent the night trying to counterpunch hunger. And when his nose tasted again the tangy smell of the poison *amanibhavam,* the sensation made his eyes water as if he had been struck.

He did not believe that he could hold himself upright much longer. But he still did not have the answer he needed. He had found no new insight, and the green handiwork of Morinmoss on his robe seemed illegible. A sure instinct told him that he could find what he lacked in the extremity of hunger. When his companions had eaten, and were ready to travel again, he climbed dully onto Dura's back and rode with them. His eyes dripped senselessly from time to time, but he was not weeping. He felt charged with passion, but could not let it out. The grief of his leprosy did not permit any such release.

In contrast to the cold ash of his mood, the day

was cheery, full of bright, unclouded sun and a warm
northward breeze, of deep sky and swift hills. Soon
the rest of the company had surrendered to the spell
of the Plains—an incantation woven by the proud
roaming of the Ranyhyn. Time and again, mighty
horses cantered or raced by, glancing aside at the
riders with laughter in their eyes and keen shimmering
calls in their throats. The sight of them added a spring
to the strides of the Cords, and as the morning passed,
Grace and Thew sang together:

> Run, Ranyhyn:
> gallop, play—
> feed, and drink, and coat-gloss gleam.
> You are the marrow of the earth.
> No rein will curb, or bit control—
> no claw or fang unpunished rend;
> no horse-blood drop without the healing grass.
> We are the Ramen, born to serve:
> Manethrall curry,
> Cord protect,
> Winhome hearth and bed anneal—
> our feet do not bear our hearts away.
> Grass-grown hooves, and forehead stars;
> hocks and withers earth-wood bloom:
> regal Ranyhyn, gallop, run—
> we serve the Tail of the Sky,
> Mane of the World.

Hearing the song, Ranyhyn pranced around the company and away, running as smoothly as if the ground
flowed in their strides.

In Foamfollower's arms, Pietten stirred and shook
off his day sleep for a while to watch the Ranyhyn
with something like longing in his blank eyes. Prothall
and Mhoram sat relaxed in their saddles, as if for
the first time since leaving Revelstone they felt that
the company was safe. And tears ran down Covenant's face as if it were a wall.

In his emptiness, the heat of the sun confused him.
His head seemed to be fulminating, and the sensation
made him feel that he was perched on an unsteady

height, where great gulfs of vertiginous grass snapped
like wolves at his heels. But the *clingor* of his saddle
held him on Dura's back. After a time, he dozed into
a dream where he danced and wept and made love
at the commands of a satirical puppeteer.

When he awoke, it was midafternoon, and there
were mountains across most of the horizon ahead. The
company was making good time. In fact, the horses
were cantering now, as if the Plains gave them more
energy than they could contain. For a moment, he
looked ahead to Manhome, where, he foresaw, a
misguided and valueless respect for his wedding ring
would offer him to the Ranyhyn as a prospective
rider. This was surely one of Prothall's reasons for
choosing to visit the Plains of Ra before approaching
Mount Thunder. Honor the ur-Lord, the Ringthane.
Ah, hell! He tried to envision himself riding a Ranyhyn,
but his imagination could not make the leap; more
than anything else except Andelain, the great, dangerous, Earthpowerful horses quintessenced the Land.
And Joan had been a breaker of horses. For some
reason, the thought made his nose sting, and he tried
to hold back his tears by gritting his teeth.

The rest of the afternoon he passed by watching
the mountains. They grew ahead of the company as
if the peaks were slowly clambering to their feet.
Curving away southwest and northeast, the range was
not as high as the mountains behind Mithil Stonedown,
but it was rugged and raw, as if high pinnacles had
been shattered to make those forbidding, impenetrable.
Covenant did not know what lay behind the mountains, and did not want to know. Their impenetrability
gave him an obscure comfort, as if they came between
him and something he could not bear to see.

They stood up more swiftly now as the company
rode at a slow run toward them. The sun was dip-
ping into the western plains as the riders entered
the foothills of a precipitous outcropping of the range.
And their backs were hued in orange and pink as
they crossed a last rise, and reached a broad flat
glade at the foot of the cliff.

There, at last, was Manhome.

The bottom of the cliff face for the last two hundred fifty or three hundred feet inclined sharply inward along a broad, half-oval front, leaving a cave like a deep, vertical bowl in the rock. Far back in the cave, where they were protected from the weather, and yet still exposed to the open air, were the hooped tents of the Ramen families. And in the front under the shelter of the cliff was the communal area, the open space and fires where the Ramen cooked and talked and danced and sang together when they were not out on the Plains with the Ranyhyn. The whole place seemed austere, as if generations of Ramen had not worn a welcome for themselves in the stone; for Manhome was only a center, a beginning for the Plains-roaming of a nomadic people.

Perhaps seventy Ramen gathered to watch the company approach. They were nearly all Winhomes, the young and old of the Ramen, and others who needed safety and a secure bed. Unlike the Cords and Manethralls, they had no fighting ropes.

But Lithe was there, and she walked lightly out to meet the company with three other Ramen whom Covenant took to be Manethralls also; they wore necklets of yellow flowers like hers, and carried their cords in their hair rather than at their waists. The company halted, and Prothall dismounted before the Manethralls. He bowed to them in the Ramen fashion, and they gestured their welcome in return. "Hail again, Lords from afar," said Lithe. "Hail Ringthane and High Lord and Giant and Bloodguard. Be welcome to the hearth and bed of Manhome."

At her salutation, the Winhomes surged forward from under the cliff. As the riders got down from their horses, each was greeted by a smiling Winhome bearing a small band of woven flowers. With gestures of ritual stateliness, they fastened the bands to the right wrists of their guests.

Covenant climbed off Dura, and found a shy-bold Ramen girl no more than fifteen or sixteen years old standing before him. She had fine black hair that draped her shoulders, and soft wide brown eyes. She did not smile; she seemed awed to find herself greeting the Ringthane, the wielder of the white gold. Carefully, she reached out to put her flowers around his wrist.

Their smell staggered him, and he nearly retched. The band was woven of *amanibhavam*. Its tang burned his nose like acid, made him so hungry that he felt about to vomit chunks of emptiness. He was helpless to stop the tears that ran from his eyes.

With a face full of solemnity, the Winhome girl raised her hands and touched his tears as if they were precious.

Behind him, the Ranyhyn of the Bloodguard were galloping off into the freedom of the Plains. The Cords were leading the company's horses away to be tended, and more Ramen cantered into the glade in answer to the news of the Quest's arrival. But Covenant kept his eyes on the girl, stared at her as if she were a kind of food. Finally she answered his gaze by saying, "I am Winhome Gay. Soon I will share enough knowing to join the Cords." After an instant of hesitation, she added, "I am to care for you while you guest here." When he did not respond, she said hurriedly, "Others will gladly serve if my welcome is not accepted."

Covenant remained silent for a moment longer, clenching his useless ferocity. But then he gathered his strength for one final refusal. "I don't need anything. Don't touch me." The words hurt his throat.

A hand touched his shoulder. He glanced around to find Foamfollower beside him. The Giant was looking down at Covenant, but he spoke to the pain of rejection in Gay's face. "Do not be sad, little Winhome," he murmured. "Covenant Ringthane tests us. He does not speak his heart."

Gay smiled gratefully up at Foamfollower, then said with sudden sauciness, "Not so little, Giant. Your size deceives you. I have almost reached Cording."

Her gibe appeared to take a moment to penetrate Foamfollower. Then his stiff beard twitched. Abruptly, he began to laugh. His glee mounted; it echoed off the cliff above Manhome until the mountain seemed to share his elation, and the infectious sound spread until everyone near him was laughing without knowing why. For a long moment, he threw out gales as if he were blowing debris from his soul.

But Covenant turned away, unable to bear the loud weight of the Giant's humor. Hellfire, he growled. Hell and blood. What are you doing to me? He had made no decision, and now his capacity for self-denial seemed spent.

So when Gay offered to guide him to his seat for the feast which the Winhomes had prepared, he followed her numbly. She took him under the ponderous overhang of the cliff to a central, clear space with a campfire burning in the middle. Most of the company had already entered Manhome. There were two other fires, and the Ramen divided the company into three groups: the Bloodguard sat around one of the fires; Quaan and his fourteen warriors around another; and in the center, the Ramen invited Prothall, Mhoram, Foamfollower, Llaura, Pietten, and Covenant to join the Manethralls. Covenant let himself be steered until he was sitting cross-legged on the smooth stone floor, across the circle from Prothall, Mhoram, and Foamfollower. Four Manethralls made places for themselves beside the Lords, and Lithe seated herself near Covenant. The rest of the circle was filled with Cords who had come in from the Plains with their Manethrall teachers.

Most of the Winhomes bustled around cooking fires farther back in the cave, but one stood behind each guest, waiting to serve. Gay attended Covenant, and she hummed a light melody which reminded him of another song he had once heard.

> Something there is in beauty
> which grows in the soul of the beholder
> like a flower.

Under the wood smoke and the cooking odors, he thought that he could smell Gay's clean, grassy fragrance.

As he sat lumpishly on the stone, the last glow of the sunset waved orange and gold on the roof like an affectionate farewell. Then the sun was gone. Night spread over the Plains; campfire flames gave the only light in Manhome. The air was full of bustle and low talk like a hill breeze rich in Ranyhyn scent. But the food Covenant dreaded did not come immediately. First, some of the Cords danced.

Three of them performed within the circle where Covenant sat. They danced around the fire with high prancing movements and sang a nickering song to the beat of complex clapping from the Winhomes. The smooth flow of their limbs, the sudden eruptions of the dance, the dark tan of their skins, made them look as if they were enacting the pulse of the Plains—dancing the pulse by making it fast enough for human eyes to see. And they repeatedly bent their bodies so that the firelight cast horselike shadows on the walls and ceiling.

Occasionally, the dancers leaped close enough to Covenant for him to hear their song:

> Grass-grown hooves, and forehead stars;
> hocks and withers, earth-wood bloom:
> regal Ranyhyn, gallop, run—
> we serve the Tail of the Sky,
> Mane of the World.

The words and the dance made him feel that they expressed some secret knowledge, some vision that he needed to share. The feeling repelled him; he tore his eyes away from the dancers to the glowing coals of the fire. When the dance was done, he went on staring into the fire's heart with a gaze full of vague trepidations.

Then the Winhomes brought food and drink to the circles. Using broad leaves for plates, they piled stew and wild potatoes before their guests. The meal was savory with rare herbs which the Ramen relished in their cooking, and soon the Questers were deep in the feast. For a long time the only sounds in Manhome were those of serving and eating.

In the midst of the feast, Covenant sat like a stunted tree. He did not respond to anything Gay offered him. He stared at the fire; there was one coal in it which burned redly, like the night glow of his ring. He was doing a kind of VSE in his mind, studying his extremities from end to end; and his heart ached in the conviction that he was about to find some utterly unexpected spot of leprosy. He looked as if he were withering.

After a time, people began to talk again. Prothall and Mhoram handed their leaf plates back to the Winhomes, and turned their attention to the Manethralls. Covenant caught glimpses of their conversation. They were discussing him—the message he had brought to them, the role he played in the fate of the Land. Their physical comfort contrasted strangely with the seriousness of their words.

Near them, Foamfollower described the plight of Llaura and Pietten to one of the Manethralls.

Covenant scowled into the fire. He did not need to look down to see the blood change which came over his ring; he could feel the radiation of wrong from the metal. He concealed the band under his fist and trembled.

The stone ceiling seemed to hover over him like a cruel wing of revelation, awaiting the moment of his greatest helplessness to plunge onto his exposed neck. He was abysmally hungry.

I'm going crazy, he muttered into the flames.

Winhome Gay urged him to eat, but he did not respond.

Across the circle, Prothall was explaining the purpose of his Quest. The Manethralls listened uncertainly, as if they had trouble seeing the connection between evils far away and the Plains of Ra. So the High Lord told them what had been done to Andelain.

Pietten gazed with blank unfocus out into the night, as if he were looking forward to moonrise. Beside him, Llaura spoke quietly with the Cords around her, grateful for the Ramen hospitality.

As Foamfollower detailed the horrors which had been practiced on the two survivors of Soaring Woodhelven, his forehead knotted under the effort he made to contain his emotion.

The fire shone like a door with an intolerable menace waiting behind it. The back of Covenant's neck was stiff with vulnerability, and his eyes stared blindly, like knotholes.

The green stains on his robe marked him like a warning that said, Leper outcast unclean.

He was nearing the end of his VSE. Behind him was the impossibility of believing the Land true. And before him was the impossibility of believing it false.

Abruptly, Gay entered the circle and confronted him, with her hands on her hips and her eyes flashing. She stood with her legs slightly apart, so that he saw the bloody coals of the fire between her thighs.

He glanced up at her.

"You must take food," she scolded. "Already you are half dead." Her shoulders were squared, drawing her shift tight over her breasts. She reminded him of Lena.

Prothall was saying, "He has not told us all that occurred at the Celebration. The ravage of the Wraiths was not prevented—yet we believe he fought the urviles in some way. His companion blamed both herself and him for the ill which befell the Dance."

Covenant trembled. Like Lena, he thought. Lena? Darkness pounced at him like claws of vertigo. Lena?

For an instant, his vision was obscured by roaring and black waters. Then he crashed to his feet. He had done that to Lena—done *that?* He flung the girl aside and jumped toward the fire. Lena! Swinging his staff like an ax, he chopped at the blaze. But he could not fight off the memory, could not throw it back. The staff twisted with the force of the blow, fell from his hands. Sparks and coals shattered, flew in all directions. He had done *that* to her! Shaking his half-fist at Prothall, he cried, "She was wrong! I couldn't help it!"—thinking, Lena! What have I done?— "I'm a leper!"

Around him, people sprang to their feet. Mhoram came forward quickly, stretched out a restraining hand. "Softly, Covenant," he said. "What is wrong? We are guests."

But even while he protested, Covenant knew that Atiaran had not been wrong. He had seen himself kill at the battle of Soaring Woodhelven, and had thought in his folly that being a killer was something new for him, something unprecedented. But it was not something he had recently become; he had been that way from the beginning of the dream, from the beginning. In an intuitive leap, he saw that there was no difference between what the ur-viles had done to the Wraiths and what he had done to Lena. He had been serving Lord Foul since his first day in the Land.

"No!" he spat as if he were boiling in acid. "No, I won't do it anymore. I'm not going to be the victim anymore. I will not be waited on by children." He shook with the ague of his rage as he cried at himself, *You raped her! You stinking bloody bastard!*

He felt as weak as if the understanding of what he had done corroded his bones.

Mhoram said intently, "Unbeliever! What is wrong?"

"No!" Covenant repeated. "No!" He was trying to shout, but his voice sounded distant, crippled. "I will not—tolerate—this. It isn't right. I am going to survive! Do you hear me?"

"Who are you?" Manethrall Lithe hissed through taut lips. With a quick shake of her head, a flick of her wrist, she pulled the cord from her hair and held it battle-ready.

Prothall caught her arm. His old voice rattled with authority and supplication. "Forgive, Manethrall. This matter is beyond you. He holds the wild magic that destroys peace. We must forgive."

"Forgive?" Covenant tried to shout. His legs failed under him, but he did not fall. Bannor held him erect from behind. "You can't forgive."

"Do you ask to be punished?" Mhoram said incredulously. "What have you done?"

"Ask?" Covenant struggled to recollect something. Then he found it. He knew what he had to do. "No. Call the Ranyhyn."

"What?" snapped Lithe in indignation. And all the Ramen echoed her protest.

"The Ranyhyn! Call them."

"Are you mad? Have a care, Ringthane. We are the

Ramen. We do not call—we serve. They come as they will. They are not for your calling. And they do not come at night."

"Call, I tell you! I! Call them!"

Something in his terrible urgency confounded her. She hesitated, stared at him in confused anger and protest and unexpected compassion, then turned on her heel and strode out of Manhome.

Supported by Bannor, Covenant tottered out from under the oppressive weight of the mountain. The company and the Ramen trailed after him like a wake of dumbfounded outrage. Behind them, the red moon had just crested the mountain; and the distant Plains, visible beyond the foothills in front of Manhome, were already awash with crimson. The incarnadine flood seemed to untexture the earth, translate rock and soil and grass into decay and bitter blood.

The people spread out on either side of the flat so that the open ground was lit by the campfires.

Into the night walked Lithe, moving toward the Plains until she stood near the far edge of the glade. Covenant stopped and watched her. Unsteadily, but resolutely, he freed himself from Bannor's support— stood on his own like a wrecked galleon left by the tide, perched impossibly high on a reef. Moving woodenly, he went toward Lithe.

Before him, the bloody vista of the moonlight lay like a dead sea, and it tugged at him as it flowed closer with each degree of the moonrise. His ring smoldered coldly. He felt that he was the lodestone. Sky and earth were alike hued scarlet, and he walked outward as if he were the pole on which the red night turned— he and his ring the force which compelled that tide of violated night. Soon he stood in the center of the open flat.

A winding-sheet of silence enwrapped the onlookers.

Ahead of him, Manethrall Lithe spread her arms as if she were beckoning the darkness toward her. Abruptly, she gave a shrill cry. *"Kelenbhrabanal marushyn! Rushyn hynyn kelenkoor rillynarunal!*

Ranyhyn Kelenbhrabanal!" Then she whistled once. It
echoed off the cliff like a shriek.

For a long moment, silence choked the flat. Striding
defiantly, Lithe moved back toward Manhome. As she
passed Covenant, she snapped, "I have called." Then
she was behind him, and he faced the siege of the
moonlight alone.

But shortly there came a rumbling of hooves. Great
horses pounded the distance; the sound swelled as if
the hills themselves were rolling Manhome-ward.
Scores of Ranyhyn approached. Covenant locked his
knees to keep himself upright. His heart felt too weak
to go on beating. He was dimly conscious of the hushed
suspense of the spectators.

Then the outer edge of the flat seemed to rise up
redly, and a wave of Ranyhyn broke into the open—
nearly a hundred chargers galloping abreast like a
wall at Covenant.

A cry of amazement and admiration came from the
Ramen. Few of the oldest Manethralls had ever seen
so many Ranyhyn at one time.

And Covenant knew that he was looking at the
proudest flesh of the Land. He feared that they were
going to trample him.

But the pounding wall broke away to his left, ran
around him until he was completely encircled. Manes
and tails tossing, forehead stars catching the firelight
as they flashed past, fivescore Ranyhyn thundered on
the turf and enclosed him. The sound of their hooves
roared in his ears.

Their circle drew tighter as they ran. Their reeling
strength snatched at his fear, pulled him around with
them as if he were trying to face them all at once. His
heart labored painfully. He could not turn fast enough
to keep up with them. The effort made him stumble,
lose his balance, fall to his knees.

But the next instant, he was erect again, with his legs
planted against the vertigo of their circling, and his
face contorted as if he were screaming—a cry lost in
the thunder of Ranyhyn hooves. His arms spread as if
they were braced against opposing walls of night.

Slowly, tortuously, the circle came stamping and

fretting to a halt. The Ranyhyn faced inward toward Covenant. Their eyes rolled, and several of them had froth on their lips. At first, he failed to comprehend their emotion.

From the onlookers came a sudden cry. He recognized Llaura's voice. Turning, he saw Pietten running toward the horses, with Llaura struggling after him, too far behind to catch him. The child had caught everyone by surprise; they had been watching Covenant. Now Pietten reached the circle and scrambled among the frenzied feet of the Ranyhyn.

It seemed impossible that he would not be trampled. His head was no larger than one of their hooves, and the chargers were stamping, skittering. Then Covenant saw his chance. With an instinctive leap, he snatched Pietten from under one of the horses.

His half-unfingered hand could not retain its grip; Pietten sprawled away from him. Immediately, the child jumped to his feet. He dashed at Covenant and struck as hard as he could.

"They hate you!" he raged. "Go away!"

Moonlight fell into the flat as if it had sprung from the sides of the mountain. In the crimson glow, Pietten's little face looked like a wasteland.

The child struggled, but Covenant lifted him off the ground, gripped him to his chest with both arms. Restraining Pietten in his hug, he looked up at the Ranyhyn.

Now he understood. In the past, he had been too busy avoiding them to notice how they reacted to him. They were not threatening him. These great chargers were terrified—terrified of him. Their eyes shied off his face, and they scattered foam flecks about them. The muscles of their legs and chests quivered. Yet they came agonized forward. Their old role was reversed. Instead of choosing their riders, they were submitting themselves to his choice.

On an impulse, he unwrapped his left arm from Pietten and flourished his cold red ring at one of the horses. It flinched and ducked as if he had thrust a serpent at it, but it held its ground.

He gripped Pietten again. The child's struggles were

weaker now, as if Covenant's hug slowly smothered him. But the Unbeliever clung. He stared wildly at the Ranyhyn, and wavered as if he could not regain his balance.

But he had already made his decision. He had seen the Ranyhyn recognize his ring. Clenching Pietten to his heart like a helm, he cried, "Listen!" in a voice as hoarse as a sob. "Listen. I'll make a bargain with you. Get it right. Hellfire! Get it right. A bargain. Listen. I can't stand—I'm falling apart. Apart." He clenched Pietten. "I see—I see what's happening to you. You're afraid. You're afraid of me. You think I'm some kind of— All right. You're free. I don't choose any of you."

The Ranyhyn watched him fearfully.

"But you've got to do things for me. You've got to *back off!*" That wail almost took the last of his strength. "You—the Land—" he panted, pleaded, *Let me be!* "Don't ask so much." But he knew that he needed something more from them in return for his forbearance, something more than their willingness to suffer his Unbelief.

"Listen—listen. If I need you, you had better come. So that I don't have to be a hero. Get it right." His eyes bled tears, but he was not weeping.

"And—and there's one more thing. One more. Lena—" Lena! "A girl. She lives in Mithil Stonedown. Daughter of Trell and Atiaran. I want—I want one of you to go to her. Tonight. And every year. At the last full moon before the middle of spring. Ranyhyn are—are what she dreams about."

He shook the tears out of his eyes, and saw the Ranyhyn regarding him as if they understood everything he had tried to say.

"Now go," he gasped. "Have mercy on me."

With a sudden, bursting, united neigh, all the Ranyhyn reared around him, pawing the air over his head as if they were delivering promises. Then they wheeled, whinnying with relief, and charged away from Manhome. The moonlight did not appear to touch them. They dropped over the edge of the flat and vanished as if they were being welcomed into the arms of the earth.

Almost at once, Llaura reached Covenant's side.
Slowly, he released Pietten to her. She gave him a long
look that he could not read, then turned away. He followed her, trudging as if he were overburdened with
the pieces of himself. He could hear the amazement
of the Ramen—amazement too strong for them to feel
any offense at what he had done. He was beyond them;
he could hear it. "They reared to him," the whispers
ran. But he did not care. He was perversely sick with
the sense that he had mastered nothing, proved nothing, resolved nothing.

Lord Mhoram came out to join him. Covenant did
not meet Mhoram's gaze, but he heard complex wonder in the Lord's voice as he said, "Ur-Lord—ah! Such
honor has never been done to mortal man or woman.
Many have come to the Plains, and have been offered
to the Ranyhyn—and refused. And when Lord
Tamarantha my mother was offered, five Ranyhyn
came to consider her—five. It was a higher honor than
she had dreamed possible. We could not hear. Have
you refused them? Refused?"

"Refused," Covenant groaned. They hate me.

He pushed past Mhoram and shambled into
Manhome. Moving unsteadily, like a ship with a broken keel, he headed toward the nearest cooking fire.
The Ramen made way for him, watched him pass with
awe in their faces. He did not care. He reached the fire
and grabbed the first food he saw. The meat slipped
in his halfhand, so he held it with his left fist and de-
voured it.

He ate blankly, swallowing food in chunks and taking more by the fistful. Then he wanted something to
drink. He looked around, discovered Foamfollower
standing nearby with a flagon of *diamondraught*
dwarfed in his huge hand.

Covenant took the flagon and drained it. Then he
stood numbly still, waiting for the *diamondraught*'s
effect.

It came swiftly. Soon mist began to fill his head. His
hearing seemed hollow, as if he were listening to Manhome from the bottom of a well. He knew that he was
going to pass out—wanted hungrily to pass out—but

before he lost consciousness, the hurt in his chest made him say, "Giant, I—I need friends."

"Why do you believe that you have none?"

Covenant blinked, and saw everything that he had done in the Land. "Don't be ridiculous."

"Then you do believe that we are real."

"What?" Covenant groped for the Giant's meaning with hands which had no fingers.

"You think us capable of not forgiving you," Foamfollower explained. "Who would forgive you more readily than your dream?"

"No," the Unbeliever said. "Dreams—never forgive."

Then he lost the firelight and Foamfollower's kind face, and stumbled into sleep.

TWENTY: A Question of Hope

HE wandered wincing in sleep, expecting nightmares. But he had none. Through the vague rise and fall of his drifting—as if even asleep his senses were alert to the Land—he felt that he was being distantly watched. The gaze on him was anxious and beneficent; it reminded him of the old beggar who had made him read an essay on "the fundamental question of ethics."

When he woke up, he found that Manhome was bright with sunshine.

The shadowed ceiling of the cave was dim, but light reflecting off the village floor seemed to dispel the oppressive weight of the stone. And the sun reached far enough into Manhome to tell Covenant that he had awakened early in the afternoon of a warm presummer day. He lay near the back of the cave in an atmosphere of stillness. Beside him sat Saltheart Foamfollower.

Covenant closed his eyes momentarily. He felt he had survived a gauntlet. And he had an unfocused sense that his bargain was going to work. When he looked up again, he asked, "How long have I been asleep?" as if he had just been roused from the dead.

"Hail and welcome, my friend," returned the Giant. "You make my *diamondraught* appear weak. You have slept for only a night and a morning."

Stretching luxuriously, Covenant said, "Practice. I do so much of it—I'm becoming an expert."

"A rare skill," Foamfollower chuckled.

"Not really. There're more of us lepers than you might think." Abruptly he frowned as if he had caught himself in an unwitting violation of his promised forbearance. In order to avoid being taken seriously, he added in a lugubrious tone, "We're everywhere."

But his attempt at humor only appeared to puzzle the Giant. After a moment, Foamfollower said slowly, "Are the others— 'Leper' is not a good name. It is too short for such as you. I do not know the word, but my ears hear nothing in it but cruelty."

Covenant sat up and pushed off his blankets. "It's not cruel, exactly." The subject appeared to shame him. While he spoke, he could not meet Foamfollower's gaze. "It's either a meaningless accident— or a 'just desert.' If it were cruel, it would happen more often."

"More often?"

"Sure. If leprosy were an act of cruelty—by God or whatever—it wouldn't be so rare. Why be satisfied with a few thousand abject victims when you could have a few million?"

"Accident," Foamfollower murmured. "Just. My friend, you bewilder me. You speak with such haste. Perhaps the Despiser of your world has only a limited power to oppose its Creator."

"Maybe. Somehow I don't think my world works that way."

"Yet you said—did you not?—that lepers are everywhere."

"That was a joke. Or a metaphor." Covenant made another effort to turn his sarcasm into humor. "I can never tell the difference."

Foamfollower studied him for a long moment, then asked carefully, "My friend, do you jest?"

Covenant met the Giant's gaze with a sardonic scowl. "Apparently not."

"I do not understand this mood."

"Don't worry about it." Covenant caught his chance to escape this conversation. "Let's get some food. I'm hungry."

To his relief, Foamfollower began laughing gently. "Ah, Thomas Covenant," he chuckled, "do you remember our river journey to Lord's Keep? Apparently there is something in my seriousness which makes you hungry." Reaching down to one side, he brought up a tray of bread and cheese and fruit, and a flask of springwine. And he went on laughing quietly while Covenant pounced on the food.

Covenant ate steadily for some time before he began looking around. Then he was taken aback to find that the cave was profuse with flowers. Garlands and bouquets lay everywhere, as if overnight each Ramen had raised a garden thick with white columbines and greenery. The white and green eased the austerity of Manhome, covered the stone like a fine robe.

"Are you surprised?" asked Foamfollower. "These flowers honor you. Many of the Ramen roamed all night to gather blooms. You have touched the hearts of the Ranyhyn, and the Ramen are not unamazed— or ungrateful. A wonder has come to pass for them— fivescore Ranyhyn offering to one man. The Ramen would not exchange such a sight for Andelain itself, I think. So they have returned what honor is in their power."

Honor? Covenant echoed.

The Giant settled himself more comfortably, and said as if he were beginning a long tale, "It is sad that you did not see the Land before the Desecration. Then the Ramen might have shown you honor that would humble all your days. All matters were higher in that age, but even among the Lords there were few beau-

ties to equal the great craft of the Ramen. 'Marrowmeld,' they called it—*anundivian yajña,* in the tongue
of the Old Lords. Bone-sculpting it was. From vulture-
and time-cleaned skeletons on the Plains of Ra, the
Ramen formed figures of rare truth and joy. In their
hands—under the power of their songs—the bones
bent and flowed like clay, and were fashioned curiously, so that from the white core of lost life the
Ramen made emblems for the living. I have never beheld these figures, but the tale of them is preserved by
the Giants. In the destitution and diminishment, the
long generations of hunger and hiding and homeless-
ness, which came to the Ranyhyn and the Ramen with
the Desecration, the skill of marrowmeld was lost."

His voice faded as he finished, and after a moment
he began to sing softly:

> Stone and Sea are deep in life—

A silence of respectful attention surrounded him. The
Winhomes near him had stopped to listen.

A short time later, one of them waved out toward
the glade, and Covenant, following the gesture, saw
Lithe striding briskly across the flat. She was accompanied by Lord Mhoram astride a beautiful roan
Ranyhyn. The sight gladdened Covenant. He finished
his springwine in a salute to Mhoram.

"Yes," said Foamfollower, noticing Covenant's
gaze, "much has occurred this morning. High Lord
Prothall chose not to offer himself. He said that his old
bones would better suit a lesser mount—meaning, I
think, that he feared his 'old bones' would give affront
to the Ranyhyn. But it would be well not to underes-
timate his strength."

Covenant heard a current of intimations running
through Foamfollower's words. Distantly, he said,
"Prothall is going to resign after this Quest—if it suc-
ceeds."

The Giant's eyes grinned. "Is that prophecy?"

Covenant shrugged. "You know as well as I do. He
spends too much time thinking about how he hasn't
mastered Kevin's Lore. He thinks he's a failure. And

he's going to go on thinking that even if he gets the Staff of Law back."

"Prophecy, indeed."

"Don't laugh." Covenant wondered how he could explain the resonance of the fact that Prothall had refused a chance at the Ranyhyn. "Anyway, tell me about Mhoram."

Happily, Foamfollower said, "Lord Mhoram son of Variol was this day chosen by Hynaril of the Ranyhyn, who also bore Tamarantha Variol-mate. Behold! She is remembered with honor among the great horses. The Ramen say that no Ranyhyn has ever before borne two riders. Truly, an age of wonders has come to the Plains of Ra."

"Wonders," Covenant muttered. He did not like to remember the fear with which all those Ranyhyn had faced him. He glared into his flask as if it had cheated him by being empty.

One of the nearest Winhomes started toward him carrying a jug. He recognized Gay. She approached among the flowers, then stopped. When she saw that he was looking at her, she lowered her eyes. "I would refill your flagon," she said, "but I fear to offend. You will consider me a child."

Covenant scowled at her. She affected him like a reproach, and he stiffened where he sat. With an effort that made him sound coldly formal, he said, "Forget last night. It wasn't your fault." Awkwardly, he extended the flask toward her.

She came forward, and poured out springwine for him with hands that shook slightly.

He said distinctly, "Thank you."

She gazed at him widely for a moment. Then a look of relief filled her face, and she smiled.

Her smile reminded him of Lena. Deliberately, as if she were a burden he refused to shirk, he motioned for her to sit down. She placed herself cross-legged at the foot of his bed, gleaming at the honor the Ringthane did her.

Covenant tried to think of something to say to her; but before he found what he wanted, he saw Warhaft Quaan striding into Manhome. Quaan came toward him squarely, as if he were forging against Covenant's gaze, and when he neared the Unbeliever, he waited only an instant before asking his question. "We were concerned. Life needs food. Are you well?"

"Well?" Covenant felt that he was beginning to glow with his second flask of springwine. "Can't you see? I can see you. You're as sound as an oak."

"You are closed to us," said Quaan, stolid with disapproval. "What we see is not what you are."

This ambiguous statement seemed to invite a mordant retort, but Covenant restrained himself. He shrugged, then said, "I'm eating," as if he did not want to lay claim to too much health.

Quaan seemed to accept this reply for what it was worth. He nodded, bowed slightly, and left.

Watching him go, Winhome Gay breathed, "He dislikes you." Her tone expressed awe at the Warhaft's audacity and foolishness. She seemed to ask how he dared to feel as he did—as if Covenant's performance the previous night had exalted him in her eyes to the rank of a Ranyhyn.

"He has good reason," answered Covenant flatly.

Gay looked unsure. As if she were reaching out for dangerous knowledge, she asked quickly, "Because you are a—a 'leper'?"

He could see her seriousness. But he felt that he had already said too much about lepers. Such talk compromised his bargain. "No," he said, "he just thinks I'm obnoxious."

At this, she frowned as if she could hear his complex dishonestly. For a long moment, she studied the floor as if she were using the stone to measure his duplicity. Then she got to her feet, filled Covenant's flask to the brim from her jug. As she turned away, she said in a low voice, "You do consider me a child." She walked with a defiant and fearful swing to her hips, as if she believed she was risking her life by treating the Ringthane so insolently.

He watched her young back, and wondered at the pride of people who served horses—and at the inner conditions which made telling the truth so difficult. From Gay, his gaze shifted to the outer edge of

Manhome, where Mhoram and Lithe stood together
in the sunlight. They were facing each other—she nut-
brown and he blue-robed—and arguing like earth and
sky. When he concentrated on them, he could make
out what they were saying.

"I will," she insisted.

"No, hear me," Mhoram replied. "He does not want
it. You will only cause pain for him—and for yourself."

Covenant regarded them uneasily out of the cool,
dim cave. Mhoram's rudder nose gave him the aspect
of a man who faced facts squarely; and Covenant felt
sure that indeed he did not want whatever Mhoram
was arguing against.

The dispute ended shortly. Manethrall Lithe swung
away from Mhoram and strode into the recesses of
the village. She approached Covenant and surprised
him entirely by dropping to her knees, bowing her
forehead to the stone before him. With her palms on
the floor beside her head, she said, "I am your servant.
You are the Ringthane, master of the Ranyhyn."

Covenant gaped at the back of her head. For an
instant, he did not understand her; in his surprise, he
could not conceive of any emotion powerful enough to
make a Manethrall bow so low. His face felt suddenly
full of shame. "I don't want a servant," he grated. But
then he saw Mhoram frowning unhappily behind
Lithe. He steadied himself, went on more gently, "The
honor of your service is beyond me."

"No!" she averred without raising her head. "I saw.
The Ranyhyn reared to you."

He felt trapped. There seemed to be no way to stop
her from humiliating herself without making her
aware of the humiliation. He had lived without tact or
humor for such a long time. But he had promised to
be forbearant. And in the distance he had traveled
since Mithil Stonedown, he had tasted the consequences of allowing the people of the Land to treat
him as if he were some kind of mythic figure. With an
effort, he replied gruffly, "Nevertheless. I'm not used
to such things. In my own world, I'm—just a little man.
Your homage makes me uneasy."

Softly, Mhoram sighed his relief, and Lithe raised her head to ask in wonder, "Is it possible? Can such worlds be, where you are not among the great?"

"Take my word for it." Covenant drank deeply from his flask.

Cautiously, as if fearful that he did not mean what he had said, she climbed to her feet. She threw back her head and shook her knotted hair. "Covenant Ringthane, it shall be as you choose. But we do not forget that the Ranyhyn reared to you. If there is any service we may do, only let it be known. You may command us in all things that do not touch the Ranyhyn."

"There is one thing," he said, staring at the mountain stone of the ceiling. "Give Llaura and Pietten a home."

When he glanced at Lithe, he saw that she was grinning. He snapped fiercely, "She's one of the Heers of Soaring Woodhelven. And he's just a kid. They've been through enough to earn a little kindness."

Gently, Mhoram interposed, "Foamfollower has already spoken to the Manethralls. They have agreed to care for Llaura and Pietten."

Lithe nodded. "Such commands are easy. If the Ranyhyn did not challenge us more, we would spend most of our days in sleep." Still smiling, she left Covenant and cantered out into the sun.

Mhoram also was smiling. "You look—better, ur-Lord. Are you well?"

Covenant returned his attention to his springwine. "Quaan asked me the same thing. How should I know? Half the time these days I can't even remember my name. I'm ready to travel, if that's what you're getting at."

"Good. We must depart as soon as may be. It is pleasant to rest here in safety. But we must go if we are to preserve such safeties. I will tell Quaan and Tuvor to make preparation."

But before the Lord could leave, Covenant said, "Tell me something. Exactly why did we come here? You got yourself a Ranyhyn—but we lost four or five days. We could've skipped Morinmoss."

"Do you wish to discuss tactics? We believe we will

gain an advantage by going where Drool cannot expect us to go, and by allowing him time to respond to
his defeat at Soaring Woodhelven. Our hope is that
he will send out an army. If we arrive too swiftly, the
army may still be in Mount Thunder."

Covenant resisted the plausibility of this. "You
planned to come here long before we were attacked
at Soaring Woodhelven. You planned it all along. I
want to know why."

Mhoram met Covenant's demand squarely, but his
face tensed as if he did not expect Covenant to like
his answer. "When we made our plans at Revelstone,
I saw that good would come of this."

"You saw?"

"I am an oracle. I see—occasionally."

"And?"

"And I saw rightly."

Covenant was not ready to push the question further. "It must be fun." But there was little sarcasm in
his tone, and Mhoram laughed. His laughter emphasized the kindness of his lips. A moment later, he was
able to say without bitterness, "I would rather see
more such good. There is so little in these times."

As the Lord walked away to ready the company,
Foamfollower said, "My friend, there is hope for
you."

"Forsooth," Covenant sneered. "Giant, if I were as
big and strong as you, there would always be hope
for me."

"Why? Do you believe that hope is a child of
strength?"

"Isn't it? Where do you get hope if you don't get it
from power? If I'm wrong—by hell! There's a lot of
lepers running around the world confused."

"How is power judged?" Foamfollower asked with
a seriousness Covenant had not expected.

"What?"

"I do not like the way in which you speak of lepers.
Where is the value of strength if your enemy is
stronger?"

"You assume there is some kind of enemy. I think
that's a little too easy. I would like nothing better than

—than to blame it on someone else—some enemy who afflicted me. But that's just another kind of suicide. Abdicate the responsibility to keep myself alive."

"Ah, alive," Foamfollower countered. "No, consider further, Covenant. What value has power at all if it is not power over death? If you place hope on anything less, then your hope may mislead you."

"So?"

"But the power over death is a delusion. There cannot be life without death."

Covenant recognized that this was a fact. But he had not expected such an argument from the Giant. It made him want to get out of the cave into the sunlight. "Foamfollower," he muttered, climbing out of his bed, "you've been thinking again." But he felt the intensity of Foamfollower's gaze. "All right. So you're right. Tell me, just where the hell do you get hope?"

Slowly, the Giant rose to his feet. He towered over Covenant until his head nearly touched the ceiling. "From faith."

"You've been dealing with humans too long—you're getting hasty. 'Faith' is too short a word. What do you mean?"

Foamfollower began picking his way among the flowers. "I mean the Lords. Consider, Covenant. Faith is a way of living. They have dedicated themselves wholly to the services of the Land. And they have sworn the Oath of Peace—committed themselves to serve the great goal of their lives in only certain ways, to choose death rather than submit to the destruction of passion which blinded High Lord Kevin and brought the Desecration. Come—can you believe that Lord Mhoram will ever despair? That is the essence of the Oath of Peace. He will never despair, nor ever do what despair commands—murder, desecrate, destroy. And he will never falter, because his Lordship, his service to the Land, will sustain him. Service enables service."

"That's not the same thing as hope." With the Giant, Covenant moved out of Manhome to stand in the sunny flat. The bright light made him duck his head, and as he did so he noticed again the moss stains which charted his robe. Abruptly, he looked back into the cave. There the greenery was arranged among the columbines to resemble moss lines on white samite.

He stifled a groan. As if he were articulating a principle, he said, "All you need to avoid despair is irremediable stupidity or unlimited stubbornness."

"No," insisted Foamfollower. "The Lords are not stupid. Look at the Land." He gestured broadly with his arm as if he expected Covenant to view the whole country from border to border.

Covenant's gaze did not go so far. But he looked blinking beyond the green flat toward the Plains. He heard the distant whistles of the Bloodguard call to the Ranyhyn, and the nickering answer. He noticed the fond wonder of the Winhomes who came out of the cave because they were too eager to wait in Manhome until the Ranyhyn appeared. After a moment, he said, "In other words, hope comes from the power of what you serve, not from yourself. Hellfire, Giant—you forget who I am."

"Do I?"

"Anyway, what makes you such an expert on hope? I don't see that you've got anything to despair about."

"No?" The Giant's lips smiled, but his eyes were hard under his buttressed brows, and his forehead's scar shone vividly. "Do you forget that I have learned to hate? Do— But let that pass. How if I tell you that I serve you? I, Saltheart Foamfollower, Giant of Searreach and legate of my people?"

Covenant heard echoes in the question, like the distant wrack of timbers barely perceived through a high, silent wind, and he recoiled. "Don't talk like a damned mystic. Say something I can understand."

Foamfollower reached down to touch Covenant's chest with one heavy finger, as if he marked a spot on Covenant's mapped robe. "Unbeliever, you hold the fate of the Land in your hands. Soulcrusher moves against the Lords at the very time when our dreams of Home have been renewed. Must I explain that you have the power to save us, or orphan us until we share whatever doom awaits the Land?"

"Hellfire!" Covenant snapped. "How many times

have I told you that I'm a leper? It's all a mistake. Foul's playing tricks on us."

The Giant responded simply and quietly. "Then are you so surprised to learn that I have been thinking about hope?"

Covenant met Foamfollower's eyes under the scarred overhang of his forehead. The Giant watched him as if the hope of the Unhomed were a sinking ship, and Covenant ached with the sense of his own helplessness to save that hope. But then Foamfollower said as if he were coming to Covenant's rescue, "Be not concerned, my friend. This tale is yet too brief for any of us to guess its ending. As you say, I have spent too much time with hastening humans. My people would laugh greatly to see me—a Giant who has not patience enough for a long story. And the Lords contain much which may yet surprise Soulcrusher. Be of good heart. It may be that you and I have already shared our portion of the terrible purpose of these times."

Gruffly, Covenant said, "Giant, you talk too much." Foamfollower's capacity for gentleness surpassed him. Muttering, Hellfire, to himself, he turned away, went in search of his staff and knife. He could hear the noises of preparation from beyond the flat; and in the village the Winhomes were busy packing food in saddlebags. The company was readying itself, and he did not want to be behind-hand. He found his staff and knife with the bundle of his clothes laid out on a slab of stone amid the flowers, as if on display. Then he got a flustered, eager Winhome to provide him with water, soap, and a mirror. He felt that he owed himself a shave.

But when he had set the mirror so that he could use it, and had doused his face in water, he found Pietten standing solemnly in front of him; and in the mirror he saw that Llaura was behind him. Pietten stared at him as if the Unbeliever were as intangible as a wisp of smoke. And Llaura's face seemed tight, as if she were forcing herself to do something she disliked. She pushed her hand unhappily through her hair, then said,

"You asked the Ramen to make a home for us here."

He shrugged. "So did Foamfollower."

"Why?"

His hearing picked out whole speeches of meaning behind her question. She held his gaze in the mirror, and he saw the memory of a burning tree in her eyes. He asked carefully, "Do you really think you might get a chance to hit back at Foul? Or be able to use it if you got it?" He looked away at Pietten. "Leave it to Mhoram and Prothall. You can trust them."

"Of course." Her tone said as clearly as words that she was incapable of distrusting the Lords.

"Then take the job you already have. Here's Pietten. Think about what's going to happen to him—more of what you've already been through. He needs help."

Pietten yawned as if he were awake past his bedtime, and said, "They hate you." He sounded as sober as an executioner.

"How?" Llaura returned defiantly. "Have you observed him? Have you seen how he sits awake at night? Have you seen how his eyes devour the moon? Have you seen his relish for the taste of blood? He is no child—no more." She spoke as if Pietten were not there listening to her, and Pietten listened as if she were reciting some formula of no importance. "He is treachery concealed in a child's form. How can I help him?"

Covenant wet his face again and began lathering soap. He could feel Llaura's presence bearing on the back of his neck as he rubbed lather into his beard. Finally, he muttered, "Try the Ranyhyn. He likes them."

When she reached over him to take Pietten's hand and draw the child away, Covenant sighed and set the knife to his beard. His hand was unsteady; he had visions of cutting himself. But the blade moved over his skin as smoothly as if it could remember that Atiaran had refused to injure him.

By the time he was done, the company had gathered outside Manhome. He hurried out to join the riders as if he feared that the Quest would leave without him.

The last adjustments of saddles and saddlebags were in progress, and shortly Covenant stood beside Dura.

The condition of the horses surprised him. They all gleamed with good grooming, and looked as well-fed and rested as if they had been under the care of the Ramen since the middle of spring. Some of the Eoman mounts which had been most exhausted were now pawing the ground and shaking their manes eagerly.

The whole company seemed to have forgotten where they were going. The warriors were laughing together. Old Birinair clucked and scolded over the way the Ramen handled his *lillianrill* brands. He treated the Ramen like spoiled children, and appeared to enjoy himself almost too much to hide it behind his dignity. Mhoram sat smiling broadly on Hynaril. And High Lord Prothall stood relaxed by his mount as if he had shed years of care. Only the Bloodguard, already mounted and waiting on their Ranyhyn, remained stern.

The company's good spirits disturbed Covenant like a concealed threat. He understood that it arose in part from rest and reassurance. But he felt sure that it also arose from his meeting with the Ranyhyn. Like the Ramen, the warriors had been impressed; their desire to see in him a new Berek had been vindicated. The white gold wielder had shown himself to be a man of consequence.

The Ranyhyn were terrified! he snapped to himself. They saw Foul's hold on me, and they were terrified. But he did not remonstrate aloud. He had made a promise of forbearance in return for his survival. Despite the tacit dishonesty of allowing his companions to believe what they wished of him, he held himself still.

As the riders laughed and joked, Manethrall Lithe came to stand before them, followed by several other Manethralls and a large group of Cords. When she had the company's attention, she said, "The Lords have asked for the help of the Ramen in their fight against Fangthane the Render. The Ramen serve the Ranyhyn. We do not leave the Plains of Ra. That is life, and it is good—we ask for nothing else until the end, when all the Earth is Andelain, and man and Ranyhyn live together in peace without wolves or hunger. But we must aid the foes of Fangthane as we can. This we will do. I will go with you. My Cords will go with you if they choose. We will care for your horses on the way. And when you leave them to seek Fangthane's hiding in the ground, we will keep them safe. Lords, accept this service as honor among friends and loyalty among allies."

At once, the Cords Hurn, Thew, Grace, and Rustah stepped forward and avowed their willingness to go wherever Manethrall Lithe would lead them.

Prothall bowed to Lithe in the Ramen fashion. "The service you offer is great. We know that your hearts are with the Ranyhyn. As friends we would refuse this honor if our need as allies were not so great. The doom of these times compels us to refuse no aid or succor. Be welcome among us. Your hunter skill will greatly ease the hazards of our way. We hope to do you honor in return—if we survive our Quest."

"Kill Fangthane," said Lithe. "That will do us honor enough to the end of our days." She returned Prothall's bow, and all the assembled Ramen joined her.

Then the High Lord spoke to his companions. In a moment, the Quest for the Staff of Law was mounted and ready to ride. Led by Manethrall Lithe and her Cords, the company cantered away from Manhome as if in the village of the Ramen they had found abundant courage.

TWENTY-ONE:
Treacher's Gorge

THEY crossed the Plains northward in confidence and good spirits. No danger or report of danger appeared anywhere along their way. And the Ranyhyn rode the grasslands like live blazonry, challenges ut-

tered in flesh. Foamfollower told gay tales as if he
wished to show that he had reached the end of a passing travail. Quaan and his warriors responded with
ripostes and jests. And the Ramen entertained them
with displays of hunting skill. The company rode late
into the first night, in defiance of the dismal moon.
And the second night, they camped on the south bank
of Roamsedge Ford.

But early the next morning they crossed the Ford
and turned northeast up a broad way between the
Roamsedge and Morinmoss. By midafternoon, they
reached the eastmost edge of the Forest. From there,
the Roamsedge, the northern border of the Plains,
swung more directly eastward, and the company went
on northeast, away from both Morinmoss and the
Plains of Ra. That night, they slept on the edge of a
stark, unfriendly flatland where no people lived and
few willingly traveled. The whole region north of them
was cut and scarred and darkened like an ancient battleground, a huge field that had been ruined by the
shedding of too much blood. Scrub grass, stunted trees,
and a few scattered *aliantha* took only slight hold on
the uncompromising waste. The company was due
south of Mount Thunder.

As the Quest angled northeastward across this land,
Mhoram told Covenant some of its history. It spread
east to Landsdrop, and formed the natural front of
attack for Lord Foul's armies in the ancient wars.
From the Fall of the River Landrider to Mount Thunder was open terrain along the great cliff of Landsdrop.
The hordes issuing from Foul's Creche could ascend
in scores of places to bring battle to the Upper Land.
So it was that the first great battles in all the Land's
wars against the Despiser occurred across this ravaged
plain. Age after age, the defenders strove to halt Lord
Foul at Landsdrop, and failed because they could not
block all the ways up from the Spoiled Plains and
Sarangrave Flat. Then Lord Foul's armies passed
westward along the Mithil, and struck deep into the
Center Plains. In the last war, before Kevin Landwaster had been finally driven to invoke the Ritual of
Desecration, Lord Foul had crushed through the heart

of the Center Plains, and had turned north to force the Lords to their final battle at Kurash Plenethor, now named Trothgard.

In the presence of so much old death, the riders did not travel loudly. But they sang songs during the first few days, and several times they returned to the legend telling of Berek Halfhand and the Fire-Lions of Mount Thunder. On this wilderland Berek had fought, suffering the deaths of his friends and the loss of his fingers in battle. Here he had met despair, and had fled to the slopes of Gravin Threndor, the Peak of the Fire-Lions. And there he had found both Earthfriendship and Earthpower. It was a comforting song, and the riders sang its refrain together as if they sought to make it true for themselves:

> Berek! Earthfriend! help and weal,
> Battle aid against the foe!
> > Earth gives and answers Power's peal,
> > Ringing, Earthfriend! Help and heal!
> Cleanse the Land from bloody death and woe!

They needed its comfort. The hard-reft and harrowed warland seemed to say that Berek's victory was an illusion—that all his Earthfriendship and his Staff of Law and his lineage of Lords, his mighty works and the works of his descendants, amounted to so much scrub grass and charred rock and dust—that the true history of the Land was written here, in the bare topsoil and stone which lay like a litter of graves from the Plains of Ra to Mount Thunder, from Andelain to Landsdrop.

The atmosphere of the region agitated Foamfollower. He strode at Covenant's side with an air of concealed urgency, as if he were repressing a desire to break into a run. And he talked incessantly, striving to buoy up his spirits with a constant stream of stories and legends and songs. At first, his efforts pleased the riders, appeased their deepening, hungry gloom like treasure-berries of entertainment. But the Questers were on their way toward the bleak, black prospect of Drool Rockworm, crouched like a bane in the catacombs of Mount Thunder. By the fourth day from Roamsedge Ford, Covenant felt that he was drowning in Giantish talk; and the voices of the warriors when they sang sounded more pleading than confident—like whistling against inexorable night.

With the Ramen to help him, Prothall found rapid ways over the rough terrain. Long after sunset on that fourth day—when the growing moon stood high and baleful in the night sky—the Quest made a weary camp on the edge of Landsdrop.

The next dawn, Covenant resisted the temptation to go and look over the great cliff. He wanted to catch a glimpse of the Lower Land, of the Spoiled Plains and Sarangrave Flat—regions which had filled Foamfollower's talk in the past days. But he had no intention of exposing himself to an attack of vertigo. The fragile stability of his bargain did not cover gratuitous risks. So he remained in the camp when most of his companions went to gaze out over Landsdrop. But later, as the company rode north within a stone's throw of the edge, he asked Lord Mhoram to tell him about the great cliff.

"Ah, Landsdrop," Mhoram responded quietly. "There is talk, unfounded even in the oldest legends, that the cleft of Landsdrop was caused by the sacrilege which buried immense banes under Mount Thunder's roots. In a cataclysm that shook its very heart, the Earth heaved with revulsion at the evils it was forced to contain. And the force of that dismay broke the Upper Land from the Lower, lifted it toward the sky. So this cliff reaches from deep in the Southron Range, past the Fall of the River Landrider, through the heart of Mount Thunder, at least half a thousand leagues into the mapless winter of the Northron Climbs. It varies in height from place to place. But it stands across all the Land, and does not allow us to forget."

The Lord's rough voice only sharpened Covenant's anxiety. As the company rode, he held his gaze away to the west, trusting the wilderland to anchor him against his instinctive fear of heights.

Before noon, the weather changed. Without warning, a sharp wind bristling with grim, preternatural associations sprang out of the north. In moments, black clouds seethed across the sky. Lightning ripped the air; thunder pounded like a crushing of boulders. Then, out of the bawling sky, rain struck like a paroxysm of rage —hit with savage force until it stung. The horses lowered their heads as if they were wincing. Torrents battered the riders, drenched, blinded them. Mane-thrall Lithe sent her Cords scouting ahead to keep the company from plunging over Landsdrop. Prothall raised his staff with bright fire flaring at its tip to help keep his companions from losing each other. They huddled together, and the Bloodguard positioned the Ranyhyn around them to bear the brunt of the attack.

In the white revelations of the lightning, Prothall's flare appeared dim and frail, and thunder detonated hugely over it as if exploding at the touch of folly. Covenant crouched low on Dura's back, flinched away from the lightning as if the sky were stone which the thunder shattered. He could not see the Cords, did not know what was happening around him; he was constantly afraid that Dura's next step would take him over the cliff. He clenched his eyes to Prothall's flame as if it could keep him from being lost.

The skill and simple toughness of the Ramen pre-served the company, kept it moving toward Mount Thunder. But the journey seemed like wandering in the collapse of the heavens. The riders could only be sure of their direction because they were always forc-ing their way into the maw of the storm. The wind flailed the rain at their faces until their eyes felt lac-erated and their cheeks shredded. And the cold drenching stiffened their limbs, paralyzed them slowly like the rigor of death. But they went on as if they were trying to beat down a wall of stone with their foreheads.

For two full days, they pushed onward—felt them-selves crumbling under the onslaught of the rain. But they knew neither day nor night, knew nothing but one continuous, pummeling, dark, savage, implacable storm. They rode until they were exhausted—rested on their feet knee-deep in water and mud, gripping the reins of their horses—ate sopping morsels of food half warmed by *lillianrill* fires which Birinair struggled to keep half alive—counted themselves to be sure no one had been lost—and rode again until they were forced by exhaustion to stop again. At times, they felt that Prothall's wan blue flame alone sustained them. Then Lord Mhoram moved among the company. In the lurid lightning, his face appeared awash with water like a foundering wreck; but he went to each Quester, shouted through the howl of wind and rain, the devastating thunder, "Drool—storm—for us! But he—mistaken! Main force—passes—west! Take heart! Augurs—for us!"

Covenant was too worn and cold to respond. But he heard the generous courage behind Mhoram's words. When the company started forward again, he squinted ahead toward Prothall's flame as if he were peering into a mystery.

The struggle went on, prolonged itself far beyond the point where it felt unendurable. In time, endurance itself became abstract—a mere concept, too impalpable to carry conviction. The lash and riot of the storm reduced the riders to raw, quivering flesh hardly able to cling to their mounts. But Prothall's fire burned on. At each new flash and blast, Covenant reeled in his seat. He wanted nothing in life but a chance to lie down in the mud. But Prothall's fire burned on. It was like a manacle, emprisoning the riders, dragging them forward. In the imminent madness of the torrents, Covenant gritted his gaze as if that manacle were precious to him.

Then they passed the boundary. It was as abrupt as if the wall against which they had thrown themselves like usurped titans had suddenly fallen into mud. Within ten stumbling heartbeats, the end of the storm blew over them, and they stood gasping in a sun-bright noon. They could hear the tumult rushing blindly away. Around them were the remains of the deluge—broken pools and streams and fens, thick mud like wreckage on the battle plain. And before them stood the great ravaged head of Mount Thunder: Gravin Threndor, Peak of the Fire-Lions.

For a long moment, it held them like an aegis of silence—grim, grave and august, like an outcropping of

the Earth's heart. The Peak was north and slightly west
of them. Taller than Kevin's Watch above the Upper
Land, it seemed to kneel on the edge of the Sarangrave, with its elbows braced on the plateau and its
head high over the cliff, fronting the sky in a strange
attitude of pride and prayer; and it rose twelve thousand feet over the Defiles Course, which flowed eastward from its feet. Its sides from its crumpled foothills
to the raw rock of its crown were bare, not cloaked or
defended from storms, snows, besieging time by any
trees or grasses, but instead wearing sheer, fragmented
cliffs like facets, some as black as obsidian and others
as gray as the ash of a granite fire—as if the stone of
the Mount were too thick, too charged with power, to
bear any gentle kind of life.

There, deep in the hulky chest of the mountain, was
the destination of the Quest: Kiril Threndor, Heart of
Thunder.

They were still ten leagues from the Peak, but the
distance was deceptive. Already that scarred visage
dominated the northern horizon; it confronted them
over the rift of Landsdrop like an irrefusable demand.
Mount Thunder! There Berek Halfhand had found his
great revelation. There the Quest for the Staff of Law
hoped to regain the future of the Land. And there
Thomas Covenant sought release from the impossibility of his dreams. The company stared at the upraised
rock as if it searched their hearts, asked them questions
which they could not answer.

Then Quaan grinned fiercely, and said, "At least
now we have been washed clean enough for such
work."

That incongruity cracked the trance which held the
riders. Several of the warriors burst into laughter as if
recoiling from the strain of the past two days, and most
of the others chuckled, daring Drool or any enemy to
believe that the storm had weakened them. Though
nearly prostrated by the exertion of finding a path
through the torrents on foot, the Ramen laughed as
well, sharing a humor they did not fully understand.

Only Foamfollower did not respond. His eyes were
fixed on Mount Thunder, and his brows overhung his

gaze as if shielding it from something too bright or hot to be beheld directly.

The Questers found a relatively dry hillock on which to rest and eat, and feed their mounts; and Foamfollower went with them absently. While the company made itself as comfortable as possible for a time, he stood apart and gazèd at the mountain as if he were reading secrets in its scored crevices and cliffs. Softly he sang to himself:

Now we are Unhomed,
    bereft of root and kith and kin.
From other mysteries of delight,
    we set our sails to resail our track;
    but the winds of life blew not the way we chose,
    and the land beyond the Sea was lost.

High Lord Prothall let the company rest for as long as he dared in the open plain. Then he moved on again for the remainder of the afternoon, clinging to the edge of Landsdrop as if it were his only hope. Before the storm, Covenant had learned that the sole known entrance to the catacombs of Mount Thunder was through the western chasm of the Soulsease—Treacher's Gorge, the rocky maw which swallowed the river, only to spit it out again eastward on the Lower Land, transmogrified by hidden turbulent depths into the Defiles Course, a stream gray with the sludge and waste of the Wightwarrens. So Prothall's hope lay in his southeastern approach. He believed that by reaching Mount Thunder on the south and moving toward Treacher's Gorge from the east, the company could arrive unseen and unexpected at the Gorge's western exposure. But he took no unnecessary risks. Gravin Threndor stood perilously large against the sky, and seemed already to lean looming toward the company as if the Peak itself were bent to the shape of Drool's malice. He urged the tired Ramen to their best cunning in choosing a way along Landsdrop; and he kept the riders moving until after the sun had set.

But all the time he rode slumped agedly in his saddle, with his head bowed as if he were readying his neck for the stroke of an ax. He seemed to have spent all his strength in pulling his companions through the storm. Whenever he spoke, his long years rattled in his throat.

The next morning, the sun came up like a wound into ashen skies. Gray clouds overhung the earth, and a shuddering wind fell like a groan from the slopes of Mount Thunder. Across the wasteland, the pools of rainwater began to stagnate, as if the ground refused to drink the moisture, leaving it to rot instead. And as they prepared to ride, the Questers heard a low rumble like the march of drums deep in the rock. They could feel the throb in their feet, in their knee joints.

It was the beat of mustering war.

The High Lord answered as if it were a challenge. *"Melenkurion!"* he called clearly. "Arise, champions of the Land! I hear the drums of the Earth! This is the great work of our time!" He swung onto his horse with his blue robe fluttering.

Warhaft Quaan responded with a cheer, "Hail, High Lord Prothall! We are proud to follow!"

Prothall's shoulders squared. His horse lifted its ears, raised its head, took a few prancing steps as grandly as a Ranyhyn. The Ranyhyn nickered humorously at the sight, and the company rode after Prothall boldly, as if the spirits of the ancient Lords were in them.

They made their way to the slopes of Mount Thunder through the constant buried rumble of the drums. As they found a path across the thickening rubble which surrounded the mountain, the booming subterreanean call accompanied them like an exhalation of Despite. But when they started up the first battered sides of the Peak, they forgot the drums; they had to concentrate on the climb. The foothills were like a gnarled stone mantle which Mount Thunder had shrugged from its shoulders in ages long past, and the way westward over the slopes was hard. Time and again, the riders were forced to dismount to lead their mounts down tricky hills or over gray piles of tumbled, ashen rock. The difficulty of the terrain made their progress slow, despite all the Ramen could do to search out the easiest trails. The Peak seemed to lean gravely over them as if watching their small struggles. And down onto them from the towering cliffs came a chilling wind, as cold as winter.

At noon, Prothall halted in a deep gully which ran down the mountainside like a cut. There the company rested and ate. When they were not moving, they could hear the drums clearly, and the cold wind seemed to pounce on them from the cliffs above. They sat in the straight light of the sun and shivered—some at the cold, others at the drums.

During the halt, Mhoram came over to Covenant and suggested that they climb a way up the gully together. Covenant nodded; he was glad to keep himself busy. He followed the Lord up the cut's contorted spine until they reached a break in its west wall. Mhoram entered the break; and when Covenant stepped in behind the Lord, he got a broad, sudden view of Andelain.

From the altitude of the break—between the stone walls—he felt that he was looking down over Andelain from a window in the side of Mount Thunder. The Hills lay richly over all the western horizon, and their beauty took his breath away. He stared hungrily with a feeling of stasis, of perfect pause in his chest, like a quick grip of eternity. The lush, clear health of Andelain shone like a country of stars despite the gray skies and the dull battle-roll. He felt obscurely unwilling to breathe, to break the trance, but after a moment his lungs began to hurt for air.

"Here is the Land," Mhoram whispered. "Grim, powerful Mount Thunder above us. The darkest banes and secrets of the Earth in the catacombs beneath our feet. The battleground behind. Sarangrave Flat below. And there—priceless Andelain, the beauty of life. Yes. This is the heart of the Land." He stood reverently, as if he felt himself to be in an august presence.

Covenant looked at him. "So you brought me up here to convince me that this is worth fighting for." His mouth twisted on the bitter taste of shame. "You want something from me—some declaration of allegiance. Before you have to face Drool." The Cavewights he had slain lay hard and cold in his memory.

"Of course," the Lord replied. "But it is the Land itself which asks for your allegiance." Then he said with sudden intensity, "Behold, Thomas Covenant. Use your eyes. Look upon it all. Look and listen— hear the drums. And hear me. This is the heart of the Land. It is not the home of the Despiser. He has no place here. Oh, he desires the power of the banes, but his home is in Foul's Creche—not here. He has not depth or sternness or beauty enough for this place, and when he works here it is through ur-viles or Cave-wights. Do you see?"

"I see." Covenant met the Lord's gaze flatly. "I've already made my bargain—my 'peace,' if you want to call it that. I'm not going to do any more killing."

"Your 'peace'?" Mhoram echoed in a complex tone. Slowly, the danger dimmed in his eyes. "Well, you must pardon me. In times of trouble, some Lords be-have strangely." He passed Covenant and started back down the gully.

Covenant remained in the window for a moment, watching Mhoram go. He had not missed the Lord's oblique reference to Kevin; but he wondered what kinship Mhoram saw between himself and the Land-waster. Did the Lord believe himself capable of that kind of despair?

Muttering silently, Covenant returned to the com-pany. He saw a measuring look in the eyes of the war-riors; they were trying to assess what had occurred between him and Lord Mhoram. But he did not care what portents they read into him. When the company moved on, he led Dura up the side of the gully, blank to the shifting shale which more than once dropped him to his hands and knees, scratching and bruising him dangerously. He was thinking about the Celebra-tion of Spring, about the battle of Soaring Woodhelven, about children and Llaura and Pietten and Atiaran and the nameless Unfettered One and Lena and Triock and the warrior who had died defending him—think-ing, and striving to tell himself that his bargain was secure, that he was not angry enough to risk fighting again.

That afternoon, the company struggled on over the

arduous ground, drawing slowly higher as they worked westward. They caught no glimpses of their destination. Even when the sun fell low in the sky, and the roar of waters became a distinct accompaniment to the buried beat of the drums, they were still not able to see the Gorge. But then they entered a sheer, sheltered ravine in the mountainside. From this ravine a rift too narrow for the horses angled away into the rock, and through it they could hear a snarling current. In the ravine the riders left their mounts under the care of the Cords. They went ahead on foot down the rift as it curved into the mountain and then broke out of the cliff no more than a hundred feet directly above Treacher's Gorge.

They no longer heard the drums; the tumult of the river smothered every sound but their own half-shouts. The walls of the chasm were high and sheer, blocking the horizon on either side. But through the spray that covered them like a mist, they could see the Gorge itself—the tight rock channel constricting the river until it appeared to scream, and the wild, white, sunset-flame-plumed water thrashing as if it fought against its own frantic rush. From nearly a league away to the west, the river came writhing down the Gorge, and sped below the company into the guts of the mountain as if sucked into an abyss. Above the Gorge, the setting sun hung near the horizon like a ball of blood in the leaden sky; and the light gave a shade of fire to the few hardy trees that clung to the rims of the chasm as if rooted by duty. But within Treacher's Gorge was nothing but spray and sheer stone walls and tortured waters.

The roar inundated Covenant's ears, and the mist-wet rock seemed to slip under his feet. For an instant, the cliffs reeled; he could feel the maw of Mount Thunder gaping for him. Then he snatched himself back into the rift, stood with his back pressed against the rock, hugged his chest and fought not to gasp.

There was activity around him. He heard shouts of surprise and fear from the warriors at the end of the rift, heard Foamfollower's strangled howl. But he did not move. He clenched himself against the rock in the

mist and roar of the river until his knees steadied, and
the scream of slippage eased in his feet. Only then did
he go to find out what caused the distress of his companions. He kept one hand braced on the wall and
moved the other from shoulder to shoulder among the
company as he went forward.

Between Covenant and the cliff, Foamfollower
struggled. Two Bloodguard clung to his arms, and he
battered them against the sides of the rift, hissing ra-
paciously, "Release me! Release—! I want them!" As
if he wished to leap down into the Gorge.

"No!" Abruptly, Prothall stood before the Giant.
The backlight of the sunset dimmed his face as he
stood silhouetted against the glow with his arms wide
and his staff held high. He was old, and only half the
Giant's size. But the orange-red fire seemed to expand
him, make him taller, more full of authority. "Rockbrother! Master yourself! By the Seven! Do you rave?"

At that, Foamfollower threw off the Bloodguard.
He caught the front of Prothall's robe, heaved the High
Lord into the air, pinned him against the wall. Into his
face, the Giant wheezed as if he were choking with
rage, "Rave? Do you accuse me?"

The Bloodguard sprang toward Foamfollower. But
a shout from Mhoram stopped them. Prothall hung
clamped against the stone like a handful of old rags,
but his eyes did not flinch. He repeated, "Do you
rave?"

For one horrible moment, Foamfollower held the
High Lord as if he meant to murder him with one huge
squeeze of his fist. Covenant tried to think of something to say, some way to intervene, but could not. He
had no conception of what had happened to Foamfollower.

Then from behind Covenant First Mark Tuvor said
clearly, "A Raver? In one of the Seareach Giants?
Impossible."

As if impaled by Tuvor's assertion, Foamfollower
broke into a convulsion of coughing. The violence of
his reaction knotted his gnarled frame. He lowered
Prothall, then collapsed backward, falling with a thud
against the opposite wall. Slowly, his paroxysm

changed into a low chuckle like the glee of hysteria.

Heard through the groaning of the river, that sound made Covenant's skin crawl like a slimy caress. He could not abide it. Driven by a need to learn what had befallen Foamfollower, he moved forward to look into the Gorge.

There, braced now against his vertigo and the inundation of the river roar, he saw what had ignited Foamfollower. Ah, Giant! he groaned. To kill——! Below him and barely twenty feet above the level of the river was a narrow roadway like a ledge in the south wall of the Gorge. And along the roadway to the beat of unheard drums marched an army of Cavewights out of Mount Thunder. Captained by a wedge of urviles, file after file of the gangrel creatures jerked out of the mountain and tramped along the ledge with a glare of lust in their laval eyes. Thousands had already left their Wightwarrens; and behind them the files continued as if Mount Thunder were spewing all the hordes of its inhabiting vermin onto the undefended Earth.

Foamfollower!

For a moment, Covenant's heart beat to the rhythm of the Giant's pain. He could not bear to think that Foamfollower and his people might lose their hope of Home because of creatures like those.

Is killing the only answer?

Numbly, half blindly, he began looking for the way in which Foamfollower had meant to reach the ledge and the Cavewights.

He found it easily enough; it looked simple for anyone not timorous of heights. There was a rude, slick stair cut into the rock of the south wall from the rift down to the roadway. Opposite it were steps which went from the rift up to the top of the Gorge. They were as gray, spray-worn and old as native stone.

Lord Mhoram had come up behind Covenant. His voice reached dimly through the river roar. "This is the ancient Look of Treacher's Gorge. That part of the First Ward which tells of this place is easily understood. It was formed for the watch and concealment of the betrayers. For here at Treacher's Gorge, Lord

Foul the Despiser revealed his true self to High Lord
Kevin. Here was struck the first blow of the open war
which ended in the Ritual of Desecration.

"Before that time, Kevin Landwaster doubted Lord
Foul without knowing why—for the Despiser had en-
acted no ill which Kevin could discover—and he
showed trust for Lord Foul out of shame for his unworthy doubt. Then, through the Despiser's plotting, a
message came to the Council of Lords from the
Demondim in Mount Thunder. The message asked the
Lords to come to the Demondim loreworks, the spawning crypts where the ur-viles were made, to meet with
the loremasters, who claimed knowledge of a secret
power.

"Clearly, Lord Foul intended for Kevin to go to
Mount Thunder. But the High Lord doubted, and did
not go. Then he was ashamed of his doubt, and sent
in his stead some of his truest friends and strongest
allies. So a high company of the Old Lords rafted as
was their wont down the Soulsease through Andelain
to Mount Thunder. And here, in the roar and spray
and ill of Treacher's Gorge, they were ambushed by
ur-viles. They were slaughtered, and their bodies sent
to the abyss of the mountain. Then marched armies
like these out of the catacombs, and the Land was
plunged all unready into war.

"That long conflict went on battle after death-
littered battle without hope. High Lord Kevin fought
bravely. But he had sent his friends into ambush. Soon
he began his midnight meetings with despair—and
there was no hope."

The seductive, dizzy rush of the river drained Covenant's resistance. Spray beaded on his face like sweat.

Foamfollower had wanted to do the same thing—
leap into the writhing allure of the Gorge—fall on the
Cavewights from ambush.

With an effort that made him moan through his
clenched teeth, Covenant backed away from the Look.
Gripping himself against the wall, he asked without
apparent transition, "Is he still laughing?"

Mhoram appeared to understand. "No. Now he sits

and quietly sings the song of the Unhomed, and gives no sign."

Foamfollower! Covenant breathed. "Why did you stop the Bloodguard? He might've hurt Prothall."

The Lord turned his back on Treacher's Gorge to face Covenant. "Saltheart Foamfollower is my friend. How could I interfere?" A moment later, he added, "The High Lord is not defenseless."

Covenant persisted. "Maybe a Raver—"

"No." Mhoram's flat assertion acknowledged no doubt. "Tuvor spoke truly. No Raver has the might to master a Giant."

"But something"—Covenant groped—"something is hurting him. He—he doesn't believe those omens. He thinks—Drool—or something—is going to prevent the Giants from going Home."

Mhoram's reply was so soft that Covenant was forced to read it on his crooked lips. "So do I."

Foamfollower!

Covenant looked down the rift at the Giant. In the darkness Foamfollower sat like a lump of shale against one wall, singing quietly and staring at invisible visions on the stone before him. The sight brought up a surge of sympathetic anger in Covenant, but he clamped it down, clutched his bargain. The walls of the rift leaned in toward him, like suffocating fear, dark wings. He thrust himself past the Giant and out toward the ravine.

Before long, the company gathered there for supper. They ate by the light of one dim *lillianrill* torch; and when the meal was done, they tried to get some sleep. Covenant felt that rest was impossible; he sensed the army of Cavewights unrolling like a skein of destruction for the weaving of the Land's death. But the ceaseless roar of the river lulled him until he relaxed against the ground. He dozed slightly, with the drums of war throbbing in the rock under him.

Later, he found himself sharply awake. The red moon had passed the crest of Mount Thunder, and now glared straight down on the ravine. He guessed that midnight was past. At first, he thought that the moon had roused him with its nearly full stare. But then he realized that the vibration of the drums was gone from the rock. He glanced around the camp, and saw Tuvor whispering with High Lord Prothall. The next moment, Tuvor began waking the sleepers.

Soon the warriors were alert and ready. Covenant had his knife in the belt of his robe, his staff in his hand. Birinair held aloft a rod with a small flame flickering from its tip, and in that uncertain light Mhoram and Prothall stood together with Manethrall Lithe, Warhaft Quaan, and the First Mark. Dim shadows shifted like fear and resolution across Prothall's face. His voice sounded weak with age as he said, "Now is our last hour of open sky. The outpouring of Drool's army has ended. Those of us who will must go into the catacombs of Mount Thunder. We must take this chance to enter, while Drool's attention is still with his army—before he can perceive that we are not where he thinks us to be.

"Now is the time for those who would to lay down the Quest. There can be no retreat, or escape after failure, in the Wightwarrens. The Quest has already been bravely served. None who now lay it down need feel shame."

Carefully, Quaan said, "Do you turn back, High Lord?"

"Ah, no," sighed Prothall. "The hand of these times is upon me. I dare not falter."

Then Quaan replied, "Can a Eoman of the Warward of Lord's Keep turn back when the High Lord leads? Never!"

And the Eoman echoed, "Never!"

Covenant wondered where Foamfollower was, what the Giant would do. For himself, he felt intuitively sure that he had no choice, that his dream would only release him by means of the Staff of Law. Or by death.

The next moment, Manethrall Lithe spoke to Prothall. Her head was back, and her slim form was primed as if she were prepared to explode. "I gave my word. Your horses will be tended. The Cords will preserve them in hope of your return. But I—" She shook her bound hair as if she were defying herself. "I will go with you. Under the ground." Prothall's protest she stopped with a sharp gesture. "You set an example I must follow. How could I stand before a Ranyhyn again, if I come so far only to turn away when the peril becomes great? And I feel something more. The Ramen know the sky, the open earth. We know air and grass. We do not lose our way in darkness—the Ranyhyn have taught our feet to be sure. I feel that I will always know my way—outward. You may have need of me, though I am far from the Plains of Ra, and from myself."

The shadows formed Prothall's face into a grimace, but he responded quietly, "I thank you, Manethrall. The Ramen are brave friends of the Land." Casting his eyes over the whole company, he said, "Come, then. The outcome of our Quest awaits. Whatever may befall us—as long as there are people to sing, they will sing that in this dark hour the Land was well championed. Now be true to the last." Without waiting for an answer, he went out of the bloody moonlight into the rift.

The warriors let Covenant follow behind the two Lords as if according him a position of respect. Prothall and Mhoram walked side by side; and when they neared the Look, Covenant could see from between them Foamfollower standing at the edge of the cliff. The Giant had his palms braced above his head on either wall. His back was to the Lords; he stared into the bleak, blood-hued writhing of the river. His huge form was dark against the vermilion sky.

When the Lords came near him, he said as if he were speaking back to them from the Gorge, "I remain here. My watch. I will guard you. Drool's army will not trap you in Mount Thunder while I live." A moment later, he added as if he had recognized the bottom of himself, "From here I will not smell the Wightwarrens." But his next words carried an echo of old Giantish humor. "The catacombs were not made to accommodate creatures the size of Giants."

"You choose well," murmured Prothall. "We need your protection. But do not remain here after the full moon. If we do not return by that time, we are lost, and you must go to warn your people."

Foamfollower answered as if in reply to some other voice. "Remember the Oath of Peace. In the maze where you go, it is your lifeline. It preserves you against Soulcrusher's purposes, hidden and savage. Remember the Oath. It may be that hope misleads. But hate—hate corrupts. I have been too quick to hate. I become like what I abhor."

"Have some respect for the truth," Mhoram snapped. The sudden harshness of his tone startled Covenant. "You are Saltheart Foamfollower of the Seareach Giants, Rockbrother to the men of the Land. That name cannot be taken from you."

But Covenant had heard no self-pity in the Giant's words—only recognition and sorrow. Foamfollower did not speak again. He stood as still as the walls against which he braced himself—stood like a statue carved to occupy the Look.

The Lords spent no more time with him. Already the night was waning, and they wanted to enter the mountain before daylight.

The Questers took positions. Prothall, Birinair, and two Bloodguard followed First Mark Tuvor. Then came Mhoram, Lithe, Bannor, Covenant, and Korik. Then came Warhaft Quaan, his fourteen warriors, and the last four Bloodguard.

They were only twenty-nine against all of Drool Rockworm's unknown might.

They strung a line of *clingor* from Tuvor to the last Bloodguard. In single file, they started down the slick stair into Treacher's Gorge.

TWENTY-TWO:
The Catacombs of
Mount Thunder

DROOL'S moon embittered the night like a consummation of gall. Under it, the river thrashed and roared in Treacher's Gorge as if it were being crushed. Spray and slick-wet moss made the stair down from the Look as treacherous as a quagmire.

Covenant bristled with trepidations. At first, when his turn to begin the descent had come, his dread had paralyzed him. But when Bannor had offered to carry him, he had found the pride to make himself move. In addition to the *clingor* line, Bannor and Korik held his staff like a railing for him. He went tortuously down into the Gorge as if he were striving to lock his feet on the stone of each step.

The stair dropped irregularly from the cliff into the wall of the Gorge. Soon the company was creeping into the loud chasm, led only by the light of Birinair's torch. The crimson froth of the river seemed to leap up at them like a hungry plague as they neared the roadway. Each step was slicker than the one before. Behind him, Covenant heard a gasp as one of the warriors slipped. The low cry carried terror like the quarrel of a crossbow. But the Bloodguard anchoring the line were secure; the warrior quickly regained his footing.

The descent dragged on. Covenant's ankles began to ache with the increasing uncertainty of his feet. He tried to think his soles into the rock, make them part of the stone through sheer concentration. And he gripped his staff until his palms were so slick with sweat that the wood seemed to be pulling away from him. His knees started to quiver.

But Bannor and Korik upheld him. The distance to the roadway shrank. After several long, bad moments, the threat of panic receded.

Then he reached the comparative safety of the ledge. He stood in the midst of the company between the Gorge wall and the channel of the river. Above them, the slash of sky had begun to turn gray, but that lightening only emphasized the darkness of the Gorge. Birinair's lone torch flickered as if it were lost in a wilderland.

The Questers had to yell to make themselves understood over the tumult of the current. Briskly, Quaan gave marching orders to his Eoman. The warriors checked over their weapons. With a few gestures and a slight nod or two, Tuvor made his last arrangements with the Bloodguard. Covenant gripped his staff, and assured himself of his Stonedownor knife—Atiaran's knife. He had a vague impression that he had forgotten something. But before he could try to think what it was, he was distracted by shouts.

Old Birinair was yelling at High Lord Prothall. For once, the Hearthrall seemed careless of his gruff dignity. Against the roar of the river, he thrust his seamed and quivering face at Prothall, and barked, "You cannot! The risk!"

Prothall shook his head negatively.

"You cannot lead! Allow me!"

Again, Prothall silently refused.

"Of course!" shouted Birinair, struggling to make his determination carry over the howl of water. "You must not! I can! I know the ways! Of course. Are you alone old enough to study? I know the old maps. No fool, you know—if I look old, and"—he faltered momentarily—"and useless. You must allow me!"

Prothall strove to shout without sounding angry. "Time is short! We must not delay. Birinair, old friend, I cannot put the first risk of this Quest onto another. It is my place."

"Fool!" spat Birinair, daring any insolence to gain his point. "How will you see?"

"See?"

"Of course!" The Hearthrall quivered with sarcasm.

"You will go before! Risk all! Light the way with Lords-fire! Fool! Drool will see you before you reach Warrenbridge!"

Prothall at last understood. "Ah, that is true." He sagged as if the realization hurt him. "Your light is quieter than mine. Drool will surely sense our coming if I make use of my staff." Abruptly, he turned to one side, angry now. "Tuvor!" he commanded. "Hearthrall Birinair leads! He will light our way in my place. Ward him well, Tuvor! Do not let this old friend suffer my perils."

Birinair drew himself up, rediscovering dignity in his responsibility. He extinguished the rod he carried, and gave it to a warrior to pack away with the rest of his brands. Then he stroked the end of his staff, and a flame sprang up there. With a brusque beckon, he raised his fire and started stiffly down the roadway toward the maw of Mount Thunder.

At once, Terrel and Korik passed the Hirebrand and took scouting positions twenty feet ahead of him. Two other Bloodguard placed themselves just behind him; and after them went Prothall and Mhoram together, then two more Bloodguard followed singly by Manethrall Lithe, Covenant, and Bannor. Next marched Quaan with his Eoman in files of three, leaving the last two Bloodguard to bring up the rear. In that formation, the company moved toward the entrance to the catacombs.

Covenant looked upward briefly to try to catch a last glimpse of Foamfollower in the Look. But he did not see the Giant; the Gorge was too full of darkness. And the roadway demanded his attention. He went into the rock under Foamfollower without any wave or sign of farewell.

Thus the company strode away from daylight—from sun and sky and open air and grass and possibility of retreat—and took their Quest into the gullet of Mount Thunder.

Covenant went into that demesne of night as if into a nightmare. He was not braced for the entrance to the catacombs. He had approached it without fear; the relief of having survived the descent from the Look had rendered him temporarily immune to panic. He had not said farewell to Foamfollower; he had forgotten something; but these pangs were diffused by a sense of anticipation, a sense that his bargain would bring him out of the dream with his ability to endure intact.

But the sky above—an openness of which he had hardly been aware—was cut off as if by an ax, and replaced by the huge stone weight of the mountain, so heavy that its aura alone was crushing. In his ears, its mass seemed to rumble like silent thunder. The river's roaring mounted in the gullet of the cave, adumbrated itself as if the constricted pain of the current were again constricted into keener and louder pain. The spray was as thick as rain; ahead of the company, Birinair's flame burned dim and penumbral, nearly quenched by the wet air. And the surface of the roadway was hazardous, littered with holes and rocks and loose shale. Covenant strained his attention as if he were listening for a note of sense in the gibberish of his experience, and under this alertness he wore his hope of escape like a buckler.

In more ways than one, he felt that it was his only protection. The company seemed pathetically weak, defenseless against the dark-dwelling Cavewights and ur-viles. Stumbling through night broken only at the solitary point of Birinair's fire, he predicted that the company would be observed soon. Then a report would go to Drool, and the inner forces of the Wightwarrens would pour forth, and the army would be recalled—what chance had Foamfollower against so many thousands of Cavewights?—and the company would be crushed like a handful of presumptuous ants. And in that moment of resolution or death would come his own rescue or defeat. He could not envision any other outcome.

With these thoughts, he walked as if he were listening for the downward rush of an avalanche.

After some distance, he realized that the sound of the river was changing. The roadway went inward almost horizontally, but the river was falling into the depths of the rock. The current was becoming a cataract, an abysmal plummet like a plunge into death. The sound of it receded slowly as the river crashed farther and farther away from the lip of the chasm.

Now there was less spray in the air to dim Birinair's flame. With less dampness to blur it, the stone wall showed more of its essential granite. Between the wall and the chasm, Covenant clung to the reassurance of the roadway. When he put a foot down hard, he could feel the solidity of the ledge jolt from his heel to the base of his spine.

Around him, the cave had become like a tunnel except for the chasm on the left. He fought his apprehension by concentrating on his feet and the Hirebrand's flame. The river fell helplessly, and its roar faded like fingers scraping for a lost purchase. Soon he began to hear the moving noises of the company. He turned to try to see the opening of the Gorge, but either the road had been curving gradually, or the opening had been lost in the distance; he saw nothing behind him but night as unmitigated as the blackness ahead.

But after a time he felt that the looming dark was losing its edge. Some change in the air attenuated the midnight of the catacombs. He stared ahead, trying to clarify the perception. No one spoke; the company hugged its silence as if in fear that the walls were capable of hearing.

Shortly, however, Birinair halted. Covenant, Lithe, and the Lords quickly joined the old Hirebrand. With him stood Terrel.

"Warrenbridge lies ahead," said the Bloodguard. "Korik watches. There are sentries." He spoke softly, but after the long silence his voice sounded careless of hazards.

"Ah, I feared that," whispered Prothall. "Can we approach?"

"Rocklight makes dark shadows. The sentries stand atop the span. We can approach within bowshot."

Mhoram called quietly for Quaan while Prothall asked, "How many sentries?"

Terrel replied, "Two."

"Only two?"

The Bloodguard shrugged fractionally. "They suffice. Between them lies the only entrance to the Wightwarrens."

But Prothall breathed again, "Only two?" He seemed to be groping to recognize a danger he could not see.

While the High Lord considered, Mhoram spoke rapidly to Quaan. At once, the Warhaft turned to his Eoman, and shortly two warriors stood by Terrel, unslinging their bows. They were tall, slim Woodhelvennin, and in the pale light their limbs hardly looked brawny enough to bend their stiff bows.

For a moment longer, Prothall hesitated, pulling at his beard as if he were trying to tug a vague impression into consciousness. But then he thrust his anxiety down, gave Terrel a sharp nod. Briskly, the Bloodguard led the two warriors away toward the attenuated night ahead.

Prothall whispered intently to the company, "Have a care. Take no risk without my order. My heart tells me there is peril here—some strange danger which Kevin's Lore names—but now I cannot recall it. Ah, memory! That knowledge is so dim and separate from what we have known since the Desecration. Think, all of you. Take great care."

Walking slowly, he went forward beside Birinair, and the company followed.

Now the light became steadily clearer—an orangered, rocky glow like that which Covenant had seen long ago in his brief meeting with Drool in Kiril Threndor. Soon the Questers could see that in a few hundred yards the cave took a sharp turn to the right, and at the same time the ceiling of the tunnel rose as if there were a great vault beyond the bend.

Before they had covered half the distance, Korik joined them to guide them to a safe vantage. On the way, he pointed out the position of Terrel and the two warriors. They had climbed partway up the right wall, and were kneeling on a ledge in the angle of the bend.

Korik led the company close to the river cleft until they reached a sheer stone wall. The chasm appeared to leave them—vanish straight into the rock which turned the road toward the right—but light shone over this rock as well as through the chasm. The rock was not a wall, but rather a huge boulder sitting like a door ajar before the entrance to an immense chamber. Terrel had taken the two warriors to a position from which they could fire their shafts over this boulder.

Korik guided Prothall, Mhoram, and Covenant across the shadow cast by the boulder until they could peer to the left around its edge. Covenant found himself looking into a high, flat-floored cavern. The chasm of the river swung around behind the boulder, and cut at right angles to its previous direction straight through the center of the vault, then disappeared into the far wall. So the roadway went no farther along the river's course. But there were no other openings in the outer half of the cavern.

At that point, the chasm was at least fifty feet wide. The only way across it was a massive bridge of native stone which filled the middle of the vault.

Carefully, Mhoram whispered, "Only two. They are enough. Pray for a true aim. There will be no second chance."

At first, Covenant saw no guards. His eyes were held by two pillars of pulsing, fiery rocklight which stood like sentries on either side of the bridge crest. But he forced himself to study the bridge, and shortly he discerned two black figures on the span, one beside each pillar. They were nearly invisible so close to the rocklight.

"Ur-viles," the High Lord muttered. "By the Seven! I must remember! Why are they not Cavewights? Why does Drool waste ur-viles on such duty?"

Covenant hardly listened to Prothall's uneasiness. The rocklight demanded his attention; it seemed to hold affinities for him that he could not guess. By some perverse logic of its pulsations, he felt himself made aware of his wedding band. The Droolish, powerful glow made his hand itch around his ring like a reminder that its promise of cherishing had failed. Grimly, he clenched his fist.

Prothall gripped himself, said heavily to Korik, "Make the attempt. We can only fail."

Without a word, Korik nodded up at Terrel.

Together, two bowstrings thrummed flatly.

The next instant, the ur-viles were gone. Covenant caught a glimpse of them dropping like black pebbles into the chasm.

The High Lord sighed his relief. Mhoram turned away from the vault, threw a salute of congratulation toward the two archers, then hurried back to give explanations and orders to the rest of the company. From the Eoman came low murmured cheers, and the noises of a relaxation of battle tension.

"Do not lower your guard!" Prothall hissed. "The danger is not past. I feel it."

Covenant stood where he was, staring into the rocklight, clenching his fist. Something that he did not understand was happening.

"Ur-Lord," Prothall asked softly, "what do you see?"

"Power." The interruption irritated him. His voice scraped roughly in his throat. "Drool's got enough to make you look silly." He raised his left fist. "It's daylight outside." His ring burned blood-red, throbbed to the pulse of the rocklight.

Prothall frowned at the ring, concentrating fiercely. His lips were taut over his teeth as he muttered, "This is not right. I must remember. Rocklight cannot do this."

Mhoram approached, and said before he saw what was between Covenant and Prothall, "Terrel has rejoined us. We are ready to cross." Prothall nodded inattentively. Then Mhoram noticed the ring. Covenant heard a sound as if Mhoram were grinding his teeth. The Lord reached out, clasped his hand over Covenant's fist.

A moment later, he turned and signaled to the company. Quaan led his Eoman forward with the Bloodguard. Prothall looked distracted, but he went with Birinair into the vault. Automatically, Covenant followed them toward Warrenbridge.

Tuvor and another Bloodguard went ahead of the High Lord. They neared the bridge, inspecting it to be sure that the span was truly safe before the Lords crossed.

Covenant wandered forward as if in a trance. The spell of the rocklight grew on him. His ring began to feel hot. He had to make an effort of consciousness to wonder why his ring was bloody rather than orange-red like the glowing pillars. But he had no answer. He felt a change coming over him that he could not resist or measure or even analyze. It was as if his ring were confusing his senses, turning them on their pivots to peer into unknown dimensions.

Tuvor and his comrade started up the bridge. Prothall held the company back, despite the inherent danger of remaining in the open light. He stared after Tuvor and yanked at his beard with a hand which trembled agedly.

Covenant felt the spell mastering him. The cavern began to change. In places, the rock walls seemed thinner, as if they were about to become transparent. Quaan and Lithe and the warriors grew transparent as well, approached the evanescence of wraiths. Prothall and Mhoram appeared solider, but Prothall flickered where Mhoram was steady. Only the Blood-guard showed no sign of dissipating, of losing their essence in mist—the Bloodguard and the ring. Cove-nant's own flesh now looked so vague that he feared his ring would fall through it to the stone. At his shoul-der, Bannor stood—hard, implacable and dangerous, as if the Bloodguard's mere touch might scatter his beclouded being to the winds.

He was drifting into transience. He tried to clench himself; his fingers came back empty.

Tuvor neared the crest of the span. The bridge seemed about to crumble under him—he appeared so much solider than the stone.

Then Covenant saw it—a loop of shimmering air banded around the center of the bridge, standing flat across the roadway and around under the span and back. He did not know what it was, understood noth-ing about it, except that it was powerful.

Tuvor was about to step into it.

With an effort like a convulsion, Covenant started

to fight, resist the spell. Some intuition told him that
Tuvor would be killed. Even a leper! he adjured himself. This was not his bargain; he had not promised to
stand silent and watch men die. Hellfire! Then, with
recovered rage, he cried again, Hellfire!

"Stop!" he gasped. "Can't you see?"

At once, Prothall shouted, "Tuvor! Do not move!"
Wheeling on Covenant, he demanded, "What is it?
What do you see?"

The violence of his rage brought back some of the
solidity to his vision. But Prothall still appeared dangerously evanescent. Covenant jerked up his ring, spat,
"Get them down. Are you blind? It's not the rocklight.
Something else up there."

Mhoram recalled Tuvor and his companion. But for
a moment Prothall only stared in blank fear at Covenant. Then, abruptly, he struck his staff on the stone
and ejaculated, "Ur-viles! And rocklight just there—
as anchors! Ah, I am blind, blind! They tend the
power!"

Incredulously, Mhoram whispered, "A Word of
Warning?"

"Yes!"

"Is it possible? Has Drool entirely mastered the
Staff? Can he speak such might?"

Prothall was already on his way toward the bridge.
Over his shoulder, he replied, "He has Lord Foul to
teach him. We have no such help." A moment later,
he strode up the span with Tuvor close behind him.

The spell reached for Covenant again. But he knew
it better now, and held it at bay with curses. He could
still see the shimmering loop of the Word as Prothall
neared it.

The High Lord approached slowly, and at last
halted a step before the Word. Gripping his staff in his
left hand, he held his right arm up with the palm forward like a gesture of recognition. With a rattling
cough, he began to sing. Constantly repeating the same
motif, he sang cryptically in a language Covenant did
not understand—a language so old that it sounded
grizzled and hoary. Prothall sang it softly, intimately,

as if he were entering into private communion with the Word of Warning.

Gradually, vaguely, like imminent mist, the Word became visible to the company. In the air opposite Prothall's palm, an indistinct shred of red appeared, coalesced, like a fragment of an unseen tapestry. The pale, hanging red expanded until a large, rough circle was centered opposite his palm. With extreme caution —singing all the while—he raised his hand to measure the height of the Word, moved sideways to judge its configuration. Thus in tatters the company saw the barrier which opposed them. And as Covenant brought more of himself to the pitch of his stiff rage, his own perception of the Word paled until he saw only as much of it as the others did.

At last, Prothall lowered his hand and ceased his song. The shreds vanished. He came tightly down the bridge as if he were only holding himself erect by the simple strength of his resolution. But his gaze was full of comprehension and the measure of risks.

"A Word of Warning," he reported sternly, "set here by the power of the Staff of Law to inform Drool if his defenses were breached—and to break Warrenbridge at the first touch." His tone carried a glimpse of a plunge into the chasm. "It is a work of great power. No Lord since the Desecration has been capable of such a feat. And even if we had the might to undo it, we would gain nothing, for Drool would be warned. Still, there is one sign in our favor. Such a Word cannot be maintained without constant attention. It must be tended, else it decays—though not speedily enough for our purpose. That Drool set urviles here as sentries perhaps shows that his mind is elsewhere."

Wonderful! Covenant growled corrosively. Terrific! His hands itched with an intense urge to throttle someone.

Prothall continued: "If Drool's eyes are turned away, it may be that we can bend the Word without breaking." He took a deep breath, then asserted, "I believe it can be done. This Word is not as pure and

dangerous as might be." He turned to Covenant. "But
I fear for you, ur-Lord."

"For me?" Covenant reacted as if the High Lord
had accused him of something. "Why?"

"I fear that the mere closeness of your ring to the
Word may undo it. So you must come last. And even
then we may be caught within the catacombs, with no
bridge to bear us out again."

Last? He had a sudden vision of being forsaken or
trapped here, blocked by that deep cleft from the escape he needed. He wanted to protest, Let me go first.
If I can make it, anybody can. But he saw the folly
of that argument. Forbear, he urged himself. Keep the
bargain. His fear made him sound bitter as he grated,
"Get on with it. They're bound to send some new
guards one of these days."

Prothall nodded. With a last measuring look at Covenant, he turned away. He and Mhoram went up onto
the bridge to engage the Word.

Tuvor and Terrel followed carrying coils of *clingor*
which they attached to the Lords' waists and anchored
at the foot of the bridge. Thus secured against the collapse of the span, Prothall and Mhoram ascended cautiously until they were only an arm's length from the
invisible Word. There they knelt together and started
their song.

When the bottom of the Word became visible in
crimson, they placed their staffs parallel to it on the
stone before them. Then, with tortuous care, they
rolled their staffs directly under the iridescent power
For one bated moment, they remained still in an attitude of prayer as if beseeching their wood not to
interrupt the current flowing past their faces. A heart-
stopping flicker replied in the red shimmer. But the
Lords went on singing—and shortly the Word steadied.

Bracing themselves, they started the most difficult
part of their task. They began lifting the inner ends of
their staffs.

With a quick intake of wonder and admiration, the
company saw the lower edge of the Word bend, leaving a low, tented gap below it.

When the peak of the gap was more than a foot

high, the Lords froze. Instantly, Bannor and two other Bloodguard dashed up the bridge, unrolling a rope as they ran. One by one, they crawled through the gap and took their end of the lifeline to safe ground beyond the span.

As soon as Bannor had attached his end of the rope, Mhoram took hold of Prothall's staff. The High Lord wormed through the gap, then held the staffs for Mhoram. By the time Mhoram had regained his position beside Prothall, old Birinair was there and ready to pass. Behind him in rapid single file went the Eoman, followed by Quaan and Lithe.

In turn, Tuvor and Terrel slipped under the Word and anchored their ropes to the two Lords beyond the chasm. Then, moving at a run, the last Bloodguard slapped the central lifeline around Covenant and made their way through the gap.

He was left alone.

In a cold sweat of anger and fear, he started up the bridge. He felt the two pillars of rocklight as if they were scrutinizing him. He went up the span fiercely, cursing Foul, and cursing himself for his fear. He did not give a glance to the chasm. Staring at the gap, he ground his rage into focus, and approached the shimmering tapestry of power. As he drew nearer, his ring ached on his hand. The bridge seemed to grow thinner as if it were dissolving under him. The Word became starker, dominating his vision more and more.

But he kept his hold on his rage. Even a leper! He reached the gap, knelt before it, looked momentarily through the shimmer at the Lords. Their faces ran with sweat, and their voices trembled in their song. He clenched his hands around the staff of Baradakas, and crawled into the gap.

As he passed under the Word, he heard an instant high keening like a whine of resistance. For that instant, a cold red flame burst from his ring.

Then he was through, and the bridge and the Word were still intact.

He stumbled down the span, flinging off the *clingor* lifeline. When he was safe, he turned long enough to see Prothall and Mhoram remove their staffs from under the Word. Then he stalked out of the vault of Warrenbridge into the dark tunnel of the roadway. He felt Bannor's presence at his shoulder almost at once, but he did not stop until the darkness against which he thrust himself was thick enough to seem impenetrable.

In frustration and congested fear, he groaned, "I want to be alone. Why don't you leave me alone?"

With the repressed lilt of his *Haruchai* inflection, Bannor responded, "You are ur-Lord Covenant. We are the Bloodguard. Your life is in our care."

Covenant glared into the ineluctable dark around him, and thought about the unnatural solidity of the Bloodguard. What binding principle made their flesh seem less mortal than the gutrock of Mount Thunder? A glance at his ring showed him that its incarnadine gleam had almost entirely faded. He found that he was jealous of Bannor's dispassion; his own pervasive irrectitude offended him. On the impulse of a ferocious intuition, he returned, "That isn't enough."

He could envision Bannor's slight, eloquent shrug without seeing it. In darkness he waited defiantly until the company caught up with him.

But when he was again marching in his place in the Quest—when Birinair's wan flame had passed by him, treading as if transfixed by leadership the invisible directions of the roadway—the night of the catacombs crowded toward him like myriad leering spectators, impatient for bloodshed, and he suffered a reaction against the strain. His shoulders began to tremble, as if he had been hanging by his arms too long, and cold petrifaction settled over his thoughts.

The Word of Warning revealed that Lord Foul was expecting them, knew they would not fall victim to Drool's army. Drool could not have formed the Word, much less made it so apposite to white gold. Therefore it served the Despiser's purposes rather than Drool's. Perhaps it was a test of some kind—a measure of the Lords' strength and resourcefulness, an indication of Covenant's vulnerability. But whatever it was, it was Lord Foul's doing. Covenant felt sure that the Despiser knew everything—planned, arranged, made inevitable all that happened to the Quest, every act and decision. Drool was ignorant, mad, manipulated; the Cavewight probably failed to understand half of what he achieved under Lord Foul's hand.

But in his bones Covenant had known such things from the beginning. They did not surprise him; rather, he saw them as symptoms of another, a more essential threat. This central peril—a peril which so froze his mind that only his flesh seemed able to react by trembling—had to do with his white gold ring. He perceived the danger clearly because he was too numb to hide from it. The whole function of the compromise, the bargain, he had made with the Ranyhyn, was to hold the impossibility and the actuality of the Land apart, in equipoise—Back off! Let me be!—to keep them from impacting into each other and blasting his precarious hold on life. But Lord Foul was using his ring to bring crushing together the opposite madnesses which he needed so desperately to escape.

He considered throwing the ring away. But he knew he could not do it. The band was too heavy with remembered lost love and honor and mutual respect to be tossed aside. And an old beggar—

If his bargain failed, he would have nothing left with which to defend himself against the darkness—no power or fertility or coherence—nothing but his own capacity for darkness, his violence, his ability to kill. That capacity led—he was too numb to resist the conclusion—as inalterably as leprosy to the destruction of the Land.

There his numbness seemed to become complete. He could not measure his situation more than that. All he could do was trail behind Birinair's flame and tell over his refusals like some despairing acolyte, desperate for faith, trying to invoke his own autonomy.

He concentrated on his footing as if it were tenuous and the rock unsure—as if Birinair might lead him over the edge of an abyss.

Gradually the character of their benighted journey changed. First, the impression of the surrounding tunnel altered. Behind the darkness, the walls seemed to open from time to time into other tunnels, and at one point the night took on an enormous depth, as if the company were passing over the floor of an amphitheater. In this blind openness, Birinair searched for his way. When the sense of vast empty space vanished, he led his companions into a stone corridor so low that his flame nearly touched the ceiling, so narrow that they had to pass in single file.

Then the old Hearthrall took them through a bewildering series of shifts in direction and terrain and depth. From the low tunnel, they turned sharply and went down a long, steep slope with no discernible walls. As they descended, turning left and right at landmarks only Birinair seemed able to see, the black air became colder and somehow loathsome, as if it carried an echo of ur-viles. The cold came in sudden drafts and pockets, blowing through chasms and tunnels that opened unseen on either side into dens and coverts and passages and great Cavewightish halls, all invisible but for the timbre, the abrupt impression of space, which they gave the darkness.

Lower down the sudden drafts began to stink. The buried air seemed to flow over centuries of accumulated filth, vast hordes of unencrypted dead, long-abandoned laboratories where banes were made. At moments, the putrescence became so thick that Covenant could see it in the air. And out of the adjacent openings came cold, distant sounds—the rattle of shale dropping into immeasurable faults; occasional low complaints of stress; soft, crystalline, chinking noises like the tap of iron hammers; muffled sepulchral detonations; and long tired sighs, exhalations of fatigue from the ancient foundations of the mountain. The darkness itself seemed to be muttering as the company passed.

But at the end of the descent they reached a wavering stair cut into a rock wall, with lightless, hungry chasms gaping below them. And after that, they went through winding tunnels, along the bottoms of crevices, over sharp rock ridges like arêtes within the mountain, around pits with the moan of water and the reek of decay in their depths, under arches like entry-ways to grotesque festal halls—turned and climbed and navigated in the darkness as if it were a perilous limbo, trackless and fatal, varying only in the kind and extremity of its dangers. Needing proof of his own reality, Covenant moved with the fingers of his left hand knotted in his robe over his heart.

Three times in broad, flat spaces which might have been halls or ledges or peak tops surrounded by plunges, the company stopped and ate cold food by the light of Birinair's staff. Each meal helped; the sight of other faces around the flame, the consumption of tangible provender, acted like an affirmation or a pooling of the company's capacity for endurance. Once, Quaan forced himself to attempt a jest, but his voice sounded so hollow in the perpetual midnight that no one had the heart to reply. After each rest, the Questers set out again bravely. And each time, their pooled fortitude evaporated more rapidly, as if the darkness inhaled it with increasing voracity.

Later old Birinair led them out of cold and ventilated ways into close, musty, hot tunnels far from the main Wightwarrens. To reduce the risk of discovery, he chose a path through a section of the caves deader than the rest—silent and abandoned, with little fresh air left. But the atmosphere only raised the pitch of the company's tension. They moved as if they were screaming voicelessly in anticipation of some blind disaster.

They went on and on, until Covenant knew only that they had not marched for days because his ring had not yet started to glow with the rising of the moon. But after a time his white gold began to gleam like a crimson prophecy. Still they went on into what he now knew was night. They could not afford sleep or long rests. The peak of Drool's present power was only one day away.

They were following a tunnel with walls which seemed to stand just beyond the reach of Birinair's tottering fire. Abruptly, Terrel returned from his scouting position, loomed out of the darkness to appear before the old Hirebrand. Swiftly, Prothall and

Mhoram, with Lithe and Covenant behind them, hastened to Birinair's side. Terrel's voice held a note like
urgency as he said, "Ur-viles approach—perhaps fifty.
They have seen the light."

Prothall groaned; Mhoram spat a curse. Manethrall
Lithe drew a hissing breath, whipped her cord from
her hair as if she were about to encounter the stuff of
which Ramen nightmares were made.

But before anyone could take action, old Birinair
seemed to snap like a dry twig. Shouting, "Follow!" he
spun to his right and raced away into the darkness.

At once, two Bloodguard sprinted after him. For an
instant, the Lords hesitated. Then Prothall cried,
"Melenkurion!" and dashed after Birinair. Mhoram
began shouting orders; the company sprang into battle
readiness.

Covenant fled after Birinair's bobbing fire. The
Hirebrand's shout had not sounded like panic. That
cry—*Follow!*—urged Covenant along. Behind him, he
heard the first commands and clatters of combat. He
kept his eyes on Birinair's light, followed him into a
low, nearly airless tunnel.

Birinair raced down the tunnel, still a stride or two
ahead of the Bloodguard.

Suddenly, there came a hot noise like a burst of
lightning; without warning a sheet of blue flame en-
veloped the Hirebrand. Dazzling, coruscating, it walled
the tunnel from top to bottom. It roared like a furnace.
And Birinair hung in it, spread-limbed and transfixed,
his frame contorted with agony. Beside him, his staff
flared and became ash.

Without hesitation, the two Bloodguard threw themselves at the fire. It knocked them back like blank
stone. They leaped together at Birinair, trying to force
him through and past the flame sheet. But they had
no effect; Birinair hung where he was, a charred victim in a web of blue fire.

The Bloodguard were poised to spring again when
the High Lord caught up with them. He had to shout
to make himself heard over the crackling of power.
"My place!" he cried, almost screaming. "He will die!
Aid Mhoram!"

He seemed to have fallen over an edge into distraction. His eyes had a look of chaos. Spreading his arms, he went forward and tried to embrace Birinair.

The fire kicked him savagely away. He fell, and for a long moment lay facedown on the stone.

Behind them, the battle mounted. The ur-viles had formed a wedge, and even with all the help of the Bloodguard and warriors, Mhoram barely held his ground. The first rush of the attack had driven the company back; Mhoram had retreated several yards into the tunnel where Birinair hung. There he made a stand. Despite Prothall's cries and the roar of the fire behind him, he kept his face toward the ur-viles.

Heavily, Prothall raised himself. His head trembled on his tired old neck. But his eyes were no longer wild.

He took a moment to recollect himself, knowing that he was already too late. Then, mustering his strength, he hurled his staff at the blue coruscation.

The shod wood struck with a blinding flash. For one blank instant, Covenant could see nothing. When his vision cleared, he found the staff hanging in the sheet of flame. Birinair lay in the tunnel beyond the fire.

"Birinair!" the High Lord cried. "My friend!" He seemed to believe that he could help the Hirebrand if he reached him in time. Once again, he flung himself at the flame, and was flung back.

The ur-viles pressed their attack ferociously, in hungry silence. Two of Quaan's Eoman were felled as the company backed into the tunnel, and one more died now with an iron spike in his heart. A woman struck in too close to the wedge, and her hand was hacked off. Mhoram fought the loremaster with growing desperation. Around him, the Bloodguard battled skillfully, but they could find few openings in the wedge.

Covenant peered through the blue sheet at Birinair. The Hirebrand's face was unmarked, but it held a wide stare of agony, as if he had remained alive for one instant after his soul had been seared. The remains of his cloak hung about him in charred wisps.

Follow!

That call had not been panic. Birinair had had some

idea. His shout echoed and compelled. His cloak hung about him—

Follow!

Covenant had forgotten something—something important. Wildly, he started forward.

Mhoram strove to strike harder. His strength played like lightning along his staff as he dealt blow after blow against the loremaster. Weakened by its losses, the wedge began to give ground.

Covenant stopped inches away from the sheet of power. Prothall's staff was suspended vertically within it like a landmark. The fire seemed to absorb rather than give off heat. Covenant felt himself growing cold and numb. In the dazzling blue force, he saw a chance for immolation, escape.

Abruptly, the ur-vile loremaster gave a barking shout, and broke formation. It ducked past Mhoram and dashed into the tunnel toward the fire, toward the kneeling High Lord. Mhoram's eyes flashed perilously, but he did not turn from the fight. He snapped an order to Quaan, and struck at the ur-viles with still fiercer force.

Quaan leaped from the fight. He raced to unsling his bow, nock an arrow, and shoot before the loremaster reached Prothall.

Vaguely, Covenant heard the High Lord gasp against the dead air, "Ur-Lord! Beware!" But he did not listen. His wedding band burned as if the defiled moon were like the rocklight on Warrenbridge—a Word of Warning.

He reached out his left hand, hesitated momentarily, then grasped the High Lord's staff.

Power surged. Bloody fire burst from his ring against the coruscating blue. The roar of the flame cycled upward beyond hearing. Then came a mighty blast, a silent explosion. The floor of the tunnel jumped as if its keel had struck a reef.

The blue sheet fell in tatters.

Quaan was too late to save Prothall. But the ur-vile did not attack the High Lord. It sprang over him toward Covenant. With all his strength, Quaan bent his bow and fired at the creature's back.

For an instant, Covenant stood still, listing crazily to one side and staring in horror at the abrupt darkness. Dim orange fire burned on his hand and arm, but the brilliant blue was gone. The fire gave no pain, though at first it clung to him as if he were dry wood. It was cold and empty, and it died out in sputtering flickers, as if after all he did not contain enough warmth to feed it.

Then the loremaster, with Quaan's arrow squarely between its shoulders, crashed into him and scattered him across the stone.

A short time later, he looked up with his head full of mist. The only light in the tunnel came from Mhoram's Lords-fire as he drove back the ur-viles. Then that light was gone, too; the ur-viles were routed. Tuvor and the Bloodguard started after them to prevent them from carrying reports to Drool, but Mhoram called, "Let them go! We are already exposed. No reports of ur-viles matter now." Voices gasped and groaned in the darkness; soon two or three of the warriors lit torches. The flames cast odd, dim shadows on the walls. The company drew together around Lord Mhoram and moved down to where Prothall knelt.

The High Lord held Birinair's charred form in his arms. But he brushed aside the sympathy and grief of the company. "Go on," he said weakly. "Discover what he intended. I will be done with my farewells soon." In explanation, he added, "He led in my place."

Mhoram laid a commiserating hand on the High Lord's shoulder. But the dangers of their situation did not allow him to remain still. Almost certainly, Drool now knew where they were; the energies they had released would point them out like an accusing finger. "Why?" Mhoram wondered aloud. "Why was such power placed here? This is not Drool's doing." Carrying one of the torches, he started down the tunnel.

From his collapse on the stone, Covenant replied in a grotesque, stricken voice. But he was answering a different question. "I forgot my clothes—left them behind."

Mhoram bent over him. Lighting his face with the

torch, the Lord asked, "Are you injured? I do not understand. Of what importance are your old clothes?"

The question seemed to require a world of explanation, but Covenant responded easily, glib with numbness and fog. "Of course I'm injured. My whole life is an injury." He hardly listened to his own speech. "Don't you see? When I wake up, and find myself dressed in my old clothes, not this moss-stained robe at all—why, that will prove that I really have been dreaming. If it wasn't so reassuring, I would be terrified."

"You have mastered a great power," Mhoram murmured.

"That was an accident. It happened by itself. I was —I was trying to escape. Burn myself."

Then the strain overcame him. He lowered his head to the stone and went to sleep.

He did not rest long; the air of the tunnel was too uncomfortable, and there was too much activity in the company. When he opened his eyes, he saw Lithe and several warriors preparing a meal over a low fire. With a trembling song on his lips, and tears spilling from his eyes, Prothall was using his blue fire to sear the injured woman's wrist-stump.

Covenant watched as she bore the pain; only when her wrist was tightly bandaged did she let herself faint. After that he turned away, sick with shared pain. He lurched to his feet, reeled as if he could not find his footing, had to brace himself against the wall. He stood there hunched over his aching stomach until Mhoram returned, accompanied by Quaan, Korik, and two other Bloodguard.

The Warhaft was carrying a small iron chest.

When Mhoram reached the fire, he spoke in quiet wonder. "The power was a defense placed here by High Lord Kevin. Beyond this tunnel lies a chamber. There we found the Second Ward of Kevin's Lore— the Second of the Seven."

High Lord Prothall's face lit up with hope.

TWENTY-THREE:
Kiril Threndor

REVERENTLY, Prothall took the chest. His fingers fumbled at the bindings. When he raised the lid, a pale, pearly glow like clean moonlight shone from within the cask. The radiance gave his face a look of beatitude as he ventured his hand into the chest to lift out an ancient scroll. When he raised it, the company saw that it was the scroll which shone.

Quaan and his Eoman half knelt before the Ward, bowed their heads. Mhoram and Prothall stood erect as if they were meeting the scrutiny of the master of their lives. After a moment of amazement, Lithe joined the warriors. Only Covenant and the Bloodguard showed no reverence. Tuvor's comrades stood casually alert, and Covenant leaned uncomfortably against the wall, trying to bring his unruly stomach under control.

But he was not blind to the importance of that scroll. A private hope wrestled with his nausea. He approached it obliquely. "Did Birinair know—what you were going to find? Is that why?"

"Why he ran here?" Mhoram spoke absently; all of him except his voice was focused on the scroll which Prothall held up like a mighty talisman. "Perhaps it is possible. He knew the old maps. No doubt they were given to us in the First Ward so that in time we might find our way here. It may be that his heart saw what our eyes did not."

Covenant paused, then asked, obliquely again, "Why did you let the ur-viles escape?"

This time, the Lords seemed to hear his seriousness.

431

With a piercing glance at him, Prothall replaced the scroll in the cask. When the lid was closed, Mhoram answered stiffly, "Unnecessary death, Unbeliever. We did not come here to slay ur-viles. We will harm ourselves more by unnecessary killing than by risking a few live foes. We fight in need, not in lust or rage. The Oath of Peace must not be compromised."

But this also did not answer Covenant's question. With an effort, he brought out his hope directly. "Never mind. This Second Ward—it doubles your power. You could send me back."

Mhoram's face softened at the need for assurance, for consolation against impossible demands, in the question. But his reply denied Covenant. "Ah, my friend, you forget. We have not yet mastered the First Ward—not in generations of study. The best of the Loresraat have failed to unveil the central mysteries. We can do nothing with this new Ward now. Perhaps, if we survive this Quest, we will learn from the Second in later years."

There he stopped. His face held a look of further speech, but he said no more until Prothall sighed, "Tell him all. We can afford no illusions now."

"Very well." Mhoram said hurriedly, "In truth, our possession of the Second Ward at such a time is perilous. It is clear from the First that High Lord Kevin prepared the Seven in careful order. It was his purpose that the Second Ward remain hidden until all the First was known. Apparently, certain aspects of his Lore carry great hazard to those who have not first mastered certain other aspects. So he hid his Wards, and defended them with powers which could not be breached until the earlier Lore was mastered. Now his intent has been broken. Until we penetrate the First, we will risk much if we attempt the use of the Second."

He pulled himself up and took a deep breath. "We do not regret. For all our peril, this discovery may be the great moment of our age. But it may not altogether bless us."

In a low voice, Prothall added, "We raise no blame or doubt. How could any have known what we would find? But the doom of the Land is now doubly on our heads. If we are to defeat Lord Foul in the end, we must master powers for which we are not ready. So we learn hope and dismay from the same source. Do not mistake us—this risk we accept gladly. The mastery of Kevin's Lore is the goal of our lives. But we must make clear that there is risk. I see hope for the Land, but little for myself."

"Even that sight is dim," said Mhoram tightly. "It may be that Lord Foul has led us here so that we may be betrayed by powers we cannot control."

At this, Prothall looked sharply at Mhoram. Then, slowly, the High Lord nodded his agreement. But his face did not lose the relief, the lightening of its burdens, which his first sight of the Ward had given him. Under its influence, he looked equal to the stewardship of his age. Now the time of High Lord Prothall son of Dwillian would be well remembered—if the company survived its Quest. His resolve had a forward look as he closed the chest of the Second Ward; his movements were crisp and decisive. He gave the cask to Korik, who bound it to his bare back with strips of *clingor,* and covered it by knotting his tunic shut.

But Covenant looked at the remains of the brief structure of his own hope, collapsed like a child's toy house, and he did not know where to turn for new edifices. He felt vaguely that he had no solid ground on which to build them. He was too weak and tired to think about it. He stood leaning where he was for a long time, with his head bent as if he were trying to decipher the chart of his robe.

Despite the danger, the company rested and ate there in the tunnel. Prothall judged that remaining where they were for a time was as unpredictable as anything else they might do; so while the Bloodguard stood watch, he encouraged his companions to rest. Then he lay down, pillowed his head on his arms, and seemed at once to fall into deep sleep, so intensely calm and quiet that it looked more like preparation than repose. Following his example, most of the company let their eyes close, though they slept only fitfully. But Mhoram and Lithe remained watchful. He stared into the low fire as if he were searching for a vision,

and she sat across from him with her shoulders
hunched against the oppressive weight of the mountain
—as unable to rest underground as if the lack of open
sky and grasslands offended her Ramen blood. Reclining against the wall, Covenant regarded the two of
them, and slept a little until the stain of his ring began
to fade with moonset.

After that Prothall arose, awake and alert, and
roused the company. As soon as everyone had eaten
again, he put out the campfire. In its place, he lit one
of the *lillianrill* torches. It guttered and jumped dangerously in the thick air, but he used it rather than his
staff to light the tunnel. Soon the Quest was marching
again. Helpless to do otherwise, they left their dead
lying on the stone of the Ward chamber. It was the
only tribute they could give Birinair and the slain warriors.

Again they went into darkness, led by the High
Lord through interminable, black, labyrinthian passages in the deep rock of Mount Thunder. The air became thicker, hotter, deader. In spite of occasional
ascents, their main progress was downward, toward
the bottomless roots of the mountain, closer with every
unseen, unmeasured league toward immense, buried,
slumbering, grim ills, the terrible bones of the Earth.
On and on they walked as if they were amazed by
darkness, irremediable night. They made their way in
hard silence, as if their lips were stiff with resisted
sobs. They could not see. It affected them like a bereavement.

As they approached the working heart of the Wightwarrens, certain sounds became louder, more distinct
—the battering of anvils, the groaning of furnaces,
gasps of anguish. From time to time they crossed blasts
of hot fetid air like forced ventilation for charnel pits.
And a new noise crept into their awareness—a sound
of bottomless boiling. For a long while, they drew
nearer to this deep moil without gaining any hint of
what it was.

Later they passed its source. Their path lay along
the lip of a huge cavern. The walls were lit luridly by

a seething orange sea of rocklight. Far below them was a lake of molten stone.

After the long darkness of their trek, the bright light hurt their eyes. The rising acrid heat of the lake snatched at them as if it were trying to pluck them from their perch. The deep, boiling sound thrummed in the air. Great gouts of magma spouted toward the ceiling, then fell back into the lake like crumbling towers.

Vaguely, Covenant heard someone say, "The Demondim in the days of High Lord Loric discarded their failed breeding efforts here. It is said that the loathing of the Demondim—and of the Viles who sired them—for their own forms surpassed all restraint. It led them to the spawning which made both ur-viles and Waynhim. And it drove them to cast all their weak and faulty into such pits as this—so strongly did they abhor their unseen eyelessness."

Groaning, he turned his face to the wall, and crept past the cavern into the passage beyond it. When he dropped his hands from the support of the stone, his fingers twitched at his sides as if he were testing the sides of a casket.

Prothall chose to rest there, just beyond the cavern of rocklight. The company ate a quick, cold meal, then pressed on again into darkness. From this passage, they took two turns, went up a long slope, and at length found themselves walking a ledge in a fault. Its crevice fell away to their left. Covenant made his way absently, shaking his head in an effort to clear his thoughts. Ur-viles reeled across his brain like images of self-hatred, premonitions. Was he doomed to see himself even in such creatures as that? No. He gritted his teeth. No. In the light of remembered bursts of lava, he began to fear that he had already missed his chance—his chance to fall—

In time, fatigue came back over him. Prothall called a rest halt on the ledge, and Covenant surprised himself nearly falling asleep that close to a crevice. But the High Lord was pushing toward his goal now, and did not let the company rest long. With his guttering torch, he led the Quest forward again, through darkness into darkness.

As the trek dragged on, their moment-by-moment caution began to slip. The full of the moon was coming, and somewhere ahead Drool was preparing for them. Prothall moved as if he were eager for the last test, and led them along the ledge at a stiff pace. As a result, the lone ur-vile took them all by surprise.

It had hidden itself in a thin fissure in the wall of the crevice. When Covenant passed it, it sprang out at him, threw its weight against his chest. Its roynish, eyeless face was blank with ferocity. As it struck him, it grappled for his left hand.

The force of the attack knocked him backward toward the crevice. For one flicker of time, he was not aware of that danger. The ur-vile consumed his attention. It pulled his hand close to its face, sniffed wetly over his fingers as if searching for something, then tried to jam his ring finger into its ragged mouth.

He staggered back one more step; his foot left the ledge. In that instant, he realized the hungry fall under him. Instinctively, he closed his fist against the ur-vile and ignored it. Clinging to his staff with all the strength of his halfhand, he thrust its end toward Bannor. The Bloodguard was already reaching for him.

Bannor caught hold of the staff.

For one slivered moment, Covenant kept his grip.

But the full weight of the ur-vile hung on his left arm. His hold tore loose from the staff. With the creature struggling to bite off his ring, he plunged into the crevice.

Before he could shriek his terror, a force like a boulder struck him, knocked the air from his lungs, left him gasping sickly as he plummeted. With his chest constricted and retching, unable to cry out, he lost consciousness.

When he roused himself after the impact, he was struggling for air against a faceful of dirt. He lay head down on a steep slope of shale and loam and refuse, and the slide caused by his landing had covered his face. For a long moment, he could not move except to gag and cough. His efforts shook him without freeing him.

Then, with a shuddering exertion, he rolled over, thrust up his head. He coughed up a gout of dirt, and found that he could breathe. But he still could not see. The fact took a moment to penetrate his awareness. He checked his face, found that his eyes were uncovered and open. But they perceived nothing except an utter and desolate darkness. It was as if he were blind with panic—as if his optic nerves were numb with terror.

For a time he did panic. Without sight, he felt the empty air suck at him as if he were drowning in quicksand. The night beat about him on naked wings like vultures dropping toward dead meat.

His heart beat out heavy jolts of fear. He cowered there on his knees, abandoned, bereft of eyes and light and mind by the extremity of his dread, and his breath whimpered in his throat. But as the first rush of his panic passed, he recognized it. Fear—it was an emotion he understood, a part of the condition of his existence. And his heart went on beating. Lurching as if wounded, it still kept up his life.

Suddenly, convulsively, he raised his fists and struck at the shale on either side of his head, pounded to the rhythm of his pulse as if he were trying to beat rationality out of the dirt. No! No! I am going to *survive!*

The assertion steadied him. Survive! He was a leper, accustomed to fear. He knew how to deal with it. Discipline—discipline.

He pressed his hands over his eyeballs; spots of color jerked across the black. He was not blind. He was seeing darkness. He had fallen away from the only light in the catacombs; of course he could not see.

Hell and blood.

Instinctively, he rubbed his hands, winced at the bruises he had given himself.

Discipline.

He was alone—alone— Lightless somewhere on the bottom of a ledge of the crevice long leagues from the nearest open sky. Without help, friends, rescue, for him the outside of the mountain was as unattainable as if it had ceased to exist. Escape itself was unattainable unless—

Discipline.

—unless he found some way to die.

Hellfire!

Thirst. Hunger. Injury—loss of blood. He iterated the possibilities as if he were going through a VSE. He might fall prey to some dark-bred bane. Might stumble over a more fatal precipice. Madness, yes. It would be as easy as leprosy.

Midnight wings beat about his ears, reeled vertiginously across the blind blackscape. His hands groped unconsciously around his head, seeking some way to defend himself.

Damnation!

None of this is happening to me.

Discipline!

A fetal fancy came over him. He caught hold of it as if it were a vision. Yes! Quickly, he changed his position so that he was sitting on the shale slope. He fumbled over his belt until he found Atiaran's knife. Poising it carefully in his half-fingerless grip, he began to shave.

Without water or a mirror, he was perilously close to slitting his throat, and the dryness of his beard caused him pain as if he were using the knife to dredge his face into a new shape. But this risk, this pain, was part of him; there was nothing impossible about it. If he cut himself, the dirt on his skin would make infection almost instantaneous. It calmed him like a demonstration of his identity.

In that way, he made the darkness draw back, withhold its talons.

When he was done, he mustered his resolution for an exploration of his situation. He wanted to know what kind of place he was in. Carefully, tentatively, he began searching away from the slopes on his hands and knees.

Before he had moved three feet across flat stone, he found a body. The flesh yielded as if it had not been dead long, but its chest was cold and slick, and his hand came back wet, smelling of rotten blood.

He recoiled to the slope, gritted himself into motionlessness while his lungs heaved loudly and his knees trembled. The ur-vile—the ur-vile that had attacked him. Broken by the fall. He wanted to move, but could not. The shock of discovery froze him like a sudden opening of dangerous doors; he felt surrounded by perils which he could not name. How had that creature known to attack him? Could it actually smell white gold?

Then his ring began to gleam. The bloody radiation transformed it into a band of dull fire about his wedding finger, a crimson fetter. But it shed no light—did not even enable him to see the digit on which it hung. It shone balefully in front of him, exposed him to any eyes that were hidden in the dark, but it gave him nothing but dread.

He could not forget what it meant. Drool's bloody moon was rising full over the Land.

It made him quail against the shale slope. He had a gagging sensation in his throat, as if he were being force-fed terror. Even the uncontrollable wheeze of his respiration seemed to mark him for attack by claws and fangs so invisible in the darkness that he could not visualize them. He was alone, helpless, abject.

Unless he found some way to make use of the power of his ring.

He fell back in revulsion from that thought the instant it crossed his mind. No! Never! He was a leper; his capacity for survival depended on a complete recognition, acceptance, of his essential impotence. That was the law of leprosy. Nothing could be as fatal to him—nothing could destroy him body and mind as painfully—as the illusion of power. Power in a dream. And before he died he would become as fetid and deformed as that man he had met in the leprosarium. No!

Better to kill himself outright. Anything would be better.

He did not know how long he spun giddily before he heard a low noise in the darkness—distant, slippery and ominous, as if the surrounding midnight had begun breathing softly through its teeth. It stunned

him like a blow to the heart. Flinching in blind fear,
he tried to fend it off. Slowly, it grew clearer—a quiet,
susurrous sound like a gritted exhalation from many
throats. It infested the air like vermin, made his flesh
crawl.

They were coming for him. They knew where he
was because of his ring, and they were coming for him.

He had a quick vision of a Waynhim with an iron
spike through its chest. He clapped his right hand over
his ring. But he knew that was futile as soon as he did
it. Frenetically, he began searching over the shale for
some kind of weapon. Then he remembered his knife.
It felt too weightless to help him. But he gripped it,
and went on hunting with his right hand, hardly knowing what he sought.

For a long moment, he fumbled around him, regardless of the noise he made. Then his fingers found
his staff. Bannor must have dropped it, and it had
fallen near him.

The susurration drew nearer. It was the sound of
many bare feet sliding over stone. They were coming
for him.

The staff!—it was a Hirebrand's staff. Baradakas
had given it to him. *In the hour of darkness, remember the Hirebrand's staff*. If he could light it—

But how?

The black air loomed with enemies. Their steps
seemed to slide toward him from above.

How? he cried desperately, trying to make the staff
catch fire by sheer force of will. *Baradakas!*

Still the feet came closer. He could hear hoarse
breathing behind their sibilant approach.

It had burned for him at the Celebration of Spring.
Shaking with haste, he pressed the end of the staff to
his blood-embered ring. At once, red flame blossomed
on the wood, turned pale orange and yellow, flared up
brightly. The sudden light dazzled him, but he leaped
to his feet and held the staff over his head.

He was standing at the bottom of a long slope
which filled half the floor of the crevice. This loose-
piled shale had saved his life by giving under the impact of his fall, rolling him down instead of holding

him where he hit. Before and behind him, the crevice stretched upward far beyond the reach of his flame. Nearby, the ur-vile lay twisted on its back, its black skin wet with blood.

Shuffling purposefully toward him along the crevice floor was a disjointed company of Cavewights.

They were still thirty yards away, but even at that distance, he was surprised by their appearance. They did not look like other Cavewights he had seen. The difference was not only in costume, though these creatures were ornately and garishly caparisoned like a royal cadre, elite and obscene. They were physically different. They were old—old prematurely, unnaturally. Their red eyes were hooded, and their long limbs bent as if the bones had been warped in a short time. Their heads sagged on necks that still looked thick enough to be strong and erect. Their heavy, spatulate hands trembled as if with palsy. Together, they reeked of ill, of victimization. But they came forward with clenched determination, as if they had been promised the peace of death when this last task was done.

Shaking off his surprise, he brandished his staff threateningly. "Don't touch me!" he hissed through his teeth. "Back off! I made a bargain—!"

The Cavewights gave no sign that they had heard. But they did not attack him. When they were almost within his reach, they spread out on both sides, awkwardly encircled him. Then, by giving way on one side and closing toward him on the other, they herded him in the direction from which they had come.

As soon as he understood that they wished to take him someplace without a fight, he began to cooperate. He knew intuitively where they were going. So through their tortuous herding he moved slowly along the crevice until he reached a stair in the left wall. It was a rude way, roughly hacked out of the rock, but it was wide enough for several Cavewights to climb abreast. He was able to control his vertigo by staying near the wall, away from the crevice.

They ascended for several hundred feet before they reached an opening in the wall. Though the stairs continued upward, the Cavewights steered him through this opening. He found himself in a narrow tunnel with a glow of rocklight at its end. The creatures marched him more briskly now, as if they were hurrying him toward a scaffold.

Then a wash of heat and a stink of brimstone poured over him. He stepped out of the tunnel into Kiril Threndor.

He recognized the burnished stone gleam of the faceted walls, the fetid stench like sulfur consuming rotten flesh, the several entrances, the burning dance of light on the clustered stalactites high overhead. It was all as vivid to him as if it had just been translated from a nightmare. The Cavewights ushered him into the chamber, then stood behind him to block the entrance.

For the second time, he met Drool Rockworm.

Drool crouched on his low dais in the center of the cave. He clenched the Staff of Law in both his huge hands, and it was by the Staff that Covenant first recognized him. Drool had changed. Some blight had fallen on him. As he caught sight of Covenant, he began laughing shrilly. But his voice was weak, and his laughter had a pitch of hysteria. He did not laugh long; he seemed too exhausted to sustain it. Like the Cavewights who had herded Covenant, he was old.

But whatever had damaged them had hurt him more. His limbs were so gnarled that he could hardly stand; saliva ran uncontrolled from his drooping lips; and he was sweating profusely, as if he could no longer endure the heat of his own domain. He gripped the Staff in an attitude of fierce possessiveness and desperation. Only his eyes had not changed. They shone redly, without iris or pupil, and seemed to froth like malicious lava, eager to devour.

Covenant felt a strange mixture of pity and loathing. But he had only a moment to wonder what had happened to Drool. Then he had to brace himself. The Cavewight began hobbling painfully toward him.

Groaning at the ache in his limbs, Drool stopped a few paces from Covenant. He released one hand from the intricately runed Staff to point a trembling finger at Covenant's wedding band. When he spoke, he cast continual, twitching leers back over his shoulder, as if referring to an invisible spectator. His voice was as gnarled and wracked as his arms and legs.

"Mine!" he coughed. "You promised. Mine. Lord Drool, Staff and ring. You promised. Do this, you said. Do that. Do not crush. Wait now." He spat viciously. "Kill later. You promised. The ring if I did what you said. You said." He sounded like a sick child. "Drool. Lord Drool! Power! Mine now."

Slavering thickly, he reached a hand for Covenant's ring.

Covenant reacted in instant revulsion. With his burning staff, he struck a swift blow, slapped Drool's hand away.

At the impact, his staff broke into slivers as if Drool's flesh were vehement iron.

But Drool gave a coughing roar of rage, and stamped the heel of the Staff of Law on the floor. The stone jumped under Covenant's feet; he pitched backward, landed with a jolt that seemed to stop his heart.

He lay stunned and helpless. Through a throbbing noise in his ears, he heard Drool cry, "Slay him! Give the ring!" He rolled over. Sweat blurred his vision; blearily, he saw the Cavewights converging toward him. His heart felt paralyzed in his chest, and he could not get his feet under him. Retching for air, he tried to crawl out of reach.

The first Cavewight caught hold of his neck, then abruptly groaned and fell away to the side. Another Cavewight fell; the rest drew back in confusion. One of them cried fearfully, "Bloodguard! Lord Drool, help us!"

"Fool!" retorted Drool, coughing as if his lungs were in shreds. "Coward! I am power! Slay them!"

Covenant climbed to his feet, wiped the sweat from his eyes, and found Bannor standing beside him. The Bloodguard's robe hung tattered from his shoulders, and a large bruise on his brow closed one eye. But his hands were poised, alert. He carried himself on the balls of his feet, ready to leap in any direction. His flat eyes held a dull gleam of battle.

Covenant felt such a surge of relief that he wanted
to hug Bannor. After his long, lightless ordeal, he felt
suddenly rescued, almost redeemed. But his gruff voice
belied his emotion. "What the hell took you so long?"

The Cavewights came forward slowly, timorously,
and surrounded Covenant and Bannor. Drool raged at
them in hoarse gasps.

Overhead, the chiaroscuro of the stalactites danced
gaily.

With startling casualness, Bannor replied that he
had landed badly after killing the ur-vile, and had lost
consciousness. Then he had been unable to locate Covenant in the darkness. Lashed by Drool's strident commands, a Cavewight charged Covenant from behind.
But Bannor spun easily, felled the creature with a kick.
"The flame of your staff revealed you," he continued.
"I chose to follow." He paused to spring at two of the
nearest attackers. They retreated hastily. When he
spoke again, his foreign *Haruchai* tone held a note of
final honesty. "I withheld my aid, awaiting proof
that you are not a foe of the Lords."

Something in the selfless and casual face that Bannor turned toward death communicated itself to Covenant. He answered without rancor, "You picked a
fine time to test me."

"The Bloodguard know doubt. We require to be
sure."

Drool mustered his strength to shriek furiously,
"Fools! Worms! Afraid of only two!" He spat. "Go!
Watch! Lord Drool kills."

The Cavewights gave way, and Drool came wincing
forward. He held the Staff of Law before him like an
ax.

Bannor leaped, launched a kick at Drool's face.

But for all his crippled condition, Drool Rockworm
was full of power. He did not appear to feel Bannor's
attack. In ponderous fury, he raised the Staff to deal a
blast which would incinerate Bannor and Covenant
where they stood. Against the kind of might he wielded,
they were helpless.

Still Bannor braced himself in front of Covenant to

meet the blow. Flinching, Covenant waited for the pain that would set him free.

But Drool was already too late. He had missed his chance, neglected other dangers. Even as he raised the Staff, the company of the Quest, led by First Mark Tuvor and High Lord Prothall, broke into Kiril Threndor.

They looked battered, as if they had just finished a skirmish with Drool's outer defenses, but they were whole and dour-handed, and they entered the chamber like a decisive wave. Prothall stopped Drool's blast with a shout full of authority. Before the Cavewights could gather themselves together, the Eoman fell on them, drove them from the cave. In a moment, Drool was surrounded by a wide ring of warriors and Bloodguard.

Slowly, with an appearance of confusion, he retreated until he was half-crouching on his dais. He looked around the circle as if unable to realize what had happened. But his spatulate hands held the Staff in a grip as grim as death.

Then, grotesquely, his laval eyes took on an angle of cunning. Twitching nods over his shoulder, he hissed in a raw voice, "Here—this is fair. Fair. Better than promises. All of them—here. All little Lords and puny Bloodguard—humans. Ready for crushing." He started to laugh, broke into a fit of coughing. "Crush!" he spat when he regained control of himself. "Crush with power." He made a noise like a cracking of bones in his throat. "Power! Little Lords. Mighty Drool. Better than promises."

Prothall faced the Cavewight squarely. Giving his staff to Mhoram, he stepped forward to the dais with Tuvor at his side. He stood erect; his countenance was calm and clear. Supported by their years of abnegation, his eyes neither wavered nor burned. In contrast, Drool's red orbs were consumed with the experience of innumerable satiations—an addictive gluttony of power. When the High Lord spoke, even the rattle of his old voice sounded like authority and decision. Softly, he said, "Give it up. Drool Rockworm, hear me. The Staff of Law is not yours. It is not meant for you. Its strength must only be used for the health of the Land. Give it to me."

Covenant moved to stand near the High Lord. He felt that he had to be near the Staff.

But Drool only muttered, "Power? Give it up? Never." His lips went on moving, as if he were communing over secret plans.

Again, Prothall urged, "Surrender it. For your own sake. Are you blind to yourself? Do you not see what has happened to you? This power is not meant for you. It destroys you. You have used the Staff wrongly. You have used the Illearth Stone. Such powers are deadly. Lord Foul has betrayed you. Give the Staff to me. I will strive to help you."

But that idea offended Drool. "Help?" he coughed. "Fool! I am Lord Drool. Master! The moon is mine. Power is mine. You are mine. I can crush! Old man— little Lord. I let you live to make me laugh. Help? No, dance. Dance for Lord Drool." He waved the Staff threateningly. "Make me laugh. I let you live."

Prothall drew himself up, and said in a tone of command, "Drool Rockworm, release the Staff." He advanced a step.

With a jerk like a convulsion of hysteria, Drool raised the Staff to strike.

Prothall rushed forward, tried to stop him. But Tuvor reached the Cavewight first. He caught the end of the Staff.

Slavering with rage, Drool jabbed the iron heel of the Staff against Tuvor's body. Bloody light flashed. In that instant the First Mark's flesh became transparent; the company could see his bones burning like dry sticks. Then he fell, reeling backward to collapse in Covenant's arms.

His weight was too great for the Unbeliever to hold; Covenant sank to the stone under it. Cradling Tuvor, he watched the High Lord.

Prothall grappled with Drool. He grasped the Staff with both hands to prevent Drool from striking him. They wrestled together for possession of it.

The struggle looked impossible for Prothall. Despite his decrepitude, Drool retained some of his Cavewightish strength. And he was full of power. And Prothall was old.

With Tuvor in his arms, Covenant could do nothing. "Help him!" he cried to Mhoram. "He'll be killed!"

But Lord Mhoram turned his back on Prothall. He knelt beside Covenant to see if he could aid Tuvor. As he examined the First Mark, he said roughly, "Drool seeks to master the Staff with malice. The High Lord can sing a stronger song than that."

Appalled, Covenant shouted, "He'll be killed! You've got to help him!"

"Help him?" Mhoram's eyes glinted dangerously. Pain and raw restraint sharpened his voice as he said, "He would not welcome my help. He is the High Lord. Despite my Oath"—he choked momentarily on a throat full of passion—"I would crush Drool." He invested Drool's word, *crush,* with a potential for despair that silenced Covenant.

Panting, Covenant watched the High Lord's fight. He was horrified by the danger, by the price both Lords were willing to pay.

Then battle erupted around him. Cavewights charged into Kiril Threndor from several directions. Apparently, Drool had been able to send out a silent call; his guards were answering. The first forces to reach the chamber were not large, but they sufficed to engage the whole company. Only Mhoram did not join the fight. He knelt beside Covenant and stroked the First Mark's face, as if he were transfixed by Tuvor's dying.

Shouting stertorously over the clash of weapons, Quaan ordered his warriors into a defensive ring around the dais and the Lords. Loss and fatigue had taken their toll on the Eoman, but stalwart Quaan led his command as if the Lords' need rendered him immune to weakness. Among the Bloodguard, his Eoman parried, thrust, fought on the spur of his exhortations.

The mounting perils made Covenant reel. Prothall and Drool struggled horribly above him. The fighting around him grew faster and more frenzied by the moment. Tuvor lay expiring in his lap. And he could do nothing about any of it, help none of them. Soon their escape would be cut off, and all their efforts would be in vain.

He had not foreseen this outcome to his bargain.

Drool bore Prothall slowly backward. "Dance!" he raged.

Tuvor shuddered; his eyes opened. Covenant looked away from Prothall. Tuvor's lips moved, but he made no sound.

Mhoram tried to comfort him. "Have no fear. This evil will be overcome—it is in the High Lord's hands. And your name will be remembered with honor wherever trust is valued."

But Tuvor's eyes held Covenant, and he managed to whisper one word, "True?" His whole body strained with supplication, but Covenant did not know whether he asked for a promise or a judgment.

Yet the Unbeliever answered. He could not refuse a Bloodguard, could not deny the appeal of such expensive fidelity. The word stuck in his throat, but he forced it out. "Yes."

Tuvor shuddered again, and died with a flat groan as if the chord of his Vow had snapped. Covenant gripped his shoulders, shook him; there was no response.

On the dais, Drool had forced Prothall to his knees, and was bending the High Lord back to break him. In futility and rage, Covenant howled, "Mhoram!"

The Lord nodded, surged to his feet. But he did not attack Drool. Holding his staff over his head, he blared in a voice that cut through the clamor of the battle, *"Melenkurion abatha! Minas mill khabaal!"* From end to end, his staff burst into incandescent fire.

The power of the Words jolted Drool, knocked him back a step. Prothall regained his feet.

More Cavewights rushed into Kiril Threndor. Quaan and his Eoman were driven back toward the dais. At last, Mhoram sprang to their aid. His staff burned furiously as he attacked. Around him, the Bloodguard fought like wind devils, leaping and kicking among the Cavewights so swiftly that the creatures interfered with each other when they tried to strike back.

But Drool's defenders kept coming, pouring into the

cave. The company began to founder in the rising on-slaught.

Then Prothall cried over the din, "I have it! The moon is free!"

He stood triumphant on the dais, with the Staff of Law upraised in his hands. Drool lay at his feet, sob-bing like a piece of broken rock. Between spasms of grief, the creature gasped, "Give it back. I want it."

The sight struck fear into the Cavewights. They re-coiled, quailed back against the walls of the chamber.

Released from battle, Quaan and his warriors turned toward Prothall and gave a raw cheer. Their voices were hoarse and worn, but they exulted in the High Lord's victory as if he had won the future of the Land.

Yet overhead the dancing lights of Kiril Threndor went their own bedizened way.

Covenant snapped a look at his ring. Its argent still burned with blood. Perhaps the moon was free; he was not.

Before the echoes of cheering died—before any-one could move—a new sound broke over them. It started softly, then expanded until it filled the chamber like a collapse of the ceiling. It was laughter —Lord Foul's laughter, throbbing with glee and im-mitigable hate. Its belittling weight dominated them, buried them in their helplessness; it paralyzed them, seemed to cut them off from their own heartbeats and breathing. While it piled onto them, they were lost.

Even Prothall stood still. Despite his victory, he looked old and feeble, and his eyes had an unfocused stare as if he were gazing into his own coffin. And Covenant, who knew that laugh, could not resist it.

But Lord Mhoram moved. Springing onto the dais, he whirled his staff around his head until the air hummed, and blue lightning bolted upward into the clustered stalactites. "Then show yourself, Despiser!" he shouted. "If you are so certain, face us now! Do you fear to try your doom with us?"

Lord Foul's laughter exploded with fiercer contempt. But Mhoram's defiance had broken its transfixion. Prothall touched Mhoram's shoulder. The warriors gripped their swords, placed themselves in grim readiness behind the Lords.

More Cavewights entered the chamber, though they did not attack. At the sight of them, Drool raised himself on his crippled arms. His bloody eyes boiled still, clinging to fury and malice to the end. Coughing as if he were about to heave up his heart, he gasped, "The Staff. You do not know. Cannot use it. Fools. No escape. None. I have armies. I have the Stone." With a savage effort, he made himself heard through the laughter. "Illearth Stone. Power and power. I will crush. Crush." Flailing one weak arm at his guards, he screamed in stricken command, "Crush!"

Wielding their weapons, the Cavewights surged forward.

TWENTY-FOUR:
The Calling of Lions

THEY came in a mass of red eyes dull with empty determination. But Lord Foul's bodiless laughter seemed to slow them. They waded through it as if it were a quagmire, and their difficult approach gave the company time to react. At Quaan's command, the warriors ringed Mhoram and Prothall. The Bloodguard took fighting positions with the Eoman.

Mhoram called to Covenant.

Slowly, Covenant raised his head. He looked at his companions, and they seemed pitifully few to him. He tried to get to his feet. But Tuvor was too heavy for him to lift. Even in death, the massive devotion of the First Mark surpassed his strength.

He heard Manethrall Lithe shout, "This way! I know the way!" She was dodging among the Cavewights toward one of the entrances. He watched her go as if he had already forsaken her. He could not lift Tuvor because he could not get a grip with his right hand; two fingers were not enough.

Then Bannor snatched him away from the fallen First Mark, thrust him toward the protective ring of the Eoman. Covenant resisted. "You can't leave him!" But Bannor forced him among the warriors. "What are you doing?" he protested. "We've got to take him along. If you don't send him back, he won't be replaced." He spun to appeal to the Lords. "You can't leave him!"

Mhoram's lips stretched taut over his teeth. "We must."

From the mouth of the tunnel she had chosen, Lithe called, "Here!" She clenched her cord around a Cavewight's neck, and used the creature's body to protect herself from attack. "This is the way!" Other Cavewights converged on her, forced her backward.

In response, Prothall lit his old staff, swung it, and led a charge toward her. With Mhoram's help, he burned passage for his companions through the massed Cavewights.

Bright Lords-fire intimidated the creatures. But before the company had gained the tunnel Lithe had chosen, a wedge of ur-viles drove snarling into the chamber from a nearby entrance. They were led by a mighty loremaster, as black as the catacombs, wielding an iron stave that looked wet with power or blood.

Prothall cried, "Run!" The Questers dashed for the tunnel.

The ur-viles raced to intercept them.

The company was faster. Prothall and Mhoram gained the passage, and parted to let the others enter between them.

But one of the warriors decided to help his comrades escape. He suddenly veered away from the Eoman. Whirling his sword fervidly, he threw himself at the ur-vile wedge.

Mhoram yelled, started back out into the chamber to help him. But the loremaster brushed the warrior aside with a slap of its stave, and he fell. Dark moisture covered him from head to foot; he screamed as if he had been drenched in acid. Mhoram barely evaded the stave's backstroke, retreated to Prothall's side in the mouth of the passage.

There they tried to stand. They opposed their blazing blue flame to the ur-viles. The loremaster struck at them again and again; they blocked each blow with their staffs; gouts of flaming fluid, igniting blue and then turning quickly black, spattered on all sides at every clash. But the wedge fought with a savagery which drove the Lords backward step by step into the tunnel.

Quaan tried to counter by having his strongest archers loose arrows at the loremaster. But the shafts were useless. They caught fire in the ur-viles' black power and burned to ashes.

Behind the company, Lithe was chaffing to pursue the guide of her instinct for daylight. She called repeatedly for the Lords to follow her. But they could not; they did not dare turn their backs on the wedge.

Each clash drove them backward. For all their courage and resolve, they were nearly exhausted, and every blow of the loremaster's stave weakened them further. Now their flame had a less rampant blaze, and the burning gouts turned black more swiftly. It was clear that they could not keep up the fight. And no one in the company could take it for them.

Abruptly, Mhoram shouted, "Back! Make room!" His urgency allowed no refusal; even the Bloodguard obeyed.

"Covenant!" Mhoram cried.

Covenant moved forward until he was only an arm's length from the searing battle.

"Raise your ring!"

Compelled by Mhoram's intensity, the Unbeliever lifted his left hand. A crimson cast still stained the heart of his wedding band.

The loremaster observed the ring as if suddenly smelling its presence. It recognized white gold, hesitated. The wedge halted, though the loremaster did not drop its guard.

"Melenkurion abatha!" Mhoram commanded. "Blast them!"

Half intuitively, Covenant understood. He jabbed at the loremaster with his left fist as if launching a bolt.

Barking in strident fear, the whole wedge recoiled.

In that instant, the Lords acted. Shouting, *"Minas mill khaball!"* on different pitches in half-screamed harmony, they drew with their fire an X which barricaded the tunnel from top to bottom. The flame of the X hung in the air; and before it could die, Prothall placed his staff erect within it. At once, a sheet of blue flared in the passage.

Howling in rage at Mhoram's ruse, the ur-viles sprang forward. The loremaster struck hugely at the flame with its stave. The fiery wall rippled and fluttered —but did not let the wedge pass.

Prothall and Mhoram took only a moment to see how their power held. Then they turned and dashed down the tunnel.

Gasping for breath, Mhoram told the company, "We have forbidden the tunnel! But it will not endure. We are not strong enough—the High Lord's staff was needed to make any forbidding at all. And the ur-viles are savage. Drool drives them mad with the Illearth Stone." In spite of his haste, his voice carried a shudder. "Now we must run. We must escape—must! All our work will go for nothing if we do not take both Staff and Ward to safety."

"Come!" the Manethrall responded. "I know grass and sky. I can find the way."

Prothall nodded agreement, but his movements were slow, despite the need for alacrity. He was exhausted, driven far past the normal limits of his stamina. With his breath rattling deep in his chest as if he were drowning in the phlegm of his age, he leaned heavily on the Staff of Law. "Go!" he panted. "Run!"

Two Bloodguard took his arms, and between them he stumbled into a slow run down the passage. Rallying around him, the company started away after Lithe.

At first, they went easily. Their tunnel offered few branchings; at each of these, Lithe seemed instantly sure which held the greatest promise of daylight. Lit from behind by Mhoram's staff, she loped forward as if following a warm trail of freedom.

After the struggles of close combat, the company found relief in simple, single-minded running. It allowed them to focus and conserve their strength. Furthermore, they were passing, as if slowly liberated, out of the range of Lord Foul's laughter. Soon they could hear neither mockery nor threat of slaughter at their backs. For once, the silent darkness befriended them.

For nearly a league, they hastened onward. They began to traverse a section of the catacombs which was intricate with small caves and passages and turnings, but which appeared to contain no large halls, crevices, wightworks. Throughout these multiplied corridors, Lithe did not hesitate. Several times she took ways which inclined slowly upward.

But as the complex tunnels opened into broader and blacker ways, where Mhoram's flame illumined no cave walls or ceilings, the catacombs became more hostile. Gradually, the silence changed—lost the hue of relief, and became the hush of ambush. The darkness around Mhoram's light seemed to conceal more and more. At the turnings and intersections, night thickened in their choices, clouding Lithe's instinct. She began to falter.

Behind her, Prothall grew less and less able to keep up the pace. His hoarse, wheezing breath was increasingly labored; even the weariest Questers could hear his gasps over their own hard panting. The Bloodguard were almost carrying him.

Still they pushed on into stark midnight. They bore the Staff of Law and the Second Ward, and could not afford surrender.

Then they reached a high cave which formed a crossroads for several tunnels. The general direction they had maintained since Kiril Threndor was continued by one passage across the cave. But Lithe stopped in the center of the junction as if she had been reined to a halt. She searched about her uncertainly, confused by the number of her choices—and by some intuitive rejection of her only obvious selection. Shaking her head as if resisting a bit, she groaned, "Ah, Lords. I do not know."

Mhoram snapped, "You must! We have no other chance. The old maps do not show these ways. You have led us far beyond our ken." He gripped her shoulder as if he meant to force her decision. But the next moment he was distracted by Prothall. With a sharp spasm of coughing, the High Lord collapsed to the floor.

One Bloodguard quickly propped him into a sitting position, and Mhoram knelt beside him, peering with intent concern into his old face. "Rest briefly," mumbled Mhoram. "Our forbidding has long since broken. We must not delay."

Between fits of coughing, the High Lord replied, "Leave me. Take the Staff and go. I am done."

His words appalled the company. Covenant and the warriors covered their own breathing to hear Mhoram's answer. The air was suddenly intense with a fear that Mhoram would accept Prothall's sacrifice.

But Mhoram said nothing.

"Leave me," Prothall repeated. "Give your staff to me, and I will defend your retreat as I can. Go, I say. I am old. I have had my time of triumph. I lose nothing. Take the Staff and go." When the Lord still did not speak, he rattled in supplication, "Mhoram, hear me. Do not let my old bones destroy this high Quest."

"I hear you." Mhoram's voice sounded thick and wounded in his throat. He knelt with his head bowed.

But a moment later he rose to his feet, and put back his head, and began to laugh. It was quiet laughter—unfeverish and unforced—the laughter of relief and indespair. The company gaped at it until they understood that it was not hysteria. Then, without knowing why, they laughed in response. Humor ran like a clean wind through their hearts.

Covenant almost cursed aloud because he could not share it.

When they had subsided into low chuckling, Mhoram said to the High Lord, "Ah, Prothall son of Dwillian. It is good that you are old. Leave you? How will I be able to take pleasure in telling Osondrea of your great exploits if you are not there to protest my boasting?" Gaily, he laughed again. Then, as if recollecting himself, he returned to where Lithe stood bewildered in the center of the cave.

"Manethrall," he said gently, "you have done well. Your instinct is true—remember it now. Put all doubt away. We do not fear to follow where your heart leads."

Covenant had noticed that she, too, had not joined the laughter of the company. Her eyes were troubled; he guessed that her swift blood had been offended by Mhoram's earlier sharpness. But she nodded gravely to the Lord. "That is well. My thoughts do not trust my heart."

"In what way?"

"My thoughts say that we must continue as we have come. But my heart wishes to go there." She indicated a tunnel opening back almost in the dirction from which they had come. "I do not know," she concluded simply. "This is new to me."

But Mhoram's reply held no hesitation. "You are Manethrall Lithe of the Ramen. You have served the Ranyhyn. You know grass and sky. Trust your heart."

After a moment, Lithe accepted his counsel.

Two Bloodguard helped Prothall to his feet. Supporting him between them, they joined the company and followed Lithe's instinct into the tunnel.

This passage soon began to descend slowly, and they set a good pace down it. They were buoyed along by the hope that their pursuers would not guess what they were doing, and so would neither cut them off nor follow them directly. But in the universal darkness and silence, they had no assurances. Their way met no branchings, but it wavered as if it were tracing a vein in the mountain. Finally it opened into a vast impression of blank space, and began to climb a steep, serrated rock face through a series of switchbacks. Now the company had to toil upward.

The difficulties of the ascent slowed them as much as the climbing. The higher they went, the colder the air became, and the more there seemed to be a wind blowing in the dark gulf beside them. But the cold and the wind only accented their dripping sweat and the exhausted wrack of their respiration. The Bloodguard alone appeared unworn by the long days of their exertion; they strode steadily up the slope as if it were just a variation of their restless devotion. But their companions were more death-prone. The warriors and Covenant began to stagger like cripples in the climb.

Finally Mhoram called a halt. Covenant dropped to sit with his back to the rock, facing the black-blown, measureless cavern. The sweat seemed to freeze on his face. The last of the food and drink was passed around, but in this buried place, both appeared to have lost their capacity to refresh—as if at last even sustenance were daunted by the darkness of the catacombs. Covenant ate and drank numbly. Then he shut his eyes to close out the empty blackness for a time. But he saw it whether his eyes were open or not.

Some time later—Covenant no longer measured duration—Lord Mhoram said in a stinging whisper, "I hear them."

Korik's reply sounded as hollow as a sigh from a tomb. "Yes. They follow. They are a great many."

Lurching as if stricken, the Questers began to climb again, pushing themselves beyond the limits of their strength. They felt weak with failure, as if they were moving only because Mhoram's blue flame pulled them forward, compelled them, beseeched, cajoled, urged, inspired, refused to accept anything from them except endurance and more endurance. Disregarding every exigency except the need for escape, they continued to climb.

Then the wind began to howl around them, and their way changed. The chasm abruptly narrowed; they found themselves on a thin, spiral stair carved into the wall of a vertical shaft. The width of the rude steps made them ascend in single file. And the wind went yelling up the shaft as if it fled the catacombs in stark terror. Covenant groaned when he realized that he would have to risk yet another perilous height, but the rush of the wind was so powerful that it seemed to make falling impossible. Cycling dizzily, he struggled up the stair.

The shaft went straight upward, and the wind yowled in pain; and the company climbed as if they were being dragged by the air. But as the shaft narrowed, the force of the wind increased; the air began to move past them too fast for breathing. As they gasped upward, a light-headed vértigo came over them. The shaft seemed to cant precariously from side to side. Covenant moved on his hands and knees.

Soon the whole company was crawling.

After an airless ache which extended interminably around him, Covenant lay stretched out on the stairs. He was not moving. Dimly, he heard voices trying to shout over the roar of the wind. But he was past listening. He felt that he had reached the verge of suffocation, and the only thing he wanted to do was weep. He could hardly remember what prevented him even now from releasing his misery.

Hands grabbed his shoulders, hauled him up onto flat stone. They dragged him ten or fifteen feet along the bottom of a thin crevice. The howl of the wind receded.

He heard Quaan give a choked, panting cheer. With an effort, he raised his head. He was sprawled in the crevice where it opened on one of the eastern faces of Mount Thunder. Across a flat, gray expanse far below him, the sun rose redly.

To his stunned ears, the cheering itself sounded like sobs. It spread as the warriors one by one climbed out past him into the dawn. Lithe had already leaped down a few feet from the crevice, and was on her knees kissing the earth. Far away, across the Sarangrave and the gleaming line of the Defiles Course and the Great Swamp, the sun stood up regally, wreathed in red splendor.

Covenant pushed himself into a sitting position and looked over at the Lords to see their victory.

They had no aspect of triumph. The High Lord sat crumpled like a sack of old bones, with the Staff of Law on his knees. His head was bowed, and he covered his face with both hands. Beside him, Mhoram stood still and dour, and his eyes were as bleak as a wilderness.

Covenant did not understand.

Then Bannor said, "We can defend here."

Mhoram's reply was soft and violent. "How? Drool knows many ways. If we prevent him here, he will attack from below—above. He can bring thousands against us."

"Then close this gap to delay them."

Mhoram's voice became softer still. "The High Lord has no staff. I cannot forbid the gap alone—I have not the power. Do you believe that I am strong enough to bring down the walls of this crevice? No—not even if I were willing to damage the Earth in that way. We must escape. There—" He pointed down the mountainside with a hand that trembled.

Covenant looked downward. The crevice opened into the bottom of a ravine which ran straight down the side of Mount Thunder like a knife wound. The spine of this cut was jumbled and tossed with huge rocks—fallen boulders, pieces of the higher cliffs like dead fragments of the mountain. And its walls were sheer, unclimbable. The Questers would have to pick their way tortuously along the bottom of the cut for half a league. There the walls gave way, and the ravine dropped over a cliff. When the company reached the cliff, they would have to try to work around the mountainsides until they found another descent.

Still Covenant did not understand. He groaned at the difficulty of the ravine, but it was escape. He could feel sunlight on his face. Heaving himself to his feet, he muttered, "Let's get going."

Mhoram gave him a look thick with suppressed pain. But he did not voice it. Instead, he spoke stiffly to Quaan and Korik. In a few moments, the Questers started down the ravine.

Their progress was deadly slow. In order to make their way, they had to climb from rock to rock, swing themselves over rough boulders, squeeze on hands and knees through narrow gaps between huge fists of stone. And they were weak. The strongest of the warriors needed help time and again from the Bloodguard.

Prothall had to be almost entirely carried. He clutched the Staff, and scrabbled fraily at the climbs. Whenever he jumped from a rock, he fell to his knees; soon the front of his robe was spattered with blood.

Covenant began to sense their danger. Their pace might be fatal. If Drool knew other ways onto the slope, his forces might reach the end of the ravine before the company did.

He was not alone in his perception. After their first relief, the warriors took on a haunted look. Soon they were trudging, clambering, struggling with their heads bowed and backs bent as if the weight of all they had ever known were tied around their necks. The sunlight did not allow them to be ignorant of their peril.

Like a prophecy, their fear was fulfilled before the company was halfway down the ravine. One of the Eoman gave a broken cry, pointed back up the mountain. There they saw a horde of ur-viles rushing out of the cleft from which they had come.

They tried to push faster down the littered spine of the cut. But the ur-viles poured after them like a black flood. The creatures seemed to spring over the rocks without danger of misstep, as if borne along by a rush of savagery. They gained on the company with sickening speed.

And the ur-viles were not alone. Near the end of the ravine, Cavewights suddenly appeared atop one wall. As soon as they spotted the Questers, they began throwing ropes over the edge, scaling down the wall.

The company was caught like a group of mites in the pincers of Drool's power.

They stopped where they were, paralyzed by dismay. For a moment, even Quaan's sense of responsibility for his Eoman failed; he stared blankly about him, and did not move. Covenant sagged against a boulder. He wanted to scream at the mountain that this was not fair. He had already survived so much, endured so much, lost so much. Where was his escape? Was this the cost of his bargain, his forbearance? It was too great. He was a leper, not made for such ordeals. His voice shook uncontrollably—full of useless outrage. "No wonder he—let us have the Staff. So it would hurt worse now. He knew we wouldn't get away with it."

But Mhoram shouted orders in a tone that cut through the dismay. He ran a short way down the ravine and climbed onto a wide, flat rock higher than the others near it. "There is space for us! Come!" he commanded. "We will make our end here!"

Slowly, the warriors shambled to the rock as if they were overburdened with defeat. Mhoram and the Bloodguard helped them up. High Lord Prothall came last, propped between two Bloodguard. He was muttering, "No. No." But he did not resist Mhoram's orders.

When everyone was on the rock, Quaan's Eoman and the Bloodguard placed themselves around its edge. Lithe joined them, her cord taut in her hands, leaving Prothall and Mhoram and Covenant in the ring of the company's last defense.

Now the ur-viles had covered half the distance to the rock where the company stood. Behind them came hundreds of Cavewights, gushing out of the crevice and pouring down the ravine. And as many more worked upward from the place where they had entered the cut.

Surveying Drool's forces, Mhoram said softly, "Take heart, my friends. You have done well. Now let us make our end so bravely that even our enemies will remember it. Do not despair. There are many chances between the onset of a war and victory. Let us teach Lord Foul that he will never taste victory until the last friend of the Land is dead."

But Prothall whispered, "No. No." Facing upward toward the crest of Mount Thunder, he planted his feet and closed his eyes. With slow resolution, he raised the Staff of Law level with his heart and gripped it in both fists. "It must be possible," he breathed. "By the Seven! It must." His knuckles whitened on the intricate runed and secret surface of the Staff. *"Melenkurion* Skyweir, help me. I do not accept this end." His brows slowly knotted over his shut, sunken eyes, and his head bowed until his beard touched his heart. From between his pale lips came a whispered, wordless song. But his voice rattled so huskily in his chest

that his song sounded more like a dirge than an invocation.

Drool's forces poured down and surged up at the
company inexorably. Mhoram watched them with a
rictus of helplessness on his humane lips.

Suddenly, a desperate chance blazed in his eyes. He
spun, gripped Covenant with his gaze, whispered,
"There is a way! Prothall strives to call the Fire-Lions.
He cannot succeed—the power of the Staff is closed,
and we have not the knowledge to unlock it. But white
gold can release that power. It can be done!"

Covenant recoiled as if Mhoram had betrayed him.
No! he panted. I made a bargain—!

Then, with a sickening, vertiginous twist of insight,
he caught a glimpse of Lord Foul's plan for him,
glimpsed what the Despiser was doing to him. Here
was the killing blow which had lain concealed behind
all the machinations, all the subterfuge.

Hell and blood!

Here was the point of impact between his opposing
madnesses. If he attempted to use the wild magic—
if his ring had power—if it had no power— He
flinched at the reel and strike of dark visions—the
company slain—the Staff destroyed—thousands of
creatures dead, all that blood on his head, his head.

"No," he gasped thickly. "Don't ask me. I promised
I wouldn't do any more killing. You don't know what
I've done—to Atiaran—to— I made a bargain so I
wouldn't have to do any more killing."

The ur-viles and Cavewights were almost within
bowshot now. The Eoman had arrows nocked and
ready. Drool's hordes slowed, began to poise for the
last spring of attack.

But Mhoram's eyes did not release Covenant. "There
will be still more killing if you do not. Do you believe
that Lord Foul will be content with our deaths? Never!
He will slay and slay again until all life without exception is his to corrupt or destroy. All life, do you hear?
Even these creatures that now serve him will not be
spared."

"No!" Covenant groaned again. "Don't you see?
This is just what he wants. The Staff will be destroyed

—or Drool will be destroyed—or we'll— No matter what happens, he'll win. He'll be free. You're doing just what he wants."

"Nevertheless!" Mhoram returned fervidly. "The dead are dead—only the living may hope to resist Despite."

Hellfire! Covenant groped for answers like a man incapable of his own distress. But he found none. No bargain or compromise met his need. In his pain, he cried out wildly, protested, appealed, "Mhoram! It's suicide! You're asking me to go crazy!"

The peril in Mhoram's eyes did not waver. "No, Unbeliever. You need not lose your mind. There are other answers—other songs. You can find them. Why should the Land be destroyed for your pain? Save or damn! Grasp the Staff!"

"Damnation!" Fumbling furiously for his ring, Covenant shouted, "Do it yourself!" He wrenched the band from his finger and tried to throw it at Mhoram. But he was shaking madly; his fingers slipped. The ring dropped to the stone, rolled away.

He scrambled after it. He did not seem to have enough digits to catch it; it skidded past Prothall's feet. He lurched toward it again—then missed his footing, fell, and smacked his forehead on the stone.

Distantly, he heard the thrum of bowstrings; the battle had begun. But he paid no attention. He felt that he had cracked his skull. When he raised his head, he found that his vision was wrong; he was seeing double.

The moss-stain chart of his robe smeared illegibly in his sight. Now he had lost whatever chance he had to read it, decipher the cryptic message of Morinmoss. He saw two of Mhoram as the Lord held up the ring. He saw two Prothalls above him, clutching the Staff and trying with the last strength of his life-force to compel its power to his will. Two Bannors turned away from the fight toward the Lords.

Then Mhoram stooped to Covenant. The Lord lashed out, caught his right wrist. The grip was so fierce that he felt his bones grinding together. It forced his hand open, and when his two fingers were spread and

vulnerable, Mhoram shoved the ring onto his index
digit. It stuck after the first knuckle. "I cannot usurp
your place," the double Lord grated. He stood and
roughly pulled Covenant erect. Thrusting his double
face at the Unbeliever, he hissed, "By the Seven! You
fear power more than weakness."

Yes! Covenant moaned at the pain in his wrist and
head. Yes! I want to survive!

The snap of bowstrings came now as fast as the
warriors could ready their arrows. But their supply of
shafts was limited. And the ur-viles and Cavewights
hung back, risking themselves only enough to draw
the warriors' fire. Drool's forces were in no hurry.
The ur-viles particularly looked ready to relish the slow
slaughter of the company.

But Covenant had no awareness to spare for such
things. He stared in a kind of agony at Mhoram. The
Lord seemed to have two mouths—lips stretched over
multiplied teeth—and four eyes, all aflame with com-
pulsions. Because he could think of no other appeal,
he reached his free hand to his belt, took out Atiaran's
knife, and extended it toward Mhoram. Through his
teeth, he pleaded, "It would be better if you killed me."

Slowly, Mhoram's grip eased. His lips softened; the
fire of his eyes faded. His gaze seemed to turn inward,
and he winced at what he beheld. When he spoke, his
voice sounded like dust. "Ah, Covenant—forgive me.
I forget myself. Foamfollower—Foamfollower understood this. I should have heard him more clearly.
It is wrong to ask for more than you give freely. In
this way, we come to resemble what we hate." He
released Covenant's wrist and stepped back. "My
friend, this is not on your head. The burden is ours,
and we bear it to the end. Forgive me."

Covenant could not answer. He stood with his face
twisted as if he were about to howl. His eyes ached at
the duplicity of his vision. Mhoram's mercy affected
him more than any argument or demand. He turned
miserably toward Prothall. Could he not find somewhere the strength for that risk? Perhaps the path of
escape lay that way—perhaps the horror of wild magic
was the price he would have to pay for his freedom.

He did not want to be killed by ur-viles. But when he
raised his arm, he could not tell which of those hands
was his, which of those two Staffs was the real one.

Then, with a flat thrum, the last arrow was gone.
The Cavewights gave a vast shout of malice and glee.
At the command of the ur-viles, they began to approach. The warriors drew their swords, braced themselves for their useless end. The Bloodguard balanced
on the balls of their feet.

Trembling, Covenant tried to reach toward the
Staff. But his head was spinning, and a whirl of darkness jumped dizzily at him. He could not overcome his
fear; he was appalled at the revenge his leprosy would
wreak on him for such audacity. His hand crossed half
the distance and stopped, clutched in unfingered impotence at the empty air.

Ah! he cried lornly. *Help me!*

"We are the Bloodguard." Bannor's voice was almost inaudible through the loud lust of the Cavewights.
"We cannot permit this end."

Firmly, he took Covenant's hand and placed it on
the Staff of Law, midway between Prothall's straining
knuckles.

Power seemed to explode in Covenant's chest. A
silent concussion, a shock beyond hearing, struck the
ravine like a convulsion of the mountain. The blast
knocked the Questers from their feet, sent all the ur-
viles and Cavewights sprawling among the boulders.
Only the High Lord kept his feet. His head jerked up,
and the Staff bucked in his hands.

For a moment, there was stillness in the ravine—
a quiet so intense that the blast seemed to have
deafened all the combatants. And in that moment, the
entire sky over Gravin Threndor turned black with
impenetrable thunder.

Then came noise—one deep bolt of sound as if the
very rock of the mountain cried out—followed by
long waves of hot, hissing sputters. The clouds dropped
until they covered the crest of Mount Thunder.

Great yellow fires began to burn on the shrouded
peak.

For a time, the company and their attackers lay in

the ravine as if they were afraid to move. Everyone stared up at the fires and the thunderheads.

Suddenly, the flames erupted. With a roar as if the air itself were burning, fires started charging like great, hungry beasts down every face and side of the mountain.

Shrieking in fear, the Cavewights sprang up and ran. A few hurled themselves madly against the walls of the ravine. But most of them swept around the company's rock and fled downward, trying to outrun the Fire-Lions.

The ur-viles went the other way. In furious haste, they scrambled up the ravine toward the entrance to the catacombs.

But before they could reach safety, Drool appeared out of the cleft above them. The Cavewight was crawling, too crippled to stand. But in his fist he clutched a green stone which radiated intense wrong through the blackness of the clouds. His scream carried over the roar of the Lions:

"Crush! Crush!"

The ur-viles stopped, caught between fears.

While the creatures hesitated, the company started down the ravine. Prothall and Covenant were too exhausted to support themselves, so the Bloodguard bore them, throwing them from man to man over the boulders, dragging them along the tumbled floor of the ravine.

Ahead, the Cavewights began to reach the end of the cut. Some of them ran so blindly that they plunged over the cliff; others scattered in either direction along the edge, wailing for escape.

But behind the company, the ur-viles formed a wedge and again started downward. The Questers were barely able to keep their distance from the wedge.

The roar of the flaming air grew sharper, fiercer. Set free by the power of the Peak, boulders tumbled from the cliffs. The Fire-Lions moved like molten stone, sprang down the slopes as if spewed out of the heart of an inferno. Still far above the ravine, the consuming howl of their might seemed to double and treble itself with each downward lunge. A blast of scorched air blew ahead of them like a herald, trumpeting the progress of fire and volcanic hunger. Gravin Threndor shuddered to its roots.

The difficulty of the ravine eased as the company neared the lower end, and Covenant began to move for himself. Impelled by broken vision, overborne hearing, gaining rampage, he shook free of the Bloodguard. Moving stiff-kneed like a puppet, he jerked in a dogged, stumbling line for the cliff.

The other Questers swung to the south along the edge. But he went directly to the precipice. When he reached it, his legs barely had the strength to stop him. Tottering weakly, he looked down the drop. It was sheer for two thousand feet, and the cliff was at least half a league wide.

There was no escape. The Lions would get the company before they reached any possible descent beyond the cliff—long before.

People yelled at him, warning him futilely; he could hardly hear them through the roaring air. He gave no heed. That kind of escape was not what he wanted. And he was not afraid of the fall: he could not see it clearly enough to be afraid.

He had something to do.

He paused for a moment, summoning his courage. Then he realized that one of the Bloodguard would probably try to save him. He wanted to accomplish his purpose before that could happen.

He needed an answer to death.

Pulling off his ring, he held it firmly in his half-fingerless hand, cocked his arm to throw the band over the cliff.

His eyes followed the ring as he drew back his arm, and he stopped suddenly, struck by a blow of shame. The metal was clean. His vision still saw two rings, but both were flat argent; the stain was gone from within them.

He spun from the cliff, searched up the ravine for Drool.

He heard Mhoram shout, "Bannor! It is his choice!" The Bloodguard was sprinting toward him. At Mhoram's command, Bannor pulled to a halt ten yards away, despite his Vow. The next instant, he rejected the command, leaped toward Covenant again.

Covenant could not focus his vision. He caught a glimpse of fiery Lions pouncing toward the crevice high up the ravine. But his sight was dominated by the ur-vile wedge. It was only three strides away from him. The loremaster had already raised its stave to strike.

Instinctively, Covenant tried to move. But he was too slow. He was still leaning when Bannor crashed into him, knocked him out of the way.

With a mad, exulting bark as if they had suddenly seen a vision, the ur-viles sprang forward as one and plunged over the cliff. Their cries as they fell sounded ferociously triumphant.

Bannor lifted Covenant to his feet. The Bloodguard urged him toward the rest of the company, but he broke free and stumbled a few steps up the slope, straining his eyes toward the crevice. "Drool! What happened to Drool?" His eyes failed him. He stopped, wavered uncertainly, raged, "I can't see!"

Mhoram hastened to him, and Covenant repeated his question, shouting it into the Lord's face.

Mhoram replied gently, "Drool is there, in the crevice. Power that he could not master destroys him. He no longer knows what he does. In a moment, the Fire-Lions will consume him."

Covenant strove to master his voice by biting down on it. "No!" he hissed. "He's just another victim. Foul planned this all along." Despite his clamped teeth, his voice sounded broken.

Comfortingly, Mhoram touched his shoulder. "Be at peace, Unbeliever. We have done all we can. You need not condemn yourself."

Abruptly, Covenant found that his rage was gone— collapsed into dust. He felt blasted and wrecked, and he sank to the ground as if his bones could no longer hold him. His eyes had a tattered look, like the sails of a ghost ship. Without caring what he did, he pushed his wedding band back onto his ring finger.

The rest of the company was moving toward him. They had given up their attempt at flight; together, they watched the progress of the Lions. The midnight clouds cast a gloom over the whole mountain, and through the dimness the pouncing fires blazed and coruscated like beasts of sun flame. They sprang down the walls into the ravine, and some of them bounded upward toward the crevice.

Lord Mhoram finally shook himself free of his entrancement. "Call your Ranyhyn," he commanded Bannor. "The Bloodguard can save themselves. Take the Staff and the Second Ward. Call the Ranyhyn and escape."

Bannor met Mhoram's gaze for a long moment, measuring the Lord's order. Then he refused stolidly. "One of us will go. To carry the Staff and Ward to Lord's Keep. The rest remain."

"Why? We cannot escape. You must live—to serve the Lords who must carry on this war."

"Perhaps." Bannor shrugged slightly. "Who can say? High Lord Kevin ordered us away, and we obeyed. We will not do such a thing again."

"But this death is useless!" cried Mhoram.

"Nevertheless." The Bloodguard's tone was as blank as iron. Then he added, "But you can call Hynaril. Do so, Lord."

"No," Mhoram sighed with a tired smile of recognition. "I cannot. How could I leave so many to die?"

Covenant only half listened. He felt like a derelict, and he was picking among the wreckage of his emotions, in search of something worth salvaging. But part of him understood. He put the two fingers of his right hand between his lips and gave one short, piercing whistle.

All the company stared at him. Quaan seemed to think that the Unbeliever had lost his mind; Mhoram's eyes jumped at wild guesses. But Manethrall Lithe tossed her cord high in the air and crowed, "The Ranyhyn! Mane of the World! He calls them!"

"How?" protested Quaan. "He refused them."

"They reared to him!" she returned with a nickering laugh. "They will come."

Covenant had stopped listening altogether. Something was happening to him, and he lurched to his feet to meet it upright. The dimensions of his situation were changing. To his blurred gaze, the comrades of the company grew slowly harder and solider—took on the texture of native rock. And the mountain itself became increasingly adamantine. It seemed as immutable as the cornerstone of the world. He felt veils drop from his perception; he saw the unclouded fact of Gravin Threndor in all its unanswerable power. He paled beside it; his flesh grew thin, transient. Air as thick as smoke blew through him, chilling his bones. The throat of his soul contracted in silent pain. "What's happening to me?"

Around the cliff edge to the south, Ranyhyn came galloping. Like a blaze of hope, they raced the downrush of the Lions. At once, a hoarse cheer broke from the warriors. "We are saved!" Mhoram cried. "There is time enough!" With the rest of the company, he hurried forward to meet the swift approach of the Ranyhyn.

Covenant felt that he had been left alone. "What's happening to me?" he repeated dimly toward the hard mountain.

But Prothall was still at his side. Covenant heard the High Lord say in a kind old voice that seemed as loud as thunder, "Drool is dead. He was your summoner, and with his death the call ends. That is the way of such power.

"Farewell, Unbeliever! Be true! You have wrought greatly for us. The Ranyhyn will preserve us. And with the Staff of Law and the Second Ward, we will not be unable to defend against the Despiser's ill. Take heart. Despair and bitterness are not the only songs in the world."

But Covenant wailed in mute grief. Everything around him—Prothall and the company and the Ranyhyn and the Fire-Lions and the mountain—became too solid for him. They overwhelmed his perceptions, passed beyond his senses into gray mist. He clutched about him and felt nothing. He could not see; the Land left the range of his eyes. It was too much for him, and he lost it.

TWENTY-FIVE:

Survived

GRAY mist swirled around him for a long convulsive moment. Then it began to smear, and he lost it as well. His vision blurred, as if some hard god had rubbed a thumb across it. He blinked rapidly, tried to reach up to squeeze his eyes; but something soft prevented his hand. His sight remained blank.

He was waking up, though he felt more as if he were dropping into grogginess.

Gradually, he became able to identify where he was. He lay in a bed with tubular protective bars on the sides. White sheets covered him to his chin. Gray curtains shut him off from the other patients in the room. A fluorescent light stared past him emptily from the ceiling. The air was faintly tinged with ether and germicide. A call button hung at the head of the bed.

All his fingers and toes were numb.

Nerves don't regenerate, of course they don't, they don't—

This was important—he knew it was important—but for some reason it did not carry any weight with him. His heart was too hot with other emotions to feel that particular ice.

What mattered to him was that Prothall and Mhoram and the Quest had survived. He clung to that as if it were proof of sanity—a demonstration that what had happened to him, that what he had done, was not the product of madness, self-destruction. They had survived; at least his bargain with the Ranyhyn had accomplished that much. They had done exactly what Lord Foul wanted them to do—but they had survived.

At least he was not guilty of their deaths, too. His inability to use his ring, to believe in his ring, had not made Wraiths of them. That was his only consolation for what he had lost.

Then he made out two figures standing at the foot of the bed. One of them was a woman in white—a nurse. As he tried to focus on her, she said, "Doctor —he's regaining consciousness."

The doctor was a middle-aged man in a brown suit. The flesh under his eyes sagged as if he were weary of all human pain, but his lips under his graying mustache were gentle. He approached along the side of the bed, touched Covenant's forehead for a moment, then pulled up Covenant's eyelids and shined a small light at his pupils.

With an effort, Covenant focused on the light.

The doctor nodded, and put his flashlight away. "Mr. Covenant?"

Covenant swallowed at the dryness in his throat.

"Mr. Covenant." The doctor held his face close to Covenant's, and spoke quietly, calmly. "You're in the hospital. You were brought here after your run-in with that police car. You've been unconscious for about four hours."

Covenant lifted his head and nodded to show that he understood.

"Good," said the doctor. "I'm glad you're coming around. Now, let me talk to you for a moment.

"Mr. Covenant, the police officer who was driving that car says that he didn't hit you. He claims that he stopped in time—you just fell down in front of him. From my examination, I would be inclined to agree with him. Your hands are scraped up a bit, and you have a bruise on your forehead—but things like that could have happened when you fell." He hesitated momentarily, then asked, *"Did* he hit you?"

Dumbly, Covenant shook his head. The question did not feel important.

"Well, I suppose you could have knocked yourself out by hitting your head on the pavement. But why did you fall?"

That, too, did not feel important. He pushed the

question away with a twitch of his hands. Then he tried to sit up in bed.

He succeeded before the doctor could help or hinder him; he was not as weak as he had feared he might be. The numbness of his fingers and toes still seemed to lack conviction, as if they would recover as soon as their circulation was restored.

Nerves don't—

After a moment, he regained his voice, and asked for his clothes.

The doctor studied him closely. "Mr. Covenant," he said, "I'll let you go home if you want to. I suppose I should keep you under observation for a day or two. But I really haven't been able to find anything wrong with you. And you know more about taking care of leprosy than I do." Covenant did not miss the look of nausea that flinched across the nurse's face. "And, to be perfectly honest"—the doctor's tone turned suddenly acid—"'I don't want to have to fight the staff here to be sure that you get decent care. Do you feel up to it?"

In answer, Covenant began fumbling with awkward fingers at the dull white hospital gown he wore.

Abruptly, the doctor went to a locker, and came back with Covenant's clothes.

Covenant gave them a kind of VSE. They were scuffed and dusty from his fall in the street; yet they looked exactly as they had looked when he had last worn them, during the first days of the Quest.

Exactly as if none of it had ever happened.

When he was dressed, he signed the releases. His hand was so cold that he could hardly write his name.

But the Quest had survived. At least his bargain had been good for that.

Then the doctor gave him a ride in a wheelchair down to the discharge exit. Outside the building, the doctor suddenly began to talk as if in some oblique way he were trying to apologize for not keeping Covenant in the hospital. "It must be hell to be a leper," he said rapidly. "I'm trying to understand. It's like— I studied in Heidelberg, years ago, and while I was there I saw a lot of medieval art. Especially religious

art. Being a leper reminds me of statues of the Cruci-
fixion made during the Middle Ages. There is Christ
on the Cross, and his features—his body, even his
face—are portrayed so blandly that the figure is un-
recognizable. It could be anyone, man or woman. But
the wounds—the nails in the hands and feet, the spear
in the side, the crown of thorns—are carved and even
painted in incredibly vivid detail. You would think the
artist crucified his model to get that kind of realism.

"Being a leper must be like that."

Covenant felt the doctor's sympathy, but he could
not reply to it. He did not know how.

After a few minutes, an ambulance came and took
him back to Haven Farm.

He had survived.

He walked up the long driveway to his house as if
that were his only hope.

Here ends
LORD FOUL'S BANE,
Book One of
The Chronicles of
Thomas Covenant, the Unbeliever

GLOSSARY

Acence: a Stonedownor, sister of Atiaran
aliantha: treasure-berries
amanibhavam: horse-healing grass, poisonous to men
anundivian yajña: lost Ramen craft of bone-sculpting
Atiaran Trell-mate: a Stonedowner, daughter of Tiaran

Banas Nimoram: the Celebration of Spring
Bannor: a Bloodguard, assigned to Covenant
Baradakas: a Hirebrand of Soaring Woodhelven
Berek Halfhand: founder of the line of Lords
Bhrathair: a people met by the wandering Giants
Birinair: a Hirebrand, Hearthall of Lord's Keep
Bloodguard: the defenders of the Lords
Brabha: a Ranyhyn, Korik's mount

caamora: Giantish ordeal of grief by fire
Caerroil Wildwood: Forestal of Garroting Deep
Cavewights: evil ceatures existing under Mount
  Thunder
Celebration of Spring: the Dance of the Wraiths of
  Andelain on the dark of the moon in the middle
  night of Spring
clingor: adhesive leather
Close, the: the Council-chamber of Lord's Keep
Cord: Ramen second rank
Cording: ceremony of becoming a Cord
Corruption: Bloodguard name for Lord Foul
Creator, the: legendary Enemy of Lord Foul

Damelon Giantfriend: son of Berek Halfhand, ancient
  High Lord
Dance of the Wraiths: Celebration of Spring

Demondim: spawners of ur-viles and Waynhim
Desolation, the: era of ruin in the Land, after the Ritual
    of Desecration
Despiser, the: Lord Foul
Despite: Power of Evil
diamondraught: Giantish liquor
Drool Rockworm: a Cavewight, finder of the Staff of
    Law
Dura Fairflank: a mustang, Covenant's mount

Earthfriend: title first given to Berek Halfhand
Elohim: a people met by the wandering Giants
Eoman: a unit of the Warward of Lord's Keep, twenty
    warriors and a Warhaft

Fangthane the Render: Ramen name for Lord Foul
Fire-Lions: fire-flow of Mount Thunder
fire-stones: graveling
First Mark: the Bloodguard commander
First Ward of Kevin's Lore: primary knowledge left by
    High Lord Kevin
forbidding: a wall of power
Forestal: protector of the remnants of the One Forest
Foul's Creche: the Despiser's home
Furl Falls: waterfall at Revelstone
Furl's Fire: warning fire at Revelstone

Garth: Warmark of the Warward of Lord's Keep
Gay: a Winhome of the Ramen
Giantclave: Giantish conference
Giants: the Unhomed, ancient friends of the Lords
Gilden: a maple-like tree with golden leaves
Gildenlode: a power-wood formed from Gilden trees
Grace: a Cord of the Ramen
graveling: fire-stones, made to glow by stone-lore
Gravelingas: a master of the stone-lore
Gray Slayer: plains name for Lord Foul
griffin: lion-like beast with wings

Haruchai: a people from whom the Bloodguard come
Healer: a physician

Hearthrall of Lord's Keep: one responsible for light, warmth and hospitality

Heart of Thunder: cave of power in Mount Thunder

Heartthew: Berek Halfhand

heartwood chamber: meeting-place of a Woodhelven

Heers: leaders of a Woodhelven

Herem: a Raver

High Lord: leader of the Council of Lords

High Wood: offspring of the One Tree

Hirebrand: a master of wood-lore

Hurn: a Cord of the Ramen

hurtloam: a healing mud

Huryn: a Ranyhyn, Terrel's mount

Hynaril: a Ranyhyn, mount of Tamarantha and Mhoram.

Illearth Stone: source of evil power found under Mount Thunder

Imoiran Tomal-mate: a Stonedowner

Irin: warrior of the Third Eoman of the Warward

Jehannum: a Raver

Kevin Landwaster: son of Loric Vilesilencer, last High Lord of the Old Lords

Kevin's Lore: knowledge of power left by Kevin in the Seven Wards

Kiril Threndor: Heart of Thunder

Korik: a Bloodguard

kresh: savage, giant, yellow wolves

Kurash Plenethor: region formerly named Stricken Stone, now called Trothgard

Land, the: generally, area found on the map

Lena: a Stonedownor, daughter of Atiaran

Lifeswallower: the Great Swamp

lillianrill: wood-lore, or masters of wood-lore

Lithe: a Manethrall of the Ramen

Llaura: Heer of Soaring Woodhelven

lomillialor: High Wood

Lord: master of the Sword and Staff parts of Kevin's Lore

Lord-Fatherer: Berek Halfhand
Lord Foul: Lords' name for the Enemy of the Land
Lords-fire: staff-fire used by the Lords
Lord's Keep: Revelstone
loremaster: a leader of ur-viles
Loresraat: Trothgard school where Kevin's Lore is studied
Lorewarden: teacher in the Loresraat
loreworks: Demondim power-laboratory
Loric Vilesilencer: a High Lord, son of Damelon Giant-friend
lor-liarill: Gildenlode

Malliner: Woodhelvennin Heer, son of Veinnin
Maneing: ceremony of becoming a Manethrall
Manethrall: Ramen first rank
Marny: a Ranyhyn, Tuvor's mount
marrowmeld: bone-sculpting
Melenkurion abatha: phrase of invocation or power
Mhoram: Lord, son of Variol
Murrin Odona-mate: a Stonedownor

Oath of Peace: oath by people of the Land against needless violence
Odona Murrin-mate: a Stonedownor
Old Lords: Lords prior to the Ritual of Desecration
Omournil: Woodhelvennin Heer, daughter of Mournil
One Forest: ancient forest which covered most of the Land
One Tree, the: mystic tree from which the Staff of Law was made
orcrest: a stone of power
Osondrea: Lord, daughter of Sondrea

Padrias: Woodhelvennin Heer, son of Mill
Peak of the Fire-Lions: Mount Thunder
Pietten: Woodhelvennin child, son of Soranal
Prothall: High Lord, son of Dwillian

Quaan: Warhaft of the Third Eoman of the Warward
Quest, the: search to rescue the Staff of Law

Ramen: a people who serve the Ranyhyn

Ranyhyn: the great, free horses of the Plains of Ra

Ravers: Lord Foul's three ancient servants

Revelstone: Lord's Keep, mountain city of the Lords

rhadhamaerl: stone-lore, or masters of stone-lore

Ringthane: Ramen name for Thomas Covenant

Rites of Unfettering: the ceremony of becoming Unfettered

Ritual of Desecration: act of despair by which High Lord Kevin destroyed the Old Lords and ruined most of the Land

Rockbrother, Rocksister: term of affection between men and Giants

Rustah: a Cord of the Ramen

sacred enclosure: Vespers-hall at Revelstone

Saltheart Foamfollower: a Giant, friend of Covenant

Sandgorgons: monsters described by the Giants

Satansheart: Giantish name for Lord Foul

Seven Wards: collection of knowledge left by High Lord Kevin

Seven Words: power-words

Sheol: a Raver

Soranal: a Woodhelvennin Heer, son of Thiller

Soulcrusher: Giantish name for Lord Foul

Sparlimb Keelsetter: a Giant, father of triplets

springwine: a mild, refreshing liquor

Staff, the: to distinguish from other staves a branch of Kevin's Lore

Staff of Law, the: formed by Berek from the One Tree

Stonedown: a stone-village

Stonedownor: one who lives in a stone-village

Stricken Stone: now called Trothgard

suru-pa-maerl: a stone craft

Sword, the: a branch of Kevin's Lore

Tamarantha Variol-mate: Lord, daughter of Enesta

Terass: a Stonedownor, daughter of Annoria

Terrel: a Bloodguard

test of truth: test of veracity by *lomillialor* or *orcrest*

Thew: a Cord of the Ramen

Tohrm: Gravelingas and Hearthrall of Lord's Keep

Tomal: a Stonedownor craftmaster
treasure-berries: nourishing fruit found throughout the
   Land
Trell Atiaran-mate: Gravelingas of Mithil Stonedown
Triock: a Stonedownor, son of Thuler
Tuvor: First Mark of the Bloodguard

Unbeliever: Thomas Covenant
Unfettered: lore-students freed from conventional re-
   sponsibilities
Unhomed, the: The Giants
ur-Lord: title given to Thomas Covenant
ur-viles: Demondim-spawn, evil creatures

Vailant: former High Lord
Variol Tamarantha-mate: Lord, former High Lord,
   son of Pentil
Viles: sires of the Demondim
Vow, the: *Haruchai* oath which formed the Blood-
   guard

Warhaft: commander of an Eoman
Warlore: Sword knowledge in Kevin's Lore
Warmark: commander of the Warward
Warrenbridge: entrance to the catacombs under Mount
   Thunder
Warward: the army of Lord's Keep
Wavenhair Haleall: a Giant, wife of Sparlimb Keelset-
   ter, mother of triplets
Waymeet: resting place for travelers
Waynhim: tenders of the Waymeets, opponents of ur-
   viles though Demondim-spawn
Wightwarrens: homes of the Cavewights under Mount
   Thunder
Winhome: Ramen lowest rank
Woodhelven: wood-village
Woodhelvennin: inhabitants of wood-village
Word of Warning: a powerful, destructive forbidding
Wraiths of Andelain: creatures that perform the Dance
   at the Celebration of Spring

About the Author

Born in 1947 in Cleveland, Ohio, **Stephen R. Donaldson** makes his publishing debut with The Covenant Trilogy. From ages three to sixteen, he lived in India, where his father, an orthopedic surgeon, worked extensively with lepers. (It was after hearing one of his father's speeches on the subject of leprosy that he conceived the character of Thomas Covenant as protagonist for an epic fantasy.) He graduated from the College of Wooster (Ohio) in 1968, served two years as a conscientious objector doing hospital work in Akron, then attended Kent State University, where he received his M.A. in English in 1971. He now lives in Albuquerque, New Mexico.

Enchanting
fantasies
from